THE *I AM MARGARET* SERIES

LIBERATION was nominated for the *Carnegie Medal Award 2016* and won 3rd place for 'Teen and Young Adult Fiction' in the *Catholic Press Association 2016 Book Awards.*

I AM MARGARET, THE THREE MOST WANTED and *LIBERATION* have been awarded the 'Seal of Approval' by the *Catholic Writers Guild* and *I AM MARGARET* was one of three finalists for the 'Teenage and Children's Fiction' *CALA Award 2016.*

PRAISE FOR *I AM MARGARET*

Great style—very good characters and pace. Definitely a book worth reading, like The Hunger Games.
EOIN COLFER, author of the *Artemis Fowl* books

An intelligent, well-written and enjoyable debut from a young writer with a bright future.
STEWART ROSS, author of *The So~~terian Mission~~*

This book invaded my dr~~e~~
SR. MARY CATHERINE BLO~~~~

D1556981

Margaret, Bane, Jon and the Major hav~~e stayed with me~~ long since I finished reading about them.
RACHEL FRASER

One of the best Christian fiction books I have read.
CAT CAIRD, blogger, 'Sunshine Lenses'

PRAISE FOR *THE THREE MOST WANTED*

I cannot reiterate enough how much I am enjoying these books and how talented this author is.
TIFFANY, blogger, 'Life of a Catholic Librarian'

The I AM MARGARET Series:

I Am Margaret
The Three Most Wanted
Liberation
Bane's Eyes

The YESTERDAY & TOMORROW Series:

Someday: A Novella

Coming soon:
Tomorrow's Dead

BANE'S EYES

CORINNA TURNER

unSeen

Cover design by Corinna Turner, Anthony VanArsdale,
and Regina Doman

A catalogue record for this book is available from the British Library.

ISBN: 978-1-910806-12-8 (paperback)
Also available as an eBook

* An imprint of Zephyr Publishing, UK—Corinna Turner, T/A

Many thanks to the developers of these beautiful Open Source fonts:
DESTROY, *Quattrocentro Roman,* Source Sans Pro, Note This, WC Rhesus A
Bta, Daniel, BPreplay, *Rosario, Aierbazzi,* DejaVu Sans Condensed,

CAPTURE IT, Inky, IMPACT LABEL REVERSED, and Windsong

"Friend and neighbor
you have taken away:
my one companion
is darkness."

Psalm 87 (88)

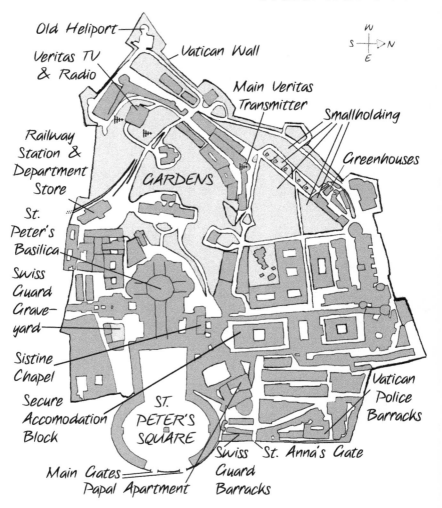

VATICAN FREE STATE

Old Heliport

Veritas TV & Radio

Vatican Wall

Main Veritas Transmitter

Smallholding

Greenhouses

Railway Station & Department Store

GARDENS

St. Peter's Basilica

Swiss Guard Grave-yard

Sistine Chapel

Secure Accomodation Block

ST. PETER'S SQUARE

Vatican Police Barracks

Main Gates
Papal Apartment

Swiss Guard Barracks

St. Anna's Gate

1

PLEASE, LORD

2 months, 21 days until the vote

"If you knew me and you really knew yourself, you would not have killed me."

This was said at the end of the twentieth century, by Felicien Ntagengwa, a survivor of a horrible genocide in what is now the Rwandan Free State. I cannot read it today without thinking: this could just as easily have been said by Polly, who was taken for dismantling the very day we arrived at Salperton EGD Facility.

This could have been said by *any* reAssignee.

Margaret Verrall—blog post, 'The Impatient Gardener'

Warm and cozy, I woke slowly. Bane lay beside me, nose tucked into my hair. Raising my head slightly, I looked across him to the bedside clock. Yep, five minutes before my alarm would go off.

I slid my arms around him, my hands rubbing his broad back and shoulders. When he woke gently, with me wrapped around him, he—usually—didn't expect to see anything when he opened his empty eyes.

A good day. Bane stirred sleepily, gathered me close and buried his nose deeper in my hair.

"Good morning, husband," I whispered in his ear.

"Good morning, wife," he murmured back.

Awake. No panic. No pain. Now we had a few blissful minutes to snuggle before the alarm.

"Love you, Margo," he whispered into my hair, as though it might make up for all the things he would probably say later.

1

"Love you, Bane." Because it almost did.

Later... Oh. Today was the big day. He hadn't remembered yet, had he?

The alarm split the peaceful silence.

With a sigh, I disentangled myself and sat up, reaching in my bedside drawer for my chart and thermometer. Time for my fertility checks. Though why I was bothering at the moment...

I pushed the self-centered complaint from my mind. At least my cycle was back to normal after all the starvation and stress of the past year. My body had finally adjusted to our relative safety: now, if only my mind would do the same... Not that safety was precisely what awaited me today.

Drawer closed again, I headed for the bathroom. Married couples got one bedroom apartments here in Vatican State. *I'd sleep in a shed in the Vatican Gardens if it got Bane his eyes back...* I pushed that thought away as well. The EuroGov weren't going to return Bane's eyes just because I agreed to bed down among the spades and pruning shears.

"Coming to Mass?" I asked casually, pausing in the doorway. Bane wasn't officially a Believer but sometimes he came to Mass, just to keep me company, as he put it.

He sat up in bed, rubbing his loose lids—they were always itchy in the morning—the familiar scowl settling on his brow. "Don't know."

"Well, I've got to get dressed, anyway."

Going into the bathroom, I washed and pulled my clothes on quickly. Seemed a million years since we'd arrived at the Vatican the first time—but it was only, what, six months? After several months hiding with the Holy-See-in-exile on Gozo, we'd returned to the Vatican about three months ago following the bloc-wide protests in January that forced the EuroGov to (among other things) withdraw from the ancient Free State.

Three long months since the EuroGov had removed Bane's eyes. How I often longed to be back in the little Citadel of Gozo, helping Bane launch the Liberations which had helped spark the protests, stressful as it had been waiting every day for the EuroGov to find us... But back then, Bane had been whole... and happy.

Bit ironic, since today I *was* off to Malta. But on my own. Well, with Pope Cornelius, but not with Bane. As Eduardo, the Head of Vatican Security, had put it with his usual lack of tact, "If you come, Bane, you'll only endanger Margo, since the guards will be looking after you as well." It had been a week before Bane had spoken to Eduardo again.

Bane was half-dressed when I went back into the bedroom—he'd decided to come to Mass. Now he'd be like a bear with a cut paw because he'd failed to overcome his dependence on me. As opposed to a bear with a cut paw because he was staying behind...

A bitter taste in my mouth, I went to join him by the bed. He'd laid two shirts on it, one red, one blue. He picked up the blue one. "This is... the red one, right?"

I wanted to tell him, *yes*—he'd spent *three hours* with Jon yesterday, learning to tell his shirts apart by feel—or trying to—but it wasn't really kind, was it? "It's the blue one, Bane," I said softly.

"Damnit!" He flung the shirt across the room.

"Well, I'm really impressed you were able to narrow it down to *two*."

"Oh, don't be stupid, Margo! I remembered where I put them, didn't I?"

I swallowed, my heart contracting in increasingly familiar pain.

His arms dropped to his sides, far too wearily for seven-thirty in the morning. "I'm sorry," he said in a low voice, as though unsure how many more apologies he was allowed. "How are you supposed to know how I knew?"

I stepped forward and tried to put my arms around him.

He shrugged me off. "Don't coddle me! I don't need a hug!"

Perhaps I do. I headed for the living room. "I've got to go, Bane."

"*Wait,* I'm coming." He pulled on the red shirt—all he needed, April being pleasantly warm here—and grabbed his stick from beside the bed. He found his way through the doorway quickly enough, then stood still, head turning from side to side.

'I'm right here' was on the tip of my tongue, but he'd just say I was coddling him. He started in my general direction, then paused. "Better put my eyes in, hadn't I?"

"However you're most comfortable."

"Don't want to *scare* people, do I?"

He went back into the bedroom and through to the bathroom. *Suck, pop. Suck, pop.* He'd a love-hate relationship with the glass eyes—in some ways his sockets felt more comfortable with them, but they irritated him too. Like a lot of other things.

Finally Bane was slipping his arm through mine, *just felt like walking arm-in-arm with my wife* projected belligerently in every aspect of his stance.

Jon waited in the main passage. He shared one of the larger 'bachelor' apartments with Unicorn, Bumblebee and Snail, who as Vatican Secret Service agents were spared barracks living. "Good morning," he said.

"Is it?" said Bane.

Ignoring this customary mutter, I said, "Morning, Jon."

"I just heard on the radio," went on Jon, as we headed off, "the EuroGov are still wriggling. But I think your Easter blog post has helped a lot."

Easter Sunday was a week behind us, now. The whole day had been a disaster. The homily had been about how much God loves us and Bane had actually walked out in the middle. I'd had to go with him because I knew he couldn't find his way across the massive basilica on his own. And when I'd tried to go to a later Mass instead, he'd been thoroughly horrible about it. I'd lost my temper and yelled back, and then I'd felt twice as bad...

Okay, I wasn't going to think about it anymore, was I?

The blog post was the only good thing that had come out of it. I'd hurled all my anger at the EuroGov, once more attacking Sorting—the practice of choosing which teenagers were 'perfect' enough to live and which would be reassigned for use as spare parts—in what everyone assured me were very well-chosen words.

"Make sure you get in a few good lines about it, while you're in Malta," Jon added, "Keep the pressure on."

"I can't believe you think this trip is a good idea,"

growled Bane, under his breath.

Jon declined to get drawn into yet another argument on the subject. "After all," he went on, "they've got two good reasons for having the referendum on Sorting and Religious Freedom at the beginning of July, haven't they? It's before exams—so it'll save them money marking future reAssignees' papers—and it's less than a complete semester for the reAssignees to catch up as far as the fitness program is concerned. The EuroGov always talk like they're going to win."

"But the *longer* they leave it, the more time they have for their propaganda machine to change people's minds," I said.

"Yeah," conceded Jon, "but we should win the religious freedom vote, whatever happens."

"True." No more risking the death penalty just for being a Believer: even that alone would be a huge victory.

"Anyway, they'll have to make the final decision soon. Unicorn says they're up to something else too, but Eduardo doesn't know what it is yet."

"*Unicorn says*," snorted Bane, concentrating fiercely on locating all the odd tables and chairs spaced along the corridor walls with his stick. "Enough with the code names! We're not doing Liberations anymore! His name's *Jack*, y'know."

"Yes, and so's Snail's, near enough." Jon refused to be drawn. "And Bee's name is Thom and I'm Jon. So we stick to code names in the flat. Hard to get those mixed up."

Bane said nothing; just reached for the call button for the lift. Started scowling again when he had to feel around. Jon could walk from our room door to the lift and put his hand straight on the button, providing he didn't stop to speak to anyone on the way, but then, he'd been blind from birth.

When we left the elevator, we walked on without talking. Things would improve soon, surely? Bane would get more confident, he'd start to be happy to go out by himself, he'd feel so much better then... Soon. *Please, Lord?*

Bane misjudged the step into St Peter's, stumbling, and I grabbed him before I could even think. He shook me off, his face crimson—picturing a load of people watching his misstep, eyes full of pity? There were only two Swiss Guards, staring unmovingly into the basilica.

"I'm *fine*, Margo!" Bane snarled, so fiercely my heart shrank again. He strode forward several determined strides—then stopped dead. Traced a large circle with his stick—encountered nothing. The emotions flitted across his face: panic, fear, and above all the pain of wounded... pride? Self-respect?

Despite the aching lump in my chest, I paused only to genuflect, then went to him and silently brushed my arm against his. He took it and we went on across the vast marble floor. In silence.

Since all the Religious Suppression laws, plus all Sorting and Dismantling, were suspended until the referendum, St Peter's Square and St Peter's itself were open to the public for the first time in decades—a security nightmare as far as Eduardo, was concerned. All access points from square or basilica into the rest of Vatican State were heavily guarded and covered with cameras, and a front section of the basilica was cordoned off for Vatican State residents only. Eduardo could still be seen at every Mass, hovering anxiously near Pope Cornelius.

A few other agents we knew from the Liberations entered, clearly off-duty: Spitfire from "Plane" team gave a wave. I waved back as he, Discus, and Croquet filed into the pews, then led Bane to our usual place, Jon following.

Kneelers and benches were arranged permanently in the Residents' part, while chairs were set out in the public section according to how many people were expected. Bane settled himself in our pew like a gloomy black cloud, turned his face down to the floor and said nothing. No apology this time. A lump filled my throat. I would have allowed him as many apologies as he liked; they were better than silence.

I knelt and tried to pray. I felt so... ragged. Desperate. Helpless.

Lord? Please let it get better soon. Really soon. I don't think I can go on like this much longer. It hurts so much. I want to pray that we'll somehow get his eyes back, but I know that's stupid. The EuroGov might have given them to someone else already. They might even have destroyed them. We have to learn to live without them. But I don't know how. Help me, Lord? Please help me, please please please?

Bother! Tears leaked from my eyes and I fought to keep my breathing steady. No use. Jon's hand touched my arm in silent comfort. Bane didn't notice, though, thank God. It would make him feel even worse...

We stood to begin Mass, and I tried to wipe my eyes surreptitiously. Didn't want everyone shaking their heads and saying *poor Margaret and Bane.*

Time for the daily battle to concentrate...

...The voice of the reader faltered. What was distracting *her?* People were looking around... Oh. A tramp was shambling up the main aisle. That wasn't unusual: the poorest were among the first through the doors when the Basilica became open to the public again. What was unusual were the two Swiss Guards discreetly trailing after him. The guards might pause an unfamiliar person to see if they knew about the Vatican homeless shelter, recently re-opened just inside St. Anna's gate, but tramps were never turned away from the house of God... this guy must've done something to alarm them.

He reached the rope barrier and moved through the central gap as though in a dream.

The guards tried to intercept him. "Sir... S'cuse me, sir, that's a restricted area..."

The man just stumbled on as if the guards hadn't spoken.

"Sir, please stop. You're not allowed in this area..." They hovered, keeping pace, reluctant to manhandle him, especially in the middle of Mass. He didn't seem to hear them. Was he deaf?

He was a mess, all right. Hair, dark with grease and filth, almost reached his shoulders and a beard grew unchecked across his lower face. His clothes were rags and he moved as though he'd crumple to the ground with each faltering step.

"*Sir!*" He was approaching the altar area now—the

7

guards' hands reached for him, hesitated, their eyes seeking the Holy Father. Pope Cornelius made a tiny gesture—*let him come.*

The man walked into the balustrade around the subterranean tomb in front of the high altar and staggered to a halt. Raised his head dazedly as though only just realizing where he was. His hoarse whisper carried in the silence. "Margaret Verrall?"

Everyone looked at me. Verrall was my maiden name, but I'd ended up keeping it after Bane's parents disowned him shortly before our wedding.

"Margaret Verrall?" A thin, desperate edge to his voice that brought me to my feet. I could almost see the strength draining out of that ragged figure...

"Catch him!" I cried, as he fell like a rag doll towards the marble floor.

One of the Swiss Guards lunged and snagged him just in time. A look of surprise crossed his face as he stood there supporting the man's weight; the guy must be light as a feather.

I slipped past Bane and hurried forward. Who *on earth*?

The Swiss Guard lowered his burden to the ground, pillowing the man's head on a kneeler cushion. I crouched beside him and Unicorn appeared at my shoulder, blue eyes even more hyper-alert than normal. Grass Snake was also heading my way. Despite all the new freedom, I was still the EuroGov's Most Wanted and was guarded accordingly.

"Sir?" I touched the man's shoulder gingerly. Was he conscious? "Can you hear me? *I'm* Margaret Verrall..."

His eyes flew open. Brilliant green eyes, like mine. Unmistakable.

2

SANCTUARY

I started back, almost falling. The guards tensed to spring, but I held up a hand quickly. "It's okay..."

They relaxed, but I could tell they didn't recognize the man. I edged forward again and those green eyes found my face. Not much sanity in them. Four months tramping around the forests of Europe clearly hadn't done much to restore his wits after all those months of torture at the hands of the EuroGov. But then his gaze wandered up to my forehead and stayed there. Fixed on the cross he'd carved into my flesh.

I swallowed. "What do you want?" Not the most gracious way to put it, but short and simple.

His brow wrinkled in an agonized attempt at thought. "I have to... I have to *know*. Have to..." His head sunk back, eyes half closing. What little skin visible under beard and grime was going dead white—was he about to pass out? A thread of compassion stirred—so hard to connect this pitiful creature with the man who'd...

My hand rose to brush the scar on my forehead. Still... I leaned closer, lowering my voice. "Say *sanctuary* and we'll look after you."

Eyelids fluttering up a little, he stared uncomprehendingly, as though I was speaking Chinese.

"Say *sanc-tu-ary*." I spoke very firmly.

He frowned like a puzzled child. "Ss... sank... ry?" His head fell to one side; his eyes closed.

I sat back on my heels. Eduardo had left Pope Cornelius corralled inside a ring of Swiss Guards and loomed on the left; more guards and a few curious enough to leave their pews gathered around elsewhere. Unicorn was hovering right beside me—no doubt he'd heard what I said.

"This man has claimed sanctuary," I said clearly. "And I

think he needs a doctor."

"Who is he?" Eduardo hadn't missed my moment of recognition.

"Major Lucas Everington. I dare say you've heard of him?"

Unamusing as it might be to have this particular individual passed out in front of me, the look on Eduardo's face *was*. "Are you *sure*, Margaret?"

Major Lucas Everington, disgraced former Commandant of Salperton Facility where I'd been imprisoned, was supposed to be rotting in a forest somewhere, several months dead, according to the best guesses of all official and non-official sources.

When I nodded, Eduardo crouched to stare at the matted collection of hair and mud that was the man's face. "How can you tell? Could be anyone."

"He has very distinctive eyes." I could clearly picture those eyes as he'd stood over me in the Lab, for once removed from his precious garden, though his gardening gloves had still been tucked through his belt, just beside his Lethal pistol.

"Well, I suppose we'll just have to take your word for it for now. Sanctuary. *Great.* "

"Personally, I think it saves everyone a lot of time and argument," I said dryly. "He's under sentence of death. No way we'll *actually* hand him over, but that won't stop some people talking about it until trumpets sound."

Eduardo shrugged, eyed me rather closely, glanced at Unicorn—whose poker-face made it clear he'd no intention of breaking bodyguard's confidentiality—and started patting down the unconscious man. One of the Major's ragged mittens fell off as Eduardo rolled him over, and I gasped. Unicorn swore, then went red and crossed himself.

"What?" Eduardo was there in a flash.

I drew up the Major's jacket sleeve to get a better look. His hand was a claw, his arm a bone with skin stretched over it. I'd never seen such emaciation, except perhaps on old video footage of twentieth-century famines.

"Where's that doctor?" snapped Eduardo.

"He's coming now," said someone, as Doctor Frederick

shouldered through the crush with his first-aid kit.

"Fellow collapsed?" He caught a glimpse of the hand and his eyes widened in incredulity. "Did he *walk* in here? Never mind, never mind... Doctor Carol?"

The couple of doctors and nurses who'd trailed in behind him got busy, and the unwelcome guest was soon whisked away.

"Do you know his name?" asked Doctor Frederick over his shoulder, "On the off chance he wakes up?"

"Uh... Lucas," said Eduardo blandly, and prowled after Doctor Frederick when he galloped off without waiting for more.

"Is it really who Jon thought you said?" demanded Bane, when I got back to our pew.

"The Major. In the flesh. In the skin and bone, anyway— he doesn't seem to have any flesh left on him. S'pose I shouldn't call him Major any more, now that he's been stripped of rank. The not-so-departed Mr. Everington, anyway."

"How on earth?" said Jon. "Four months in the forest? What did he eat?"

"Nothing, by the look of him."

"He must've eaten something."

"Well, yeah... oh, shhh, I think we're carrying on."

Eduardo hadn't returned by the time morning Mass ended, but Grass Snake, a VSS agent and former "Animal" Liberation team member who'd been my bodyguard on the other three trips to Free States that I'd made since Bane was well enough to be left, came over to me as soon as I got up from the kneeler. "Have you got your suitcase ready, Margo?"

"It's all packed. But we're not leaving for an hour and a half, are we? So I've got time to pop and see what's going on with our... um... guest. I'll be there at VSS HQ on time, don't worry."

Bane was glowering at the marble floor...

"Um... coming, Bane?" I asked as brightly as I could.

For a moment it seemed he'd agree, then... was he recollecting all those long, unfamiliar corridors, leading to the place where he'd spent an agonizing few weeks waiting for a miscellaneous patchwork of skin grafts to grow into place? Or just too furious with me for going on this trip, period?

"No. Think I'll go back to the apartment until it's time to see you off. Jon... are you... going back that way?"

From his expression, Jon had been planning to hotfoot it to the hospital with me. But he just said, "Yeah, I'm going back that way. See you in a few minutes, Margo. Or maybe not, I'm on cleanup duty after breakfast." Tactfully telling me he couldn't stay with Bane for long. Not quite tactfully enough: Bane bristled at the reminder that Jon was proficient enough to be part of a cleanup team. Feeling useless and angry all over again?"

"Okay. I won't be long, Bane."

Not right *now*, said the grumpy twitch of his brows, but what do you call a three-day trip to Malta? He didn't say anything, but his face wore that familiar expression of hurt that I was leaving him and anger that it bothered him so much.

Uh oh, my brother Kyle was moving in my direction,.... With a hasty mutter of, "I'm off then, see you in a minute," I headed for the door into the private section of the Vatican.

But Kyle caught me up just inside the corridor, cassock swishing around his legs. "Margo! Wait up! I want a word..."

"*Another* one?"

"You're my sister. I'm allowed to want to talk to you, aren't I?"

"Talk, yes. Lecture, no." I tried to keep my voice down.

"I'm not going to lecture you. Look, Margo, seriously," he dropped his voice, "how's Bane treating you these days?"

"Everything's fine, Kyle."

"Don't give me *everything's fine*, Margo. You were crying in Mass; what was that about?"

"Look, I've got to go..."

"Did Bane upset you again?"

"We upset each other regularly, it's called marriage, as you will no doubt understand when you're ordained and get to counsel married couples..."

Kyle looked annoyed. "What you were talking about in

February didn't sound like normal marital spats, and I told you my concerns then..."

I whirled on him, but spoke as calmly as I could. "Look, Kyle, you seem to forget that a year ago, I was locked away waiting to be chopped up as spare parts and the only reason I'm not still there in Salperton Facility—or already dismantled—is Bane. Bane got me out. Me, Jon, everyone in that place. He got me and Jon all the way across Europe with the EuroArmy hot on our heels. Then he started the Liberations and freed thousands more reAssignees—he was *your* Liberation team leader, for pity's sake! And you think I should abandon him just because he's hit a rough patch? Have you forgotten *why* he lost his eyes? Because he handed himself over to the EuroGov to try and whip up dissent and save everyone in the Citadel—and it worked! He saved us all! But at such a terrible cost! And *now* I should turn my back on him?"

"Past goodness is no excuse for what's going on now, and if you'll only stop defending him and look at the situation for a moment..."

"I'm sorry, I haven't got time right now." I walked determinedly away from his infuriated, "*Margo!*"

I knew, deep down, that he was just worried. But he was only focusing on how the situation affected me; he didn't seem to be able to open the eyes he was lucky enough to still have and see Bane's needs as well. He acted as though Bane should've simply had a good cry, then shrugged and said, "Well, it was only my eyes," and gone on just as normal...

Of course, the other reason I was getting so angry with him these days was because I was trying not to lean too hard on Jon, and I desperately needed Kyle's support instead—but all I was getting was criticism of my husband. By now I'd about given up on getting anything else.

I galloped on up to the hospital wing, trying to work off some of my annoyance with my brisk pace. When I arrived, it was an oasis of calm. Just what I needed. Did they know, yet, who they'd admitted? The nurses directed me to a private room at the end of the corridor, next to the one Jon had had, a million years ago, when we'd first stumbled into the Vatican, refugees ourselves.

The frail figure in the bed scarcely raised the blankets. Eduardo was examining the mound of removed clothing—the remains of a lady's all-weather jacket among other things, its lining stuffed with pine needles for extra insulation, needle-tips sticking through the fabric. "Margaret? All ready?" When I nodded, he went on, "So what was the fellow's state of mind, would you say?"

"He's still out of it—that's the impression I got, anyway."

The fellow in question lay in a nest of tubes. Some familiar, from Bane's and Jon's stays in hospital—oxygen and fluids and stuff—and another tube that must be a feeding tube. The nurses had shaved him and hacked off most of the excess hair, probably to make it easier to get the tubes in place—the cadaverous face now sparked a ghost of recognition of the man I had known. Ghost was the word: I'd never seen anyone so fragile...

"Well, I'm putting a guard on the room," said Eduardo. "Mad or not, this guy waltzed out of a high-security detention Facility, survived for four months on the run, and found his way here, so forgive me if I'm slightly cautious."

"Cautious, fair enough," snorted Doctor Frederick, coming in, "but the guy's got no muscles left. He's not going anywhere."

"He just walked across St Peter's Square and into the basilica under his own steam, muscles or not. The guard stays."

Doctor Frederick shrugged. "Well, I doubt it will be a long assignment."

"What do you mean?" I asked.

Doctor Frederick looked surprised. "Well, he'll be dead by morning. We've done what we can, but he's about had it." He shot me a quick look. "Er... not a friend of yours?"

I stared at the almost-dead man in the bed, whilst Eduardo tried not to look amused. "No. Not exactly."

"Look, you're going to hear it from somewhere fairly soon," said Eduardo. "His name's Lucas Everington, but I don't want that to affect the care he receives in any way."

Doctor Frederick looked affronted, then the name registered. "Everington? That EGD Security man?"

No doubt he, like practically everyone in Europe, had watched the televised show trial where the EuroBloc Genetics Department attempted to prove that Everington was the mastermind behind the mass breakout actually engineered by two teenagers—Bane and me. They'd eventually succeeded in reducing the Major to a pathetic deranged figure huddled in a corner of the courtroom whispering a mantra of, "I need to know, I *need* to know, I need to *know*"—but never managed to make him look at all guilty.

Eduardo clearly remembered the show trial too. "That's the one. He's claimed sanctuary."

Doctor Frederick scowled, his eyes moving from the man in the bed to my forehead. As my doctor, he knew better than most what I'd been subjected to. Perhaps it was time for the unsaid to be said: it might clear the air a bit.

"Thousands of innocent reAssignees owe this fellow their lives, you know," I told him.

Doctor Frederick looked at me as though I'd taken leave of my senses. "Owe him their lives? He *oversaw* the *deaths* of hundreds of reAssignees, to say nothing of all the Underground prisoners that were executed on his watch."

"But the Liberations were dead in the water and going nowhere until that top secret EGD Security manual was anonymously mailed to me—I'm not sure if you ever heard about that? We had to keep it pretty quiet. I don't know why Everington did it, but I know it was him."

"Indeed," Eduardo backed me up. "All but one of the Liberations were planned with the information provided by the—once—Major Everington. But that's still confidential, just in case we lose the vote and have to start Liberations again, so I'm afraid you can't pass it on."

"Well, we'll do all we can for him," Doctor Frederick sniffed, his Hippocratic impartiality returning. "But he'll probably die, and you can't blame us for that."

Would simplify my life—and quite a few other people's—if the man did just die. All the same... Bane had wondered out loud while watching the trials what the man wanted to know so badly, and I was getting quite curious myself.

* * *

I was going to head straight back; have a spot of breakfast with Bane before I left, but one of the nurses commandeered my assistance with washing the patient's hair; I'd helped with Bane often enough. I'd really no doubt Everington would have been looked after anyway, but it still felt like I'd dropped a load of extra work on the hospital, so I didn't like to say no.

"The water must be good and warm," she said briskly, "and then you must blow dry his hair—at once—he's no energy to spare getting cold. But it's got to be done, and it'll be a much nicer job now than when he's... well, grab that bowl."

Than when he's dead. Right. He was so pale and still, it was uncomfortably like preparing a corpse as it was. I imagine.

It took three washes and even more rinses, but finally his hair was clean and I set to work with the hairdryer. Fortunately, there wasn't too much hair after its impromptu trim—kind of satisfying watching it dry to that familiar pale blond.

"You know, I'm not sure I like you much," I found myself murmuring to him, not that he could hear me over the hairdryer, "but I do wish you'd live. Seems rather sad for you to make it all the way here, only to die in this hospital bed, y'know?

"Anyway... that's all dry and fluffy as a baby chick's down..." A flattering way to put it—his hair was thin and dry, as starved as the rest of him. I tried to flatten it into its customary neatness but it was no use. "Oh well. That's my duty done. I'd better... Oh Lord, the time! I've got to get back!"

I dumped the hairdryer on the bedside table and scampered.

"Where have you *been*?" snapped Bane. "I thought you were leaving anytime now?"

I fought not to bristle. He was sitting alone on the sofa and must've been there for almost an hour. "I'm sorry, every person I met on the way back wanted to talk about this morning's little drama. And I was longer at the hospital than I expected. I'm back now. I'll have to make do with a coffee and biscuit for breakfast. Do you want the same?"

"No," he said sulkily.

I waited a beat, heart aching. I didn't want to go off with things like this between us...

He hung his head and said almost inaudibly, "Yes. Please."

I went into the kitchenette and put the blind up to let the daylight in. "Coming right up. Do you think you could open the curtains? It's dark in here."

Another moment's silence. A rather flat, "Okay." At least he was up and doing something. There were so many things he *could* still do, but he was so fixated on what he couldn't...

We sipped and munched in mutual silence, mine hurried, Bane's moody.

"How's our mysterious benefactor, then?" he asked at last, wiping his face with repeated—almost paranoid—swipes of his hands to make sure he'd removed any biscuit crumbs. He looked like a mouse washing its whiskers, but I wasn't going to say it.

"Doctor Frederick doesn't think he'll make it. He's almost starved to death—body's eaten up his own muscles to stay alive. No protein, you know."

"Huh. Know all about that, don't we? So how was he walking around this morning?"

"Stubbornness, I suppose."

"Yeah, he is stubborn, isn't he?"

Thinking about that farce of a trial? "He's that, all right. But he's like a skeleton. As much as Doctor Frederick tends to the negative, I've a nasty feeling he may be right."

Bane shrugged. "Oh well. It's one final poke in the EuroGov's eye that he made it this far. He must've walked straight past the EuroArmy."

The section of wall and the gates that sealed off the square, though originally built by the EuroBloc, had been turned over to the Vatican. But the EuroGov maintained their white line a few meters away, guarded at all times, especially in front of the gates. What for, who knew? Did they think I'd try and stroll out past them, or something?

"He'll certainly have given them a red face. Again."

"So why was he looking for you, Margo?"

Should've seen that coming. Lots of people had expressed puzzlement as to why Everington had asked for me, but it hadn't occurred to any of them that I might know any more than they did... until now.

Bane's ears were practically pricking up as he strained for any clue why I hadn't replied. "I can see why he'd throw himself on the Underground's mercy, in his situation," he persisted, "but I'd have thought you're the last person he'd dare get near."

What to say?

Bane's voice held certainty, and the beginnings of anger. "You *know* why he asked for you, don't you?"

"Sorry. Yes. Um, during my interrogation, after he... well, when he was about to leave... I said... Well, I didn't even think about it, it just popped out, so it sounds better than it really is—but... I said I forgave him."

"You *what?*"

"I told him I forgave him, okay?"

"*Not* okay! That bastard carved up your face and you told him you *forgave him?*"

"Love your enemy, Bane. Anyway, it was mostly the Holy Spirit, I think. But I imagine that's why he's looking for me. Assuming he's got a rational reason. He's still loopy."

Bane continued spluttering his indignation.

"Look," I said firmly, "I've never said anything about this because you haven't exactly been very understanding where that man is concerned, but I'm pretty certain he was actually trying to help me avoid Conscious Dismantlement by torturing me, okay? In a really twisted way, but he's a twisted guy."

"*Help* you? By cutting you up?"

"He was trying to force me to answer his questions—but if I answered them, he was going to give me the normal anesthetic. Then I would've been out like a light during the Dismantling, instead of conscious as the EuroGov intended."

Bane stopped spluttering, the memory of the three long *days* of torture he'd endured pinching his temples. How he must've longed for the anesthetic... "Would he really have

18

given it to you?"

"Yes. I was sure he was going to, at the end, even though I wouldn't answer. I think the questioning was mostly an excuse. But *dear Doctor Richard* interfered."

Bane was silent for a long time. I'd thought nothing could reconcile him with Everington, not with this scar on my forehead for him to feel every day. But... he understood so much better, now.

"Is the guy comfortable?" he asked at last.

"He's unconscious. He'll go peacefully, no doubt about that."

Bane nodded, once, and felt cautiously for his coffee mug. Subject closed. The animation left his face, and he just looked glum again. I checked my watch. Time to go.

"You *know* these trips are stupid," said Bane, as we walked down to VSS HQ.

"Bane..." I protested. Were we really doing this *again*, right now? On a good day he would admit that his opposition to my trips out of the Vatican was based almost entirely on a selfish fear for my safety. But good days were so rare, just now... "They're not stupid. Why did we stay in Gozo instead of going to Africa? Because refusing to run away inspires people. And they're not *that* dangerous. I'm going to a Free State; it's not like I'm going into the EuroBloc. That *would* be stupid."

"The EuroGov *hate your guts*, Margo!"

"Yes, but they don't want bad press right now, do they? Assassinating me in a Free State would not go over well. You know how touchy everyone is about the autonomy of independent states after their little spate of annexations."

"In other words, you're staking your life on the Euro-Gov's good sense," he said sarcastically.

"Eduardo agrees, Bane," I said tiredly. "And so does Pope Cornelius. He's the one who suggested the trips, after all."

"And their opinions count for far more than mine, naturally," snapped Bane.

"*Bane*. I value your opinion more than anyone else's. But when it comes to *this*, you're just not thinking objectively..."

Here we were at the door to VSS HQ. Thank goodness.

Bane let the subject drop as we showed our pass cards and went in.

Sister Krayj was waiting with my disguise. The trim eastern European Sister wasn't Vatican Secret Service, but until the vote was decided, the State was being run by the minimum number of staff possible—since if we lost the EuroGov's retribution would be inevitable—and lethal. With her ex-Resistance past, she'd been a key member of the Liberation teams, and Eduardo had no hesitation about calling on her skills.

"There," said Sister Krayj, holding up a mirror a few minutes later.

I checked myself carefully. Blonde wig pinned over my fastened-up hair. Glasses with blank lenses. My scar covered with makeup, with a sun hat over it, just for good measure.

"So convincing, my own mother wouldn't recognize me," I said to Sister Krayj. My mother... Bad choice of metaphor. I still didn't know if my parents were dead or alive. I swallowed and turned to Bane. "I'm all disguised, love. Nothing to worry about."

He simply scuffed a shoe moodily on the floor. He knew he was being selfish. He just needed me so much right now...

A bearded older man swept in from a side room, dressed in a lightweight summer suit. A new arrival? Oh... No. It was my 'Uncle Conrad.' Belatedly, I bobbed a curtsey. "I didn't recognize you, your Holiness."

"That's the whole idea, isn't it?" Pope Cornelius smiled.

"Everyone ready?" Eduardo stuck his head into the room. "Good, come along..."

When we reached the entrance to the secret passage, and Eduardo swung the huge old painting away from the wall, Bane unbent enough to give me a long hug and kiss me goodbye. "Please be careful..." The shaky appeal in his voice made my heart ache again.

Grass Snake stepped up to me and gave Bane's shoulder a quick, comradely bump with his fist. "Don't worry, Bane; no one will hurt her while there's breath in my body."

Bane managed a silent smile of thanks and tried to look

reassured. Where was... ah, finally. Jon was just coming along the passage. "Bye, Jon," I called, as Eduardo shepherded me impatiently through the hole in the wall. "No wild parties, you two! I don't want to find the place a mess when I get back..." Bane really couldn't manage everything by himself yet, so Jon was staying at our apartment while I was away.

Bane managed a rather forced laugh, and Jon sniggered at this, then Eduardo shut the portrait again, and it was just Pope Cornelius and his two Swiss Guards, Fox and Foxie, plus Unicorn and Grass Snake, who were my bodyguards, though Unicorn was in overall charge of Pope Cornelius's security as well. Hard to be stealthy with any larger party.

As we set off along the dimly-lit passage, I tried not to feel like I'd got an unexpected reprieve from lessons or something. *It's just something you've got to do, Margo...* In truth, despite what I'd said to Bane, I'd much have preferred to stay within the Vatican. I wasn't so worried about something happening in the Maltese Free State, but we had to cross a thirty kilometer strip of EuroBloc territory to reach Ostia and the boat...

"Almost no one knows we're going, Margo," said Grass Snake. The light level clearly wasn't quite low enough to hide my face. "No way the EuroGov could know."

"I'm fine, Snakey. That's just my default expression when I think about the trip to Ostia. You should know that by now!"

Grass Snake grinned, the glow from the wall lights bouncing off his shaved head. He'd been so supportive of Bane, these last few interminable months. Some of the guys clearly felt awkward around Bane now, not knowing what to say. But Snakey and the Foxes, and Unicorn, of course, had been brilliant.

"Here we are," said Unicorn after a while, unlocking a door. We went out into a basement garage, and got into the large people carrier parked there. "Everyone got their ID cards?" Fakes, needless to say. We all nodded, so he aimed a key fob at the garage doors and they began to open.

Here we went again...

3

UNWANTED GIFTS

"See," said Grass Snake, completing his security sweep of the cabin and letting me enter at last. "Safe and sound on the boat, yet again."

"It's an ocean liner," I corrected him, "but so we are. Thank you."

Grass Snake waved this away. "We've booked the whole corridor, so no one should be coming along here. There's a kitchenette-lounge-type cabin two doors along, if you're hungry. We'll bring you and your Uncle Conrad something from the cafeteria at meal times, like last time."

Stay out of sight, in other words. I concurred with that. On this big, slow, passenger ship, we wouldn't reach Malta until the following morning. But it was by far the most discreet way to travel.

I removed the few things I'd need from my case, then went along to the kitchenette. Coffee and a biscuit wasn't really enough on a day like this.

I met my 'Uncle Conrad' in the passage, heading the same way. "Ah, Margaret. I think I can guess where you're going," Pope Cornelius smiled.

I had to smile back. His was such a cheerful, tranquil presence. "Can you really?" I joked back.

He held the door open for me, then ushered me to a seat. "I saw Kyle trying to waylay you after Mass."

The smile slipped from my face. "Yes. Again."

"Do I get the impression you're not too keen to speak to your brother these days?"

"Yes. He's so..."

"So?"

"Unsympathetic."

Pope Cornelius looked surprised. "Really?"

"To Bane. They used to get on okay when we were

children, but now... Well, anyway."

"Oh. Toast?"

"Please."

Filling the toaster, he came to join me at the table. "I've always been under the impression Kyle liked Bane."

"He does. Or he *did*. I made the mistake of unburdening to him one day back in February, and he didn't take it very well."

"He's worried about Bane's behavior towards you." Statement not question. Had Kyle had the Holy Father's ear? Or had the Holy Father himself noticed? "How bad is it?"

I swallowed. "Bane's hurting, which hurts me to start with. Then *he* hurts me all the time—I mean, just saying hurtful things—*because* he's hurting, which hurts me even more. It hurts *him* when he hurts me, which hurts still *more*. So it's... it's not a barrel of laughs for us at the moment." My voice was choked.

"I imagine not."

"Kyle thinks—I don't know, that I shouldn't be putting up with it."

"What do you think?"

"*I think*... if I'd been tortured like he was, and lost my eyes, I'd like people to be really, really patient with me, for quite some time." I shot an anxious look at him, afraid he might side with Kyle.

He caught the look and gave me a reassuring smile. "You're both right, you know."

"We are?"

"Yes. It's a big danger with a life-changing injury like Bane's—that the pain's so bad they lash out at everyone around them, especially their nearest and dearest—often the only ones they dare let it out on—and sometimes they actually drive their loved ones and friends away when they need them most. And then they plunge still further into despair and loneliness. Things can end very badly."

I gulped. "You mean... with them doing... bad things to themselves."

"Yes. So you're absolutely right how important it is to stick with the one you love through something like this, even putting up with pretty much anything—up to a point—

in order to bring them through it. But you mustn't act as if his behavior is okay."

"He's always sorry," I said quickly. "He wants so much not to say these things to me, and then over and over he does it anyway. I don't dare let on how bad he makes me feel sometimes, because he's feeling so bad already, I don't think he could take it."

"Well, you're in the best position to decide how much he can bear. But as much as you can, as soon as you can, you need to make it quite clear when he's behaved badly and hurt you. Because you can't allow this to become permanent."

"He doesn't want to be like this..."

"I'm quite sure he doesn't. So make sure you help him *not to.*"

I nodded, reassured. I wasn't wrong. Glad of that bit of advice, though.

"And you know," Pope Cornelius went on, "the two of you don't need to do this alone. Bane could probably use some help from other people, you both could."

"You mean... counselors? I don't think Bane would..."

Pope Cornelius flapped his hand, "Something for him to consider, surely? But even just reaching out to people who care about you both. Let them help."

I nodded again, politely, and made a few 'message received' noises, but... Other people? I was trying not to load Jon down with our troubles, and look what had happened when I tried Kyle! I wasn't making that mistake again.

"Well, now..." Pope Cornelius fetched the toast and gestured invitingly to the row of three jars on the table— marmalade, honey, jam. "I suppose you saw the good news in the papers yesterday that the United States of South America have decided to support a permanent ban on Sorting?"

"So it's not a rumor?" It was hard to believe everything you read in the EuroBloc papers.

Pope Cornelius beamed. "No, it's true. They're actually sending over a delegation to present their arguments to the EuroGov, and they've asked to meet with us beforehand, in the Vatican. It's fantastic news—well, except perhaps for

Eduardo, who is already working on the security angle! Until recently, the African Free States were practically the only Bloc who still opposed both Sorting and the Suppression of Religious Practice, so it's heartening to see the tide turning."

Another entire Bloc really had thrown their support behind our cause. Fantastic news indeed!

2 months, 20 days

"Historic wrongs and injustices can only be overcome if men and women are inspired by a message of healing and hope, a message that offers a way forward, out of the impasse that so often locks people and nations into a vicious circle of violence."

Pope Benedict XVI—quoted on 'The Impatient Gardener'

People lined the road as we walked up from the harbor to the Maltese capital of Valletta. Crowd control barriers had been put up to deal with the numbers, and the place was crawling with police. Despite Religious Suppression having never become law in this Free State, it had been over fifty years since the government had dared to accept a Papal Visit.

Fortunately for us, after the way the EuroGov had violently tried to annex the State three months ago, the Maltese government no longer cared what the EuroGov thought. In fact, anything that would weaken the EuroGov had their support.

Flanked by Fox and Foxie, resplendent in their Swiss Guard uniforms, Pope Cornelius walked ahead, back in his Papal whites and distinctive red shoes, pausing often to bless babies and accept flowers and hugs from small children. I trailed along behind at a distance with Unicorn and Grass Snake, dressed now in my Sunday best—the blue blouse and skirt with the embroidered waistband that I'd been married in—and doing my best to be inconspicuous: much chance of that! Frequently the cries of welcome and invocation to Pope Cornelius became screams of support directed at me, and I had to smile and wave acknowledgement. I ended up with a good armful of flowers myself.

The main public event was Mass in the Cathedral of St John. No acting skills were required on my part for me to gaze with admiration at the beautiful old church, modest in size compared to many European cathedral buildings, but richly decorated—and still in use for its intended purpose. I made appreciative remarks to the microphones shoved in my face, and smiled a lot. The reporters, to my bemusement, smiled back, their voracious hunger for once seeming to be for more than just a good front page.

After Mass, we went out into the nearby main square and Pope Cornelius mounted a podium to speak to the crowds. No matter that we weren't *actually* in the EuroBloc, this would go out EuroBloc-wide, all the same!

"Second chances," concluded Pope Cornelius, "are something of quite incomparable value and in our world they often come far too few and far between. But something amazing is happening in the EuroBloc in two months' time. Every man and woman is getting a second chance. A chance to re-enshrine the right to life in law and to affirm the fundamental value of the human person. Because the right to life is the most fundamental right of all. If a person does not have life, no other rights or virtues are of any importance whatsoever. For this reason, all human beings must first and foremost protect the right of every last person simply to live.

"So I urge all of you to support the citizens of the EuroBloc in every way you can, and to miss no opportunity to encourage them to make the right choice on the first of July. Now is their chance to make history! Let them not fail to take it!"

The applause bounced off the tall stone buildings around the square and shook the windows of the little enclosed wooden balconies sticking out from some of them. Uh oh, now it was my turn. Pope Cornelius was heading off for a serious conference with the government, leaving me in the square to occupy the crowd.

I checked my notes nervously. No reassuring words from Grass Snake or Unicorn this time, they were in full alert mode, eyes never still as they searched the square for danger. *Yeah, Margo, don't think about the fact that one of those people might be pointing something worse than a camera your way...* Too late...

No, I must simply trust Snakey and Unicorn to do their job and concentrate on doing mine. I mounted the podium, wincing internally at the roar from the crowd. It made me feel like some sort of rock star.

But as usual, once I started talking, it was fine.

"...Ask yourselves this," I demanded as I neared the end of the speech. "Ask yourselves this question, and answer it honestly, whether you are here, living free in the Maltese Free State, or living under oppression in the EuroBloc. Answer this: *would you* still think Dismantling was okay if *you*, or *your child*, or *your grandchild* failed Sorting? Would you *really* still think it's okay?

"*That* is the only question you should ask yourselves, when deciding—honestly—whether you think Sorting is acceptable in a supposedly-civilized Bloc. It is the only question you need to ask! And out of the entire world's population, I don't think more than a bare handful of utter fanatics, if that, could answer *yes*, not if they were truly being honest with themselves!

"So if you want to know how to decide which way to vote, there you are; that's it. *Could you send your own child to the Facility with a clear conscience?* Could you? And if not, why were you happy to send *me*? To send *Jon*? To send Sarah and Jane and Rebecca and Bethan? To send anyone's child? Perhaps you will say that you never really thought it was right, you just never had a choice! Fair enough. But you have a choice now! Make it the right one!

"Thank you. Thank you all." I stepped back from the lectern, but of course I wasn't getting off that easily. Question time.

"Mrs. Verrall, what do you think will happen if the Religious Suppression is lifted? The EuroGov have killed tens of thousands of your fellow believers, and the population have stood by and let it happen. Do you think there will be a violent backlash from people of faith?"

"Well," I took a deep breath, "I certainly hope not.

Certainly not from my stream of the Underground. Definitely not from me. Our faith teaches us to forgive our enemies and to love those who have harmed us."

More hands shot up.

"Mrs. Verrall, does that mean you love and forgive Major Lucas Everington? The man who oversaw your incarceration in Salperton Facility. A member of EGD Security for over fifteen years?"

Fortunately I'd seen that one coming, and I'd spent some of yesterday on the boat... sorry, ocean liner... trying to figure out how I felt about the whole thing.

"Concerning Lucas Everington, well... in case any of you don't know, yesterday morning, a dead man—or at any rate, a man believed to be dead—walked into St Peter's and asked to speak to me. And yes, (Former) Major Lucas Everington was the Commandant of Salperton Facility, where, as most of you probably know, I was incarcerated for four months after failing my Sorting before, as the EuroGov like to put it, 'illegally absenting' myself." The crowd tittered and whooped at this.

"Anyway, to suddenly meet Everington—well, imagine one of those Jewish concentration camp survivors from the Great Wars coming face-to-face with one of their Nazi guards, and that's about how I felt, as would any former Salperton reAssignee.

"However, as I have mentioned on my blog, Lucas Everington was in fact tortured and sentenced to death for a 'crime' he didn't commit. In light of which, I think I was far from the only one to be quite delighted at the way he managed to slip from a top security Detention Facility and disappear into thin air, leaving his captors looking remarkably stupid. And this while off his rocker, too!" From the screams of approval, the crowd had found it rather delightful too...

"As a result of this, I cannot help but feel that whatever his other sins, those four months at the tender mercies of the Department for Internal Affairs must've gone a good way towards atoning for them. He's in the Vatican hospital now and I'm glad to have him there, even if, as the doctors fear, he will not survive long.

"But since he's claimed sanctuary, regardless of the uncharitable mutterings likely to arise from some, or even vengeful demands for him to be given up—we are, I'm afraid, only human—I know the majority of Believers will never find it in their hearts to hand a man over to certain death. So if he lives, he stays, and if he dies—he gets the grave he wanted.

"And yes, I do forgive him, and yes, I will do my utmost to love him like the brother human being he is, for as long as he is with us."

Hands shot up again.

"Mrs. Verrall, *how* can you forgive that man?"

"It's not easy, but it is very important. Refusal to forgive harms *us* even more than it harms the person who wronged us."

"Mrs. Verrall, if you hold such an opinion, how can you ally yourself with the Resistance? They make it quite clear that forgiveness and reconciliation are not on their agenda, only justice and retribution."

"And only *their* notion of justice!" I said fiercely. "I will say it yet again, I am *not* allied with the Resistance. The Underground are most certainly not allied with them. Myself, personally, with Bane and Jon, have on a couple of occasions worked with them through extreme necessity and only then when assured that their goals were restrained and moderate."

"But Mrs. Verrall, what about the helicopter pilot killed at Salperton Facility, and the four guards killed on the Channel Bridge by the Resistance during your escape?"

"No one regrets those unnecessary deaths more than I do. They only go to confirm me in my view that the Resistance's methods make them an organization I can in no way support or endorse. In fact, I see the EuroGov and the Resistance as two heads on the same snake of violence. Both heads need to be destroyed, to get rid of the snake. In this case, I believe that if we de-fang the one head—the EuroGov—the other head will quite simply wither away."

"Mrs. Verrall..."
"Mrs. Verrall..."
"Mrs. Verrall..."

* * *

I collapsed onto a sofa as soon as we'd boarded the (different) ship that would take us home. We'd be sailing to Pescara this time, on the opposite side of the Italian Department, a bit over two hundred kilometers from the Vatican, and most importantly, not Ostia, where the EuroGov would no doubt be eagerly awaiting us. One of Eduardo's guys would have dropped off a vehicle.

"I hear you gave a wonderful speech," said Pope Cornelius. He glanced at Unicorn and Grass Snake. "Was it good?"

Grass Snake shrugged. "I honestly wasn't listening; no offense, Margo."

Good thing, considering what I'd said about snakes!

"Glad to hear it," said Unicorn approvingly to Snakey, being the senior of the two, then smiled apologetically. "You know we have to watch the crowd, Your Holiness. I doubt Fox and Foxie heard a word you said, either."

"Did he say something?" said Foxie, widening his eyes and looking astonished. His older brother laughed.

"All right, fair enough," said the Holy Father, laughing too. "I'm asking the wrong people."

"*Your* speech was amazing," I told him.

He shrugged this off. "Well, I think it *all* went very well. Now we can sit back and relax."

"*You* two can," said Unicorn. "Not *you* three. Though I know I don't need to say that," he added, as Grass Snake and the Foxes turned indignant looks on him. "Though, actually, Snakey and Fox, you're on half-watch now, so stay with your Principals. Foxie, we're on duty."

Foxie followed him out. They were using cabins at each end of the corridor as guard posts. With the doors open, they could see if anyone came along, without having to stand outside in a suspicious-looking manner. On 'half' watch, Snakey and Fox could relax, sit down, have a coffee, but they had to remain with us, just in case someone decided to rappel down the side of the ship, or something.

Snakey was already heading for the kettle. "Coffee, everyone?" he asked. "Or tea, for Your Holiness?"

"Tea, please."

"It's only a tea bag, there's no loose tea."

"I'll live," smiled the Holy Father.

Fox sat in a corner and pulled a bookReader from his pocket. Snakey handed him a mug, then joined Pope Cornelius and me at the table.

"By the way," I asked him, "what were you telling Bane the other day when I was in the kitchen? It sounded really interesting but I couldn't catch it all. I mean... unless it's private!"

"Hmm? Oh, do you mean the story about the itsy-bitsy cross the Lord gave me to carry? That's no secret." Clearly reminded, Snakey pulled a tube of cream from his pocket and slathered a layer over his shaved head. If he didn't do it every few hours, patches of his scalp began to flake off and get sore. "Have you really not heard that yet? I first told Bane ages ago. He keeps getting me to repeat it. I can only hope the Lord's speaking to him in some way."

"I really haven't heard it," I told him.

"Okay, well, uh, when I was growing up in Spain, I dreamt of having long hair like a hero in a historical film— but my *madre* wouldn't let me until I became a teenager. At which point I developed this scalp condition of mine and my hair was soon falling out in patches: it was hopeless."

I couldn't help wincing in sympathy. Imagine having to go to school with a condition like that.

He just smiled ruefully, "It seems so unimportant now, but at the time I got so angry with God about it, I actually stopped practicing my faith for over a year.

"But one day, I realized what a vain fool I was being. Realized that I was treating my aunt, who gave me some horrible unwanted present every Christmas, better than I was treating God. Because I thanked her for the awful gift, and tried to appreciate it. And I'd not once tried to do that with... well, this," he waved to his head.

"Once I'd figured that out, I threw away all my hair concoctions and I realized what a good gift it really was. It had brought me far, far closer to Him than I'd been before, and gone at least some way towards curing my excessive vanity."

"So when did you come to the Vatican?"

"Not long after, actually. There was a devastating raid on our Mass center, during a Mass, the worst possible time. Either through chance, or providence, we weren't there, but after that, my parents just lost their nerve. Wouldn't go to Mass any more, wouldn't allow me to go. Eventually I couldn't bear it any more. I already knew I wanted to give my life to God. Not as a priest or religious brother, I didn't feel that call, but in some way. So one day, when I was fifteen, I just packed a rucksack and left. Got to the Vatican State okay and managed to persuade them to let me stay, rather than being sent on to Africa."

"Like Eduardo," I remarked. Eduardo had been even younger when he arrived, fleeing the far distant Sorting he knew he would fail on account of his borderline autism.

"Rather like, yes." Grass Snake grinned, clearly not minding this association with his much more senior fellow Spaniard. "In fact, I was planning to apply to the Vatican Police when I turned sixteen, but Eduardo used me a lot for errands and little jobs, and shortly before my birthday asked me if I'd thought of applying to the VSS. I realized then that he'd been testing me all along. It was clear it would suit me much better, so I applied. And here I am, seven years later."

"With quite a reputation for slithering in and out of the EuroGov."

He looked embarrassed, waved this away, and sipped his coffee.

Personally, I thought he made too light of his story. It had obviously been a huge struggle for him at the time. No wonder Bane found it so interesting.

2 months, 19 days

I was expecting that everyone would read all about Everington's arrival in the newspapers, but the details have been a bit thin on the ground. The EuroGov do seem to be tightening up their censorship an awful lot, don't they?

Margaret Verrall—blog post, 'The Impatient Gardener'

"Margo!" Bane crushed me to him in a tight embrace.

I hugged him back. "See, home safe and sound. And very glad to be back. I'm always afraid the crowd is going to eat me alive."

Jon laughed. "You make mincemeat out of them, Margo. I don't know why you worry so much."

"I worry," I said rather hotly, "because if I answer even a single question badly, it will be over the front of every newspaper by the next morning, providing selfish people with excuses to vote the wrong way..."

"All right, keep your hair on," said Jon, face sobering. "You're right. It is important. In fact... you know you won't have made any friends among the Resistance with that little, er, *diatribe*, right?"

"It's the truth," I said, "and I'm fed up with people associating me with them."

"True, I just don't see any huge benefit in ticking them off, that's all."

"Have you eaten, Margo?" asked Bane quickly, when I drew in a rather deep breath. "Eduardo said you were stuck in traffic, so we had lunch."

I tried to let my annoyance go. The EuroGov's constant insinuations that we were allied with the Resistance had been bugging me for ages. "Snakey slithered into a service station and bought sandwiches. And cake. And coffee. I'm stuffed. But... I could drink another coffee," I added quickly, when his face fell. Then I'd have to get back to my blogging, I didn't need to say that.

"I need to get home, actually." Jon excused himself with more tact than honesty, I suspected, and picked up his night bag from the sofa.

"Oh, right, 'til later, then," said Bane.

"Bye, Jon," I said, making sure my smile entered my voice. "Thanks."

I made coffee—a small one for me—and sat on the sofa beside Bane. "I hear Everington is still alive," I remarked. "That's unexpected."

"Yeah, he's still taking delight in pissing off even his allies," said Bane dryly, "at least in the form of Doctor Frederick. Jon dragged me up there yesterday and we met

33

Doctor Frederick and he was like, 'Well, he *should* be dead. Don't ask *me* to explain it.' Clearly they don't cover stubbornness in medical school."

That made me laugh. "Apparently not."

"You gave a great speech, Margo," Bane said abruptly. "Changed some minds and hearts, from the newscasts afterwards. I'm sorry I was so grumpy about you going. I..." His voice went almost inaudible. "I miss you so much when you're not here, that's all."

He'd said much the same after my last trip. Still, it was nice to see him in such a good mood. Shame I couldn't be freshly returned from a journey every day... I pushed the thought away and rested my head on his shoulder. But all too soon, the mugs were empty.

"I'll wash up in a minute," Bane said. "I know you need to get on."

Anything Jon can do...

I bit back, *careful with the hot water.* "Okay, thanks. I had better get blogging."

I went over to the table by the window and switched on my laptop. Our apartment in the Secure Accommodation Block looked out onto an internal courtyard of flagstones and the odd potted plant, amongst which roamed the ever-present guard. All the rooms with good views overlooking St Peter's square or the Vatican walls were occupied by people the EuroGov didn't know from Adam and cared about even less. In fact, most were empty, just at the moment.

While waiting for the laptop to wake up, I stuck a finger in the soil of the one and only plant on the windowsill. Too dry? It'd felt soggy from overwatering before I left—now it was all dried out! The little fuchsia, grown from the packet of seeds that had arrived tucked inside the EGD Security Manual, had inspired the name of my blog: "The Impatient Gardener." I'd been so impatient for it to grow and confirm my suspicion about the identity of the sender, but now I had to keep it alive, which was not going so well.

I watered it with a glass of water that had been standing forgotten on the desk since before my trip, and what was left of the afternoon passed normally enough, except that

Bane remained in slightly higher spirits. I edited the blog post I'd prepared before leaving, belatedly adding a bit about Mr. Everington's arrival, clicked 'Post' and set to work again, writing tomorrow's blog: all about the Papal visit. Then I answered comments. Read a couple of blogs that Eduardo and Sister Mari's prayer team had flagged up for me to challenge, one pro-Sorting and another cautiously (or cowardly, as I made sure to point out!) neutral, and commented on them. Answered more comments.

After a couple of hours, I went down to St Peter's for evening prayer, carefully collecting my Divine Office token: I was saving up to get my own book from the Vatican's limited supply. Bane came; he *was* in a good mood. He went back to the apartment with Jon while I stayed to pray through some of the prayer lists. Moratorium on Sorting or not, we still had prayer requests pouring in.

When I got back to the apartment, I found Jon taking advantage of Bane's liveliness to teach him—or start teaching him—how to cook pasta with cheese sauce. I bit my tongue some more, picturing the burnt fingers to come. Bane could do things, slowly, with Jon there, but then he'd go and immediately try to do them on his own, and fail, and be more depressed than ever... I almost wished Jon wouldn't try so hard, but I suppose he was taking the long view.

"Well, that was tasty." I finished off the last bite. "Thanks for cooking, you two."

"A compliment," said Bane. "That just proves Jon did most of it."

"I don't know, maybe your cooking's finally improved," teased Jon.

"Unlikely. Father Mark used to say he should be, what's it... canonized?... y'know, made a saint, for living on my cooking for four months."

"He was joking, Bane," I laughed. "You have to be..." I broke off. *...dead to be canonized.*

Bane put down his fork, leaving his last few pasta swirls uneaten. How badly did he miss Father Mark? Even worse than me? I couldn't help remembering all those months Bane had put his life on the line hiding Father Mark, when things had got tough back in Salperton. Not because Father

Mark was a priest, but because he was Bane's friend. His death during the Liberations was something we never talked about.

I sought something cheerful to say—we'd been having such a nice evening—but a knock on the door cut me off. Most people didn't keep their doors locked here, but for certain people, Eduardo insisted on it. I went to look through the peep hole—speak of the devil...

"Hello, Eduardo."

"Can I come in for a minute?"

"Of course. We've just had pasta. There's some left, have a bite..."

Eduardo waved the offer away with the bug sweeper he'd just pulled out and began circling the room, but Jon was already heading for the kitchen. He brought a plateful back and held it near Eduardo's nose as he pocketed the sweeper again. "Go on; you never eat."

"Fine." Eduardo pulled out two EuroGov ID cards and slapped them down in the middle of the table, then accepted the plate. "That's why I came." He broke off to insert a forkful into his mouth.

I picked them up. Frowned at the pictures. One of Bane, hair slightly lightened. One of Jon, with brown hair. Apparently they were Blaine Kerby and Tom North. My stomach went cold. I had a fake ID, but why did *they* need them?

"EuroGov IDs?" My voice was thin. "We're not going into EuroGov territory! Not... properly?"

"No, I certainly hope you're not," Eduardo agreed. "It's just precautionary. Very unlikely we're in the slightest danger until the first of July. After that... well, if we lose, it's both certain and, I imagine, imminent. If we win, we should be safe for the indefinite future. There's a little motivation for your blogging.

"On the subject of which," He put down his fork, folded his hands and stared at me. "I want to emphasize again that the EuroGov are looking for something, anything, that they can use to sway people's opinions against you. Against us. That includes reporting any scandal—or creating one."

"Margo was talking about that earlier today," said Bane

pointedly.

I just nodded. Eduardo looked from me to Bane and said, "Yet after Mr. Everington's little interruption at Mass the other day, Jack confiscated a camera from someone and deleted some rather emotive photographs of Margaret's tear-streaked face. Given your respective facial expressions on that occasion, I imagine they were planning on splashing it across the front page of the next day's newspaper."

"Oh." I could picture it all too clearly. TROUBLE IN PARADISE, across the headlines. MARGO'S MARRIAGE ON THE ROCKS? Yet another attack on my credibility. It didn't help that many people had placed me on an unreasonably high pedestal. "U didn't... mention that."

"I said I'd speak to you about it."

Bane was scowling. "It's none of their business."

"No, it's not, but they'll print it just the same," said Eduardo. "So may I suggest that you try to keep your private matters, shall we say," he glanced at me meaningfully, "a little more private? I trust there aren't actually any big marital problems?"

His usual tact. Jon turned his head away, as though he could hear something very interesting anywhere but here, and Bane's scowl deepened.

"I'm surprised you want to hear about our little troubles," I said hastily. "But since you do..."

Eduardo flinched. Emotion of any kind left him completely out of his depth. "I was going to say that if there are, talk to a shrink. But for goodness's sake keep it out of the public eye, hmm? And all of you, keep your EuroIDs on you at all times. If the EuroGov decides to overrun us, it'll all be individual efforts, and the best-known faces need all the help they can get."

My EuroID card was still in my pocket from my trip—clearly Eduardo not taking it back had been no oversight. I pulled it out and turned it in my hand, feeling a little guilty at having such an advantage. Still, Eduardo was right: we'd need all the help we could get. I put the card away again. The thought of trying to reach Africa with Bane and Jon—*both* unable to see now. I swallowed.

"Right." I picked up Bane's and Jon's and handed them

to them. "Come on, you two, put these away safe—keep them on you, but make jolly sure no one gets a look at them."

They both accepted them, wearing near-identical expressions of doubt and bitter amusement. Oh Lord, if the EuroGov broke in, they'd both ditch me at once, wouldn't they? Try to leave me free to escape the only way I'd have any real chance—by myself. And I'd be running around looking for *them*. We'd *all* be caught. The cards were a waste of time.

Eduardo looked from them to me and gave a tiny grimace: he saw it too. "Well, anyway," he said. "You've got them."

When he'd gone, Bane scowled. "Dear Eduardo," he said sarcastically. "Good at his job, yes, but..."

"Tad insensitive?" Jon said wryly. "True. But you know he can't help it. Well, I'll see you two tomorrow."

After seeing him off, I closed the door, feeling numb. Why'd Eduardo chosen tonight to issue the things?

Afraid Everington's arrival might provoke something, as ours had once done? But he'd been here several days by now. All the same...

Lord, please keep us safe tonight...

4

THE NOT-SO-DEPARTED

2 months, 18 days

So alive or dead, Lucas Everington will be remaining under our protection. Just in case anyone was wondering.

Margaret Verrall—blog post, 'The Impatient Gardener'

His good mood already flagging, Bane stayed determinedly in bed the following morning. He'd be grumpy with nerves by the time I got back from Mass, but what could I do?

"How are things?" asked Jon, once we were in the lift.

"Oh, fine. What are you up to, today?"

"I'll be going down to the library archives again, trying to find Braille books. The archive caretaker's sure there must be some—the old records give some idea where to start, but it's so long since they've had time to organize things properly, pretty much the only thing to do is hunt for them."

Braille, like so many other inventions to help the disabled, had fallen into disuse after Sorting was brought in. With an end to Sorting in sight *(please, Lord?)* Jon felt it was time to bring such things back into the public eye. "But... you don't know Braille, do you?" I couldn't help saying.

He pulled a face. "Never had a chance to learn. But hopefully there'll be a 'learn Braille' book. Or I'll have to treat it as a code to be cracked."

"Well, good luck," I said, as we stepped into St Peter's.

"Has he woken up yet?" I asked Doctor Frederick, as I took a peep through the observation window at the sleeping figure after Mass.

"No, there's a mild sedative in the drip to discourage it. The patient has no energy to spare on anything other than breathing and keeping his heart beating. He's picking up a little now, so we may withdraw the sedation soon."

"Uh-huh." The feeding tube was clearly doing its work. Speaking of work...

I went back to the apartment.

"*Where* have you...?" Bane broke off mid-sentence and chewed his lip.

"I don't suppose you'd care to rephrase that? It would make it so much more pleasant to be around you." I was insisting on a little more respect after my chat with Pope Cornelius.

"Sorry, Margo," he muttered. Not sullenly. Just... guiltily. Or what would've been guiltily if there'd been even a spark of energy in it. He was down again. More down.

"Well, have you had breakfast?"

"No. Jon's on breakfast duty in the cafeteria."

"Right." I headed for the kitchenette. "You know, I don't know why you're not on that rotation, come to think of it."

His bitter bark of laughter followed me, though he didn't. "Me? What would I do, Margo?"

"They seem to keep Jon busy enough. You could've gone along with him. At least you wouldn't have had to wait to eat."

"Well, pardon me for waiting until you got back so we could eat together."

"That's *not* why you're here," I said firmly around the doorframe. "You just didn't want to go to the cafeteria."

"And that's illegal, is it?"

"It's not that scary, y'know."

"Oh? And what the hell do you know about it?"

I couldn't argue with that one, and he knew it. I'd tried to join in a few of Jon's lessons in independent living as a blind person, but even with a handkerchief tied over my eyes, I couldn't even begin to do half the things. Which was in itself proof of how far Bane had already come, but try telling him that.

Two mugs of coffee, two bowls, two spoons, a box of cereals and a jug of milk on a tray and I went back into the living room, transferred it all to the table. "There's cereal if you want it."

When Bane dragged himself off the sofa and found his way to the table, sighing as though being forced to walk the plank, I added, "I said *if you want it*."

"That's what you *said*." He groped for the cereal box. "But if I didn't come and start eating, you'd be on at me fast enough, wouldn't you?"

"Obviously if you didn't eat *anything* I'd be worried," I said stiffly.

I'd basically just conceded the point but he didn't even smirk, gloomily guiding cereals into his bowl with a cupped hand. Smothering a sigh of my own, I poured milk onto mine. I'd just got a spoonful raised to my lips when there was a wild hammering on the door.

"Oh, now what..." I went to look through the peephole—Jon, beaming. I opened the door.

Jon found my hands at once. "Margo, you won't believe it!"

"I expect I *will*, but come in and tell Bane too."

"Right... Bane, you won't believe it!"

Bane took the Lord's name in vain and ignored the swipe I landed on the top of his head. "*What?* You found a Braille book or something?"

"Huh? Well, actually, yes, I did find one right before Eduardo popped down to see me—just the one... But it's my *parents*—they've found them. They're safe!"

2 months, 14 days

"[Married love] is above all fully human, a compound of sense and spirit. It is not, then, merely a question of natural instinct or emotional drive. It is also, and above all, an act of the free will, whose trust is such that it is meant not only to survive the joys and sorrows of daily life, but also to grow, so that husband and wife become in a way one heart and one soul, and together attain their human fulfillment."

Pope Paul VI, 'Humanae Vitae'—quoted in a blog post on 'The Impatient Gardener'

41

If only Jon's parents had known a bit more. They'd written the letter the moment they got to African soil, from the Moroccan immigration hall, even breaking off in the middle when it was their turn to be processed. Jon had immediately asked Eduardo if they could come over here and Eduardo had used that really dry tone of his and said, "That's *really* what you want? *At the moment.*" And of course Jon had thought better of it.

As ever, a cold prickle ran down my spine at the thought of the first of July... But Jon was still walking around with a spring in his step—his parents would be safe and sound in a Free Town by now. Perhaps they were even at Kanju with Jane and Sarah and the others. Their next letter would tell us—or they might be able to call.

I'd spoken to the others on the phone a few times since we got back to the Vatican, and they were still happy, loving adult life and their jobs. Jane had already left the weaving shed and joined the town police force, whilst Sarah had celebrated being promoted to weaving on the high quality looms by buying another 'hamster,' and was now running her own little business selling baby Desert Jerboas...

But, as it had constantly for the last few days, my mind returned to one particular paragraph of the letter: "We set off with George and Elizabeth Verrall, as planned, but we split up a week or two later. Four of us was just too great a strain on local Underground networks."

In other words, they didn't know *anything*... The EuroGov, or more specifically, Reginald Hill, the hard-faced, soft-voiced Minister for Internal Affairs, had tried to blackmail me back when we were on Gozo, even sending me a box supposedly containing the ashes of one of my parents, but all the evidence—or the lack thereof—suggested it had been a bluff...

Bane drew me from my thoughts by asking, "How's Everington, by the way?" Trying to distract himself from the whole, *going to the cafeteria for breakfast* ordeal?

"Doctor Frederick was talking about trying to wake him up," I said, "but I don't know how it's going. I didn't go along yesterday, I was on cafeteria duty."

"Oh, right. Don't know *what* we're going to do with him,

if he does recover."

"Not a lot, I imagine. He's gaga, isn't he?"

"True. S'pose we could walk him on the Vatican wall each day—y'know, nah, nah, na, nah, nah."

"Somehow I don't think that's the best idea you've ever had," said Jon dryly. "Us being in a position of such military superiority and all that."

Bane shrugged, trying to look nonchalant as we headed off the familiar route between apartment and basilica—he'd ventured out to Mass this morning, so I'd pressed my advantage and persuaded him to come along to breakfast.

No one in the cafeteria bothered him, and he was actually in quite a good mood when we arrived back home. But he'd have forgotten by tomorrow. Forgotten he always enjoyed it once he got there.

I opened my laptop and a metaphorical avalanche of earmarked comments and blog posts poured out and swallowed me...

"They should give you a pay raise." A mutter from Bane. "Or at least that Divine Office book you want so much."

"Huh?" I blinked and looked at the clock. Oh. I'd not said a word to him for three hours. I turned slightly to face him and answered jokingly, "Come on, we have a comfortable home, ample food, access to a store for whatever else we need, and great job satisfaction. How much better paid do we need to be?"

"We? And what's my job description: official dead weight?" He spoke bitterly, but worse was the despair creeping into his voice.

I turned right away from the computer. "As far as I'm concerned, you have the most important job in this place."

"Job? What *job*? How many blind commando teams have you seen lately? Even on the *big screen!* Mr. Useless, that's all I am."

I went to sit beside him. Didn't hug him, that might've been coddling. Did venture to take his hands in mine. "The very most important job, Bane. More important than anyone else. You're my husband."

"Oh *God*..." He turned his head away in something so close to physical pain that I didn't have the heart to cuff his tousled hair for taking the Lord's name in vain. "Don't say that. Anything but that..."

"Why *anything but that...*?" I couldn't keep the hurt from my voice.

"Because I'm making such a mess of it, aren't I? And don't try and tell me I'm not, 'cause I know I am. S'like Beauty and the bloody Beast. I don't know how you put up with me."

I did hug him now. "Because I love you, silly," I whispered into his neck. His arms snaked around me in return and he sighed into my hair, remaining still in my arms. Was he convinced? *Lord, if only we...*

Ring, ring. Ring, ring.

Damnit!

I eased reluctantly from the first out-of-bed cuddle we'd had for weeks and went to answer it. "Yes?"

"Margaret? It's Eduardo."

"Are we being *invaded?*"The sarcastic words escaped.

"No." Unperturbed. If I was going to snap at an innocent party, I'd chosen the right one. "We could use your help at the hospital, that's all."

What the...? "I'm not that good a nurse!"

"No, it's Everington. They've had him awake a few times but he just goes crazy and pulls out the feeding tube. They can't reason with him—he doesn't even seem to know they're speaking to him. Doctor Frederick tried to ditch the feeding tube and hand feed him—but he won't touch a bite. Just cowers away like they're going to eat *him*. They don't know what to do. But Jack seems to think the man might listen to you, for some reason?" Eduardo made that a question.

I *had* told him to say 'sanctuary' and he *had* obeyed. I could see Unicorn's reasoning, but... not convinced.

"Well... all right, I'm coming." I put down the phone with something close to a huff and looked glumly at Bane. "I'm sorry, I have to go to the hospital. Mr. Everington is causing some crisis that for some reason *I'm* apparently supposed to be able to solve. You can wish me luck with *that*."

"Good luck, then," he said dully.

I hurried to the hospital, half my mind on Bane—who I'd

clearly failed to convince in any way that he was not-useless—and half on the only-partly-excavated avalanche. An anxious huddle waited outside Everington's room. Nurse Poppy, clutching a dinner tray, Doctor Frederick, Eduardo, Doctor Carol, and several other hospital staff. Unicorn stood by the room door, clearly on guard, but his blue eyes turned my way when I approached.

"Oh, Margo," exclaimed Nurse Poppy, "won't you make him eat?"

I couldn't help a slight snort of disbelief. Did she think I was a super-nanny to the mentally disturbed or something? Looking through the observation window, there was no discernible difference in the unmoving figure, except for the absence of the feeding tube.

"He's still awake?" I asked doubtfully.

"According to the monitor," said Doctor Frederick. "He doesn't let on, it's true."

"Have you tried simply leaving it on the bedside table? Would he be strong enough to eat it by himself?"

"He's strong enough to swipe it across the room as soon as we've gone."

"Oh..." How many meals had they gone through? "Well, I'll give it a go, but I don't imagine I'll have any better luck." I took the tray from Poppy and slipped into the room, sat in the chair by the bed and put the meal on my knees. Tried to forget the audience.

"Mr. Everington? Mr. *Everington?*" Not a flicker. Could have been unconscious, or even dead. Tentatively, I tried, "Lucas...?" Did his eyelids twitch, just the tiniest bit? Strange to even think of him by his first name, like he was just someone else... "Lucas? It's Margaret. Margaret Verrall." Did he raise his eyelids just a fraction, to peep at me?

He didn't seem frightened, anyway, so I pressed on. "I've brought you some nice cottage pie. You only get cottage pie here when the British cooks are on duty. D'you want some?"

Definitely peeping now, a thin, eyelash-shrouded gap visible between his lids. *Hungry?* I held out a spoonful of cottage pie invitingly—only to start and almost drop it as he recoiled violently. *Maybe not.*

"It's perfectly safe. See?" No hardship to pop the

45

spoonful in my own mouth; it was lunchtime and I was hungry. "Umm, lovely. Don't you want some?" I advanced a spoonful determinedly towards his mouth, hoping to entice him with the smell—he almost fell out the other side of the bed and I withdrew it again hastily. What could I do? It wasn't me he was scared of, was it? It was the *food*.

Really? Could he just be scared of me reaching towards him? I put the plate on the bedside table and he relaxed into a safer, more central position on the bed. Went back to peeping at me between his eyelashes and otherwise playing dead. When I reached out under the pretext of drawing the blanket back up over him, he didn't move a muscle.

A food phobia? Perhaps he just didn't like being offered stuff. Was there anything else to try? "Lucas Everington," I said sternly, "eat your lunch at once."

His eyes widened slightly, in... anguish? Then he closed them tight and turned his face away. So much for Unicorn's theory. *Any other bright ideas, Margo?*

I ate the meal myself. Occasionally offering him some, but only verbally. Even that made him twitch, so I wasn't too surprised when the food was gone and he'd accepted none of it—but at least I'd given him the clearest possible demonstration that there was nothing to be afraid of.

"Well, perhaps you'll feel hungry later," I said, by way of a goodbye. But I did look closely at his face before leaving.

"As you probably saw, no luck," I said, as Poppy took the tray from me. "But it's the food he's scared of, not the people, in my opinion."

"The food?" echoed Doctor Carol. "Why would he be scared of the food?"

"I've a nasty idea... Doctor Frederick, is there something wrong with his mouth?"

"It's not *damaged*," replied Doctor Frederick. "But there is a great deal of faint scarring on his lips and around his mouth, from repeated injuries of some kind. Perhaps minor burns or scalds."

I bit my lip. "Then I dare say the Ministry for Internal Affairs could tell us why he's scared of a harmless cottage pie! *Bastards!*"

Nurse Poppy looked faintly shocked at my language.

She'd not been on Gozo with us, and had no doubt bought into the whole 'Saint Margaret' reputation that I'd acquired through my online persona—and perhaps even more from the sort of photos Eduardo liked to send to the press. Well, she'd have to get used to the real me.

Then her face crumpled in horror as she took in what I meant. From the slight downturn at the corner of Eduardo's mouth, he'd already reached the same conclusion. And been sparing the medical staff's delicate sensibilities? Oops.

"So, uh, what will you do?" I asked the doctors.

Doctor Frederick pulled a face. "We'll have to sedate him once a day and put the feeding tube in for a time. But it's not good for him."

"The tube *or* the sedation," agreed Doctor Carol grimly.

"But," I frowned, "can anyone go four months without food?"

"Certainly not whilst walking across Europe," said Doctor Frederick. "He must have been eating something. We'd better figure out what as quickly as we can."

"Well, good luck. But I've got to go..." The avalanche would be renewing itself as we spoke...

I'd kind of hoped after the success of the January protests that my blogging workload might ease off a bit, but if anything it only seemed to increase. Or perhaps, with Bane now so much better, at least physically, I just felt there was more and more of it I ought to do myself, rather than leave to my prayer team. With what was at stake... it was going to be a long two months until the first of July.

2 months, 12 days

Torture is one of those things people often secretly feel isn't really so utterly terrible so long as it's done to bad people for good reasons.

So tell me: who gets to decide who is bad, and what is a good reason?

Margaret Verrall—blog post, 'The Impatient Gardener'

"All right, I'm here..." I hurried into the hospital and took the lunch tray from Nurse Poppy. They persisted in sending me in with the man's meals, as though I had some magic touch.

"At least he looks at you," Doctor Frederick had said.

"Just barely!"

"Well, he doesn't give any sign the rest of us exist. So in you go..."

In I went, my stomach rumbling. Only one meal on the tray. Putting two out just meant one wasted.

Mr. Everington looked no better. Satisfied the patient was emptying the glasses of water left on the bedside table, Doctor Frederick had now removed the last couple of external drips but the regular insertion of the feeding tube, though keeping him alive, was also rubbing his throat raw, and just one feed a day wasn't enough to put weight on him.

"Hello, Lucas." That name drew a response, if only a slightly startled flicker of the eyelids. "Look, here's a nice baked potato and salad. I'll certainly be happy to eat it if you don't want it." I sat down, picked up my fork and bowed my head to say grace. Looked up to find a skeletal hand creeping towards the plate. When my eyes widened it was snatched away again.

"It's all right..." I hid my surprise under a smile. "It's your food. Here, do you want it...?" I slid the plate onto the bed beside him, rather expecting it to go flying across the room. A panicked swipe sent the potato rolling right off the bed—I just managed to catch the squidgy handful—he was already grabbing a lettuce leaf. He peered, sniffed like a rabbit and finally nibbled... then he was grabbing handfuls of salad and it was all gone in about fifteen seconds.

"*Au naturel!*" Of course, no baked potatoes and cottage pie lying around in the forest! "Did you like that? I'll get you some more."

Doctor Frederick was in the hospital corridor when I returned from the kitchen storerooms, the baked potato transferred to my stomach and the plate piled high with raw fruit and vegetables. I'd brushed dirt from carrots but left the bushy green bits on top, and lightly cracked the shells of nuts but left them in place. All very natural and untouched.

48

"What on earth?"

"Watch this," I invited them, including today's guard—Bumblebee—in my look. "I *hope* it'll be worth watching, anyway..."

It was. The man almost leapt from the bed when he saw the plate. Fortunately for the monitor cable, I managed to set it down in his lap before he'd freed himself from the blankets. He tucked in with none of his earlier suspicion, and I left him munching like the world's largest and skinniest rabbit, albeit a happy one.

"Could he have got here just on plants?"

"No." Doctor Frederick was categorical. "Short of a miracle, he has to have had some better source of protein than that, at least now and then."

Tell me about it. Bane, Jon and I had barely kept mobile after a month of limited protein, let alone none at all...

Doctor Frederick was thinking out loud. "But we tried plain steak the other day, and plain chicken the day before that..."

"Acted like it was poison," I agreed. "He must be craving protein, though."

"Quite. We can't stop the tube feeding until he'll eat it by himself. Oh... Poppy, Carol, come and look at this..."

Soon everyone clustered around, watching the man eat—I slipped off back to my computer.

But it niggled at me all day. He wouldn't touch meat, and he wouldn't have had access to lentils or beans or anything like that. But he'd been eating *something*.

I made sure to have a cup of tea with Bane mid-afternoon, since I'd be leaving him to eat with Jon again, and tried to pick his brains. But he just said "I don't know" over and over, until I switched to worrying about him instead.

2 months, 11 days

Feeding the birds is also a form of prayer.

Pope Pius XII—quoted on 'The Impatient Gardener'

Coo, coo. Tap, tap. Coo, coo.

Looking up from my screen, I tried to feel pleased rather than irritated. "Bane, you've got visitors."

"Is there anything for them?" Bane asked apathetically. At least he asked.

"Crusts in the usual place."

"Right."

I let Bane fetch the crusts himself and open the window before going to join him. Time for a little break. The doves hopped straight onto his arm to take the bread, cooing gently. Some of the tension drained out of him as their blunt beaks tickled at his palms. "Don't know how they can still fly," he said, not for the first time. "I mean, they just go round all the best windows *all day*, don't they?"

"There's quite a lot of them, though... watch it, that's a pigeon..." But Bane had shaken the bold interloper off. I made an impressed noise

"They sound different." He looked slightly pleased with himself.

"Your ears are really getting good." I stroked a dove's soft white feathers with a finger. So nice to be able to enjoy animals' company again. Right after our trek they hadn't looked like anything other than...

I started, making the dove flutter over to Bane. "*That's it!* I'll be back in a bit, Bane..."

"What...?"

"Nothing's wrong. Be back soon."

I headed for the Vatican Gardens. Once large and wholly ornamental, judging from the old photographs, what was left of the ornamental part now doubled as a graveyard and the other half was a small farm. Antonio, a young lay Franciscan, managed it and did much of the work, but he was nowhere in sight—perhaps fortunately.

The hen coops were easy enough to locate, and I was soon hurrying down the main hospital corridor with a plump hen under my arm.

"Margo!" exclaimed Nurse Poppy. "You can't bring that in here!"

Snail muttered, "*Pourquoi?*" and tried not to stare, as Doctor Frederick came over to see what had made Poppy yelp.

"It's okay, Doctor Frederick; it's just a little experiment," I assured him. "It won't be around for long."

I went to Mr. Everington's room and checked the external monitor screen. I'd learned to interpret the readings enough to know the man was indeed awake. Though playing as dead as usual. Could he be aware the 'mirror' was a one-way window?

Opening the door a crack, I pushed the bird through the gap and shut it again. Moved to the window to see if anything happened or if I was about to have a very red face. Looking perplexed, the two medical staff joined me and Snail's head turned several degrees before he managed to overcome the distraction.

The chicken's questioning clucks came over the little speaker as it stalked slowly forward, head stretched up as it peered around. But I wasn't really watching the chicken. The thin figure in the bed had become motionless. The green eyes opened, fixed on the intruder. One skeletal hand slid under the pillow. Came out holding something long and silver.

"How the hell did he get a knife!" said Doctor Frederick, as Mr. Everington hefted the thing as though to get the weight.

Snail was suddenly peering in as well. "*Qu'est-ce que...?* Oh, a table knife..."

Table knife or not, a flick of the man's hand and it flashed across the room... a thud and a strangled *glurk* attested to its adequacy as a weapon.

"Oh my God!" gasped Nurse Poppy, in a tone of shocked appeal.

"Eduardo's not going to like this," muttered Snail, mind clearly still on the knife.

Mr. Everington scrambled along the bed on hands and knees, yanked the monitor band from his wrist, tumbled to the floor and crawled the last few feet to where his catch lay twitching. Grabbing it, he ripped several handfuls of feathers from its breast and raised it to his mouth...

"See," I said triumphantly. "I said he must be craving protein!"

Poppy made a weak, deflating sound and crumpled.

5

BAD NEWS

Mere hundred-and-eight-acre state or not, Antonio was nowhere to be found. The apology for the missing hen would have to wait. I galloped back to the hospital to clean up—I'd told the staff I'd do it. Everington was back on the bed, lying on his side as usual, his hands tucked up in front of his face as though he were hiding behind them from the world, a broken chicken bone clasped in one. He must've been sucking on it when he fell asleep—getting the marrow out?

But the room... was spotlessly clean.

I went back out, where Snail informed me that no one else had been in, "*Non, nul,*" enjoying my astonishment.

Interesting. The man had always been very neat. Was he tidying his environment in unthinking reflex, or was there proper thought behind it? Well, it'd saved me a job. I raced homewards.

I'd actually reached our corridor when Unicorn appeared from the stairwell, saw me and let out a relieved breath.

"Margo, I was hoping to find you." His upper class British voice was grim.

"Is something wrong?"

"Jon's had some rather bad news. You know how with the moratorium all the Underground's communications are flowing a bit easier, and all sorts of updates are trickling in? Well, it just trickled in that... his sister was executed in Lincoln two years ago."

"Oh no!" Jon's sister had joined the Anchoresses of Our Lord, also known as the Prayer Warrioresses, who were an enclosed order that established convents behind enemy lines, as it were. Trouble was, sooner or later someone tended to figure out that there were more people living in a particular house than just the couple of lay sisters who came and went for groceries. So not a surprise, exactly, but still...

"I've got to relieve Snail," Unicorn went on. "Jon's gone to St Peter's..."

"I'll go and see how he is."

Unicorn made a speedy escape and I hurried off to the basilica, heavy-hearted. Jon was in the pews near the dove-shaped tabernacle where it hung over the high altar. I sat beside him and touched his shoulder gently, making him raise his head. Beneath his sightless eyes his cheeks were damp.

"Jon?"

"Oh, hi Margo. You heard, then?"

"Unicorn just told me."

"Oh. Right." He wrapped his arms more tightly around himself. "I don't know why I feel like this. I knew when she left we'd never meet again. In this life. Knew I'd never know when... Well, I thought I'd mourned for her already. I suppose... *knowing*... And now I've actually got to forgive them for what they... did..." His voice wobbled.

I put my arms around him and hugged him tightly. The mere fact that his sister was a nun would have made her guilty in the eyes of the EuroGov not merely of 'Practicing Superstition,' but of 'Inciting and Promoting Superstition'. And that carried the highest penalty of all: Conscious Dismantlement. Like Uncle Peter, whose death I'd witnessed in its every last, agonizing detail. My heart ached in sympathy for her...

Anger flared too. How could they *do* this to people? *No, Margo.* I pushed the anger down. *Remember Uncle Peter. He forgave them...* And what had I told that journalist?

I *had* to let this go, like Jon...

"Where have you *been*?" snarled Bane, as soon as I'd shut the door. "You just ran off without a word! Been gone for *hours!* I could've been lying dead on the floor for all you care!"

"Why on earth would you be lying dead on the floor? You're in perfectly good health."

A book whacked into the wall five meters away.

"*Perfectly good health?*" Bane poked his fingers into his

empty sockets and waggled them grotesquely. "*This* is your idea of perfectly good health?"

"Bane!" I went to retrieve the book. "You almost hit the plant! I wasn't making light of your loss, for pity's sake! I just meant, as far as *falling down dead* is concerned..."

"Like I'd *care*. And where the hell *have* you been?"

"Bane, calm down, I'm sorry I rushed off like that, it was stupid. But I'd have been back sooner if it wasn't for... Well, Jon's had some bad news."

"You've been with *Jon?*"

"For a little while, yes. He just heard his sister was executed. Two years back."

Bane frowned and was silent for a moment. "That's a shame."

"Well," I tried to be positive, "She's a martyr. In fact," my positivity flagged, "it would have been... the worst..."

"Bastards," spat Bane, so fiercely I couldn't help adding, "Jon's already trying to forgive them."

"Huh. Well, if anyone can manage it, he can. Though I reckon you all need to get practicing. Decades and decades worth of forgiveness coming up, if we win. Like that reporter said. Do you *really* think it's going to happen?"

If we managed to end injustice through a simple, democratic vote, we'd be following a path too little travelled. We *must not* allow ourselves to stray off that path into hatred and revenge.

"It has to happen," I said firmly. Which meant I had to forgive the murderers of Anne Revan, Jon's sister. Right here, right now. Surely I could do that? I mean, for all my empathy with her fate, I'd never even met her...

"So Jon's sister is now a statistic," said Bane bitterly, flopping limply back onto the sofa. His voice came, muffled by cushions. "This day officially sucks."

"Bane..." I went around the table; knelt and put a hand on his shoulder. "Bane, I am sorry I went off like that. I was kicking myself afterwards. But I figured it out, you see. Mr. Everington's been eating whatever he can catch raw; that's how he survived."

"Yay for him," said Bane blackly. "Tells me where I stand in the scheme of things, doesn't it? Blogging, church, Mr.

Everington, Jon, Bane. So glad you can fit me in *somewhere*."

"Bane, don't be silly..."

"Am I?"

"Yes! Look..." I checked my watch. "I'm sorry, but we need to hurry up—we've got to go to the cafeteria for dinner. I have to own up to stealing a chicken."

Bane twisted over to scowl in my direction, curiosity getting the better of him. "What'd you want with a *chicken?*"

"Fed it to the Ma... to Mr. Everington."

"Raw?"

So he had been listening. "And with feathers on. Catch your own."

"Bet the hospital staff loved that."

"Poppy fainted."

"She would." He'd had plenty of time to get acquainted with all of them.

"Yeah, well, it was all rather, um, *feral.*"

"Gory, you mean. Well, that's nature, isn't it? Look, go to the cafeteria, I'm not hungry."

"*Bane...*"

"Oh, clear off!"

I stood up abruptly. So much for the chicken story having calmed him down... "Look, I'll go and see if Antonio's there, then I'll come back and cook us something nice..."

"I *said*, I don't want anything. You going to force-feed me?"

I turned and marched out of the apartment again.

Antonio was just finishing his meal when I entered the cafeteria. "One of your hens has been eaten by a hospital patient," I told him, well past mincing my words by now. "So you haven't lost one. I'd have asked but I couldn't find you, and the guy's really ill, so it couldn't really wait."

Antonio, gaping at me, muttered something about *egg-layers,* and to my horror, began to run through a list of *names*, with descriptions.

"Antonio, I'm really sorry." He seemed so distressed, I felt bad about it, despite my foul mood. "I honestly didn't know they had names. But, uh, I don't know, so, perhaps you should go and look for yourself...?"

Phew! Antonio rushed off, presumably to do just that.

"You could've put that more tactfully." Eduardo came up beside me.

"*You're* telling *me* about tact?"

"It's a first, I know."

"I really didn't mean to hurt his feelings. I never imagined... He's got about a hundred hens! I didn't want to take one of Father Mario's doves..."

"I'm not saying it wasn't a *rational* choice, Margo. Anyway, is Jon all right?"

"I think so. I mean, he's upset, of course."

"Umm. Bane?"

"*Fine.*"

"Uh-huh? Well. See you around." He headed off, and Sister Krayj and Sister Mari, an African friend, came to sit with me.

"Is it true?" Sister Krayj's eyes glinted with amusement. "You really fed a live chicken to the Major?"

So... actually, I'd spent the day trying to figure out how to feed a man who'd spent his life keeping reAssignees imprisoned ready for the dismantlers' blade, to say nothing of keeping the Facility secure and operational for all those executions of people like Uncle Peter... and Jon's sister... Huh.

I focused on telling them the story, which amused Sister Krayj mightily, former Resistance commander that she was, and rather shocked Sister Mari.

"Are you two going to night prayer later?" I said as soon as I'd finished, wanting to change the subject. "I think I'll go tonight, I only need one more token and I can get my first Office book." There were four Divine Office books and to get your own physical copies, you collected a token at every office you attended until you had the required number. Stopped short-term residents carrying the books away with them. One could also collect Mass tokens for a Missal or put either kind of token towards a physical copy of the Holy Scriptures—but to my guilty delight Pope Cornelius had already given me a Bible to help with the blog.

Sister Mari smiled. "Yes, we're going, but don't you want to get back to Bane?"

"He was having a lie down when I left." Besides, I really did need some prayer time.

Thinking about what will happen if we lose the vote is something I'm trying not to do. But I think you should. All of you. Especially all you pro-Sorting bloggers. Think about things going on as they are, on and on, for the rest of your lives, your children's lives, their children's lives, with every reassigned child's blood on your hands.

Of course, if I were you, I imagine I'd be trying not to think about that either.

Margaret Verrall—blog post, The Impatient Gardener'

"Look, we've found out what he'll eat," I told Doctor Frederick the next day, "I don't see that I need to keep coming. I've hardly had a meal with Bane for a week."

I'd just delivered Mr. Everington's dinner, and he was quite obviously eating on his own now. Out of danger. My job was done, and thank goodness for that.

Doctor Frederick frowned. "Margaret, I can understand how you feel, but the fact remains that the patient only responds to you."

"*Responds!*" I snorted. "Big response!"

Food eaten, he just lay there, eyes closed to a thin slit, not responding to anything I said. But watching me.

"It is, *comparatively*. Look, every psychologist and counselor in the state has gone in there and tried to get him to speak to them—or give even the slightest sign they exist—but *nothing*. Someone else can take him his meals but in my capacity as his doctor I must ask that you continue to visit him, at least once a day. You really are our best chance of getting through to him."

He was right, I could see that. With a sigh, I nodded and headed for Jon's apartment. But, passing a crucifix set into a niche in the wall, my frustration suddenly boiled over. I dropped onto the kneeler in front of it, clenching my hands together in something of a death grip.

"*Why*, Lord?" The words slipped through my gritted

teeth. "I mean, which part of *can't deal with what I've got on my plate already* was so *unclear?*"

I seethed in silence for a moment, as though waiting for Him to answer the question there and then... But as I slowly focused on the crucifix—on the Man in agony there—my anger died. I wasn't being asked to hang on a cross. I wasn't lying on a gurney. I wasn't blind or a widow. Lucas Everington was a fellow human being in more than usual need. Our Lord had died for him as well. What was I complaining about?

"Sorry..." I whispered. "*Your will, Lord...*" I pressed a kiss to the carved feet, and went on my way.

Jon and Bane were the only ones in the sitting room when I reached Jon's apartment.

"Hi, Bane, hi, Jon. How's your morning been?" They were poring over a book that contained no words but seemed to have a terrible case of measles.

"Hi, Margo. Bane's been helping me translate this book. I think we've nearly cracked it."

"Oh, that's the Braille book, right?" I ran my fingers over the little dots. "Gosh, that looks difficult."

"Oh, not really. You've just got to learn what each letter feels like and then it's no different to the normal alphabet. Right, Bane?"

Bane nodded half-heartedly. "It's really not that bad."

"Well, I've got a new book too! My first Office book," I waved it proudly—but pointlessly—at them. "Finally. And they even had one with English on the facing side." They both made polite *we're happy for you* noises. Fair enough; it didn't mean much to them. "So have you eaten yet?" I asked.

"There's something in the oven," said Jon. "The Major behave himself?"

"Ate his raw chicken cold, thank goodness. We could hardly chuck live animals in there all the time."

"The press would just love that, wouldn't they?" Jon's smile was only slightly subdued. He picked up his stick, stood and headed for the kitchenette, stopping to bang on Unicorn's door. "Lunchtime, U, wakey-wakey." Unicorn must've been on a night shift.

I almost got up to help, but Bane was sitting there so

quietly. I sat in Jon's vacated seat and tried to drape my arm casually around his shoulders rather than grabbing like a limpet. "I'm not going to have to take Everington his food anymore, so I'll be able to eat with you again." I tried to put how happy this made me into my voice.

Bane just frowned faintly. "Oh. Good."

"I thought you'd be pleased."

Bane rubbed irritably at a glass eye, as U came out in his dressing-gown, neatly folded clothes under his arm, smiled a greeting, and disappeared into the bathroom.

"I am pleased, Margo." Bane slipped his arm around me in return and gave me a quick squeeze. "I am pleased."

My heart lifted, but only a little. Was there no way I could raise his spirits any more?

We were all finishing a tasty home-cooked meal when there was a knock at the door. Unicorn went to answer it. "Oh, hello, sir. Do you need me?"

"No, Jack. I'm here to see Margaret."

No, *is Margaret here*? My location was tracked on the security cameras these days.

"Hi, Eduardo." Always incredibly hard to read, but he looked... *excited?* But a little tense... "Is something wrong?"

"Not at all." He held up a piece of paper, rather triumph-antly. "*This* is an invitation for you to speak at a rally in *Monaco.*"

My heart went *thunk* in my chest.

Monaco. Clinging to the very edges of the EuroBloc itself...

6

THE MOST BEAUTIFUL THING IN THE WHOLE WORLD

"Monaco..." I checked. "It *is* a..."

"It is a Free State, yes. But it's about as close to the EuroBloc as you could *possibly* get."

"She's closer here, surely?" said Jon. "Monaco is what, the second smallest Free State? We're the smallest, right?"

Eduardo flapped a hand dismissively. "So, technically, you are actually closer to the EuroBloc at this very moment. But people are used to you being here. But in Monaco, people will be able to simply drive or walk across the EuroBloc border to hear you speak. This is a great opportunity."

"For the *EuroGov*," said Bane, scowling. "The assassins can stroll in too! In fact, their snipers can probably take her out without even crossing the border themselves!"

Eduardo shot Bane a rather impatient look. "Naturally trajectories and cover provided by buildings will be considered before I approve any location for Margaret's speech."

"What does Pope Cornelius think?" I asked.

"They haven't invited him. But he's happy for you to go."

"What? Why haven't they invited him?"

"For Monaco, this is not about morals, this is about making a fast buck." When I looked bewildered, he went on, "Thirty-five percent of the Monacan population are millionaires. They've never fancied living under other people's rules—especially Religious Suppression—so they've kept their State free by greasing the EuroGov's palm whenever necessary. However, their money may have kept them free, but one can't help feeling they've become rather too fond of it in recent decades. Anyway, they've obviously realized that by inviting you to speak, they can make a killing flogging food, drink, accommodation, souvenirs... They're even charging an entrance fee."

I frowned. "I don't think I like that. Look, can you tell them I'll come and do the speech: but only on the condition that they don't charge people—not above their entry visa fee—and that Pope Cornelius comes as well."

Eduardo was shaking his head. "Quit while you're ahead, Margaret. I think they'll swallow the first condition: a smaller slice of pie is better than no pie at all. But there's no way they are going to let Pope Cornelius visit."

"Why not?"

"Because he is a Head of State, and the moment he steps foot on Monacan soil the whole thing changes from a simple money-making scheme to something of an entirely different order. Admittedly, I think the Monacan government may be underestimating just how large a cut they're going to have to give the EuroGov, to earn their forgiveness over this—even bearing in mind that they can do no wrong in the eyes of the Chairman."

"*The* Chairman? Of the EuroBloc High Committee? Reginald Hill's boss? Why not?" asked Bane, frowning.

"Oh, he loves his Monacan holiday villa far too much to risk any long-term strife between EuroBloc and Monacan Free State. All the same. Welcoming the Holy Father just at the moment would put it beyond any backhander."

"Should we be... encouraging this?" I asked uncertainly.

"Their greed is their problem," said Eduardo bluntly. "As far as we're concerned, this is simply an unparalleled opportunity to speak near-as-possible to the EuroGov itself. You will not get a better chance than this."

"Then I'll go," I said. Bane's face closed in hurt and anger. *Oops...* "I mean, Bane and I should talk it over. But I'll probably go."

"That means she's going," snarled Bane. "Like anything I say is going to make any difference!" He got up, grabbed his stick, walked into the kitchen, and slammed the door behind him. Hard.

"I'll make the arrangements," said Eduardo.

"Everyone always refers to 'Sorting' but what we're really talking about is Dismantling. Because that's what happens to those who fail sorting—and to unRegistered children, whose fate is even worse. ReAssignees are only taken after Sorting, but most kids like me don't even make it to eighteen, even if we're 'perfect' enough to pass Sorting no problem, if only given the chance.

Here's what happens to the unRegistered: someone else's preSorting little darling (registered and not a preKnown, and therefore provisionally 'human') needs an organ, so a child like me is snatched from their family with zero warning and chopped up to supply it. Feeling queasy? Clearly you've had your head in the sand, because it's been going on for years and you know it!"

Janita (Jane) Patel, former Salperton Facility ReAssignee and unRegistered child—quoted on 'The Impatient Gardener'

"This thing is looking droopy again," I said glumly, alternately watering the fuchsia plant and prodding the soil in an effort to determine whether it was now 'moist but not damp', whatever that was supposed to mean.

"At his trial, you should've submitted the fact that he sent *you* seeds as evidence he didn't know you at all," said Bane, a little more sarcastically than necessary. "That should've cleared him of all charges of conspiracy."

"Ha ha," I said, dismally. What was I doing wrong?

"There's probably nothing the matter with it," Bane added, "You're just paranoid about that thing. If you're really worried, why don't you go and ask him?"

"He doesn't *speak* to me. He won't communicate..." I broke off, staring at the purple flowers. Had Everington really put the seeds in with the manual simply to identify himself? Or had it been an attempt to save the plant he loved so much? Or both... *Wait...* "My goodness, I'm an idiot! I'm worrying about how to get a reaction out of him and here I've got *the most beautiful thing in the whole world!*"

"*Seriously?*"

"According to *him*. One of the few things he said during one of our *actual* meetings. I know it's not the usual time, but d'you mind if I go see him now?"

"Whatever. You'll go anyway."

I paused before answering, struggling to keep hold of my patience. "It doesn't have to be *now*. That's why I *asked* you. I'm just keen to try this, that's all."

"Haven't they got experts for this sort of thing?"

"Yes," I said gloomily, "and they all keep telling Doctor Frederick to send *me* in."

"Well, you'd better go, then, hadn't you?"

I ventured to go across and give him a quick peck on the cheek. "I'll try not to be too long. I'm cooking lunch today. U's on duty but Sister Krayj's coming, and Snakey, and the Foxes." Since Bane was refusing to go to company, I'd bring company to him. I added casually, "Oh, and Calla Aguda—you know, that nice African girl who's come over to join the VSS? And Jon, of course."

"You just happened to invite Jon *and* Calla, did you? Good luck with that." Bane gave a rather grumpy snort of laughter. "As well try to set Calla up with *U.*"

I picked up the fuchsia and let myself out, frowning. Jon didn't share the inclinations Unicorn—universally-respected for his chastity and self-control—had mastered so thoroughly, so... Did Bane think that Jon still liked me so much he wouldn't be interested in anyone else? What was *funny* about that?

Lord, don't let it be true!

The longer I was married to Bane, the more clearly I could see what I must've put Jon through, back at the Facility, when he and I had to pretend to be lovers, even sleeping in the same bed. Okay, so it wasn't all my fault; circumstances had forced it on us and Jon had suggested it in the first place, but still. I shouldn't have snuggled up with him the way I did. Talk about dangling something under his nose that he could never have. His self-restraint had been positively saintly. Bane wouldn't have managed to be that hands-off in that situation. No way.

But even now, it still kind of felt like Jon was fettered to me. Okay, so it was *Bane* he came around to see, *Bane* he came to help, but... it would be so nice if he and Calla...

I wanted to be just friends with Jon. *Really* just friends. On both sides.

Grass Snake was on duty when I got there, trying not to look bored and failing. Proof of which was, he actually spoke to me. "Guess what I found under his pillow this morning."

"Another knife?"

"*Sí.*" He handed me a table knife, the blade rather the worse for wear but peculiarly sharp.

"All that work sharpening them on the bed frame, and then you go and nick them," I teased.

Snakey gave me a responsible frown. "Mad, Margo, remember?"

"Can't the hospital staff count, though?"

Snakey grinned. "Actually, it's not their fault. I managed to spot it this morning. Nurse Poppy went in there for the tray. I saw her check the knife and fork because she touched them both very deliberately, then when she turned her head for just a second to get the last cup, this bony hand whipped out and removed the knife. And Nurse Poppy being much nicer than she is observant, carried the tray out without noticing it was gone."

"Sneaky, isn't he?"

"I'll say. And I need to get that other knife before you go in there." He glanced at the window and muttered something rude in Spanish. "Not again!"

The curtains were drawn over the window.

"I can't blame him. Would you want people staring in at you?"

"He's not supposed to be able to tell!"

"Yeah, well, I think he figured out the one-way glass first thing. I know Doctor Frederick thinks he's completely out of it—what did he say the other day?" I put on a German accent. "*Chimpanzees make tools.* But the longer I spend with Mr. Everington the more I'm convinced he's thinking plenty—he's just really good at not letting on."

"Except by shutting the curtains and sharpening the cutlery."

I rolled my eyes, but returned the lethalized table knife and stayed where I was as Grass Snake rattled the door knob, waited a moment, then opened the door, cautiously locating the patient before stepping inside. The persistent cutlery theft was making him jumpy. But Everington was on the bed and playing dead. He'd taken over all his own hygiene needs as soon as he could get as far as the room's little bathroom, but if someone came in while he was out of bed, he just dropped right down on the floor and played dead there instead—so everyone had taken to rattling the door handle to let him know they were coming.

Snakey retrieved the latest knife, opened the curtains and stuck his head back out the door. "I've had a thought; why don't I just take the blasted things down?"

"Oh, come on, that's a bit grim, isn't it? He's a patient, not a prisoner."

Snakey threw up his hands. "Fine, you're the boss."

"No, I'm not."

"You are as far as this guy is concerned." He came out and waved invitingly to the doorway. "All yours."

Unfortunately that seemed to be true at the moment. I went in.

"Hi, Lucas, how are you today?" Still unaware each piece of meat was slightly—and at this stage *slightly* was the word—less raw than the one before? Hopefully. He peeped at me in his usual way—then his eyes suddenly widened and fixed on what I held. "I wanted to ask your advice on something, actually. My plant's looking droopy."

I placed the fuchsia on the bedside table. A moment later two thin hands whipped out and snatched it into the bed. Tucking one arm securely around the pot, he ran his fingers delicately over leaves and flowers, breathing in deeply.

"Is it okay? I'm worried it's looking peaky."

He—of course—ignored me, his fingertips in the soil, running up the stems, checking the leaves, inspecting flowers. Apparently there was nothing to be alarmed about, because eventually he just settled back on the bed, hugging the pot, and gazed at the fuchsia. That was me upstaged.

"I came a bit early today because of the plant. Can you suggest anything?" No response. Time for drastic action. "Oh dear, I'd better take it to the gardener, then." I reached out and took hold of the pot—his grip tightened. "Perhaps he'll know."

I heaved; he clung on with surprising strength, but there was a slight give. Another effort on my part, and I held the pot. He scrambled up onto hands and knees in pursuit—perhaps realized he hadn't a hope in his condition because abruptly he spread his clenched fingers and pressed his hand very deliberately to his chest, looking me right in the eye for the first time since St Peter's.

"What's that?" I immediately turned back to him. "Do you mean you'll look after it for me?"

He pressed his chest more urgently, and stretched out his other hand towards the pot. *No*, he was jolly well going to communicate properly, I knew he could...

"*Are* you going to look after it for me? I need a yes or a no..."

He sank back on the bed, eyes round with anguish. Much the same look he'd given me when I'd tried ordering him to eat his lunch.

"Just tell me yes or no," I coaxed. "It's not that hard."

Yes, yes, it is, said his eyes. *I must not speak...* That was the huge barrier he was staring out at me from behind, wasn't it? Silence so long self-imposed during his captivity it now held him prisoner. But he could break through it; he'd done so at his trial and again in St Peter's. *So hold firm, Margo. It's for his own good.*

"I'll have to take it to the gardener, then." I began to turn away.

His hand flew out in a clear, *wait*, gesture—I stopped. Again he tapped his chest.

"Are you going to look after it for me until tomorrow?"

Clearly—painfully—he nodded. It wasn't words, but it was certainly communication.

I handed him the plant. "I'm very glad," I said calmly—the psychologists advised me to act as though he'd done something perfectly normal when he... did something perfectly normal. "I'm sure you know what to do for it. If you need anything, let me know." I had a thought. "I'll get you a pencil and paper in case you want to write anything down."

His lip curled up slightly—he probably had an equally deep-rooted aversion to *signing things,* come to think of it—and he retreated back to the center of the bed, nursing the plant. Ignoring me again. Still, he'd communicated. And he'd jolly well do it again tomorrow if he wanted to keep the thing another day...

2 months, 4 days

So how many of you have really thought about why you think it's okay for people who believe in God to be executed? (I'm talking to everyone, now, not just the anti-God bloggers.) Or do you not think that it's okay, and therefore simply try not to think about it?

Margaret Verrall—blog post, 'The Impatient Gardener'

Someone was hammering on the front door. I lurched into a sitting position, blinking in confusion, and switched on the bedside light.

Bane sat up as well, groping at his bedside table, where no lamp stood. "Margo, put the light on, I can't find mine..."

My stomach dropped. Bad morning.

I leaned around him and caught his hands in mine. "Bane, stop, there's no lamp there."

"Yes, there is." His voice gone thin and petulant with fear... Remembering. "*Why wouldn't there be?*"

I pulled my arms in, hugging him tightly. "You can't see, Bane," I said just as gently as I could. "Remember, love?"

"No... No..." he whispered it a couple of times, brokenly, and finally put his hands to his empty sockets. "*Damnit!*"

Someone was still thumping on the door. I scrambled out of bed and hurried through to the living room, shut the bedroom door behind me, checked the peephole—Jon. Who ought to know better. I yanked the door open. "What do you want? The alarm would've gone off in about five minutes! Couldn't you wait?"

Jon lowered his fists and winced slightly. "Oh, sorry. But you won't believe what the EuroGov have done, Unicorn just came off shift and told me, the bastards!"

He was mad as a hornet, and upset too. Must be something bad. I braced myself. "Go on, then."

"Where's Bane?"

"He's... having a minute to himself, *Mr. 'oh, sorry.'* You might as well tell me first."

I moved backwards and he followed me in, pacing up and down the room, stick lashing in front of him like the tail of an angry cat.

"They're only having one question on the referendum. *Just the one.*"

"What? But they promised..."

"Oh, they're covering both the issues, but in only *one question*. It's going to be 'Do you want Sorting and the Eradication of Superstition to continue? Yes or no?'"

"I was expecting they'd want the positive response in their favor," I said slowly, "'cause shrinks always reckon people prefer to make a positive response, but..."

"Think it through, Margo!" Jon almost yelled it.

I *was* thinking it through, and I didn't like it. "Anyone who was prepared to vote for Religious Freedom but who wasn't prepared to give up their unlimited supply of organ transplants will be tempted to vote Yes. And anyone who wanted to vote to end Sorting but who actually believes their anti-Superstition stuff is—what do they call it?—'ultimately beneficial to mankind', will be tempted to vote Yes. But some of them *will* vote the other way, especially in the second category..."

"Well, they'd better!" Jon stopped pacing as his stick smacked squarely into a cupboard front. "Uh, sorry... 'Cause I think this wrecks our clear majority big time!"

"I wasn't even confident we'd still have a *clear* majority by July. It's a long time for people to go off the boil. This just makes it even more dicey. *Blast.*"

"You'd better give a really good speech in Monaco next week," said Jon. "Because I can't help thinking that this is going to lose us a lot of votes!"

The Monaco visit. The one thing he could have mentioned to make Bane's morning even better.

As soon as Jon had left I tapped on the bedroom door. "Are you okay, Bane? Did you hear that?"

"I'm pretending I didn't and I'm going back to sleep," came a rather small voice. "Perhaps this is all a dream..."

I winced. Very bad morning.

"... and it wasn't any better when he woke up again. He's *so* down this morning, and I just can't get through to him. *I* don't know what to do." I glanced at Everington, who was listening—or at least staring—intently.

"And why I'm going on about this to you, I don't know," I said, rather self-deprecatingly. "Probably because you're a captive audience." Did his expression change, fractionally? "...In the metaphorical sense, of course. You're not a captive, obviously, just a... I think the technical term would be 'supplicant,' but 'guest' is a lot simpler."

Must watch my wording—it was me who insisted he understood more than he let on. Come to that, I ought to be a little bit careful what I said to him. Some days I thought he understood every word, other days that maybe he just wanted to.

Anyway, time to go. I'd read the midday office to him in English, as usual, before I began essentially to think out loud. "Well, I must be off." I touched a hand to the fuchsia's pot. "Will you look after this for me until tomorrow?"

Dutifully, he made eye contact and nodded. He seemed to be finding it easier with practice. Probably better raise the bar soon.

Today I just picked up my nice new Latin-English Office book, thanked him politely, and departed.

2 months

Safia lives in the Free Town of Sankiwa, African Free States, and she was born deaf. How can she possibly make a living, you ask? So crippled, so handicapped? Well, Safia runs her own pottery company—and so far her beautiful pots grace the homes of no fewer than seven State leaders.

Margaret Verrall—blog post, 'The Impatient Gardener'

Mass over, I hurried straight back to Bane. Please, Lord, let him be feeling a little better today? He'd not come to Mass for over a week now, despite how stressed it made him to be left behind, and he'd got so badly into one of his *not wanting to do anything* dips.

"Hi, Bane." He was actually up, if still in his pajamas, and sitting in the living room. Thank goodness, I was off to Monaco in four days' time, and I wanted to leave him a bit happier.... *Oh.* His expression—as bleak as I'd ever seen it. "*Bane?*"

He flicked a hand in the direction of something lying on the table. A micro audioPlayer with earphones attached. "Someone chucked that onto the window ledge."

"They *what?* Who?"

"Obviously I couldn't *see* who!" His voice was knife-sharp. "And they didn't stop to tell me."

An audioPlayer. "It's for you?"

He nodded.

"Is it... private?" Once, I'd have just asked what was on it, but he was so prickly these days...

He jerked a hand at it again. "*Listen.* Please."

I went to sit beside him. Slipped the earphones in and found the controls.

"Dear Mister BLANK-BLANK," said a cold voice, using Bane's official EuroBloc name.

I stiffened in recognition. "Reginald bloody Hill!"

Bane said nothing.

The cold voice of the Minister for Internal Affairs continued, "I've had to adopt this novel way of communicating with you since you, hmm, seem to have misplaced your eyes. How careless of you. Happily for you, I have found the aforementioned ocular organs and would be very happy to return them to you, in full working order, in return for one small favor. Your unofficial registered partner causes us some small inconveniences with her blog, speaking, and other activities. Persuade her to cease such activities ASAP, and you will receive your lost property on the twenty-third of June.

"Hoping to be securely packaging your retinal equipment soon, yours very sincerely, Reginald Hill."

7

MY ONE COMPANION IS DARKNESS

I pulled out the earphones and sat there, head buzzing, my mouth dry and my stomach ice-cold. I sat quite still and waited. Waited to hear what Bane said. Waited in terror and utter confusion. What if he asked? What if he expected me to *offer?*

After a moment he frowned. "Margo? You okay?"

Had Reginald Hill been there, when they took his eyes? The way he'd presided over my own interrogation? "Not sure. I feel sick."

"Oh." His brow creased slightly. Still he said nothing.

"Bane?" My voice sounded strangled.

"Yes?"

"What are you... going to do?"

He found my hand, took the audioPlayer from it. Placed it on the floor, and with the aid of his fingers, positioned his heel with great precision, then stamped down hard. "That."

Relief washed over me, and guilt too, that I'd thought he might consider... I wrapped my arms around him, shaking. "Bane, Bane, you're so wonderful."

He laughed bleakly, so bleakly, but at least he hugged me in return. "I'm not wonderful, Margo," he whispered back. "I've been sitting here, thinking about it, have I just. But I know if I betray the very thing I gave my eyes for just to get them back, life won't be worth living at all. Even though it's barely worth living now."

A choking cold ball of fear blocked my throat, hearing him talk like that. I hugged him tighter as he went on, "And with you silenced, we lose the vote, which means in a couple of months I'd die anyway. But not only me. You. Jon. Everyone in the state."

I swallowed. A thought I'd been trying very hard to put out of my mind for months escaped my mouth at last. "Are we sure we can't... try to get them back?" This message... it made it very likely indeed they *did* still have them. It'd always been most likely.

Bane said nothing for a long time, his eyelids scrunched tightly shut. Like one wrestling with temptation. "D'you know how many times I've thought of getting the old team together and asking them—begging them!—to give it a go?"

"If it's as often as I've considered it, quite often."

"Yeah. So why haven't you?"

"You know why. Someone could die. Probably would." I couldn't help thinking of Father Mark, the only person killed during the Liberations.

From Bane's expression, he was thinking about Father Mark too. "Yeah. Then I'd spend the rest of my life knowing I'd valued my *sight* more than someone else's *life*. Don't fancy that vision of the future any more than the current one."

"Twenty-third of June," I muttered, more to myself. "No use..."

"They're not idiots."

"No." With the vote on the first of July, faking compliance—or rather, complying just until Bane had his eyes back—was definitely out. Especially since I'd have to miss the Monaco visit...

"It's no good, Margo," said Bane. His voice sounded so... empty. No hope in it. "Well, we'd better go and see Eduardo."

Eduardo swept the fragments of audioPlayer into a small zip-lock bag, then pushed a nonLee pistol across his desk towards me. "I'm posting an additional guard on the roof—opposite side of the courtyard, so there's a clear view of all the windows on your side—and I'm issuing that to you, Margaret."

"A nonLee?" I said, more for Bane's benefit. "I don't have to... *carry it around* with me, do I?" A nonLethal was much better than a Lethal pistol, but still...

Eduardo appeared to give this idea serious consideration, but finally shook his head. "At the moment I'd like you to simply have it in the apartment with you, just in case. And perhaps you should redo the Personal Protection course."

"I only did the original course two months ago!" I pointed out. Eduardo had given the course to me, along with a handful of other high-risk residents. All about finding escape routes, using what your environment provided, and operating various types of weapons, with a bit of target practice thrown in.

"Well, we'll see. A refresher never goes amiss. I at least want to see you down at the firing range now and then, keeping your hand in. We can see how much they want you silenced," he gestured to the plastic bag. "This was clearly an inside job. We've had some indication over the past month that a EuroGov agent—or agents—have infiltrated the State. This confirms it. When they realize it hasn't worked, they may resort to... less subtle... means. So keep that handy, especially when opening the door. Even if you think you know who it is. Just in case they've got a gun pointed at their head."

I frowned. A spy in the Vatican. Or *spies*. Something already unpleasant and emotionally excruciating was taking a very serious turn. "You really think they'll... try for me?"

Eduardo tilted a hand from side to side. "Maybe, maybe not. They'll be reluctant to face the bad press, but they might think shutting you up was worth it, all the same. So don't get totally paranoid, but if in doubt, assume the most sinister interpretation until it's proven otherwise."

I raised an eyebrow. "Explain how to reconcile that with 'don't get totally paranoid'?"

"Fine, *be* totally paranoid; just don't get assassinated. Please."

"It's not her job to make sure she's not assassinated," snapped Bane. "It's yours!"

"I can assign a bodyguard to tag along after her..."

"Oh, come off it!" I said.

"...but I don't think she'll like the idea."

"She doesn't! Please, no bodyguard unless it's really

necessary."

"There we go, then," said Eduardo to Bane. "Now, off you two go, I've got some spy hunting to do. Talk about the worst possible time: the ambassadors from South America are due to arrive about the same time as you get back from Monaco, Margaret." We turned to go. "Oh, and Bane?"

"Yes?"

"Next time you hear something land outside your window, pick up the phone and call security, please. Before opening the window and handling the object."

Bane flushed crimson. "Okay," he muttered. "Come on, Margo..."

After that little burst of energy, Bane sat on the sofa with his head in his hands and said almost nothing for the rest of the morning. I was still waiting for him to bring up Monaco, but since his outburst in front of Eduardo, he hadn't said a word about it. He must realize that the EuroGov would take my visit to there as an absolute rejection of their offer. But he'd turned it down anyway, so it didn't really make any difference, did it?

Jon came around, but it was me who explained what'd happened, and his attempts to interest Bane in a new audioTrack failed completely. He was still trying when I left to see Everington.

Quite nice to just sit quietly and read the Office to an apparently appreciative audience. Something about the way Everington relaxed when I opened the book, shifted, turned his head... Of course, no way to know if he was actually looking forward to it or if he just knew I was going to read it and he might as well make himself comfortable!

Physically speaking, he was making good progress. He'd even managed to shift his—admittedly, wheeled—furniture around so the bedside table—or rather, the precious plant pot—stood just so in front of the window, with the bed at an easy fuchsia-grabbing distance close beside.

"Lord my God, I call for help by day; I cry at night before you..." I read. Uh-oh... *Couldn't we have had a cheerful one, Lord?*

Everington listened attentively.

"For my soul is filled with evils; my life is on the brink of the grave..."

A bleak psalm, this one.

"You have laid me in the depths of the tomb, in places that are dark, in the depths..."

I'm really not in the mood for this one today, Lord. Bane hates this one.

I plowed on. "...You have taken away my friends and made me hateful in their sight. Imprisoned, I cannot escape; my eyes are sunken with grief..."

A slight sound made me glance at Everington—a deep line of pain ran across his brow and tears trickled silently down his cheeks. He stared at me—or at the book—with miserable but expectant eyes, so after a shocked beat I managed to carry on.

"...Wretched, close to death from my youth, I have borne your trials; I am numb. Your fury has swept down upon me; your terrors have utterly destroyed me. They surrounded me all the day like a flood, they assail me all together. Friend and neighbor you have taken away: my one companion is darkness."

I stopped at the end; my companion's anguish was all too clear. What chord had this psalm touched inside him?

He reached out a hand and pointed to the book, touched his chest. More sign language. At least he was trying to communicate, though his eyes were still on the book. He gestured to it again, brought his hand back to his chest once more—looked up at me, eyes pinched with pain. And said, "*Me.*"

Knowing he could talk and hearing him do it after near enough three weeks of absolute silence were two different things. I blinked. Act normal, remember? "The psalmist... the person speaking in the psalm... reminds you of yourself?"

He nodded. The tears were still running, unheeded, down his face. "Me," he confirmed in an agonized whisper, tapping his chest yet again.

"A lot of people identify with this psalm when they've been through a really bad time. Or when they're going through it. Bane... my husband... he can't even listen to this one. He... lost his sight, y'know." Still hard to say, even for me.

Everington made a slight sideways movement of his head, whether in sympathy for Bane or just as an outlet for his own pain was unclear. After a moment he reached out a hand and touched the book lightly. "I have?"

"He spoke to me," I told Grass Snake, who was on guard again when I went out.

He looked startled. "I'm surprised you don't sound more pleased. That's a *huge* breakthrough."

"I know, I am pleased." I meant it, though it'd come out a bit unenthusiastically the first time.

"Where's your *nuevo* Office book?"

"His *nuevo* Office book now," I said glumly.

Oh well. I'd just have to collect some more tokens. It'd go quicker this time, without all the Offices missed when out on Liberations and then looking after Bane in the hospital.

When I'd held out the book to Everington he'd accepted it hesitantly, eyes wide with shock, as though unable to believe his wish had been granted. From the way he'd stroked the pages and run the bright ribbon bookmarks through his fingers, it looked like the book would have a careful owner, anyway. Would he be able to read it? Not the Latin, obviously. Though according to Eduardo—or rather, Everington's ID database entry—he spoke fluent Italian and intermediate Spanish. Or had done.

"Try and spot if he reads it, why don't you?"

Snakey snorted. "Fat chance of that. Any moment now he's going to come creeping up to that window and inch the curtains across again. I've spotted him at it a few times now, he really is a sneaky blighter."

"Doesn't like living in a fish tank, is all. He could have his own room soon, couldn't he? No reason for him to be cluttering up the hospital now he's eating properly."

"I suppose not. Perhaps with a security camera and a lock on the door, please Lord." Snakey sounded fervent. "I think he's harmless enough. I'll suggest it to the boss." He glanced at me, not failing to miss, VSS boffin that he was, that my chagrin wasn't just over losing my new office book.

"Well, congratulations on the progress," he said sympathetically, "but it looks like you're stuck with him now."

Yes, among my genuine delight at the breakthrough was a very selfish streak of dismay. Because Snakey was right: no way would I be able to turn his care over to the experts now, would I?

When I got home I found Jon sitting there in a defeated silence and Bane still with his head in his hands. Would Bane bite my head off if I tried to tell them about Everington? In this mood, probably more likely he wouldn't respond at all.

"I think he's actually recovering," I said, taking the armchair.

"Really?" said Jon.

"Showing signs."

"What we *are* going to do with Major blinking Everington walking around in full mental health..."

"Quite some way to go before you need to worry about *that*. Anyway, they can just ship him off to Africa or something."

"S'pose. Good riddance."

"Forgiveness, Jon," I chided, slightly amused. Perhaps it was easier when it was your own forehead that had been decorated with a primitive tattoo, rather than that of someone you cared about...

"I'm working on that one," he said, rather grimly. "But it's hard to even hear about him without remembering the Facility, and everyone who died there, on his watch."

He turned his head towards me as though trying to summon a little more interest. "What happened, anyway?"

"He cried, and then he spoke to me."

"That's good, I suppose," said Jon.

"Er, *yes*, voluntary speech, very good."

Jon tilted his head meaningfully at Bane. "We could use a bit more of it in here, come to that."

I smothered a sigh. Could be a long day.

Everyone is asking about Safia. Well, I passed your
questions on to her and she says, "Actually, I don't think
of myself as handicapped at all. I think of my deafness as
a gift. It allows me to focus so much on the visual and
tactile elements. If I could hear, my work would lose so
much power. In fact, if I was 'perfect,' I truly don't think
my pots would be anything special."

Margaret V. & Safia K.—blog post, 'The Impatient Gardener'

It was several long days. Bane's withdrawal slid into a
mood so black I longed for services, even for my daily visit
to Everington, anything to get me out of the apartment for a
spell. The only positive was that Everington spoke to me
several more times. Apparently the breach in the barrier
was permanent.

"Lucas," I said one day, after I'd been telling him a little
more about part of the Office and he looked sufficiently
engaged to maybe answer. "Could I ask what it was you
wanted to know so badly?"

He stared at me for so long that if it was anyone else, I'd
have assumed they weren't going to reply. As it was, I just
waited patiently.

At last he said, as though it should be obvious, "If you
forgive me."

I blinked. "If... *I forgive you?*"

He nodded.

"But... I told you so, right back... *then.*"

More silence. Finally, "You *said* it. Did you mean it?"

"Of course I meant it. D'you think I'd be here," I waved
around the room, "if I didn't?"

He stared at me intently, head tilting slightly to one side.
"I don't know. Maybe. I don't..." He touched a couple of bony
fingertips to his heart. "Don't *believe* it."

I frowned, dismayed, and rather lost for words. He
didn't feel like I really forgave him?

Instead of replying, he turned his eyes longingly to the
Office book, which he'd handed to me when I came in. He

looked exhausted—we had just had what was, for him, an extremely lengthy conversation. Time for a break, then. I opened the book and hunted out the right page—the six ribbons were always in different places.

"Oh, Lucas, before I forget," I said after I finished. "I won't be able to come and see you tomorrow, I'll be away. Nothing to worry about, I'll be back the day after."

Lucas looked as though 'won't be able to come and see you' and 'nothing to worry about' simply couldn't fit in the same sentence. He grabbed the fuchsia with shaking hands and hugged it close.

Oh dear, it was only one day... "I know!" I suggested. "How about they bring a TV in here, so you can see me give my speech? Then I can still visit you... sort of."

He greeted this with a dubious look, but his outright panic subsided.

"So how was he?" demanded Bane, in what, at the moment, actually counted as quite a mild voice. I was still waiting and waiting for him to say something about the Monacan trip, but he just got grimmer and grimmer, the more often it was mentioned. Which meant he'd been pretty grim the last couple of days, what with all the preparations.

"Oh, he's fine," I said.

"What's wrong, then?" He really was getting quite sensitive to my tone. "Second thoughts about tomorrow?"

Uh oh... "He thinks I don't really forgive him," I said quickly.

"I wonder why."

"What's that supposed to mean?"

"You know what it means. You talk about him like he's a lab animal. Something to look after and train but not become emotionally attached to."

"I don't treat him like a lab animal!"

"Whatever you say, Margo. Guess any warmth you feel towards him must be showing only on your face and not in your voice, 'cause I'm not hearing it."

Warmth? "I'll get you your coffee..." I said, changing the subject.

"I'm not a bloody invalid!" Bane's snarl jerked me from my thoughts.

"Sorry... You just normally like one while I make lunch..."

"Well, perhaps I *don't* want a coffee today!"

"Bane, calm down, *please*. I didn't mean to..."

"*I* didn't mean to be a bloody cripple for the rest of my life, but here I am!" He kicked out at the coffee table, sending it tumbling across the carpet.

I stood, gripped with an increasingly familiar feeling of helplessness bordering on panic. Once I'd have just gone and taken his arm, spoken to him, calmed him, but it didn't *work* anymore. *Coddling...* "Bane..." I tried softly. I was leaving *tomorrow*, surely he wasn't really going to...

"Was it worth it, Margo?" he snapped. "You and your bloody cause!"

It was your cause too, whispered my aching heart. *You said so.*

"I'm going to make the lunch. Jon'll be coming over soon with his Braille books." Nothing to do but let him calm down. "I presume you don't want a coffee. Let me know if you change your mind."

A thud from behind me as he tried to kick the armchair after the table. I shut the kitchen door behind me and started chopping carrots and onions, stopping often to wipe my streaming eyes.

Bane refused to eat what I'd cooked, so I ate by myself, then stole away to the Sistine Chapel. I prayed for Bane and myself for a while, and for the success of the Monaco visit, then, since there was nothing I could do about Bane, I just sat there, chewing over the whole *forgiveness of Mr. Everington* question.

Tap. Tap. Tap. Jon came in and found a pew. Knelt with his head in his hands and let out a long, long sigh. No one else was there, so I asked softly, "Bane?"

"*Bane*. I don't know how you stand it, Margo." Jon moved to sit on the bench.

"He's feeling bad today."

"*He's feeling bad today* ceases to be an excuse when today is every day. I don't know whether to punch him or hug him. No way will he let me hug him, so while you're away I'll probably punch him..."

"Oh, don't get in a fight with him, Jon. You'll win, you know you will, and then he'll feel even worse..."

Jon gave a rather irritable "huh," then added, "I wouldn't count on it, the mood he's in."

"Well, beating you to a pulp will also not make him feel better, not afterwards."

"Probably would *during*. But I'm not offering. He never did pull his punches." Jon sighed, staring towards the altar.

There was something I wanted to bring up with him, actually... and this was unusually private. "Jon...?"

"Hmm?" He turned his face toward me.

"Well, I've been wanting to say... I am *really* sorry about everything that happened at the Facility. You know, all the... snuggling. It was horribly unfair of me. I feel like I... used you, and that... you're maybe still paying the price." He'd been friendly enough to Calla—but it had reminded me of the way he was with all our eager dorm-mates in the Facility, cordial but no more.

Jon frowned slightly. "You said something like this already, remember? Right after we escaped?"

"Yes, I know, but I've... only gradually realized *just how* unfair it was and... how strong you were in resisting any temptation you... you know, *felt.* "And still feel?

Jon sighed again. "Margo, we got a bit close, and I came to care for you a bit more than I should have done, yes, but it's okay now, all right? You and Bane are married, just as you should be, and everything is fine. And if we win the vote, who knows what the future might hold for me? Please stop beating yourself up about it—clearly you are!"

"I just feel bad..."

"Then stop! *Anyway*..." Jon changed the subject firmly, "Bane said the Major upset you?"

"What? Oh, not upset, exactly. I'm more bemused. He doesn't think I really forgive him, would you believe? And Bane thinks the same!"

"*Do* you forgive him?"

"Oh, not you too!"

"Well, you're very dutiful in doing what Doctor Frederick asks you to do, but there's never... never any *genuine feeling* when you speak about him. Like you could come back and say he'd died in the night with about as much emotion as you report on any other development."

"But..." I trailed off. How bothered would I be if the man died? Quite a lot? Only moderately?

"Anyway, I've got to go," said Jon. "Washing-up duty calls. Your best beloved left me with a strong need for a moment or two's quiet. Or at least a few minutes to vent. Bye."

He tapped his way out of the chapel, leaving me to my uncomfortable thoughts.

Bane sat around like a gloomy cloud for the rest of the day, being very quiet, and very polite, like he knew he'd upset me earlier, but unaffected by all my attempts to lift his spirits. I went to bed tired, but couldn't stop my thoughts churning, round and round. Bane—Everington—Bane—Everington—Bane—Bane—Bane...

I thought he was asleep, but he heard me sniff and wrapped his arms around me, gathering me in. I held him tight. Why did we ever have to get out of bed? In the dark, tucked up together, he seemed to feel his blindness less keenly. Not that he was often in the mood for anything more than a good cuddle, these days...

But tonight, when I got the sniffle under control, he began to nose gently around the edge of my face, circling it with kisses. My hands slid inside his pajama top, tiredness forgotten.

"All clear?" he murmured.

I pictured my chart... technically my infertile time started tomorrow morning, but we were close enough, surely? I mean, I was off tomorrow and Bane was actually... "Just about."

In other circumstances he'd have picked up on that, but as it was... his lips moved to mine, and his hands to other places...

1 month, 27 days

"The notion of forgiveness needs to find its way into

international discourse on conflict resolution, so as to transform the sterile language of mutual recrimination which leads nowhere."

Pope Benedict XVI—quoted on 'The Impatient Gardener'

My alarm went off at three in the morning. Bane woke with a jolt and thrashed around for a moment, swearing, before sitting up, shivering slightly.

"Sorry, love." My apology was heartfelt. "You know I have to catch the boat..."

"Are you really going to do this?" he demanded, his voice tight.

"Of course I am," I said, then added gently, "what happened to, 'You gave a great speech, changed some minds and hearts'?"

"That doesn't mean I think you should go off again! Especially not to *there*. So close to..."

"Eduardo's been over all the security arrangements with the Monacan police, Bane. And I'll have Unicorn and Snakey with me."

"We both heard Eduardo say that it's impossible to make an event like this totally safe. Did we not?"

"It's worth the risk, Bane."

"Well, perhaps it isn't to me!"

"I'm sorry," I said softly. I slipped out of bed and began to get dressed.

Bane lay there for a while, clearly still shaken by his bad awakening and mired in terror for me. But finally he got up as well, pulled some clothes on and joined me by the door. "I'll take that for you," he said, when I let go of his arm and bent to pick up my bag.

"Thanks." I yielded it to him and we set off for VSS HQ. For this trip, I had only the one small bag, containing my best skirt and blouse, which I'd wear for the speech. We were going to travel on a highPropulsion speedboat, like the ones we'd used for the Liberations, arriving in the early afternoon. I'd do my speech, answer some questions, then we'd slip onto a different speedboat—just in case anyone had recognized me when I arrived—and head home.

Bane didn't speak again until we'd almost reached VSS HQ. "I really don't like this, Margo."

Lord help me, what could I say? "I know. And I'm really sorry we don't agree about it."

"You don't care what I think."

"*Bane...* I *do* care what you think. Very much. But I've *got* to go."

"You haven't *got* to go." A thread of anger in his voice. "You're just *choosing* to go."

That was true as far as it went, I suppose. "For good reasons, Bane."

"What will it do to your precious cause if you get yourself killed; have you thought about that? Since you clearly don't care what it would do to *me.*"

"You had to do this now, didn't you?" I snapped, in a whisper. "It's too late to call it off! Why couldn't you just hug me and say, 'Good luck'!"

"Because it's *not* too late!" he hissed.

I pushed open the door to HQ and went in, showing my pass to the alert night guard. I'd told Sister Krayj I could do my own disguise this time, but she was there waiting to help me. She tactfully ignored the distress I couldn't entirely conceal, though when she'd finished she did say quietly, "Are you okay, Margo?"

"Fine," I said. "Thank you for getting up."

She made a dismissive gesture. "Good luck with your speech," she said.

Jon was there with Bane when I went back out with Eduardo, Grass Snake and Unicorn. We'd told him not to bother getting up, either...

At least Bane was still there. Since he hadn't followed me in, I'd been horribly afraid he might have stormed off. When we reached that old portrait, his hug was stiff, but there was a desperation in his kiss. "Come back, Margo," he whispered.

"I will," I whispered back, as though saying it could provide some guarantee of it actually happening.

"Margo..." Snakey was shaking my shoulder. "We're coming in sight of the coast. You'd better straighten your wig."

I sat up on the speedboat's padded bench. However had I fallen asleep? What with my emotional turmoil from that row with Bane, and the violent smacking of the speedboat as it skimmed the waves, I'd have thought it impossible.

I took a small mirror from my bag and sorted out my disguise, swapping the fake glasses for sunglasses—the sun was blazing down—then stared at the approaching land. "Is that Monaco?"

"That's the French Department," said Raphael the boatman, who I knew from the Liberations.

I swallowed. "Oh."

"We're not making landfall there, Margo," said Unicorn, reassuringly.

"It's going to turn into Free State really soon," added Grass Snake. "Look at all the boats..."

Wow... yes, there were literally hundreds of little boats, all streaming along the coast in the same direction as us. Fishing boats, speedboats, a few yachts, little sailing boats, and closer in, I even spotted rowing boats and inflatable dinghies. For the first time I understood why Eduardo was so confident we'd be able to slip in unobserved.

"I'm glad they've got robust crowd control plans in place," said Unicorn dryly.

But... if this many people were heading in just from the *sea*... "Exactly how large is this main square?"

"Not large enough by half," grinned Snakey. "Quite small, actually, as these things go. They're setting up screens all over the State. People could just as well watch from the comfort of their own homes, of course, but they won't feel like they were really there."

"But they *were* really there," said Unicorn, looking bemused by this.

"*Sí*, but they won't have *seen* the speech *in person*."

"Hardly anyone does, at a big event like this."

"True."

"Monaco," grunted Raphael, pointing at the coast.

My heart leapt.

Acting just like everyone else, we joined the queue of

vessels that was forming, and waited to enter the main harbor. And waited. Raphael directed us to a large cooler that proved to contain a packed lunch for four. My stomach was beginning to flutter with nerves, but I tried to eat with carefree abandon—boats floated close on every side, now. I'd surely be glad of the meal later.

Snakey and Unicorn talked and laughed in Esperanto convincingly enough for all of us, calm as two ultra-competent cucumbers. Raphael leaned on the wheel, chewing on a licorice stick, unmoved as ever by all this cloak and dagger stuff.

"I heard they're charging three times the usual visa fee," said someone in a neighboring boat.

"That much?" said Snakey, in apparent dismay. "I *really* hope Margaret Verrall shows up!" He took his wallet out and began to count the money in it. If I hadn't been so nervous, I'd have died of laughter. As it was, I only suffered a minor outbreak of choking.

Finally we reached the jetty. We didn't need a mooring spot, since Raphael was taking our apparently tatty boat away again. Good thing: it looked as though there were hardly any berths left, for love or money.

"IDs," said the bored border guard, as we reached one of the weaponScanner arches. He swiped our cards uneventfully, then unfolded the papers Unicorn handed to him—and started. Most people arriving weren't presenting him with official Monacan Government carry permits for nonLethal weapons. He eyed me rather closely after that, but let us pass through the arch, silencing the buzzer quickly and being noticeably careful not to make a big thing of it when searching Unicorn and Snakey to ascertain that they were only carry the weapons covered by their paperwork.

And we were in.

The *Place du Palais* was teaming with people, though it really was quite a small square (though presumably the largest the tiny state had to offer). The space was impressively well-organized, with no fewer than five cordoned off access-ways of a good width: they clearly didn't risk things like crowd stampedes here; bad for business, no doubt. Or more likely, the people here had—despite my efforts—paid for the pleasure (over and above the hiked up visa charge), and didn't want to have to wait around to leave afterwards.

I'd left the wig and sunglasses with my bag in the room inside the Presidential Palace where I'd changed into my speaking outfit, and I was all unencumbered and ready to go. And already starting to sweat in the light-weight jacket. But without it my outfit looked too eveningish with the blouse tucked into the embroidered waistband of the skirt, and too everyday with it untucked. I was going on stage any moment, anyway, and the huge construction of metal girders and black plastiCloth had a roof to keep the sun off.

Even in my Sunday best I felt decidedly drab compared to the celebrities who'd wrangled private introductions to me while I was inside the Presidential Palace. But I wasn't going to worry about that. I hadn't been invited here to speak because I was glamorous or powerful, had I?

Almost time. I swallowed hard, trying not to destroy my notes by twisting them in my hands too much. It was easier having Pope Cornelius go first. He was usually the main event. Now I was. In fact, I was the only event, period.

Unicorn and Grass Snake paid no attention to my fidgeting. Their eyes were hyper-alert, ever moving, as they searched for danger. I eyed the stage again. It had been constructed up against the main gateway of the palace that dominated the square—or which *had* dominated the square. The stage looked like something that would be erected for a EuroGov Annual Summit, not *one speech.*

"I can't see all these supposed plainclothes policemen," Unicorn said to Snakey under his breath, eyes never leaving the square. "Hopefully that means they're really good at their jobs, but you'd think they'd want more uniformed officers at an event like this."

"The boss fixed it all up ever so carefully," said Snakey.

"Yes, he did..."

The Monacan organizer-fellow was beckoning me up the side stairs. Unicorn went ahead and Snakey followed behind.

Florestan the third, the Sovereign Prince of Monaco,

had just finished giving me such an—apparently—heart-felt welcome that I couldn't help suspecting that he was not quite so focused on the material advantages of my visit as his government. He clearly felt it politically imprudent to actually stay for my speech, though, since he shook hands with me, letting the cameras get some good shots, then excusing himself with—apparent—sincerity, disappeared down the stairs, and got into a limo.

Over to you, Margo...

I waited for the limo to make it out of the square along one of the fenced-off roadways, then I stepped up to the podium, arranged my notes and smiled at the crowd.

Lord, be on my lips...

"I'd like to thank you all for coming. Although I'm sure many of you are keen to hear about the events of the past year, right now I want to look to the future. I know that a lot of you have made a great effort to be here today, and I find that really, really, heartening. Because great effort is going to be necessary in the days ahead. Great effort, and great resolve. Resolve to make a better world, through *peaceful, democratic* means. Whatever happens on the first of July, whether we win the vote, or lose it, we must not allow ourselves to slip into mindless violence, through frustration or anger. We will need this resolve just as much if we win. We must be absolutely committed to putting the wrongs of the past behind us, and moving forward. *Forgiveness* will heal our continent, not justice, and certainly not vengeance! Win or lose, forgiveness is the answer!

"We must all..." I lost my place, distracted, as Snakey suddenly moved closer to my shoulder, drawing his nonLee and staring at one corner of the square. A ripple in the crowd.... *Just carry on, Margo, they'll tell you if you need to leave.* "We must all consider..."

Screams suddenly broke the listening hush. I lost my place again as a camo-painted army truck swung into the square, tearing straight towards the stage. Shots rang out... I just glimpsed the Monacan police, firing at the truck, then Snakey was rushing me full tilt towards the back of the stage—heading for the stairs? No, for the great gateway of the palace, where glass doors were set a meter back inside the arch, leaving a sort of pit between them and the stage. I concentrated on not tripping over my feet, my heart pounding in my chest.

We almost made it, but we couldn't quite out-run the truck. The square just wasn't that big... The stage shuddered under our feet as the truck plowed into it, I stumbled and almost fell... then I did fall as Snakey let out a yell and shoved me to the side.

I hit the ground hard, as the floor seemed to rise up to meet me and the world turned into a maelstrom of plummeting girders and plastiCloth. Something painfully solid surged up and over me, crushing me to the ground... people were screaming... I had no air left in me with which to scream...

Finally the clatters and thuds and cries died away. Slightly more distantly I could hear the sound of a very large number of people all trying to vacate an area at the same time, but it seemed like something happening in another world.

My world had shrunk to square wooden panels, heaped up in front... oh, it was dislodged stage flooring... and behind too, piled over my legs, pinning me down. I tried to sit up, gasping for breath, and the panels lying across my back shifted slightly. I'd been lucky. I was a bit stuck, but I hadn't been crushed.

Lucky? No, not luck... *Snakey?*

I peeped over the wood.

Oh Lord, save us!

The impact of the truck had driven the stage flooring up against the palace to form a ridge-like heap, and the roof had collapsed completely. A tangle of roof girders lay atop the heap of splintered wooden squares—and the malevolently-steaming truck. My heart seemed to stop. *Was U somewhere under all that?*

And where was...?

There... Snakey was up against the other side of the palace gateway, a few meters away, legs pinned by the heap, but still on his feet... *Oh no!* He was only standing because one of the fallen roof girders was pinning him upright! One of the Monacan policemen was propped there beside him, ominously still. Snakey's face was white, and blood was trickling from his lips. Perhaps he'd just hit his mouth... *Please, Lord...*

His dazed eyes fell on me, and a spark of alertness flared. "Run," he whispered.

Run? Only then did I realize that a man was trying to kick open the buckled door of the truck. A man dressed in Resistance-style incogniCam and holding a gun.

8

THE FIELD DRESSING

I tried frantically to sit up, and the wood slid a little from my back. But... my feet were still trapped... I shoved with my legs, but the panels were too thoroughly wedged and interlocked, and they wouldn't budge. Not large enough to crush me, but quite large enough to pinion me...

The man had got the door partially open... he could shoot me through the gap—*Oh Lord!*—but he didn't raise the gun yet, intent on getting out of the vehicle... Oh, the lattice-like roof girder lay between us. Why would he risk a ricochet when he could walk up and shoot me at point blank range?

Oh God! Help me!

I yanked as hard as I could; flung myself from side to side. Nothing! Wait... had the panels moved...? Skin tingling horribly in anticipation of the imminent bullet, I twisted around, putting my back to the man, and got my knees against the heap, pushed with my hands as well... Yes! They were moving. And that pit-like space under the gateway was just behind the heap of broken stage flooring in which I was trapped! If I could just get free, I could throw myself over and into it... I heaved. I heard the door creak all the way open... footsteps approached quickly... The heap shifted...

A shot rang out. I flinched, but when I looked around, it was the man who was clutching his arm and swearing. Yes! One of the policemen had come! No... it was Snakey, still pinioned but holding a Lethal pistol—the policeman's gun?—in one shaking hand, struggling to take aim again... but the man stepped to one side just as he fired, then casually raised his own gun and shot Snakey in the head.

My mouth opened on something that might have been going to be "NO!" but never came out because the man was turning back to me and I was too busy diving up and over the top of the heap. If I showed up right behind him at the pearly gates, Snakey was going to be *very* peeved...

I fell head first, managing to break the impact with my arms. But as soon as I sat up, I realized that I'd just swapped one trap for another. There were iron bars on the outside of the huge glass doors, and the stage I'd hoped to hide under was solid all the way down to the ground, its panels undislodged. The inside of the archway itself provided some shelter, but not enough—the man would just walk to the other side and shoot me like a fish in a barrel... And he'd be over the top of that heap any moment...

Wait... There! Snakey's nonLee lay in the bottom of the pit where it must've been flung from his hand when the girder struck him. I snatched it up, snapped off the safety catch, and leapt up the back of the stage to aim through a gap in the heap. I pulled the trigger just as the man spotted me.

Nothing happened. I looked at the nonLee properly and saw battery acid leaking from the crushed power magazine. On no...

The man's momentary expression of fear had turned to derision. "Stupid pacifist bitch!" he sneered. He glanced over his shoulder at the truck. "This is taking too damn long!" He hurried forward again, pistol raised, and I dropped back down into the pit, my heart racing.

Lord, what do I do! Belatedly, something I'd just seen sank in... The Lethal pistol lay near Snakey's feet, where it had fallen from his hand. But it was near the bottom of the heap... on the assassin's side. By the time I'd hauled myself over and reached it, the man would have shot me at least three times... Bent double, I darted to the correct end of my little pit, just the same. It was literally the only chance I had.

No chance at all... *Oh, Bane*...

Get ready, Margo. Try for it before he's close enough to see over...

I drew a shuddering breath, psyching myself up... The footsteps were almost here... I heard him push aside the girder...

Then a thud and an oath...

"Yeah, you bastard, up here!" Unicorn's voice... I pulled myself up and risked a look... There he was, on top of that heap, blood streaking his face, still half trapped, by the look of it... And... oh no, his hands were empty! Like Snakey, he'd lost his nonLee in the chaos. "Yes, you son of a bitch...!" Unicorn directed a stream of even ruder names at the man, clearly trying to divert his attention from me.

But the man just glanced at the truck again and moved towards me, raising his gun when he saw me peeping out. Then swore again, hand flying to his head and coming away stained with blood. U must have thrown a jagged piece of wood, or something. As U readied another improvised missile, the man swung around, raising the gun...

No! Not U as well!

I launched myself up and over, diving full-stretch, reaching... my hand closed around the butt of the pistol—I rolled onto my back, already pointing the gun... the man had turned, his pistol was almost in line with me... I aimed for the center of his body, the way Eduardo had taught me to do when using an unknown weapon, and pulled the trigger.

Crack.

Red blossomed on the man's shoulder—his gun spun from his hand and slid to rest against the truck.

"Bitch!" But he gasped it this time, face whitening.

I scrabbled back up the slope and tipped myself into the pit as he staggered forward. "Back off!" I yelled, pointing the gun again as he loomed over the top.

He just directed yet another look at the truck, and stumbled forward. I pulled the trigger again...

Nothing.

Either it was jammed, or the policeman had fired off most of his mag earlier...

Drawing a knife from his belt with his left hand, the man half-fell into the pit. *Yikes!* I started to scramble out, then paused as I caught the look of triumph that flitted across his face, even as he sagged against the wall and slid into a sitting position. Still clutching the knife, he promptly crawled around into the shelter of the gateway... *What...?*

Unicorn had finally pulled himself completely free of the heap and scrambled down it, immediately moving towards the truck to get the gun...

The truck...

"*U! There's a bomb in the truck!*"

He lurched across the stage, stopping only to lift Snakey's head long enough to see his blank eyes, before leaping into the pit beside me. He landed with an involuntary gasp of pain, and immediately dragged me behind the archway and plastered me to the wall with his body.

Panting and shaking, we both waited.

And waited.

And waited.

It was starting to get a bit embarrassing, being in this position with a man, even U. Clearly I was wrong. Nothing was going to ha...

BANG...

It felt like the very stone of the arch jolted against my cheek. Something slammed into the glass doors with a huge smack—a spider's web of cracks suddenly marred their smoothness. The air seemed to shiver as the noise echoed back from the buildings opposite. My ears rang. My head rang.

When everything was still and silent again, U pushed away from the wall and staggered to his feet. "Margo, please stay here, okay?" he said, very loudly and very clearly.

Moving wasn't something my numb mind was quite considering yet, anyway...

The haze receded slightly when I realized U was approaching the assassin opposite as warily as a man creeping up on an adder.

"U... be careful..." I croaked. My throat seemed full of gun smoke and dust and, well, bomb smoke.

The man glared at Unicorn, but seemed hardly able to lift the knife any more. His shirt was soaked in blood. With a swift step, U pinned his knife hand. Bent rather stiffly and twisted the knife free. His fingers went to the man's neck, squeezing very precisely: the assassin's eyes rolled up and he went limp.

U put the knife in his own belt, and came back over to me. He looked very unsteady—definitely hurt worse than he looked. "Margo, please stay right here for a little longer, okay?" he said. He tried to shrug off his jacket, went white as a sheet, and desisted. "Could I have your jacket, please?"

"What?" I whispered.

"Your jacket? Please?"

Trying not to wince—he was definitely hurt worse than me—I slipped it off.

"Thank you. Here," he handed me a lumpy object he'd just taken from his pocket. "If you want to do something with that, feel free. Otherwise I suppose I'll do it in a minute." I'd never heard him so grim. "But... just stay right there for a moment longer..."

He moved to the stage and hauled himself up with another involuntary grunt of pain. Did he think there was a second bomb? I shifted to peep around the gateway. Oh... He'd just laid my jacket over Snakey. He didn't want me to see what... what the explosion had done...

Swallowing, I turned my eyes to the thing in my hand. A field dressing. Slowly, I looked up at Snakey's murderer, bleeding to death opposite.

Lord, do I really have to?

I swallowed again, fighting a hot, sick rush of hatred that made the blood pound in my head. The bastard had killed Snakey as casually as though he were swatting an insect... He didn't *deserve* to be helped...

But what had I just said on stage? What was it I'd thought about Everington? Our Lord had died for this murderous bastard too...

Breathing hard with rage as well as pain, I crawled across to the other side of the archway and ripped the man's shirt open, placed the pad on the wound and pressed down as hard as I could. If he died, I would have killed him. However much he *deserved* it, I didn't want that.

Blood spilled over my hands; the smell filled my nose. I slumped tiredly, still keeping up the pressure, and rested my cheek against the crazed glass, my heart aching, my eyes closing in silent misery. *Snakey...*

When Unicorn came back a few moments later, Monacan police were right behind him. And press, no surprise... The camera flashes blinded me as I crouched over the wounded bastard.

Police... In fact... where the *hell* had the police *been* all this time? Although, it had probably *actually* all happened within the space of about a minute or two, if not less. But still...

"My bodyguard needs medical attention too..." I said, as the laggard police took rather disorganized charge of my patient.

"I'm fine," said Unicorn tersely. "Excuse me, I need to speak with Mrs. Verrall for a moment... Come on, Margo..."

"What? But you need..."

"Come on over here..." Unicorn let some of the milling policemen boost me up onto the stage, then hustled me away down the sagging steps.

"Where are we...?"

"Shhh, just come with me..."

We went around the side of the palace and into the side streets and found ourselves among the distraught and shell-shocked crowds. We mingled with them, moving down from the *Plais du Palais*, up on its little fortified plateau, and towards the waterfront. When our particularly blood-stained and tattered appearance began to risk attention, U steered me into a public rest room, checking the cubicles quickly before moving a 'closed for cleaning' sign into the doorway.

"Quickly, wash your face," said U, moving to the wash basin himself.

I was still dithering by the door. "U... this is the *Gents*..."

"I'm not going in the Ladies!" U looked shocked. "Wash, quick. And change your parting: you know, your hair..."

I complied, still too shaken to argue. Apparently we weren't going back for my wig. Changing my parting was the most rudimentary of all possible disguises, but when I looked in the mirror it was astonishing what a difference it made. U pulled out his omniPhone while I was finishing up, and called Raphael, using a prearranged and totally innocuous code phrase to request an immediate pick up.

"Just keep your head down and don't look at anyone," Unicorn said as, still a bit tattered, but somewhat less gory, we headed on to the waterside.

Now I was glad I wasn't wearing anything fancier. I'd untucked my top from my skirt to hide the embroidered waistband, which seemed to have survived fairly unscathed—I should have felt pleased about that, it being my wedding outfit and all, but it seemed meaningless, in the circumstances... *Snakey*... I didn't blend in too badly, anyway, and we reached the boat—a different one—without hiccup.

"Lie down in the bottom," U told me, and he lay down on the opposite side of the boat, and got Raphael to chuck a tarp over us. The engine roared and we were away.

"U, what's going on?" I whispered, once we'd cleared the busy marina.

"That whole thing stank, couldn't you see? There wasn't the agreed number of police—plainclothes, my foot!—the ones actually there mostly just ran away, except for a few unlucky ones... The square was rigged to allow the public to escape in the quickest possible time... I think it was a bloody set-up! I wasn't staying a second longer than necessary."

"Are you alright? Let me take a look at you..."

"You stay right under there, until we reach the Italian Department," said Unicorn firmly.

"But you're hurt..."

"I'm fine..."

"You are not!"

"The boy's hurt inside, *cara mia*," Raphael interjected. "There's nothing you or I can do for him, except get him home."

That was hours and hours away! How could I have let U rush us off like that? He needed a doctor... Too late now. No way would I get this boat turned around.

"We left Snakey..." I said in a small voice.

"They'll send him back to us." Unicorn's voice was tight with pain. "It was... far too late to help him... But not us. Seriously Margo, we're *both* safer getting out of there."

Far too late. Far too late. I couldn't tell if the dampness on my cheeks was tears, or bilge slime.

"Wake up, *cara mia*." Raphael's voice. "We're here..."

The motion of the boat, and utter exhaustion, must've

finally combined to lull me into blessed oblivion. I pushed aside the tarpaulin, unable to suppress a wince. I ached all over. There was the shore... the lights of Civitavecchia glowing in the darkness. I checked my watch. One in the morning. We'd made good time. Of course, we'd left sooner than we'd expected...

"*U?*"I pulled the tarpaulin off him and he blinked at me blearily. "How do you feel?" I asked anxiously.

"As soon as we get you inside the Vatican wall, I will feel just wonderful," he said rather hoarsely, and tried to sit up. "*Oh God...*" It hissed through his teeth, prayer rather than profanity.

I slipped an arm around his shoulders and helped to slowly sit him upright. By the time he was sitting on the bench, his face was gray in the boat's lights and he looked like he was about to be sick.

Slipping a little medical pouch from his pocket, he took out a couple of strong painkillers and a stimulant, and gulped them down. "By the time we dock, I'll be all ready to go," he assured me. "Don't look so worried, I think it's mostly busted ribs. Hurts like hell, but not very serious."

"Don't overdo it," I said helplessly, knowing perfectly well that until I was safe, he wasn't going to pay any attention in the slightest.

He made it up the ladder to the jetty, but he wasn't at all steady on his feet. Raphael chucked the cooler up after us. "Carry that, *cara mia.*"

Good idea. People would assume we'd been out picnicking, and that U was drunk.

We reached the car park fairly quickly, in the circumstances, but... "I'll have to drive," I told Unicorn.

No argument from Unicorn. "Keys are in my pocket," he gasped.

I fished them out and pressed the button... there was the car. We managed the painful business of getting U into the vehicle—I insisted on pulling an afghan from the back and tucking it over him: he was going so cold and clammy—then I eased gingerly behind the wheel. How long had it been since my last driving lesson with Dad, on the quiet roads of the Fellest?

It was only an hour's drive. There was no one else on the road. I could do this. "You'd better put your seatbelt on, U. I never actually took my driving test."

He began to shake his head, then seemed to think better of it. "I really can't, Margo. Just drive carefully."

I frowned, but pressed the accelerator, gently easing up on the clutch. What it would do to U just now, if I kangaroo-hopped down the road... But the car moved off smoothly. *Thank you, Lord.*

Just concentrate on driving, Margo... But once we'd left the built-up area behind us there was nothing to distract me from my thoughts. Especially the thought that Snakey had just died to save my life. I knew he was doing his duty, but...

"Protecting you is our way of fighting the EuroGov, you do know that, don't you?" asked Unicorn. My expression must be betraying me. "Snakey died fighting the EuroGov. He's a hero."

A dead hero...

"I know," I said quietly. "It's just... it's hard being the one people feel they should die for. It doesn't feel... fair. My life is worth no more than Snakey's."

"Well, if you want to get metaphysical about it. But *practically* speaking, you're worth more to our cause just now—alive—than virtually any of the rest of us. So we're going to carry right on dying for you, if that's what it takes to defeat them."

I'd feel that way too, if I wasn't me, no doubt about it.

Thank you so much, Snakey, I thought to him. *And I know you'll wave it away, but... I'm really sorry.*

By the time we reached Rome, Unicorn was fighting to stay awake. His breathing sounded so painful. But he fished in his pocket for the garage door control and soon I was easing the car inside.

We hobbled slowly along the secret passage, desperate to reach the place, and more importantly, the people, at the end, but too sore to hurry. But soon brisk footsteps and tense voices approached. They'd seen us on the cameras.

Eduardo was at the front. Unicorn stopped dead when

he saw him, and his face wobbled... For the first time I wondered how U felt about this... Grieving for Snakey, yes, but... did he feel guilty? He'd been in charge...

But his face straightened as he succeeded in fighting back the tears. "*Sir*..." he choked.

Eduardo gave him a slightly jerky nod. "We saw it all on TV," he said tersely. "You did... really well. You... both did." His unconscious glance upwards included the absent Snakey in this. Then he glanced at me. "All three of you, in fact."

I let out a breath. Thank you Lord, that even Eduardo realized this wasn't the time for a blow-by-blow critique of Unicorn's every decision...

"I think it was a set-up..." Unicorn's voice was still very strained.

"It looks that way. I'll worry about that. You go to the hospital straight away." Eduardo looked at me. "You too."

"Margo?" Bane pushed his way through the crowd of VSS guys, head turning from side to side. "*Margo?*"

"Here..." He hurried forward. "Don't hug me, Bane!" I said quickly. He stopped, looking hurt. "I'm a bit sore," I added, grabbing his hands in mine and squeezing. "I do want a hug, actually, just... gently..."

He obliged.

1 month, 26 days

Murder can often be rationalized—does that make it okay?

The same goes for Sorting.

Margaret Verrall—comment on "A Rational Defense of the Sorting Program"

I slept late in the morning, and stopped only to gobble a light breakfast before hurrying up to the hospital to see how Unicorn was.

"He's okay, Margo," Bane told me, as we went. "Jon saw him earlier. Quite a few broken ribs and a couple of small lung contusions, but his abdomen escaped serious damage.

Doctor Frederick wants him out of bed within a day or two, and moving around. Something about preventing fluid build-up in the lungs. U said good, he'd get back to work as soon as the pain was a little less distracting."

"What did Doctor Frederick say to that?"

"He just shrugged. I gather making people move around is the bigger problem, with this type of injury."

"Really? When *you* broke *your* ribs you stayed in bed for precisely two days before getting bored."

Bane's turn to shrug. "Anyway, long-term, no harm done. Unlike..." He broke off and clamped his lips together.

Unlike Snakey... Poor Bane. Losing another friend, so soon after Father Mark...

"You'd better see the Major afterwards," he added rather reluctantly.

Lucas... *Oh no!* "Please tell me Snail forgot to put the TV in his room?"

"Nope."

"Uh oh... how did he take it?"

"Did what we all wanted to do, apparently. Tried to climb through the front of telly, he was that interested in what was happening—then shot out of the room and off through the state as though he was going to run all the way to Monaco and save you. Snail chased him for a while, tried to reason with him—Everington wouldn't listen to a word, of course—so Snail shot him with his nonLee. For his own good, but the man's been glowering at Snail through that window all morning."

I blinked. "He can't see through the window."

"That's not stopping him. Suppose it's a good sign, really. Reacting to someone other than you, and all that."

Hmm.

When we reached Unicorn's room, Eduardo was there, and Jon was there again, as well. "Do you know anything yet?" I asked Eduardo. "Hi, Jon; hi U, how are you?"

"I feel just wonderful," Unicorn assured me, grinning positively sunnily. Huh? Was he okay? He seemed a bit... "See, here you are, back in the Vatican. Plus, I'm on morphine," he confided. Ah... that explained it. "Oh, sorry, sir. What were you saying?"

Eduardo nodded to me in recognition of my question. "I was just telling Jack that the EuroNews are screaming—rather too loudly, in my opinion—that it was the Resistance, in retaliation for you criticizing them, but despite the fact that the assassin does *appear* to be a member of the Resistance, I'm quite certain he's a EuroGov mole. But proof? No chance.

"However, the bomb was highly directional, more like a Claymore mine than a normal bomb, hence the lack of fatalities among the crowd, which strongly suggests that there was some sort of EuroGov-Monacan collaboration, though whether at the highest levels of the government or just a handful of people bribed, well, we're not going to find out."

"How does that support it being the EuroGov?" asked Jon. "Deliberate indiscriminate bombing of civilians is one thing the Resistance have never sunk to. Sounds more like proof it *was* the Resistance."

"I did badmouth them..." I added.

Eduardo shook his head. "No, what I mean is that the directional bomb is proof of *Monacan* involvement. Left to their own devices, yes, the EuroGov would be quite happy to let the Resistance take the blame for the maximum carnage. But the Monacan element would most likely have insisted that none of their own citizens or visitors be killed."

"But why are you so sure it wasn't the Resistance?" I asked.

Eduardo made a rather dismissive noise. "You've brought the Resistance more recruits in the last year than anyone has in the last ten. It was the EuroGov, with the Monacan element providing at least a breath of morality, thank God, and they meant business. A truck, *and* an assassin, *and* a bomb: they had every reason to be confident that you'd be dead by the end. And if it wasn't for Javier, Jack and the combined efforts of all your guardian angels, you would've been."

Javier. I'd hardly ever heard Snakey's real name. In fact...

"What's Snakey's surname?" I asked, in a small voice.

"Alvarez," said Eduardo shortly. "Excuse me, I need to get on." He hurried out.

Javier Alvarez. So how did *Eduardo* feel about losing

one of his young agents?

Unicorn was suddenly looking glum, despite the morphine. And very tired.

"Perhaps we'd better come back later," I said.

He gave us an apologetic look. "Perhaps. Oh, don't go without seeing the newspapers, though..." He nodded to the bedside table. "Did you notice that freestanding video tower? The whole fiasco was live, even after the stage collapsed. Even after the bomb. The tower tilted sideways a bit, but most of the cameras stayed on.

Bane shuddered, at that. "The one thing worse than having to listen to Snail and Bee narrate what was happening would have been if the damn thing had cut out before we knew you were safe..."

I took his hand for a moment. "I'm sorry. It must have been awful..."

Bane yanked his hand free. "Don't coddle me!" he hissed, under his breath.

"I wasn't..." I began. Unicorn was politely looking at the opposite wall, pretending nothing was happening in finest British fashion. Choking back a sigh, I went to examine the newspapers. Soon started reading the headlines to Bane.

RESISTANCE IN M.V. DEATH ATTEMPT

HORROR IN MONACO: M.V. ALIVE, THREE DEAD

M.V. VANISHES AFTER MONACO ASSASSINATION CHAOS

But most of them, to my shock, were eschewing the more dramatic headlines and photographs in favor of a shot of me bending over that assassin with a bandage in my hand.

M.V. PRACTISES WHAT SHE PREACHES

WE NEED FORGIVENESS, SAYS M.V., THEN FORGIVES KILLER

M.V. SHOOTS ASSASSIN! THEN GIVES FIRST AID!

"They dug two policemen and the compère out alive!" I said, reading a paper in more detail. "That end of the stage collapsed partially, and what with all the floor panels, it was enough to protect them from the blast... Oh... enough to save their lives, anyway. Sounds like they're pretty badly hurt. Two policemen died, one hit by the truck, the other by that girder. A few cuts and bumps and twisted ankles among the crowd. Well, that bit could be worse."

I skimmed on. So little about Snakey! Or the two policemen who'd died. Horrible. Typical press. The paper did have a close-up of Unicorn half in, half out of the heap, arm raised to launch a bit of broken metal at the assassin. 'M.V.'s crazy bodyguard,' said the caption.

"That's a bit harsh," I remarked. "I thought it was incredibly brave of you."

Unicorn sniffed dismissively. "Nonsense. What else could I do? Wouldn't have been much point my going off to find a better weapon, would there? It would all have been over by the time I came back. By the time I got myself free of that mess, even. Anyway, *you* saved us both, in the end."

"Me? I was only alive by that time because you and... and Snakey... had both risked your lives for me."

"It's our job, Margo." He really did look tired, now.

"I know," I said miserably. "Well, we'd better go."

"Hi, Margo," said Snail, when I approached Lucas's door. His voice was strained.

I managed a subdued, "Hi."

"Snakey *a fait très, très, bien, oui?*"

"*Oui,*" I agreed. Snakey did very, very, good...

Snail opened the door without further comment, thank goodness. Lucas glared at him from the bed.

"Look, for the third time this morning," said Snail, "If

you'd run across that white line, you'd have got yourself executed!"

"He's right, Lucas," I said, slipping past Snail. "You really should thank him."

Lucas's glare disappeared like magic. Relief took its place.

"You, uh, did tell him I was okay, right?" I muttered to Snail.

"Till I was blue in the face, Margo. He doesn't listen to me. Have fun." He stepped back out and shut the door.

"I, uh, I'm sorry about yesterday," I said, sitting in my usual chair by the bed. "With hindsight, the TV was a bad idea."

Lucas was staring at me so intently. Afraid I would disappear? Or trying to tell if I was okay?

"I really am fine, Lucas," I said. "Just like Snail told you." Last night Doctor Frederick had diagnosed extensive bruising and a hairline fracture of one rib in my back, and allowed me to go straight home with Bane.

Looking a little skeptical, and a little wary, as though still thinking I might just go poof and be gone, he offered me the office book.

My mind strayed back to the forgiveness question as I read. Surely I *did* forgive him? I mean, if I could bandage that beastly assassin, surely I forgave Lucas?

"Lucas," I asked him, once I'd finished the Office, "why don't you think I've forgiven you?"

He frowned at me—wondering if he could face a long conversation after all that stress yesterday? But he finally spoke, very bleakly. "How could anyone? It's not possible."

"Not possible? Of course it's *possible*. However can you think it's not?"

He gazed at me, or rather through me, for a long time, even for him, as though seeking in his own mind for the reason. A look settled on his face, a look of anguish that made me not really want to know the answer.

"My own mother couldn't forgive me," he whispered at last. "She hated me for seven years. She died hating me." His face crumpled, slowly, as though this time he were fighting it, then he put his hands to his face as the sobs began.

I watched him, shifting uncomfortably on my seat, then wincing as it jostled my bruises. Never had that long-growing awareness that adults were actually just like me—making mistakes, being afraid, *crying*—been forced on me so clearly. 'Course, I was an adult too, now. Still hard to remember... I was only nineteen, after all.

He cried and cried, as though some dam had broken inside him and there was far, far too much stored-up pain trying to force its way out in one go. My heart twisted in response, and something around it cracked. Oh, Lord forgive me, Bane and Jon had been spot on, hadn't they? My heart was enclosed like a granite egg as far as Lucas was concerned. So much for my forgiveness.

Still he wept, and it was painful even to watch. Moved by I know not what, I leaned forward and put my arms around him, rubbing his back as though comforting a little child. His bony hands moved timidly to knot in my sleeves, then he was clinging tight, his tears soaking my shoulder. I gritted my teeth against the pain and let him cling. And something gave a little more inside me.

Finally he ran out of tears and lay back against the pillows, face drawn and tired. "I think I was happier not remembering," he whispered. For a moment, he sounded so sane, we could've been standing in his little courtyard garden back at the Facility as he extolled the virtues of fuchsias.

It was only a flash. He gathered the Office book to his chest, hugging it, and fixed his eyes on the fuchsia. Within a few moments, his eyes closed and he slept—peacefully.

Peaceful was the last thing I felt. I'd just understood the depth of my failure—and taken the first step towards rectifying it?

Lord, finally I understand—it's not as simple as just saying the words, or going through the actions, or even wanting to mean them. I didn't really forgive that assassin yesterday, because there's no forgiveness without love. You have to mean it with your whole heart. Can I do that? It's so easy to think of these people as monsters, whatever we say... but there's nothing monstrous about wanting your mother to forgive you...

A Monacan hearse brought the body of Javier Alvarez, the dear friend I knew best as 'Snakey,' home yesterday afternoon. They'd put him in an incredibly fancy casket, as though that might make up for his death in some way. They made a great deal of panoply about the handover, too. But perhaps I'm being cynical and uncharitable. Perhaps it really was their way of honoring our fallen soldier. Either way, we kept Snakey and sent that ridiculous casket back with the hearse.

Today, he was laid to rest after a beautiful (and packed) Requiem Mass, in a simple wooden coffin (much better suited to his ideas about avoiding vanity) in the ancient graveyard of the Swiss Guards, now the resting place of all 'military operatives of the superstitious rebel organization known as the Underground' as the EuroGov would put it. An 'organization' to which Javier was proud to belong, and in the service of which he gladly gave his life.

We know that his faithfulness and generosity will not go unrewarded.

Margaret V.—blog post, 'The Impatient Gardener'

I sat among the crush of palm trees and headstones in the little courtyard garden, beside the fresh grave. I'd slipped away from the reception being hosted by the Swiss Guards in their barracks, desperate for a few moments' peace and quiet. By myself. Since I'd got back from Monaco, Bane had been combining his unrelenting black mood with a smothering level of overprotectiveness. I couldn't blame him for feeling that way, but he was driving me crazy. And... I just wanted some time to think.

The press were still going on about me helping the assassin. I'd been so pleased with myself, for managing to do it. Now, after what I'd realized the other day, I felt such a hypocrite. I'd *helped* him, but I hadn't *forgiven* him. Not properly. And the other thing...

"I shot that guy, Snakey," I whispered. "With a Lethal. I had to do it, he was about to kill U." And me... "It's just... horrible to think how close I came to killing him. I can hear you saying, *you weren't trying to kill him, you were trying to stop him from shooting U.* It's just... sobering, I s'pose. I've always admired those who refuse to harm others, even to save their own life. The ultimate in loving the other as yourself. But we have a duty to protect life. So that meant I had to do it. Whereas if it had just been me..."

I fell silent, remembering U's words in the car: *we're going to carry right on dying for you, if that's what it takes to defeat them.* Right now, in light of that, could high-mindedly refusing to exercise my legitimate right to self-defense ever count as anything other than completely selfish?

After what Snakey had done... Maybe not.

"Margo? *Margo?*"

"Hi, Bane." I smothered a sigh.

"See." Jon's voice. "I said she'd be here. No need to panic."

"*Who said I was panicking?*"

Smothering another sigh, I murmured, "Bye, Snakey," and got stiffly to my feet, wincing as my cracked rib and bruises made their presence felt.

1 month, 21 days

So I'm going to do a series of posts on organ donation because people seem hardly to know what it is. Basically, it means using an organ to cure someone, in much the same way as EuroBloc hospitals do today, but the organ has been donated—voluntarily—by a person who has died naturally, through ill health or accident. For many of those in the Underground, of course, 'organ donation' carries negative connotations, similar to 'abortion' or 'euthanasia', since it was these three things that led to the acceptance of Sorting. But organ donation in itself wasn't a bad thing.

Margaret V.—blog post, 'The Impatient Gardener'

Coo, coo. Tap, tap.

I stopped typing and glanced at Bane. "They're asking for you, Bane."

He didn't move from the sofa. "They want food, not me."

"Aren't you going to give them any?"

He flopped face forward on the sofa and pulled a cushion over his head.

Now he wouldn't even speak to the doves. Getting me back alive really hadn't done anything at all to raise his spirits long-term. What with Snakey's death, very much the opposite...

After a moment's hesitation, I clicked to save the draft post about organ donation that I'd been working on for a couple of days prior to the trip, and went to sit beside him. "Bane, please talk to me..." I didn't touch him or do anything that could be interpreted as *coddling*. "Don't shut me out like this."

"What is there to say?" he said blackly, though he rolled over slightly to free his mouth from the cushions.

"Just... *talk* to me. Tell me how you're feeling."

"Trust me, you don't want to know how I'm feeling."

"Then tell me how I can help you..."

"*Seriously?*" He sounded so bitter... "Not that there's even any chance of the EuroGov's offer still being available, after... well, Monaco. Not that you cared about that..."

"But... I thought you didn't *want* to accept it!"

"I don't." He sat up abruptly. "And I *won't* stoop to it; I'd rather die. Not that that's saying much, just at the moment."

"Please don't talk like that, Bane."

"See, you don't want to know how I'm feeling. You just want me to say something that will make *you* feel better."

"No, I don't! Bane, I don't want you to lie to me! I just... I wish you didn't feel that way. You were so much more positive to start with..."

"Ignorance is bliss, isn't it? I thought I could learn to be like Jon, all happy and fulfilled—but I'll never be able to do things the way Jon can. I'll never be able to forget what he's never known. I'm useless and I'll be useless for the rest of my life..."

"No, you're not! You're being too impatient! Maybe you'll never be quite as good at stuff as Jon is, but you'll be almost as good one day, if you just keep trying!"

"It's not that simple! You just don't *understand. Snakey* understood better than you do! But you went and got him killed, didn't you? "

I felt like he'd just punched me in the stomach. That false guilt which I'd been trying so hard to suppress surged up inside me. "Bane... How can you even say that?"

"It's true, isn't it?" he snapped. "You wouldn't listen to me and now he's dead!"

"I didn't *make* him go with me! He did his duty, Bane! Would you have had him *not do his duty?* Had him simply let me die?"

Bane was silent. I stared at him, still stunned by his attack. Was this what he'd been thinking? That my going to Monaco meant I didn't care about his eyes? That Snakey's death was *my fault?* I felt sick. But Snakey hadn't just done his duty, he'd also kept his word to Bane...

It was like someone had switched a light on in my head. Bane didn't think it was my fault. He thought it was *his* fault, because of Snakey's promise to him: *no one will hurt her while there's breath in my body.* No wonder he was so depressed! He couldn't cope with the pain of that guilt, so he was pushing it off onto someone else...

The realization lessened my hurt—at least slightly. "Snakey died because of the EuroGov, Bane. Not because of me, not because of him, and certainly not because of you."

"How did we get on to it being *my fault?*"he practically yelled. "We were talking about you nagging me all the time!"

"I'm just trying to *understand,* Bane, but you won't talk to me anymore!"

"Because all I get back is, *'Don't say that, Bane'* You want the truth? I wish they'd killed me! I wish they'd finished the job, one piece a day or whatever, it would be better than this!"

My chest was tight, heart thudding, a cold prickling over my entire body. "You don't mean that..."

He was silent for several long, shuddering breaths. "Maybe not the bit about one-piece-per-day. But I wish I'd died there. Then I wouldn't be this... this millstone around your neck."

I grabbed his shoulders and made a futile attempt to shake him, only succeeding in making my fractured rib twinge. "Don't you dare say that, Bane Verrall! I'll say if you're a millstone around my neck, and you're no such thing! And I won't let you give up whilst there's breath in my body!"

"And how does that not make me a millstone?" he asked sarcastically.

"You just want an excuse to give up because it's easier than carrying on!"

"EASY? Nothing about this is easy!"

"Well, I thought hell would freeze over before you gave up on *anything!*"

"*I* never said I was giving up!"

"Well, you've certainly got everyone else ready to give up on *you!* The Foxes only came around the other day to commiserate about Snakey, and even Jon thinks..."

"OH, SHUT UP ABOUT WHAT JON THINKS!" His clenched fist rose... and stopped suddenly in midair.

His face froze with it, turning automatically towards his upraised hand as he tried to see it.

"Bane!" I protested, shocked.

He flexed the clenched fist as though surprised to find it attached to his body, his lips shaping something that might've been, "Oh God," then he buried his face in his knees.

I put my arms around him and rubbed his back and kissed his hair, and eventually he managed to cry. He'd wept a few times right at the beginning, but never like this. Nothing I said or did seemed to comfort him. Eventually he fell asleep with his head in my lap and I sat there stroking his hair for a long, long time.

9

UNFORGIVEABLE

Since my post about organ donation yesterday, I've actually had some people asking how organ donation, abortion and euthanasia led to Sorting. Well, if you can get access to a computer with internet, the information is all there, and you'll find links to some comprehensive sites at the end of this post. But the short version is this:

Back before the EuroBloc took on its current form, the introduction of abortion eroded respect for life, opening the door to euthanasia. The 'option' of euthanasia for the disabled and mentally ill quickly became the expected thing. And it's a very short step from 'expected,' to 'mandatory.'

At the same time, advances in organ donation alternatives were stalling due to the world's unstable economic situation. The rise of hard-line governments such as the EuroGov quickly led to the re-introduction of the death penalty in Europe—and to the appropriation of the organs of death row prisoners, in imitation of the system in use in less ethical states, where for decades organ transplant waiting times had been months, not years.

Racial tensions among the (then) multi-racial continents of Europe and North America provided the final impetus for the rise of our dear friends the EGD—the EuroBloc Genetics Department—and their USNA equivalent. Regardless of their claims that they wanted *all* races to be pure, they gained popular support because it was clear that their goals would necessitate the large-scale emigration of non-white citizens back to their ancestral countries of origin.

But for the EGD, the elimination of the 'imperfect' was also vital for their racial purity program. Since the use of death row prisoners couldn't meet the still-increasing demand for organs as the population lived longer and more treatments that used transplants were developed, this, plus huge advances in the medical industry's abilities to store organs for future use, provided a powerful incentive for the population to accept the gradual implementation of Sorting.

It started, of course, with the most severely disabled, the ones society viewed as being 'better off dead', the ones society expected—indeed, considered *should be*—killed anyway: so why waste their organs? And, inevitably, inexorably, it expanded, inch by inch, until we get to today, when failing one single test might be enough to get you included in the school's quota for reAssignees.

As I well know.

Margaret Verrall—blog post, 'The Impatient Gardener'

Taking the thermometer out of my mouth, I glanced at it, marked the result on my chart and made to put both back in my drawer... paused, frowning at the graph. My temperature should be gradually dropping at this point in my cycle—but it had just taken quite a sharp leap *upwards*. I glanced at the thermometer. No, I'd not misread it...

So what did this mean?

Natural variation? I'd only charted my implant-free cycle for about three months... I flicked quickly back through the previous pages of my chart book. This was totally new. Think, Margo. What did Mum teach you? Other than the cardinal rule about not anticipating, which I'd broken the other week...

My breath caught, stolen by shock and delight—and a healthy dose of terror.

A sharp increase in temperature several days after the infertile time starts is a strong indicator of pregnancy—I could remember Mum saying it.

Was I...?

Tentatively, my hand went to my stomach, exploring its flatness. I struggled to hold down an overwhelming surge of joy. *It's not conclusive, you need to do a test...* A shard of guilt made itself felt as well. After all, we'd agreed we weren't going to try for a baby until the vote was settled... But it was hard to feel too sorry.

Bane cocked an ear towards me. "Margo? Everything okay?"

Hastily I closed the chart book and replaced everything in the drawer. "Yes, yes, just... just daydreaming." Even if I *was*, it must be *so* early... I didn't want to say anything until I was sure of at least this much.

I hurried into the bathroom, for once hoping he wouldn't come to Mass so I could slip up to the hospital afterwards. Not that there was much chance of it, the way he was feeling at the moment. A slight stab of doubt cut through my happiness. Would this news—*if it's really happening, steady, Margo*—give him a boost, or just cause him further worries about his helplessness? Surely it would help—and help with his temper, too...

He was just so down at the moment... I would say fair enough, what with Snakey, but he'd been like this before as well... I put it from my mind, or tried to. He'd be overjoyed, on fire to be the best dad possible, blindness or no.

By the time I was hurrying along the hospital corridor after Mass, my mind was throwing up baby names, however much I tried to rein it in. It was only when I stopped in the waiting area—deserted, good, all the staff were at breakfast—that I wondered which sort of pregnancy tests they had. I remembered seeing them... yes, there, in that box. I dived across to them—all the same type, yes—snatched one, pocketed it and tried to slow to a saunter as I left the wing again. I went into the first ladies' room I came to and shut myself in a cubicle. Pulled out the box and examined it.

Yes! *Thank you, Lord!* It was the slightly more expensive kind, that worked after only seven days, not like the cheap ones we'd had at the Facility. I wouldn't have to wait.

I pulled the little device out of the box and forced myself to read the information leaflet. Right, I just stuck my finger in the end, it would give me a little prick and then after a minute or two, show the result. Simple enough. And... *oh*. If I was using it during the first two weeks after the likely date of conception I was strongly advised not to tell *anyone* until these fourteen days were up because... I gulped. *Up to fifty percent of pregnancies miscarried during this time.* Only, the leaflet assured me, until this better test came along, most women never even knew. Was that a good thing or not? It actually suggested that I might prefer to wait two weeks after the day I thought I might have conceived and only use the test then...

No. Even if the baby didn't make it, I wanted to know it had been there. I stuck my finger in the indent.

Ouch.

It flashed up the message to remove my finger again. Now I had to wait. I stared hungrily at the screen until my eyes began to ache. Right, I was going to say a few Hail Marys. What for, though? Positive or negative?

Despite our responsible intentions, there was only one answer to that. It was one thing not to try for a child, it was another to have one dangled in front of me...

Beep.

I'd left it too long. The gadget had finished its deliberations. Holding my breath, I looked at the tiny screen...

Positive!

"Margaret?"

I focused on the earnest green eyes. Lord help me, I *was* distracted if even the madman was noticing. "I'm fine, Lucas. Sorry, you were trying to show me something?"

He nodded and tilted one of the fuchsia's stems gently towards me.

"Oh, it's... budding, is that the word?"

He nodded again.

"Good." The plant was certainly thriving. He'd used to take it to bed with him some nights, which drove the nurses mad—soil on the sheets—but the Office book had spared the plant further duty as a teddy bear—with its leather cover zipped up around it, the book didn't mind in the slightest.

The green eyes were shooting me a sidelong glance.

"It's Bane," I said apologetically.

"Always."

"Well, yes. I'm so worried about him." The truth, just not the whole truth, today. My mind was full of our baby. The next seven days were so fraught with risk. What if I miscarried...? I shuddered. I just didn't dare tell Bane about the baby yet. I mean, what sort of black depression would *that* throw him into?

Lucas had spread his hands and raised them ceiling-wards in a very apologetic manner.

"I know there's nothing you can do," I said quickly. "Sometimes I'm afraid there's nothing anyone can do..." *Something's* got to be done, though, now he's a father... "Well, maybe there is. We'll see."

He picked up the Office book, unzipped it and selected a bookmark. Pointed to a line on the page. I read, "It is the Lord who gives sight to the blind, who raises up those who are bowed down." Well, I was in no doubt by now that he was both reading and understanding. I'd caught him poring over both the English and the Latin—he was already coming out with the odd Latin word—s'pose it was so similar to Italian.

"Yes," I told him. "But it doesn't happen very often, *physically,* though you do get the odd miracle. It's normally interpreted spiritually. Spiritual sight. Which, as it concerns the next world, is way more important. Not that both physical and spiritual sight aren't needed in this world. Well, ideally..."

The usual slight thought-frown appeared on his face. Had he understood all of that?

"Thank you for marking it, though."

The frown eased. He was satisfied. Alas, I couldn't imagine the psalm providing any comfort to Bane, just at the moment. I wasn't even sure how he felt about God now. After everything that had happened since the escape, I'd begun to hope he might finally be leaving his stubborn agnosticism behind, but now that he'd lost his eyes... Even if he had come to believe fully in God, did he feel anything towards Him but rage? No, the psalm wouldn't help. But perhaps the baby might give him some comfort; soothe his anger. *Please, Lord?*

"Do you know who the Lord is, Lucas?" I asked curiously. He couldn't be reading and understanding the psalms without some concept of the 'Lord' they spoke of so often...

He took his usual time to respond, then pointed up at the ceiling and drew a hand eloquently across his throat.

"God?" I interpreted. "The God you get executed for believing in?"

He nodded.

"That's exactly... right." Didn't mean he believed God was there... I almost asked, then held my tongue. He might be getting better by the day, but best to leave big existential questions a little longer.

"Lucas, can I ask? *Why* is it so important you know whether I forgive you? I mean, what you've gone through, to get here... was it for that? Or did you just know we'd help you?"

"Came to find out," he said after a moment. "Don't care about the rest."

If he didn't care about his own survival, then... "How can it matter so much?"

"Because it's how I'll know."

"Know what?"

"About God."

I blinked as that big existential question popped up and smacked me in the face. *Oh well.* "What about God? Do you... believe in God?"

"God's *there.*" He spoke very definitely. "Always known *that.* Looked into it when I was younger. Every argument for... not God... *has* a God. Just not *called* God. Multi-verse, Universe, Laws of Science, Fundamental Principle... *same thing,*" he said emphatically.

I nodded in agreement. "So you've always been honest enough to call this ultimate reality God?"

After another moment's intense thought, he nodded. "But I've never known what God *is.* Never known... only one thing that matters. Does God *care?*"

"Is God a loving personal God or just some uncaring—or even insentient—multi-verse entity?"

He nodded. "*That.*"

"So..." I tried not to frown too hard. Many, many people came to the same conclusion, but fear stopped them pursuing the subject any further. "So... how will whether I forgive you help you figure this out?"

His eyes filled with a bleak misery that reminded me for a moment of Bane. "No one could forgive me. My mother couldn't. It's not possible. Not for... a human. Not without... *help.*"

It felt like someone had just chucked ice-cold water over me.

This man had hung his belief in the true and living God on *my* ability to forgive him. Not that his reasoning was wrong, as far is it went, but...

"The Holy Spirit works wonders," I said weakly, "but... human beings have free will, y'know? When we're sorry, God forgives us utterly, but if a *human being* chooses not to pass that forgiveness on to us, God won't... force them. Do you understand *that?*"

"*Do* you forgive me?" he countered.

I felt sick; I felt like a mountain of responsibility was crushing me. Would I be held responsible for this man's soul?

I reached out and caught both his hands; pressed them. "Lucas, I want to forgive you with my whole heart, but... it's a little lengthier a process than I realized—I mean, I really thought I *did* forgive you, until you asked me the other day..." I trailed off; my turn to eye him anxiously for once. Mostly, now, I felt very friendly towards him—quite concerned about him—*except* when I thought about what he'd done. Then the anger that still rose to the surface frightened me...

He squeezed my hands, just a little. "So wait and see."

Phew. I had time, then.

We sat quietly for a moment, both lost in thought. Then he selected another bookmark and pointed to, "The fool hath said in his heart, there is no God."

I smiled. "I was thinking of that when you were talking."

Had he come up with this plan for determining the existence of God whilst under torture with the EuroGov? Must've been then.

"Lucas... if you thought there *might* be a God who cared about things, how could you work at the Facility?"

His eyes widened the way they had when he'd remembered about his mother. He shook his head violently, clawing at his face, barely intelligible words keening from his throat... "*No, no, not that one, not... no...*"

Blood sprang up on his cheek as a nail tore the skin... Quickly I held the fuchsia in front of him but his eyes didn't focus. Help them come back *gently*, the shrinks had said, when I'd told them I thought he had some memory loss. *How* had been my first thought... *How, how, how?*

Dumping the fuchsia back on the bedside table, I dashed out of the room—Bumblebee started—"*Margo?*"—I'd already darted down the corridor to the nearest window. Some sort of bright orangey-yellow flowery thing sat there in a pot—I grabbed it and dived back into the room. Shoved it in front of Lucas. "Look, Lucas, isn't it beautiful? *Look...*" His cheeks were smeared with blood and his head thrashed from side to side as though fighting something off...

His gaze passed over the plant without stopping—blast, it'd have to be Doctor Frederick and a sedative and he'd *hate* that—then his eyes flicked back, fastened on the flowers. He snatched the pot from me, burying his face in the blooms, and gradually he quieted, sinking back into himself. As though the bad memory had caught him like a rabbit too far from its burrow...

Then he was ignoring me again—at least, he'd gone into that near-catatonic state I'd come to understand as his way of hiding from the world—from *everything*. Even the rest of himself.

"Things okay in here, Margo?" Bee looked in, frowning at the blood.

"I think it is now," I said shakily.

Talkative he certainly wasn't, but in our little half-mimed, half spoken conversations about fuchsia and Divine Office Lucas seemed so normal, *comparatively*, my question about the Facility had come so naturally... After all, we'd talked so much about my forgiving him, surely he remembered what he'd done to me, and *where?* So whatever terrible memory my question had stirred must be something else... something from... long ago?

The thing his mother had been unable to forgive him for?

"Well, it's not like they've given you any training," said Bane, when I returned home after seeing Lucas cleaned up and sleeping.

"That's what Bee said. But still, I keep thinking that a real counselor wouldn't have put their foot in it like that..."

"Well, they're the ones who keep saying you should be doing this, not them."

"Umm. Though, to be fair, they do talk to me, give me a few pointers, y'know?"

"He's improving. So you must be doing it right."

"Who knows? Perhaps he'd improve if he were just left to his own devices. I think he's more disturbed and traumatized than mad, in many ways."

"Er, define *disturbed*," said Bane pointedly.

"You know what I mean."

"Quietly cuckoo rather than deranged and raving."

"Something like that." Baby, baby, baby! *Shhh, Margo, you can't tell him yet!* But there were things I could try to sort out. Bane seemed to be trying very hard not to play the bear with the cut paw today... Enough gentle hints. They just weren't working. I had to take the bull by its horns. "Y'know, I do wish he'd talk to the experts. I think anyone with... oh, any kind of problem... would get a lot of help from them."

"Really," said Bane flatly. "Are we having lunch?"

"In a minute. You know there are a couple of psychiatrists here—y'know, proper doctors—as well as a handful of counselors, to say nothing of several sisters and priests with no formal qualifications but a lot of experience and hearty recommendations. Lucas... or anyone... could take their pick."

"Yay for Lucas and anyone. Lunch?"

His shoulders were getting very tense, but I plowed on, "Some of them do trauma counseling, and some even

specialize in torture victims. And a lot of them deal with...
um... anger management and uh, bereavement and working
through issues to do with that..."

"Who cares! Are we having lunch or not?"

"When we've finished talking. I, uh, I made a little list,
actually. Of the ones who specialize in, um, certain things.
The anger management and..."

"As far as I'm concerned, we've *finished* talking!" A
thundercloud had taken up residence on his forehead and
all the muscles in his neck were knotted up.

Please, Bane, listen to me... "Bane, are you sure you
wouldn't like to hear a little bit about some of them?"

"*I am not interested.*" He bit off each word like it was
one of Reginald Hill's fingers.

"Bane, I know this is difficult, but it could really help..."

"*Help with what?*"

I took a deep breath. Never had I seen him so angry
with *me*, but I had to try, for both—for *all*—our sakes...
"You've got a problem with anger, Bane. We both know it,
and we both know that since... well, it's getting worse, isn't
it? You *need* to see someone."

"*I need you to shut up and stop talking nonsense!*" He
jerked to his feet. "I don't need a *shrink;* there's nothing
wrong with me!"

"I don't mean wrong in a... in a guilty way..." I stood up as
well, my hands reaching towards him in unseen appeal. "I
just mean... you don't have to struggle with this all by
yourself. Let someone help you..."

"I don't need *help!*" His face was dark with anger,
embarrassment, shame—did he hear what I was saying at all
or did he just hear me saying I thought he was... what...
inadequate?

I winced. "Bane, you're so strong, you're so, so strong,
I'm not saying you can't get through this by yourself, but
they're *experts.* Make use of them!"

"*Shut up!*" he shouted.

"Bane, will you just have a *think* about..."

"No! Shut up about it! Just *shut up about it!*"

He really wasn't going to listen. Despair welled up
blackly inside, because I was lying: I wasn't sure he could

get through this by himself, and I needed him, I *really, really* needed him now, and so did our baby—I was going to be tired, and tearful, and throwing up, and unable to bend down, and... How could I do it without him? "*Bane, please...*"

"NO!"

"Oh for goodness sake! It's not the end of the world!"

"NO? Hearing you talk like this feels awfully like it! What are you going to do, have me committed?"

"Bane, don't be *stupid!*"

"*Stupid?* You're the one who's being stupid!"

"I am not being stupid, Bane! For pity's sake, you think *Jon* wouldn't see someone? Wouldn't *admit* he had a problem?"

His hand swung out of nowhere and smashed into my face. I reeled back, tripped over the coffee table, crashed off the corner of the cupboard and came to rest with my face mashed against the wall. Lay there gasping, every nerve in my body tingling with shock, agony knifing my back from my jolted rib. A fiery, throbbing ache began to spread across my face and something trickled down my lip.

My heart insisted on my mind replaying the last few seconds, over and over again, unable to believe my memory of how I'd ended up down here on the floor.

Eventually I got my breath back a bit and my mind stopped looping. I pushed off the wall, rolled over and sat up, wiping something drippy and crimson from my face before it could get on the carpet. "*Bane...!*" I snarled furiously, "You *hit* me!"

How could he? What if he'd hurt the baby!—then I stopped... His face...

"*Bane, I'm okay...*" The words tumbled out instead of... whatever I'd been going to say next.

He stood there, empty eyes wide and face ashen-white. Clutching his guilty, shaking hand to his chest.

"Bane?"

He grabbed his stick from the sofa, turned, and ran for the door.

"*Bane?* Stop...!"

He was through the door and gone. Ice-cold dread gripping my insides, I scrambled to my feet, kicked away the

123

entangling coffee table and lurched dizzily after him. *Move, Margo...*

I stumbled out into the corridor and straight into Antonio, almost knocking a stack of egg boxes from his hands. His eyes widened and for once he forgot to glare at me.

"Where's Bane?" I demanded.

The lift door was closing at the end of the corridor...

"Why didn't you *stop* him?" I rushed forward... the destination number on the lift screen was seven.

The roof.

I took off up the stairs as though all the hounds of hell were behind me. I could beat the lift, I could... Still half-winded from the fall, my chest burned, rib screaming—my head spun and ached but if I didn't get up these stairs fast, fast, faster than I'd ever gone, none of it would matter ever again...

I slammed through the door at the top of the stairwell, my eyes racing over the rooftop. Bane was already there, sprinting for the parapet—the roof was flat, nothing to trip him, I'd never catch him...

There! A Swiss Guard stood by the roof access, frowning at Bane.

"*Foxie, stop him!*"

10

DAY AND NIGHT

Foxie gave me a puzzled look, but I was already beside him. I yanked the nonLee from his holster— *"Margo!"*—aimed and fired twice.

Bane crumpled like a dropped doll; half-rolled, half-skidded along until his head bumped into the parapet. I was already racing after him.

"Margo! Give that back!" The voice barely penetrated. It went on behind me, more softly, "Stair Six to Officer of the Watch. Have a situation. Request your presence. Just you, Fox, no one else, discretion required. Please confirm?" He was calling his brother on his wristCell...

I fell to my knees beside Bane—heaved him over onto his back. Unconscious. As I dragged him into my lap, drops of scarlet splashed onto his white face. Swiping at my bleeding lip with my sleeve, I wrapped my arms around him, fighting to keep sobs from escaping. I'd stopped him. He was safe...

Dimly aware of Foxie picking up his nonLee from where I'd dropped it beside me... of him checking Bane's pulse... An indeterminate period of anxious repetitions of "Margo?" and gentle touches, then Fox was there, pulling more insistently on my shoulder.

"Margaret, what's going on?" His hand snaked in, fingers also pressing against the pulse on Bane's neck, then he began prying me determinedly from Bane. "Come on, Bane's okay, Marg ..." He broke off, staring at my face. "Margo, who hit you?"

Unable to look at him, I saw his younger brother's face crumple in sudden understanding and disbelief.

"Didn't say anyone hit me," I muttered.

"No, but the hand print on your face says it for you."

Bugger. "Could we concentrate on Bane? He hit his head

when he fell."

After another quick, critical glance at my face, Fox probed Bane's forehead for a moment. "I'm guessing he'll just have a nasty headache from the nonLee, right, Foxie?" he queried his brother.

"Yeah, I really think he's fine." Foxie assured me.

"Now, what happened?" demanded Fox.

"Well," said Foxie, "Bane came through the door and started running full out across the roof, which seemed strange behavior for a blind... for someone who can't see... then Margo bursts out and shouts something about stopping him, and while I was trying to figure that out she snatched my gun and shot him. At which point it dawned on me that... um... Bane kinda... didn't look like he was planning on... *stopping*. If you get my drift."

Fox glanced at the thigh-high parapet, face twisting in understanding. "Discretion. Quite," he said grimly. "*Oh, what a mess.*"

That summed it up.

"What's going to be done about it?" asked Foxie uneasily.

"That's Margo's business, I suppose, like it or not. We'd better think about getting Bane off this roof before anyone comes up to take the air. This mustn't end up in the newspapers, especially not at the moment. How many times did you shoot him, Margo?"

"Twice," I muttered. "In case I missed."

"Doubt you did, so." He looked at his brother, "can you grab the EVAC stretcher from the top of the stairwell?"

Foxie hurried away.

"Where do you want him taken, Margo?" asked Fox.

Where? "Home, of course..."

"If you're sure."

"Where else?"

"Well... the holding cells are both free." He saw my expression and hurried on, "But I suppose that's not what he needs, in his... condition."

"Of course it's not!" I snapped, beginning to shake again.

He crouched beside me and put an arm around my shoulders. "Okay, Margo?"

"Yeah, it's just... just... I *know* Bane's done something terrible..." My hand gingerly probed my sore face... "But when he realized what he'd done, he almost... he *almost...*" I found myself crying into a stripy red, blue and orange uniformed shoulder.

"I know," sighed Fox. "I know. I'm sorry."

Foxie was soon back with the stretcher and Bane was quickly lifted onto it. Fox took one end and Foxie the other and we all squeezed into the lift. Reaching our floor, we hurried along a mercifully empty corridor—except... bother, Antonio was peeping around the corner... But we had Bane inside before anyone else appeared. They rolled him off onto the bed and stood there rather awkwardly.

"Um... I've got to get back to my post, but... what do I put in my report?" asked Foxie rather plaintively.

"Nothing!" I said at once.

"I don't know if I can do that, Margo. I mean, my weapon's been fired. Twice."

I'd scarcely had time to think about *what next*, but the thought of this being reported, of other people knowing... "Well, mine hasn't!" I went back into the living room and took my nonLee from the drawer in the cupboard by the door, popped out the power mag and offered it to him as they followed me through from the bedroom. "Swap?"

"Margo..."

"Oh, come on, Foxie," I said, making sure to speak calmly. "I thought Bane was your friend. Didn't you see the state he's in? It's not like he isn't sorry. Didn't he just prove that? He needs TLC, not an interrogation! Just take this power mag, give me yours, and forget what you saw, both of you, please?"

Foxie looked at his older brother. Fox frowned. "We've sworn to..."

"You've sworn to defend the Holy Father with your lives. Keeping quiet about Bane isn't going to interfere with that! Perhaps you're not in the need to know, but there's a spy in the Vatican, and they haven't been caught yet. If you put this in a report, if you tell *anyone*, it's going to get out. It's going to be all over the newspapers and you know what the reaction from the public will be. Now that really will put the Holy Father in danger, just at the moment, won't it? *And the rest of us. Promise* you won't tell?"

Fox's frown deepened. "We're not going to *promise*, Margo—but we'll avoid saying anything about it if we can. If Bane's as sorry as he... seems to be... and he makes amends and preferably agrees to get some help... we'll take it to our graves. But if he so much as clenches his fist at you, well, we don't care what trouble we'll be in for not reporting it sooner. Is that clear?"

· "Of course," I said quickly. This was probably the best I was going to get. "Foxie?"

Foxie looked relieved to have the decision out of his hands. That was why he was still a happy-go-lucky private and Fox was the Officer. "Okay by me." He unholstered his nonLee and removed the power mag, swapping it with mine.

Fox was frowning again. "You get that charged as soon as you can, Margo. They don't hold many shots at the best of times."

"I know, I know."

"D'you want me to send someone round? Jon, perhaps?"

I shook my head. Despite my efforts to shrink his uniform with my tears a few minutes ago, I really didn't want anyone here just now. "No, thanks. I'm fine."

He gave me a disbelieving look, but they let themselves out.

I put Bane properly to bed, then sat on the sofa and cried some more. I'd left the bedroom door open in case Bane started to wake up, but... I *had* hit him with both shots. It would be some hours before he woke. The real reason I'd fired twice...?

A leaden ache of fear and pain seemed to reach from my forehead to my chest to my stomach. My stomach... I pulled my blouse up and inspected my belly anxiously. There was a red mark to one side, where I'd hit the cupboard, perhaps I'd have a bruise? But the baby must be absolutely miniscule at this point, surely the impact wouldn't be enough to do any harm? *Please, Lord? Please, please, please...* Fifty percent was too high already...

Eventually I went into the bathroom to wash my face.

And inspect the damage. Looking in the mirror, I winced. There really *was* an identifiable hand mark. Had Antonio seen it? He'd seen the whole show, hadn't he? Or enough to figure it out. Nothing I could do about that... but if he said anything, and then I went out like this, it would confirm it all... The way people would look at Bane. Unbearable.

Perhaps he didn't mean to. Didn't mean to actually *hit me... He was just lashing out, because I hurt him...*

Lashing out *at me.* Perhaps he wouldn't have dreamt of doing it the moment before or the moment after, but *right then...* He *had* meant to hit me. He had.

Oh, Bane...

I ran some water and washed off the mingled blood and tears. My cheek was swollen but the cut on my lip wasn't really all that big. It bled again after its dousing with warm water, so I held a piece of toilet paper to it until it stopped, wiped the rest of the water from my face with a towel and eyed my reflection critically.

It'd definitely be a few days before I could go out. Anyone who saw this would guess what Bane had done, whether Antonio told tales or not... Shame curdled in my stomach. And fear. *Bane... they'll hate you forever... everyone will hate you... from hero of the Liberations to criminal and coward, that's how they'd see it...*

No! No one must know!

What else could I do? Anyway, we really didn't want the EuroGov getting a picture of me like this for the front page. They'd neglect to mention I'd looked ten times worse after *their* specialCorps captain got through with me.

I shouldn't have kept on at him like that... This is my fault...

No. I shoved the thought away. That just wasn't true. Bane did this, not me. I rested my hands on the washbasin and bent over as a fresh wave of anguish swept over me.

Bane, how could you?

How, beloved?

How...?

Eventually I found two painkillers and a glass of water and went back to the bedroom. Bane was still deeply asleep. I put the pills ready on the bedside table—he'd have a terrible headache when he woke up—and slipped under the covers beside him, wrapping my arms around him and resting my head on his chest, listening to his heart drumming under my ear.

"Bane, please don't let this destroy you!" I whispered to his sleeping ear. "Please... You're more than just your eyes, can't you see that?" I whispered it to him, over and over, until I felt tears coming again.

Baby, please be okay. Please, Lord? Please...

...Bane was stirring beside me. Daylight streamed in. What time was it? I was fully dressed, *what*... I rolled over and flinched as my cheek touched the pillow. My cracked rib ached worse than it had for days.

Oh.

I put an anxious hand to my stomach, but all felt normal. No cramping, no bleeding. Okay so far...

Settling my arms back around Bane, I waited, my nerves screwing themselves up in anticipation. *Lord, please help him to deal with this...*

Finally his hand went to his forehead and his empty eyes opened. "Aww, I feel like someone shot me with a nonLee," he groaned.

"Someone did," I said softly.

"*Huh?*"

"Here, take these..." I pressed the tablets to his lips.

He took the glass when I touched it to his hand and washed them down. "Thanks. Who shot me?"

Well, it could be worse. At least he hadn't woken up expecting to see. "I shot you, Bane."

"Why on *earth*..." He stopped. The blood drained from his face. When he spoke again, his voice was barely audible. "I didn't, did I? Tell me it was a nightmare..."

"I'm sorry, Bane. I'd be lying."

He closed his eyelids tight and turned his head away. The look on his face—too much like his expression before running for the roof.

I hugged him and spoke as lightly as I could. "It's going to be all right, Bane. We'll get through this. There's no such thing as an unforgiveable sin, you know."

130

"No?" His hand crept towards me, found my shoulder, sought my face. I pulled away gently—he'd only feel worse, touching the damage. He drew his hand back abruptly, shaking. "Why did you stop me?"

"Bane! Why do you *think?*"

He kept his face turned away and said nothing. I held him, pretending I couldn't see the tears of despair running down his cheeks, until finally he sank asleep again.

Sick to my core with dread, I got up and scoured the apartment, removing curtain cords and belts, moving all the remotely sharp knives into a box on top of the highest kitchen cupboard and locking the windows and pocketing the keys. I was still quartering our four rooms, uneasily certain a smart guy like Bane would find something I'd missed if he really wanted to, when the phone rang.

"Hello?"

"Margo?"

"Hi, Jon." Now that I'd had a bit of time to myself, his calm, friendly face would be a very welcome sight. Though... I wanted to pour my heart out to him, yet if I wanted to get rid of his attachment to me, that probably wasn't a great idea. But it would still be good to see him.

"Are you all right, Margo?"

What? Surely Fox hadn't... "I'm fine, Jon. Why wouldn't I be? D'you want to come round?"

A brief silence. "Bane's there, is he?" Jon's voice was oddly hard.

I frowned at the wall. *He knew.* How did he *know?* "Of course. He's having a nap, actually. Well, he was, the phone may have woken him..." Which made me desperate to go and check on him...

"I don't think I will, then." Jon's voice cracked with unaccustomed anger. "Look, call me if you need anything." He hung up.

I stood with the phone clutched to my chest. Jon. *Jon?* The one person I would have trusted to stand by us—to stand by Bane... To be *reasonable,* to *forgive...* So his feelings for me might still be slightly more than mere friendship, but... he was Bane's friend first. His best mate growing up. He'd been Bane's best man, stood in for Bane's parents...

how could he just turn his back on him now?

How did he *know?*

My eyes were pricking again, but I fought it. I'd get de-hydrated if I carried on like this!

Ramming the phone back into its cradle, I went back to the bedroom. Bane sat on the edge of the bed holding a wire coat hanger. He'd straightened the hook and was rubbing the end with a finger as though testing its sharpness.

I dived across the room and snatched it from his hands. "Don't you dare! Don't you dare, d'you hear me? You want to make it up to me? Well, *don't do this!*" Had the dark spirit that had once made him so determined to kill me himself rather than let me be Consciously Dismantled now driven him to this? *Holy Michael the Archangel, please protect him... Protect us both...*

He just sat there and said nothing at all. Sat there un-moving as I emptied the wardrobe of coat hangers and threw them out into the corridor. Rushed back... still just sat there. I scribbled "unwanted, please take" on a piece of paper, tossed it out the door and rushed back again.

Still sat there. Had he taken in what I said?

From his expression... no.

I grabbed the phone and dialed the numbers for two of the counselors, one after the other, but no one answered. I began to dial a third and slammed the phone down suddenly. What was I *doing?* They would see my face. They would know. They would tell someone, and other people would find out. They might even *be* the spy. Or *a* spy. Eduardo thought there could be more than one... *No one* could see me until my face was better, *no one!* Bane's future depended on it... the *vote* might even depend on it...

There was a rattling sound from outside, as though someone had just stepped into a pile of coat hangers and got tangled up. The sounds of someone extricating them-selves, then a knock at the door. I froze, panicking again.

Another knock, and a voice called, "Margo?"

Jon... who couldn't see me...

I let out the breath I was holding, went to the door and peeped out, making sure to stay far enough back to be invisible to the corridor camera. There was no one there apart from Jon.

"I thought you weren't coming round," I said rather shortly. The hurt was still fresh in my chest.

"After what Antonio told Kyle, is that any wonder?"

That's how he knew. Oh no. Was Antonio going to tell everyone? Was Kyle? Was it already too late?

"What on earth did Antonio tell Kyle that put you in such a funny mood?" Somehow I managed to sound merely slightly miffed.

Jon frowned. "He said Bane hit you."

"He *said what?*" My outrage was fairly convincing—I hoped.

"Is it true?"

"Jon, Antonio has never forgiven me about that chicken. I suppose you can't see it, but he glares at me like mad whenever we meet."

"So he made this up completely, did he?"

"Look," I sighed and let myself sound a bit less happy. "Bane and I just had a really nasty fight, Jon. It wasn't nice, okay? We were talking about anger management and stuff, and Antonio caught the end of it when Bane stormed out of the apartment and I ran after him. Maybe he got totally the wrong impression."

Jon had a mulish look on his face. "Kyle said Antonio saw you with blood on your face, and a big mark as though someone had hit you. He was quite specific."

"Perhaps he has a good imagination."

"Or perhaps..."

"What? Perhaps your best friend is a wife beater? An abusive bastard? Is *that what you think?*"

Jon was silent for a long moment. It was one of those moments when I could practically see him sucking every auditory clue in through his ears, and I struggled to breathe normally.

"I don't think my best friend is an abusive bastard," he said at last, slowly. "But I think... it's not impossible... just at the moment... that he might... *really* lose his temper. And... you're not denying it, are you? I'm not stupid, Margo. Tell me the truth."

If I tell you the truth... you'll be sucked in. I'll cry all over you, you'll comfort me... it's not fair to you. And... I can't bear for you to know. Not even you. Not this...

"Antonio has blown it out of all proportion. It was a horrible, horrible argument, Jon. But I'm going to go and join Bane for a nice, um, *making up session* as soon as you remember how upset Antonio was that I fed his precious hen to Mr. Everington and stop taking him so seriously."

Jon hadn't entirely lost his frown, but he said nothing, flushing slightly.

"And for pity's sake, if you hear Antonio—or Kyle!—spreading those rumors around, squash them, will you? You know what people are like! If this gets about, well, Bane could save the Holy Father's life or achieve world peace, and to his dying day people would still think of him as... you know."

Jon's frown deepened for a moment. He wasn't convinced, I could tell. But after a moment he said, "True. Well... bye then. But you know where I am if you need me."

"And if Bane needs you? You know how depressed he's been..."

"Oh, *don't talk to me about Bane!*" He marched off down the corridor.

He didn't believe me. But he would keep the secret. Thank God.

I rushed back to the bedroom. Bane was jiggling the window handle. *If I hadn't already taken the keys...* I dragged him into the living room and sat him on the sofa. "Bane? Bane? Please talk to me...? Please?"

No reply.

I choked back tears as there was another knock at the door. *Now what?* "Who is it?"

"Margo, are you all right?"

Kyle.

Bugger.

I marched up to the door and yelled at it with all the anger I could muster, which was rather a lot, just then. "My own brother is spreading the most vile rumors about my husband, and you ask if I'm all right? No I am not all right! I am really pissed off with you! So *go away!*"

"Did Bane hit you, Margo?"

"I can't speak to you right now, I'm too angry! Just clear off!

"Margo... *let me in!* Antonio said you were bleeding."

"I'm sure he said a lot of things, but I fed one of his not-supposed-to-be-pet chickens to someone, unless you've forgotten! He is *not* one of my fans!"

"If there's nothing wrong, then let me in!"

"There *is* something wrong: my brother is spreading gossip from people who don't like me! I mean it, Kyle, if you tell anyone else, I don't think I'm ever going to speak to you again."

Silence for a moment, then he said, "You've spoken to Jon, have you?"

"Yes, thanks to you filling him up with this stuff!"

Another silence. "Look... I'm going to go away and let you calm down. But Margo, if Bane's hitting you, you have to..."

"Bane is not hitting me!" I snarled. Hit, yes, but not *hitting...* "Is that clear? Now *go away!*"

"Okay, okay. I'll come back another day." He sounded much less certain, all of a sudden.

"Good riddance!" I snapped.

He went away, thank God, and I glanced around to check on Bane, feigned anger at Kyle quickly turning into the real thing. He hadn't so much as asked if Bane was okay! Not a *word!* Antonio must've told him what Bane tried to do. Didn't he care even the tiniest, tiniest bit?

I sat beside Bane and put my arms around him. "It's going to be all right," I whispered to him. "Jon and the Foxes aren't going to talk, and Kyle isn't sure enough of what he knows to make trouble. We'll just stay in here for a few days until my face is okay and then we'll find someone to help, okay? Pope Cornelius, maybe. You wouldn't mind if we spoke to him, would you? He'll know what to do. I know we'll both feel better if we talk to him. Bane? What do you think?"

He just bowed his head a little lower and said nothing. I wasn't getting through to him.

Oh Lord, help us, please? What do I do?

135

* * *

I watched him. Day and night. He'd drawn away from me into a frighteningly Lucas-like indifference to life and everything in it. I didn't dare leave him alone for a moment. He'd raise his arm when asked as I dressed him, but he wouldn't talk to me, except the occasional mutter of "What's the use?" or a broken whisper of "I'm so sorry..." I'd sit him at the table but he wouldn't eat. I'd try shoving food into his mouth but he didn't want it.

I phoned Doctor Frederick to ask for advice, telling him Bane had got rather down and lost his appetite. He reckoned I should concentrate more on getting water into him and that he'd improve in a few days; if not, get in touch and perhaps he'd have to be admitted to the hospital wing. I hung up, sweating at the thought. I couldn't go to the hospital with my face like this! But if I didn't go with him and they took their eyes off him for an instant... so after that, I told everyone we were fine. I was fine, he was fine. A terrible lie.

Because I said everything was fine, Doctor Frederick started calling every day, wanting me to go and see Lucas. I told him I was too busy and hung up. I longed to ask him to send one of the counselors around *here*, but they could be the spy, and even if they weren't... as soon as they saw the state Bane was in, they'd have him off to the hospital, wouldn't they? And then... All the counseling in the world would be no use if he wasn't alive to benefit from it... No, I just had to manage until he snapped out of it, or my face was fit to be seen. Then it would be safe to see about some proper help.

I'd park Bane on the sofa like a huge doll and try to write my blog, looking over my shoulder about every ten seconds to check what he was doing. Before long I dragged my desk around so I could see him as I worked—I told him I'd moved it so he wouldn't bump into it, but he didn't walk anywhere, period. Didn't do anything. He just seemed to want to die.

Fox phoned every morning for three days in a row, to check I was okay. Me, not Bane. I told him I was. It was almost a complete lie—but not quite. The baby was like my

136

personal sun. A sun trapped behind thick black clouds on a dull day, but still a comforting presence providing a little warmth. Every morning a ray of light peeped right through when I woke up and found no blood, no cramps. *Thank you, Lord.*

My daily look in the mirror gave me no such feelings. The bruise had gone technicolor and my lip wasn't healing as fast as I'd hoped. I traced the finger marks on my face every morning, frowning. *Fade, come on, fade... then we can speak to Pope Cornelius...*

The next morning, it occurred to me that I could invite Pope Cornelius *here. Yes! That was it!* I picked up the phone at once and dialed Sister Immanuela.

"Hello?" Eduardo's voice!

"Oh... I... must've dialed the wrong num..."

"No, you haven't," said Eduardo. Was he going to ask me a load of questions? But he went on, "The delegation from the United States of South America have arrived. They're meeting with some of the leaders of the African Free States while they finalize the details for their deputation to the EuroGov, who are now kicking up a fuss about this first meeting, complaining about some trade agreement with Africa and threatening not to allow the visit from the South African delegation at all. Of course, there's no doubt about the outcome—the EuroGov are too keen to keep the USSA sweet because of all their mineral resources—but they're clearly trying to punish them for their support for the referendum."

"Oh," I said. "So the Holy Father..."

"Is meeting with them all right now, trying to ensure that the South American visit to Brussels goes ahead. Sister Immanuela is busy interpreting, so her calls are coming to me. Anyway, security's very tight, right now, and I want anyone who's a possible target to stay out of the way. So could I ask you to stay in your apartment for the next few days until this is all sorted out, and the EuroGov representatives have cleared off?"

"Of course," I said, all too readily.

"Did you want to leave a message for the Holy Father?"

"No, not now..." I said quickly.

Eduardo hung up without saying goodbye, of course, and I sank back down on the couch and looked at Bane helplessly. No question of speaking to Pope Cornelius until it was all over. But probably the Foxes and everyone else would be too preoccupied to worry about us either... For a few minutes, I was relieved, but...

Come on, Bane, just snap out of it, please?

Every time I thought he might be calming down I'd find him holding some object I'd overlooked and examining it in that disturbing manner, and I'd have to confiscate it. I couldn't sleep more than ten minutes without starting awake in a sweat of terror and turning on the light to check on him. Soon I just left the light on.

Blogging became difficult, then slow torture, then almost impossible. Fortunately the South American situation was hogging the press's attention for now, and I could just keep my series of posts on organ donation going, ask for prayers, and report the Pope's public comments on the current situation. Good thing too, since I could hardly keep my eyes open, but every time they closed my subconscious sent a spurt of pure fear to yank them up again. I felt like a zombie. I prayed almost constantly, haphazard, frantic, erratic prayers, and I longed to attend Mass, but even leaving aside Eduardo's request, there was no possibility of leaving Bane alone.

"What do I do, Lord?" I whispered, flat out on the floor with arms outstretched, and not for the first time, but the answer just wouldn't come... Everything I could do seemed to threaten either Bane's life, his future, or the vote—but not acting left Bane in danger too. Pope Cornelius was the only answer. He was so wise and compassionate, he'd know what to do... We just had to hang on until we could speak to him... Bane would be fine until then, so long as I kept my eyes on him...

Had I fallen into a nightmare?

Kyle kept coming to the door, but since he was demanding I charge Bane with assault and have him hauled off to the cells, I didn't even let him in. He seemed to want to believe Antonio. He didn't send any counselors around, or anything like that, so either he was still a bit unsure, or he didn't care two hoots about Bane. His attitude towards Bane hurt more than anything else.

He wasn't the only one. Jon called regularly, but the conversations became increasingly mono-syllabic. I was so hurt and angry with him for showing zero concern for Bane's condition, and he was hurt and angry with me for refusing to confide in him. But I'd a feeling he was part of the reason why Kyle remained nicely uncertain about what had really happened.

On Monday, after I'd been a no-show at every Sunday Mass, Sister Eunice rang to ask if I wanted Holy Communion brought to my apartment. *Wanted it?* Oh, how I wanted it, but I had to say *no, please, don't trouble yourself.* That blasted mark on my face... still far too clear. Everyone would know... they'd put Bane in the hospital and he'd...

I hung up, fighting back tears at that vision of Bane being taken away...

Hurrying back around the sofa to look at Bane, who lay motionless on his back, face turned to the ceiling, my head swam and I dropped abruptly into the armchair.

Oh God! I've got to sleep! I'm going to faint if I carry on like this! Then there'd be no one to watch Bane! In desperation, I yanked out the nonLee I'd taken to carrying around... just in case... took wobbly aim and fired twice. Lay down on the carpet beside the sofa...

...Darkness shrouded the apartment. It was near dawn. We'd slept away the rest of the day, and almost all the night. The nonLee had satisfied my subconscious as well as I could possibly have hoped. *Was this day number...? Yes, it was!* Any blood...? Nothing...? Nothing! The two weeks were up! It felt like a huge weight had just lifted... until I remembered Bane. Still asleep...

I rubbed my belly gently. "Daddy's going to be okay," I whispered. "He's going to be okay..." Should I tell Bane, now? Would it snap him out of it? Maybe... But he'd realize, wouldn't he? That I'd already been pregnant when he... The Lord only knew what he'd do if he found that out, just now. And what if I did lose the baby? There was still a twenty percent chance, until ten weeks were up, according to that leaflet. No, I couldn't tell him, not at the moment.

Baby probably had nothing at all like ears yet, but I talked to our little one a bit more, until Bane began to stir. Then fetched painkillers to feed to Bane and managed my first half-decent blog post for a week, thank goodness. I'd nearly finished my series on organ donation, and I wanted it to end well.

I'd no sooner posted it than the phone rang. "Hello?"

"Hi, Margo." Even in the circumstances, the well-bred British voice wasn't entirely unwelcome.

"U! How are you?"

"Oh, I'm fine. Back at work. I'll be stuck behind a desk for another week or so, but it's better than wandering around all day with nothing to do and people trying to fuss over me. How are *you*, anyway? I didn't see you at Mass yesterday. Or on Sunday. Eduardo didn't mean you couldn't go to Sunday Mass, you know."

Had Eduardo set Unicorn on me? No, he was surely too wrapped up in that meeting... *please Lord?* But if U was back at work, how did *he* have time to call me? Panic swirled inside—the pressure from concerned parties was growing, and yet they were only concerned for *me*, I just didn't *dare*... "No, I was feeling a bit below par. But I'm much better today. I've just posted my blog. Have a read if you've got time."

"Of course. I always read it." I could hear tiny clicking sounds, he must be by a computer, then a few moments of silence as he scanned the beginning. "Looks good, Margo." He sounded considerably less anxious. "Glad you're feeling better."

I breathed out a sigh of relief when he hung up. That improved blog post would reassure people better than any assurances from me.

Another few days of somewhat less mediocre blog posts and our baby was well, but I was running short of painkillers for Bane and the nonLee was getting dangerously low on charge. The things didn't have many shots in them at the best of times, and if an assassin did come through the door, a full power magazine could mean the difference between life and death.

I went into the bathroom and looked at my face yet again. It *was* much better. Still a fading bruise and a tiny mark on my lip, but the handprint was getting very hard to make out. With a quick glance at Bane, I reluctantly picked up the phone and dialed Jon's apartment.

"Hello?"

I let out a breath in relief. French accent. "Hi, Snail, it's Margo."

"Margo! Are you all right? We heard some... nasty things... Jon says they're just rumors but..."

They weren't convinced. Bother. "I'm fine, Snail."

"*Oui?* How's Bane?" A hard edge to Snail's voice.

Was *everyone* going to be like that? *Yes.* That's why I'd been hiding, wasn't it... "He's... um... fine. Is Unicorn there?" Probably a fool's hope, actually, though the meeting was finally finishing today...

"Yeah, hang on, you just caught him..." His voice called distantly, "U, it's Margo..."

"Hello?" Unicorn's voice came down the wire.

"Hi, U. Um... I need a quick word with you. Don't suppose you've got time to come over?"

A moment's awkward silence. "Margo, if I go see Bane just now, my flatmates will disown me."

"I'm asking you to come see *me!* We can talk in the corridor, if you like!"

"You're able to show your face in public?"

"Are you coming or not?" I asked after a moment's silence.

"All right, I'll be round in a minute."

As soon as I'd put the phone down, I checked Bane. He gave no sign of having heard what I was saying. Had he totally given up?

After a few minutes there was a tap at the door, so with one last glance at Bane, I tiptoed across the room and slipped out into the passage. "Hi, U, how are you?"

He'd still been very pale and prone to wincing as he breathed when I'd last seen him. There was more color in his cheeks now, and though his movements were rather controlled, the pain had clearly eased a lot.

"I'm well on the mend, Margo, honestly."

"Well, thanks for coming."

"I'm not mad at *you*, Margo." His clear blue eyes inspected the left side of my face and his brow darkened. "What can I do for you? Drag your husband to the cells?"

"Oh, shut up!" I hissed, "You're as bad as Kyle!"

He shrugged. "Just offering. What, then?"

I opened the apartment door, peeped at Bane and eased it closed again. Then took out the nonLee. "I need this charged and I can't really go see Eduardo at the moment..."

Unicorn's eyes widened. "I hadn't heard there'd been an incident..."

"No, there's been no... *incident*. Everything's fine."

Unicorn frowned. He inspected the gauge. "That's, what... at least six shots fired, maybe more like eight. That doesn't look like 'everything's fine' to me. What do I tell the boss? He'll want to know."

Damn. Here was hoping Unicorn would just take it and charge it for me. "Just... just tell him... look, I *just need it charged.*"

"*Just need it charged?*" Unicorn looked at me in disbelief. "Margo, what *have* you been using it f..." He broke off and went *white* with rage—took a step towards our door.

I flattened myself against it and didn't budge.

"Are you using it on *Bane?* I'll knock the bastard's block off! I thought it must be a one-off; I thought things were getting better, that's the only reason I haven't told...! Why don't you leave him, Margo?"

"Don't be so horrible...! I thought you were our friend...!"

"I *am* your friend, Margo! That's why I don't like to see you putting up with his behavior!"

"You know how depressed he is! What else can I *do?* I'm terrified of losing him!"

"Right now, he wouldn't be much loss..."

I started forward, hand upraised... remembered his ribs and tried to stop myself... but the next moment I found myself in a gentle but firm immobilizing hold. I tried to shake him off, quite ineffectively, then froze as I heard him give a little 'oof' of pain.

"For pity's sake, Margo, calm down! Look, I'll take this to Eduardo, but I think you can expect a visit from him, okay?"

He released me. "Look, let's do it this way…"

He unholstered his own nonLee, popped out the power mag, switched it with mine, reholstered his own and returned mine to me, just as I had with Foxie. My face went red with remorse and shame. After what Bane had done to *me*, how could I fly at him like that…?

"I'm so sorry," I whispered, wiping tears from my eyes. "Did I hurt you? Is… is there no way you can get it charged without telling him?"

His brow twisted. Asking him to hide stuff from Eduardo was a tall order…

I stared at him, my heart in my mouth, swallowing back a sob. Lord help me, it wasn't just Bane, *I* was a mess too…

Unicorn sighed. "All right, I'll charge it as though it were my own, okay? But you can't carry on like this with Bane, Margo. Promise me you'll think things through?"

"Fine, I promise." Wasn't going to take long. Bane dead in someone else's care or alive in mine. Difficult decision.

Unicorn's lip twisted, but he headed off along the corridor in the direction of VSS headquarters. I bit my lip. Had I made a big mistake in asking him? U was Eduardo's heir-in-training—thinking I could outmaneuver him was probably about as sensible as thinking I could win against the world Chess Grandmaster. Too late now… Still, the meeting was almost over. Tomorrow I might be able to see Pope Cornelius… *Please, Lord…*

I was almost calm again—until I went back into the apartment and saw Bane standing by the window, fingers to the glass, about to push out a pane.

"Stop it, Bane!" I raced over, grabbed him and dragged him back to the sofa. Sat beside him and took his shoulders and shook him so hard I actually made his head wobble a little. "Please! Stop it! And say something, please! *Talk to me?* Just talk to me, please, Bane, please, please, please… Just *SPEAK TO ME!*"

No response. I buried my face in his chest, feeling as though my head would split open with anguish. His hands moved slightly, as though they would wrap around me—I raised my head, heart thrumming with agonizing hope… and his hands fell to his sides again.

* * *

...What the? A surge of panic brought me fully awake. I'd been asleep slightly more than twenty minutes—but Bane hadn't moved. Perhaps I should try sleeping *on* him in future. Wrapping my arms around him, I rested my cheek against his stubbly one. Time to shave him again.

"We'll see Pope Cornelius tomorrow, Bane," I whispered. "That's what we'll do..."

The phone rang.

Reluctantly, I went to get it. "Hello?"

"Margaret"

My stomach dropped. *Unicorn, you promised!* I put on a cheerful voice. "Hi, Eduardo. How are you?" *Still too busy to worry about me, I hope...*

"Other than the fact that people are lying to me and my power magazine records are shot to hell, I'm fine. I think the real question is, how are *you?*"

I froze, my thoughts racing. U hadn't told him, had he? No, he just hadn't gone to any effort to make Eduardo believe what he *had* said. Sneaky VSS unicorn. And the power mags all had serial numbers... now that Eduardo had looked, he knew that not just one, but two, people had turned in mags originally issued to... someone else. Eduardo had probably just had an intensive catch-up session about where I'd been and what I'd been doing recently. Which would have been rather revealing in a completely different way than he expected...

"Oh, I'm fine. Bane and I have been keeping to ourselves as you requested. It's nice to have some couple time."

"I'm so glad to hear it. However, the EuroGov representatives just left. So you'll be able to go up to the hospital and see your patient before he succeeds in starving himself to death."

"I can't... *What?*"

"Mr. Everington hasn't touched his food in over a week. Just throws the plates at any counselor who comes into the room. He's on a hunger strike: he wants you back, and Dr. Frederick says you won't answer any of his messages telling you so."

"But..." My thoughts whirled. Tomorrow, tomorrow I

144

could see Pope Cornelius; he'd know what to do! Then, maybe... "Tomorrow, I should be able to ..."

"When I spoke to him just now, Doctor Frederick said if he couldn't get you to come today, he was going to sedate the man and put the feeding tube in."

"Oh, he hates the tube..." But... Lucas was still in too bad a shape to miss this many meals...

"Indeed. But fortunately," said Eduardo silkily, "you are fine, and can therefore go and see him."

"Today? Um..." I struggled to think.

"Should I come around, then, so we can discuss how fine you may or may not be?"

He didn't believe a word I said; he was just trying to force me to tell him the truth. And I didn't, didn't, didn't dare do that. Pope Cornelius wouldn't take Bane away, I was sure of it. But Eduardo might, without a second's hesitation. And he wouldn't be amenable to argument.

"That would be a waste of your time, wouldn't it?" I struggled to sound light and unconcerned. "I'll pop up to the hospital within the hour, I hadn't realized how serious the situation was—I've been so busy with the blog and everything."

"You're a terrible liar, Margaret Verrall. You haven't left that apartment for two weeks—popping out for five minutes this morning to almost assault one of my agents doesn't count. I'll check with Doctor Frederick later and if you haven't been out, we'll be having a little chat. I'm not too sure what's going on, and you know how much I like that."

"I *said*, I'll go up to the hospital!" I slammed the phone down. Damn those security cameras!

I went a few steps across the room to get a better look at Bane, who still sat there harmlessly, then started chewing on my fingers. How to be in two places at one time? Well, there was bilocation, but one had to be a saint, and like there was any chance of that the way I was going at the moment... Then there was asking for help. From a less dangerous source—one who didn't have the power to click his fingers and have Bane taken away, even if he did genuinely think he was acting for my own good.

I didn't want to ask, but what choice did I have?

I went back to the phone. Whispered a prayer and dialed a number.

"Hello?"

"Jon? It's Margo."

11

SOMETHING AMAZING

"Margo? Are you okay?"

"I'm fine, but... I do need your help. Really need it." My heart sank even as I spoke. With Bane like this, how could getting involved right now do anything other than draw Jon closer to *me?* But Bane's life was more important. "Will you please... come and speak to me?"

A moment's silence. "All right."

I spent the next couple of minutes quietly arranging all our spoons along the window ledge with a row of saucepans underneath, so I'd hear if Bane got near it again. When there was a quiet knock on the door I slipped out into the corridor. "Hi, Jon. Thanks for coming."

"Of course I came, Margo. I'm here if you need me."

"And Bane? Are you here if *he* needs you?"

"Stop talking to me about Bane!"

"Oh, he's only your best friend; why would you care?"

"I *know* what he did to you, Margo."

"Yeah? Y'know, I kind of noticed myself. Exactly how sorry does he have to be before you can forgive him?"

"*Is* he sorry? From what U says..."

"Is he *sorry?*" I exploded, then dropped my voice to an intense whisper. "Oh, *no,* not *at all sorry,* he's trying to do himself in because he just feels *mildly bothered!*" At that I opened the door a crack to check... all okay... closed it again.

Jon's expression had gone rather funny, kind of frozen. "What did you say?"

I stared at him. "You must know about that! Surely Kyle told you?"

"Told me what?" He looked very anxious now. "He burst in, all furious, told us Antonio said Bane had hit you, that's all..."

"God forgive him, he didn't *tell* you? Bane did hit me, I

won't deny it, but as soon as he realized what he'd done he ran right up to the roof and tried to throw himself off. Would have managed it, if I hadn't shot him with Foxie's nonLee. And since then..." My voice shook as I tried to keep hold of myself. Clearly other than Antonio and Kyle, only the Foxes knew that part of the story, and they *had* kept their mouths shut. "Bane won't speak to me, he won't eat, he won't do *anything*... except try to do himself in if I turn my back for thirty seconds..." I peeped into the room again. All fine.

"And I'm terrified to let anyone know because they'll take him and put him in the hospital and if the staff there are anything like you *horrible lot*, they won't care and he'll... he'll manage it..." I clamped a hand over my mouth.

Jon's blue-gray eyes were wide with dismay. He reached out, found my shoulders and drew me firmly in for a hug. "Margo, I'm so sorry, I didn't know... Oh, you poor thing, I'm so sorry! I thought he'd hit you, and you were just defending him even though... well, U came back earlier *ever so worried* and said Bane's absolutely terrorizing you and you *still* won't consider separation!"

"He said *what!*" Oh no! Unicorn's odd reaction... Too late, I realised what he'd thought. "He totally misunderstood! And... then he went and communicated it all to Eduardo... oh no! No wonder Eduardo's on my case!"

"Unicorn said you made him say he wouldn't tell Eduardo. But he thought he'd managed to give Eduardo a heads-up anyway."

"I noticed, the sneaky blighter."

"Yeah. Look... I mean, Bane still did something *awful*, but you're right, it sounds like he's so sorry it's..."

So sorry it's destroying him.

"...well," Jon finished awkwardly. "How can I help?"

"If I don't go up to the hospital, Eduardo's going to come here and see me, and I can't let that happen. Will you just stay with Bane while I'm gone? Keep an... I mean, keep your ears open, make sure he doesn't hurt himself?"

"Of course. But what's so urgent about going to the hospital?"

"Apparently Lucas Everington has pretty much gone on

hunger strike in protest at my disappearance."

"That guy's nuts."

"He's getting better. Or he was," I added glumly.

"All right, well, I'll stay with Bane."

"Come on in, then." I opened the door again, my eyes darting to Bane. Still okay. Letting out a breath, I walked across to the sofa, Jon following. "Bane? I've got to pop out for a minute but Jon's come to visit."

"Hi, Bane," said Jon.

No response from Bane. Jon sat on the sofa beside him. "Go on, then, Margo, you go and tell the Major he's being a naughty boy. We'll just have a little chat about the stupid way Bane's behaving."

Good luck with *that*. I managed a cheerful, "I won't be long, Bane. Bye, you two."

Walking away down the passage was an awful lot harder than I expected. I wanted to turn and sprint home—it took all my willpower to go into the lift and press the button.

Nurse Poppy came running over to me as soon as I entered the hospital. "Margo! You're here! Are you okay? Where have you b...?" She broke off, her eyes searching my face. "What happened?"

"I fell over." That was true, after all.

By Lucas's door, Snail raised an eyebrow at this piece of sophistry, but Poppy greeted it with a look of sympathy and no sign of suspicion. Had the rumors not reached her? Was it possible that not everyone knew?

"Well, I'm so glad you're here," she said. "It wasn't too bad the first couple of days; he just picked at his food, but since then he's refused to eat anything. He's all right with us nurses, but if anyone goes in there trying to do your job—well, he doesn't need to speak to get the message across. Not a happy bunny."

"So I hear. Well, if you've got a meal for him, I'll take it in."

Poppy ran her eyes up and down me in professional disapproval. "I'll get a meal for *you* as well." She bustled away.

I went to look through the window, trying to ignore the

way Snail was peering at my face. The curtains were open, probably because, looking at the skinny form lying disconsolately on the bed, Lucas was feeling too tired and hungry to keep closing them. He'd the Office book tucked to his chest and he looked utterly miserable. Guilt wriggled inside me, but... how could I have left Bane; let people see my face?

Pretty soon I was slipping into the room, balancing a tray containing one nice cooked meal—pasta and sauce—and one almost-raw Lucas special. His head turned slightly, expression downright fierce, hand twitching as though to grab some piece of ammunition... then his eyes filled with relief.

"Hi, Lucas. I'm really sorry I haven't been to see you for a while." I put the tray down on the bedside table and pulled up the chair to the bed. "I've brought you some lunch..." But when he weakly pushed himself up into a sitting position—*so* weakly—my fragile calm snapped. "*For pity's sake, Lucas,* do I really have to stand over you just to make you *eat?*"And... oh, Lord, no! I burst into tears.

His eyes went wide with horror, like his world was shaking on its foundations—the look of a small child who sees the unthinkable sight of a parent weeping.

Helpless at that moment to get a grip on myself, I just went on sobbing into my sleeve—he grabbed the fuchsia, offered it to me—I waved it away. His eyes darted around, then with a look of desperation on his face, he seized the cooked meal, dug the spoon in and, panting, began to eat. He ate and ate until it was all gone, flung the bowl away and sat staring at me hopefully.

For some reason, I wanted to laugh. Fortunately my tears were trailing off and I was able to reward his momentous effort by getting hold of myself and wiping my eyes. "I'm sorry," I told him. "I'm so sorry, I'm not really angry with you, it's just... it's been a really, really bad couple of weeks and... I can hardly *think straight* or... *anything* right now..."

He took my hand and pressed it between his, giving me a look of totally heartfelt sympathy. "I know," he said simply.

Oh. A tiny taste of what it was like to be in *his* head? I

put my other hand over his and pressed back. In a weird way, I think I'd almost missed him.

After a few moments, he freed one hand and lifted it, palm up, in his usual questioning gesture. *What happened?* As an afterthought, he pointed to my face and raised his palm up again. *What happened to your face?*

"It's kind of the same thing. Bane lost his temper and hit me and... oh, don't look like that, you can't throw stones!" I said irritably, because his expression had gone positively murderous. I tapped my scarred forehead and he'd the grace—and the sanity—to look abashed. Then he gave me an enquiring look.

"Um, well, after he hit me, he tried to throw himself off the roof in remorse—it's an eight story building—I managed to stop him, but to cut a long story short, he's been trying to find another way to do it ever since, and I've been trying to prevent him. Which hasn't left me much time for eating or sleeping or... well, let alone leaving the apartment!"

He pointed at me and raised his palm up again. *How was I here today?*

"Jon's finally forgiven him and agreed to help. Turned out we'd had a bit of a misunderstanding."

"So better now?"

"Yes, Margaret is feeling much better. I'm sorry about just now, I think it was partly the relief—making up with Jon, y'know."

He stared at me solemnly for a while. Thinking about what I'd told him? Then he brightened, unzipped the Office book and held it out to me. Oh dear, I really wanted to get back to Bane, but... I had neglected Lucas terribly. I accepted the book and sat there trying to remember what day it was until he took it back and found the place himself.

"Oh, Margo!" said Poppy in dismay, when I took the tray back to her. "He wouldn't even eat for *you?*"

"Rather the opposite." I smiled in spite of myself. "He ate the cooked one."

"He *what?*" She gaped at me.

"*Very* keen to please me, poor thing."

I raced home without seeing many people. Trying not

to hold my breath, I unlocked the apartment door and went in. Bane and Jon were still sitting on the sofa—Bane had his head tilted back, fingers pinching his nose, other hand clutching a bloody tissue—despite which it looked like they'd been talking animatedly before I came in.

I shut the door and hurried forward. "*Bane*... Jon, did you hit him?"

Jon looked sheepish. "Um, yeah."

"I deserve it." Bane stuffed some tissue up each nostril so he could put his head forward.

I stared at him—he'd spoken—I was almost afraid to breathe...

"I didn't hit you because of that, and you know it," said Jon firmly. "I hit you because of what you've been doing to Margo *since.*"

"Well, if you're right, I still deserve it," said Bane in an undertone, but he sounded skeptical.

"Yes, you do. Margo, this big idiot is convinced you're terrified of him and the only reason you haven't kicked him the hell out is because you're too good a Believer to let him commit self-murder."

"He thinks *what?*"

Bane flinched from my shriek.

Not a lot of space on the sofa so I flung myself half on top of him and seized two handfuls of his shirt. "You think *what*, Bane Verrall?"

"Um..." He seemed bewildered, shocked that Jon might in fact be right. *"Yeah?"*

My hand flew up to slap him—I stopped suddenly—with an effort I clenched it back in his shirt. No more hitting in this marriage—from either of us. "Bane, you are an *idiot.* Haven't you been listening to *a word I've said?* Did it *sound* like I was terrified of you?"

"But... when I tried to touch you, you drew away..."

"'Cause my face was swollen and I didn't want you to be upset! *Bane*... how could you think I didn't want you?"

Ever so shyly, he raised a hand to touch my hair, and I knew why. Because he'd been seeing the world through an impenetrable morass of guilt, drowning in it...

"I love you, Bane." I maneuvered around the tissue to

kiss his rather salty lips. "I love you, and I don't ever want to lose you!"

"Well, on that score," said Jon, "it may interest you to know he's not actually all that desperate to reach the next world."

"What?" My heart lurched in timorous hope. "He could've fooled me! Bane?"

"Um. Well, I *was*, right after, I really was. After I'd had a day or two to calm down, the, er, enthusiasm wore off rather—I just know... knew... *whichever*... I had to... *free* you."

"*Free* me?" I snarled.

"That's when I hit him," said Jon.

"Free me!" I spluttered. "Bane, you fool, I don't want to be free of you! I want us to live to a hundred and die in bed, *together.*"

"Do you really mean it?" The uncertainty in his voice was like a knife thrust to my heart.

I slipped my arms around him and kissed him, and kissed him, and kissed him. When his arms rose to encircle me, I was dimly aware of someone getting up from the sofa and leaving the apartment but I was too busy trying to communicate to Bane how much he meant to me to pay any attention.

Eventually, after a very great deal of communicating, something amazing happened—his hands slid under my blouse. I mirrored him and slowly his kisses grew more confident, more urgent... we struggled off the sofa and when he grew uncertain again I towed him into the bedroom and then...

Praise the Lord!

1 month, 6 days

Well, I think we've covered organ donations backwards and forwards by now. We'll be moving on to a new topic tomorrow—and you might want to get your hankies ready.

Margaret Verrall—blog post, 'The Impatient Gardener'

The sun shone on my face. I opened my eyes. Why hadn't I closed the curtains? I turned to check on Bane and the sheet slid away... what the! I was stark naked! Memory rushed back and I sat up, hugging the sheet to my chest. Was I awake? Please let me be awake?

I *felt* awake—Bane was there sleeping beside me, his chest rising and falling steadily. We'd been asleep for hours and hours.

I touched my stomach gently. All well. Did I dare leave Bane while I cooked some breakfast? I chewed my lip for a minute, then slipped into the bathroom to wash and dress. Came back and sat on the bed again. Bane was still out like a light. Not been sleeping any better than me—or I'd kept waking him up by moving to check on him.

I headed to the kitchen.

The food was almost ready to serve when I popped back to check on Bane yet again and saw him roll over sleepily. Hurrying to the bed, I climbed onto the covers and slipped my arms around him, stroking his dark locks. "Good morning, husband," I said softly.

His eyes opened, he remained still for a moment—brain having a rapid catch-up session? At last, timidly, "Good morning, wife."

My heart lifted as though a million tons had been taken from it. No relapse. "I've made a really nice breakfast, Bane. Will you come and eat with me?"

He pushed himself up into a sitting position; rubbed his eyelids for a moment. "Would you... like me to?"

Not totally better, then. I gave him a quick kiss, careful not to knock his nose, which wasn't broken but was definitely sore. "I would like it very much."

"Okay. I suppose... I'd better get dressed."

"Most people do, y'know."

He got out of bed and started hunting for clothes. I watched him anxiously. How badly had all this knocked his confidence, already hit so hard by his blindness? Strange to hear him so... hesitant.

He ate, though, praise the Lord—in fact, when I kept refilling it, he cleared his plate three times. Yes! Might not even matter if Eduardo came around now. Seeing Pope

Cornelius suddenly seemed much less urgent—now that he might finally be available!

After breakfast I sat beside Bane on the sofa and snuggled up until he—tentatively—put his arm around me. "You... don't have to do your blog?"

"It'll keep. I think I'm entitled to a couple of hours off to celebrate my husband's return to the world of the living."

He winced slightly—my dry tone hadn't quite disguised the slight tremor in my voice. "Do you know the other reason why I knew I had to... you know..."

"There was another reason as well?"

"I thought I'd lost you—thought you couldn't love me anymore—so I knew there was no point trying to go on..."

I cut off the last syllable of that by pressing my lips to his. "You haven't lost me," I told him intently. "You know that now, right? How could you think I could stop loving you just like that?"

"It was a pretty huge *that*."

"The number of times I've thumped you or smacked your face, Bane. Did you suddenly stop loving me?"

"That's different."

"Oh, how?"

"Well, no offence, you've got girly fists."

"You've gone *ouch* often enough."

"Mostly for dramatic effect. You've never even left a *mark*."

"So how bad the action is depends on whether there's a mark?"

"Don't start twisting my words around!" A welcome flash of spirit. "It's not the same and you know it!"

"Well, you'll be glad to hear I am totally resolved not to ever whack you again, so we can call it quits and forget it."

"Forget it? Just like that?"

"Obsessing over it won't help." *Seeing someone might, but I don't want to mention that until you're feeling a bit better...*

"No..." But he looked anxious and uncertain again... So I cuddled up to him—huh, my rib was all better, when had that happened?—and tried to kiss the expression away. For several hours.

Eventually there was a knock at the door. Probably Jon... Well, I did find myself in the most unexpected position of needing to thank him for punching my husband.

Dragging myself away from Bane, I took out the nonLee, slipped off the safety catch and went to the door. Hated having to do it this way, sent a prickle of fear down my spine every time. I looked through the peephole...

Kyle.

I sighed. Opened my mouth to tell him to go away, then shut it again. He was just worried. I suppose it was natural for him to care more about me than Bane. Okay, so I was furious with him for withholding information from Jon and the others, as well, but... perhaps we should just sit down and talk about it. Look what had happened when I spoke to Jon properly, after all...

"Fine," I said, opening the door. "Come in."

12

THAT

Looking rather surprised, Kyle stepped inside—staring hard at my face. "I thought you said Bane didn't hit you?" he demanded at once.

"You asked if Bane was *hitting* me. He's not hitting me. He hit me, *once*. One single time. Now come and sit down so we can talk properly, please?" I slipped the safety catch on and stuffed the nonLee in my pocket, then turned back to Bane. Oh dear, he wouldn't mind me letting Kyle in, would he? He was still sitting right there on the sofa, groping for his stick, looking lost and almost... afraid? Having Kyle there to confront him was probably a bit too like having my parents there...

"I have absolutely no wish to sit down with a wife-beater!" snarled Kyle. I glanced back at him. Uh oh. His face had darkened with rage. "He shouldn't even be in the same room with you!"

"He is *not* a wife-beater!" I snapped.

Kyle caught my shoulders. "Margo, you're clearly *completely in denial* about his behavior. I suppose that's natural, but we've got to get you some help, because it's very important you understand that the way he's been treating you is totally..."

"Wife-beater?" said Bane hoarsely, his face pale. "Is that what they're saying about me? Is that what everyone thinks?"

"From what Antonio says—and by the look of Margo's face—they have every reason to think that!" Kyle retorted.

Bane flinched—his face crumpled. "Oh, God. Oh God." He slumped forward and buried his face in his knees. "I wish I was dead," he moaned.

Terror gripped my belly like a tiger's jaws; the world spun as though the tiger was shaking me. "*Look at what*

157

you've done!" I pulled free of Kyle and ran to Bane. "I don't care what you—or *anyone*—says!" I put my hands on Bane's shoulders and faced Kyle. "He's my husband. We're married. We're one flesh! So if you're trying to force me to choose between you and him, I'm choosing him!"

Kyle lowered his voice, looking at me. "Margo, I don't blame you for wanting to be loyal. But you're only nineteen, and you're just not mature enough to realize...."

"Mature enough? You're only two years older than me!" I yelled, losing it entirely. "And if you think I'm just a starry-eyed child with a crush you obviously don't know me at all! And you think Bane's a wife-beater? Clearly you don't know *him* either!"

"You know our parents always had reservations about you two getting married. Mum spoke to you about it before, and I raised the subject again before your wedding, but you wouldn't listen..."

"What?" That was Bane. He was rigid with shock. "You never told me. I thought..."

"You thought they loved you like you were their own son," I said quickly. "And they do, Bane! Kyle's making it sound worse than it is. Somehow the minor fact that you risked your life to save me—and hundreds of others!—from certain death has slipped his mind!" How could I ever forgive Kyle for revealing this to Bane?

"Bane *did* rescue you," said Kyle, obviously making an effort to speak more calmly. "And of course I'm grateful. But that doesn't mean he's the right husband for you. Mum and Dad never thought that."

My heart twisted inside me, yet again. "And who *would* be the right husband for me, tell me that? Bane rescued me from the Facility, saved me from Dismantlement—Conscious Dismantlement, mind you!—carried me half-way across Europe, never once pushed me to go further than my faith allows, then set about rescuing thousands of... well, do I really need to go on! Just *who would* satisfy you? So he sacrificed his eyes to save us all, and he's finding it difficult to adjust. Wouldn't *you?* What sort of wife would I be if I abandoned him just when he needs *me?*"

"That's irrelevant!" said Kyle. He took hold of my hand.

"It doesn't change how he's behaving now! In light of everything he's done for you I'm not demanding that you charge him if you really don't want to, Margo, but it's quite clear that he's a danger to you. You cannot possibly spend another night with him until he's had some serious psychiatric help, at the very least."

I yanked my hand free. "You can't be serious!"

"I'm quite serious, Margo." He grabbed my wrist and started towing me towards the door. "Just come with me, now..."

I twisted free, and I'd had far too much experience in the last year with my inability to fight bigger, stronger men hand-to-hand that when he reached for me again I snatched out the nonLee at once. "Get away from me and get out." When he hesitated, I snapped off the safety catch. "Get out of our home right now and leave us alone!"

Kyle looked furious. "Margo, *put* that down..."

"GET OUT OF OUR HOME!" I yelled. "Get out before I shoot you and drag your body out the door and never let you in again until you start acting like a Believer! *GET OUT!*"

Another voice broke in suddenly, a voice shockingly calm. "Margo, it's all right." Bane turned his face towards my furious brother and his voice went a bit fiercer. "Would you please *leave?* Can't you see you're upsetting her?"

Upsetting me? Upsetting *me?* What he'd just done to *Bane!* Why wouldn't he *leave?*

Before I could speak, Bane went on, "You really should leave, Kyle: I think you both need to calm down. There'll be a better time to talk."

"Better time?" I yelled. "*I never want to see him ever again!*"

"Margo, love, put down the gun. You know it's for assassins, not relatives," said Bane quietly. "If he won't go, just pick up the phone and have the guard come and remove him."

"You wouldn't dare," growled Kyle.

"I would," said Bane coolly. "Margo, hand me the phone and I'll do it."

Kyle moved as though to launch himself at Bane and I leveled the nonLee hastily. Kyle jerked to a halt, looking at

159

us both with such fury... then he abruptly swung on his heel and strode out of the apartment, grim-faced. I leapt to the door and slammed it. Hard. "I mean it!" I yelled through the crack. "I never want to see you again!"

I dropped the gun and crumpled to the floor. My heart felt as though it was breaking... So much for little Miss Forgiveness. When someone really hurt me, like now, could I forgive? No. I just screamed horrible things. I was such a colossal hypocrite.

Then Bane was there, gathering me into his arms and soothing me. It was so long since he'd comforted me like this that I just cried even harder.

"How could he?" I sniffed. "How could he behave like that? I thought... I thought if we just sat down and talked, it would all be okay... like with Jon! But he just wouldn't *listen!* And he tried to take me away from you... How could he do that! And now... Have I driven him away for good?"

Bane didn't say anything, but I felt a couple of tears trickle through my hair and touch my scalp.

"Are you ok?" I asked anxiously.

"I'm fine, Margo."

"What... what happened to you?" I asked, once my heart was beating a little slower. "One moment you were... well, *down,* and the next... you were there, you were... wonderful..."

He rested his forehead against mine. "I suppose... when you went for him like that... I believed that it's true. You really do want me. You do still need me. I've been an idiot to think otherwise."

Bane held me close for a while, before finally drawing away slightly. "You never told me that your mum... said that to you."

No need to ask which 'that' he meant. "Bane, it wasn't that they didn't care about you, it was just..."

"They were worried I'd hurt you," he said flatly. "They were right, weren't they?"

"We've got the rest of our lives to prove them wrong, Bane."

"Right. And we will. Did you... say you have a list?"

I stared at him, not daring, just now when somehow

miraculously everything was all right, to risk a misunderstanding. "Um... list?"

"The list of... *shrinks.*"

"Um. Yes, yes I do."

"Well, d'you want to get it so we can have a..." The usual pause as he sought a sight-free alternative phrase—and failed, in this case. "Oh, so you can look and I can listen?"

"Yep. Okay." I hurried to get the well-thumbed piece of paper from beside the phone, heart pounding. He wanted to... *hear...* the list! Despite my seesawing heartbreak and anger about Kyle, joy bubbled up inside.

"Are you, um, thinking about speaking to one of them?" I asked casually, as I joined him on the sofa. *Please, please, please Lord?*

He nodded. "You're dead set on keeping me, so I have to make sure I'm safe to be around you. 'Cause I swear, Margo, if I did that again I'd... I'd chew through my bloody wrists, if that's what it took..."

I clutched him suddenly. "No!"

He found my head and kissed it. "Well, anyway, we need to prove it to your parents, don't we? And Kyle."

"Who cares about Kyle?" I snapped. "After the way he just behaved?" I felt flayed inside.

"I still care," said Bane softly, squeezing my hand. "If only because I know you do really. So let's go through the list, hmm?"

1 month, 5 days

Well, at least you're honest about it. After reading your arguments, that's the one and only positive thing I can say.

Margaret Verrall—comment on 'An Unashamedly Selfish Defense of Sorting'

"And in the end we asked Unicorn—you know, the polite British guy with the blue eyes who saved me by chucking stuff at that assassin—which counselors had the highest security clearance, and that cut the list down to just three names, so we simply put the names into a bowl and I said a prayer and Bane pulled one out!" I told Lucas. "I'd like to say it was proof of his faith in the power of prayer, but the alternative was to meet with more than one and then choose, which was not his idea of an easier option!

"Anyway, she's a trained counselor, Bane spoke to her on the phone yesterday and we're going to see her this afternoon. I'm really hoping it goes well."

Lucas made a series of gestures I interpreted with no difficulty whatsoever to mean he was pleased for us and hoped it went well too. But... no one else would've got all that, would they?

"Out loud, Lucas?"

He gave me a puzzled look and signed, *you understood.*

"Yes, I did, but no one else would. You've got to use words, Lucas. Don't look at me like that, I'm not being mean."

Why, he signed.

"*Because* no one else will understand what you are saying."

He made a gesture I'd never seen before, but which was perfectly eloquent. *I don't care.*

I started to frame arguments about the long-term, and his future well-being, then thought better of it. "I care," I said simply.

His brow creased slightly. Kind of scary how important my opinion was to him. If I begged him to leap out the window he'd probably do it unhesitatingly.

"Why?" he asked. Out loud. In Latin. He was getting pretty good at the language. Half the time I forgot to speak to him in English. Fairly sure he was using the bilingual Office book as a Latin textbook.

"Because I care what happens to you. And everything will be so much easier and nicer for you if you're prepared to speak to people."

The idea of *speaking* to other people made his eyes widen. Before I could reply, there was a knock at the door.

"*You* should answer the door. It's your room," I told him, when he looked at me.

It *was* his room. He'd literally just today moved from

the hospital to this pleasant, south-facing room, with a private bathroom and a little kitchenette. Just right for Lucas. Even more perfectly, it had wide windowsills for lots of plants, and a little balcony for even more. It was in the most secure section of the high security block in which Bane and I also lived, as befitted a recovering madman—safe from others and hopefully from himself too. Though if he wanted to get out, it would probably be next to impossible to stop him. It wasn't more secure than the EuroBloc detention facility he'd vanished from!

Reluctantly, Lucas went to the door and opened it.

"Oh, hello Mr Everington." It was Eduardo, with a networkAccessor in his hand, here to check the newly-fitted camera was functioning correctly. "Hello, Margaret," Eduardo went on. "Is this room all right for you, Mr. Everington? Margaret picked it out for you."

The room wasn't that large, despite the private facilities, but the solid old bed had drawers built in underneath it and there was space for a little table and a couple of soft chairs.

Surprise, surprise, Lucas ignored Eduardo, skittering over to the window to inspect the new array of plants there.

"Where did all those come from?" asked Eduardo.

"Various windows between here and the hospital," I said guiltily. Lucas had been collecting them as we went along, until I made him stop "D'you think I should take them back?"

Lucas flinched slightly.

"I wouldn't worry," said Eduardo. "We may not have quite the huge Vatican gardens of old, but there are plenty more where those came from. I take it he's happy, anyway."

"Lucas," I said firmly, remembering Eduardo's question. "Eduardo asked you if you're happy with the room?"

He eyed me sideways, clearly remembering the whole 'out loud' conversation, but only managed a nod—very slightly in Eduardo's direction, good enough.

"Okay then," said Eduardo. "Sorry about the camera, Mr. Everington, but it's as much for your security as anything."

So far no one with a grudge against the EuroBloc Genetics Department had done anything more than mutter and moan and bend Pope Cornelius's ear but some people's grievances were very real, and very raw. Tens of thousands of children had been murdered in EGD facilities, including relatives of some living here.

No response from Lucas.

"Margaret, I need to have a word," said Eduardo.

"Okay. Lucas? This is the clothes trolley I mentioned. Pick out some things you like, then wheel it back out the door and someone will take it away, okay? And later on they'll be bringing around a food trolley with milk and things for your kitchen. I'd better get home after speaking to Eduardo. Arranging this room has taken a bit of time, so I'll see you tomorrow. There's a phone there—it won't bite you!—and my number's on the pad beside it, so call me if you need anything, okay? I'm just one floor up."

Lucas dragged his attention away from one of his new plants long enough to shoot me a look. "Yes," he said after a moment.

"Good. Okay, bye, then."

I followed Eduardo out into the passage—a little nervously.

"Is everything all right now, Margaret?" he asked.

"Yes, it is. And I'm not just saying that."

"But not with Kyle," he said.

"No, not with him," I admitted. Every time I thought about Kyle, I wanted to cry or throw things.

On the plus side, clearly Jon and Unicorn had been quick to update Eduardo about the misunderstanding. *Thank goodness.* And it was beginning to look like Antonio had only told Kyle—genuinely concerned, rather than gossiping?—and Kyle had passed on the edited version to Jon and his flatmates—but only to them.

"A nasty business," went on Eduardo. "I wish I had known. But I hear Bane's doing better?"

"Much better. And we're going to see Karen North this afternoon."

Eduardo's eyes widened the tiniest fraction. I wasn't exactly planning on spreading it around that Bane was seeing someone, but Eduardo—well, it was worth telling him. He looked more relaxed already. "That *is* good news. My respect for that young man has just risen several more notches. I hope it goes well."

"Thank you. I'm very proud of him too."

"Hello, I'm Karen, you must be Bane..." The slim, neat lady shook Bane's hand and turned to me. "And you're Margaret, of course!"

"I am." I shook her hand. Nice that she spoke to Bane first. So many people treated him as an appendage of me now he was blind. "Come in and please sit down." She gestured inside the office so I led Bane in. From the look of the room, she was here in the State as an administrator of some kind, not as a counselor, but she still did counseling on the side, as a ministry.

She made instant coffee using a kettle in the corner—she was definitely from the British department of the EuroBloc—then brought her own chair out from behind the desk, no doubt trying to avoid the interview/interrogation feeling. She made polite conversation for a few minutes as we sipped our mugfuls—my blog, the Liberations, the vote... Bane was soon getting restive. Wanting to get it over with.

"So," she said at last. "If I understood correctly, Bane, you're looking for some general counseling for stress and more specifically for anger management, and for a touch of bereavement-related guilt, yes?"

"Yes," muttered Bane.

"Well, you'll be glad to hear that pretty much the most important step in just about any problem of this kind is to admit the problem is there and to seek help. It's also the most difficult step and very many people don't have the courage to take it. So you'll be glad to hear, in a sense the worst is over!"

"Yes, thank you for the pep talk," said Bane, rather cuttingly. "Moving on?"

Karen just smiled slightly. "Moving on. There's no magic cure for problems like this; that's the next thing I have to make sure you understand. You have to be honest with me, you have to work at any exercises I set you, but above all, you have to carry on wanting to change with all your heart."

"Wasn't expecting you to snap your fingers."

"That's all right, then. Well, let's start with some general

165

questions. You and Margaret grew up together, I understand?"

"Yes."

"And you've been in love a long time?"

"Haven't you read Margo's book?"

"I want to hear it from you."

Getting him used to answering her questions, wasn't
she?

"Fine, yes, a long time."

"And how would you describe your relationship with
your wife?"

"Relationship?" Bane looked appalled, as though afraid a
wrong answer might get me taken away from him. His arm
slipped around me convulsively and his other hand
clutched mine, so I squeezed back. "I love her!"

"Yes, I'd gathered that. Could you enlarge at all? Do you...
trust each other?"

"Yes. Well... I trust her."

"And I trust you," I told him. *And I want so much to tell
you about our baby.* Kept waiting for the right time...

"No jealousy?" put in Karen.

"No!" After a long hesitation, Bane muttered, "Yes. But
not the kind that has anything to do with my head thinking
she'd ever.... just the stupid feelings that have more to do
with... with *my* bloody insecurity!"

Karen raised her eyebrows. "Well, I can't fault your self-
awareness on that one."

Bane said nothing, face turned down. I wrapped my
arm more securely around him.

"So," went on Karen, "tell me about your relationship
with your parents."

"*We don't need to talk about that!*"

"Looks like we *do.*"

13

CUCUMBER SANDWICHES

"Well, that was fun," growled Bane, as we walked home.

"I know it's difficult but I thought you handled it really well."

"Well, that's nice to hear," he said more lightly, "what with you being well on your way to getting *your* counselor's credentials, from what I hear."

"Hardly. Lucas is fixated on me like... well, like an imprinted duckling or something. That's the only reason I've been able to help him at all."

"I s'pose you were the only one who ever forgave him."

The only one who even *wanted* to...

When we got home, Bane sat down on the sofa as though he'd no intention of moving from the apartment until our next session with Karen the following afternoon. I made coffee and had just sat beside him, wondering if this were a good moment, when the phone rang. With a groan, I went to answer it.

Sister Immanuella. "Hi, Margaret, you're in now!"

"Obviously," I grinned.

"Well, yes! I've been trying to reach you. His Holiness has been really wanting to have you round for tea but he's been so busy. But this afternoon's just opened up, d'you think you could come up in about, um, half an hour?"

"Both of us?" Things all seemed to be sorting themselves out now, but it would still be good to have a talk. Come to that, just how coincidental was the 'opening up' of this afternoon?

"Oh... sorry Margaret, he didn't mention Bane this time."

I glanced at Bane on the sofa, trying not to chew my lip. He seemed all right now. All the same... I really wasn't sure I wanted to leave him... But... what had Eduardo told Pope Cornelius? Had he brought him up to date yet? We needed

167

to catch up a bit, even if Bane couldn't come.

"He needs to discuss his trip to Brussels with you," added Sister Immanuella.

"His *what?*"

"Oh, I probably shouldn't have mentioned it. Don't pass it on. But he does need to see you."

"Right... um...." Had she really just said *Brussels?* Well, I'd just have to get Jon to come and sit with Bane again. He'd come this morning, so I could go to Mass, a thousand blessings on him, and stayed until I got back from seeing Lucas at midday. "Okay, I'll be along."

"Great."

I stared at the phone for a moment after she'd hung up, my insides churning. Could the Holy Father *actually* be going to the capital of the EuroBloc? Surely I'd misheard. And surely, surely, there could be no question of *me* going with him? She had referred to *the Holy Father's* trip, not *my* trip.

Yet he wanted to speak to me...

Lord, please no. Not the EuroBloc itself!

Shaking off the clinging dread, or trying to, I dialed Jon's apartment. No answer. Oh no... *Of course*, no answer. He was doing a talk to interested persons, including some members of the press, about his Braille finds. He'd wanted Bane to go, and I'd wanted to go, but Bane really hadn't wanted to brave the crowd.

Still no answer. His flatmates must be on duty. I ticked people off on my fingers... Fox and Foxie, on duty; Sister Krayj, at Jon's talk; Sister Mari—busy, busy, busy with all the stuff I ought to be getting on with... so who? Try to park Bane on Eduardo? I winced.

Oh Lord! Help? I really *don't want to leave him on his own so soon! There's got to be* someone...

Yes. Oh dear. I picked up the phone and dialed. *Come on, pick up...*

Eventually, when I'd about given up hope, someone picked up.

"Lucas? It's Margaret. Talk to me?"

"Hello?"

"Hi. See, the phone didn't eat you. How are you?"

Silence. "The plants like the room."

"Oh, good. Everything else okay?"

Silence. "I took food like you said."

You actually did? Act normal, Margo... "Oh, good. Listen, um, I've got a rather big favor to ask you."

Silence. "Yes?"

"I have to go and have tea with Pope Cornelius. I don't want Bane to have to sit around on his own. Could he come around to you for half an hour?"

Dead silence this time. Silence that said *NO, NO, NO but I'm incapable of refusing you anything...* I cringed inside. But... it wasn't like it would do Lucas any harm.

Finally, "Important?"

"Yes. Remember what we talked about, the day before yesterday?" *Remember, please?*

Eventually Lucas said, "Yes. And yes."

"Well, it's better than sitting around on your own," I said lightly, as Bane and I headed down to Lucas's room.

From Bane's expression, he totally disagreed, but didn't feel he could argue after what he'd put me through for the last two weeks. "Sure he won't *stab me* and *eat me raw?*"

"I really don't think so. And don't you do anything to him, *either.*"

Bane flapped a hand reassuringly.

When Lucas opened his door at my knock, I flinched—dressed neatly in shirt and trousers, he looked much more like the Facility Commandant I'd once... barely known. Or his ghost. For a moment I was back on that gurney as his knife bit into my forehead, remembered terror threatening to engulf me...

"Margo? Are you okay?" Bane's grip on my arm tightened, helping me break free of the whirlwind of emotions.

"I'm fine."

Lucas was shrinking into himself, he'd seen my fear—and my anger. *Blast.*

"Hello, Lucas," I said cheerfully. *He was trying to help you, remember? And he's definitely doing you a favor now.* "This is Bane, my husband. Bane, this is Lucas."

Lucas uncoiled slightly, his alarm fading as I tried my

169

hardest to project normality. He looked at Bane, then at me, then another sidelong look at Bane. Finally managed a quiet, "Hello."

I checked my watch. Time to go. "Okay, I've got to be off. Um, I hope you have a nice time, you two."

I left them both wearing near-identical expressions of resigned skepticism.

"Margaret, my dear, come in." Pope Cornelius ushered me inside and took my hands, his eyes running over me anxiously. "You look so pale and thin."

"It's been a bad two weeks."

I don't know what he saw in my eyes, but he drew me in for a rare—but very welcome—hug. Held me at arm's length and looked me over again. "Well, come and have some cake." His gaze paused on the left side of my face, but he made no comment.

"Actually, uh, could I use your phone for a moment?"

"Of course."

I dialed Eduardo's number quickly. "Hi, Eduardo, it's Margaret. I've just left Bane with Lucas—I really don't think they're going to do anything to each other, but... well, I just thought I'd call it to your attention."

"Scraping the barrel, weren't you? I could've sent someone up." There was a pause as Eduardo navigated to a screen, "Just now Mr. Everington is offering Bane a plate of sandwiches—cucumber, by the look of it—so relax."

"Oh, great. Um, thanks."

Eduardo always forgot to say goodbye, so I just hung up and went back over to where Pope Cornelius had two cups of tea and plates of cake waiting.

"How is that fellow doing, by the way?"

"Lucas? Very well, actually. I was afraid he might have gone backwards after—well, I couldn't visit him for two weeks—but actually he didn't at all. Not... after I reappeared, anyway," I said guiltily. "The guards were that fed up of watching him behaving himself that he moved into his own room today."

"Still, he and Bane, don't sound the safest combination to me—at least, if certain things I've heard are correct," he finished delicately.

I winced. Who'd been speaking to him? Kyle? Antonio? Eduardo? "Yeah, I know they've both got a reason to be mad at the other, but that's just it: they can't throw stones and don't want to upset *me*, I think they're safe. I really hope so because I can't help feeling Bane would come off worst."

"If you think that, why risk leaving Bane there?"

How much *did* he know? "Look, I'd really like to bring you up to date on... everything that's been going on these hellish two weeks. If we've got time? Though it sounds like you've heard most of it already."

"Today I've been hearing a number of things people know or think they know, but I'd much rather hear it from the horse's mouth."

"Right." I told him all about it. He listened without interrupting. "...And some of the stuff I said to Kyle I really didn't mean and pointing the nonLee at him—I don't know what came over me! I think I really need to go to confession..."

"Oh dear," he sighed, when I fell silent at last. "It really has been a bad patch, hasn't it? Poor lamb, have another slice of cake..."

I hadn't eaten much that day, and it was a nice English fruitcake, so I accepted without hesitation.

"You can confess now, if you like," he told me. "I mean, after you finish your cake, no rush. But I'm sure reconciliation with Kyle will come soon enough, if you both want it." He gave me rather a close look. "Is there anything else that's bothering you?"

"What, other than the life-and-death vote in just over a month?"

He grimaced. "Other than that, yes."

I found myself tracing a circle on the table. "Well, yes, there is. You see I... well, I'm... not sure I've really forgiven Lucas. Let alone that assassin!"

Instead of looking surprised and saying, "But the whole world knows you have," he just gave a sad smile. "Ah."

I rushed on, voice wobbling, "I thought it was going so well... but just now, I remembered that time in the Lab and... I wanted to just... hit him ...and hit him..."

I didn't want to feel like that about anyone. "Now I

realize I can care about him and look after him and feel like I've forgiven him, but *only so long as I don't actually think about how he hurt me...* that can't be forgiveness!"

Pope Cornelius sighed again. "True. To forgive someone completely you must be able to face them with the hurt and pain they caused you alive in your mind and still love them."

"How am I ever going to do that?"

"Love is an act of the will, and forgiveness is little more than love given to someone who has hurt us. Your forgiveness may not be complete, yet, but never think, for that reason, that it is not there at all."

I frowned. Love was an act of the will, yes, so if I already willed to forgive Lucas, then to some degree, I *did* already forgive him. Just not completely. I'd a nasty feeling he needed *completely*—or close to it.

"In both cases," Pope Cornelius added, "in order to do someone good, you must first will to love them, even if you don't feel full of warm emotions towards that person. Since you have acted for the good of both Lucas Everington and, what's his name, Georg Freidrich, the assassin, I think your forgiveness of them is well underway."

I thought about that a bit more, beginning to feel more cheerful. At least until Pope Cornelius said, "Anyway, on to what I really need to discuss with you."

My heart went *thunk* down to the floor. *Please Lord, not me...* I tried to look attentive rather than terrified.

"The discussions between the USSA delegation and the EuroGov representatives were concluded successfully. More successfully than we could possibly have hoped. I will be accompanying the USSA delegates to Brussels in three days' time, as part of their delegation. Thus sharing their diplomatic immunity."

I hadn't misheard. Excitement surged in me, despite my trepidation. He was going to Brussels itself! What an opportunity! But... oh no, he was eyeing me gravely. An ice-cold tingle began to creep up from the base of my spine... *No, no, no...*

"The USSA delegation," he went on, "have also issued the invitation to *you*."

14

BRUSSELS

Full of cake and freshly shriven, but with my mind in turmoil, I made my way back to Lucas's new room and knocked. Lucas opened the door warily, a plant in his hand, his face brightening when he saw me. Bane sat at the table, cleared of tea things and now covered in plants, face turned hopefully in my direction.

"Hi, I'm back." I managed to keep my voice steady. "Sorry, I think I was a bit longer than I expected."

"It's all right." Bane sounded surprisingly relaxed. "I've been learning about plants. They're actually more interesting than I realized," he added grudgingly. "They all smell different."

I tried not to sigh too noticeably—or audibly—in relief. Lucas had found something he was willing to talk about, even to a stranger, and letting Bane smell and feel each one, he'd probably got out of having to say much. "They are quite nice, aren't they?"

Lucas shot me a look—clearly to his mind 'quite nice' was akin to blasphemy. Bane was getting up, clearly not that sorry to leave, and Lucas rushed to shield the table's load from any mishap.

"Thank you for the tea, Mr. Everington," said Bane. "And for the, er, horticultural lesson."

"You're welcome."

"Or Margo is," said Bane wryly.

We said goodbye, and Lucas saw us out.

"Well," said Bane, once we were in the lift. "Never thought I'd say this when I can feel what he did to you every day, but he's actually not so bad. Not mad-mad, you're right. Definitely peculiar, though."

"How would you be after four months of *that*?"

"True."

173

"Did he drink the tea?"

"Um... sounded like he poured two cups. Ages before I heard any sipping though. Must've been stone cold."

So. He'd drink it if he made it himself? And food he'd made himself? "Did he eat the sandwiches?"

"Well... I hope I didn't eat the whole plateful!"

I managed a laugh.

"Are you okay, Margo?"

"Fine... But, uh, I need to talk to you about something when we get home."

I put the kettle on straight away and made two coffees, then joined Bane on the sofa.

"So?" inquired Bane, frowning slightly.

"Well..." I told him what Pope Cornelius had just told me.

His face had gone very closed, by the time I finished. "The *EuroBloc?* What did you tell him?"

"I said I couldn't possibly give any answer until I'd discussed it with you."

He brightened like a smoldering log in a sudden draft. "Well... It *is* a good opportunity," he said reluctantly.

"Good?"

"Alight, downright incredible opportunity. I suppose the question is: just how much will the EuroGov *actually* respect this diplomatic immunity?"

"I don't know the answer to that."

"Nor do I. Do you think Eduardo wants a coffee?"

Not entirely to our surprise, considering the import-ance of the issue, Eduardo came around immediately.

"They *have* to respect diplomatic immunity," he said, accepting a mug of coffee and putting it straight down on the table, intent on what he was saying. "No other bloc will maintain relations with them if they violate it. Pope Cornelius is leaving a letter of conditional resignation, just in case, yes, but it's only a precaution. I never thought I'd say this concerning either you or him entering the EuroBloc right now, Margaret, but this really is comparatively safe. I wouldn't entirely put it past them to try a well-staged accident, mind you, but outright assassination? No."

"And what about another well-staged supposed *Resistance* assassination attempt?" demanded Bane. From his tone, he was still a bit miffed with Eduardo for failing to somehow anticipate the first one.

"The Resistance have been denying Monaco until they're blue in the face. They're so unamused at being framed for a deliberate bombing near a crowd of people that even they consider to be civilians that they're positively singing Margaret's praises: hasn't your wife been reading the papers to you? *We may have our differences with Mrs. Verrall, but we share a common enemy, blah, blah.* Plenty of people are suspicious enough about the official take on Monaco—doing it again just won't wash."

He turned to me. "No, Margaret, I predict that the EuroGov will seek to best or humiliate you in public debate. Discrediting you and your cause would do them more good in those circumstances than trying to convince everyone that they had nothing to do with you ending up dead right there in Brussels, the heart of their bloc. But God is on our side, so as long as you pray and prepare yourself properly for any speeches or debates, it will be fine."

This startlingly simple declaration of faith in the Lord—and in me—from Eduardo brought a lump to my throat. And a surge of terror. What if I went, and *I* messed it up, somehow?

"Does diplomatic immunity extend to someone who has previously been found guilty of a crime in the EuroBloc and sentenced to death?" persisted Bane.

Eduardo rolled his eyes, just a fraction. "Strangely enough, that was the first thing I checked. Yes, it does. The USSA delegation's immunity will extend fully to all Vatican Free State members of their party, and to all Vatican employees present: our bodyguards, essentially."

"Yes, what about security?" went on Bane. "No question of relying on EuroBloc security forces, even before what happened in Monaco, right?

"EuroBloc security? Heaven forbid," Eduardo actually shuddered. "No. Both we and the USSA delegates are permitted two bodyguards for each member of the group."

Bane's eyes narrowed. "So... can I come?"

"Yes, I think that would be a good idea."

What? What happened to, *you'll endanger Margo?*

"I bet Jon would be prepared to come," said Bane.

"I'm hoping so," said Eduardo. "Sister Krayj will come, too, as Margo's PA."

I stared at him blankly. "Why on earth would I need a personal assistant?"

"You don't. But all my best bodyguards are men and they can't, for example, go into the ladies' room with you. Sister Krayj is going to be like your very shadow, you understand?"

"And as a member of the delegation," grinned Bane, "she can also bring two guards, right?"

"Exactly." Eduardo smiled too. For once, he and Bane seemed to be in perfect understanding. "Cardinal Akachi and Cardinal Janusz will be accompanying the Holy Father, along with Sister Immanuela, as his actual PA. And I expect you know Dr. Sarai Okiro of the International Theological Commission, who is also the African Free States ambassador to the Vatican. She's coming, and I will also be attending as a member of the group."

"That's six in Pope Cornelius's group," muttered Bane, "and four in Margo's. Twenty guards for Margo, good."

"What?" I still felt like I was missing half of this conversation. "*Two* guards for me, surely..."

"Why do you think Eduardo's allowing me to come?" said Bane, rather gently. "So you can have my guards, of course! Same with Jon and Sister Krayj. Not that *she* needs any."

"No way!" I exclaimed. "Your two guards should be for *you!* And Jon's for him! To say nothing of Pope Cornelius!"

"Relax, Margaret," put in Eduardo. "Bane is essentially correct about the strategy, though a little single-minded about its ultimate application. Yes, the idea is that the larger the group, the more guards we can take along. However, the exact deployment of those guards will depend entirely on what is going on at the time. I do not intend to leave any member of the group unguarded at any point, I assure you. So: are you prepared to come?"

Such an opportunity, but... the *EuroBloc...* I just

managed to stop my hand from going to my tummy. How could I take our baby into the EuroBloc? On the other hand... if we lost the vote, Baby had no future anyway...

I glanced at Bane. Though his tension betrayed his worries, his face was lit with excitement in a way I'd not seen for months... Finally he felt he could actually *do something* for the cause again.

"Yes, I'll come," I said.

1 month, 3 days

And just to conclude, for those of you who are following Lucas Everington's progress, he's out of hospital now and has a room of his own. He has some new plants and is happy and doing well. If you're a praying person, please continue to pray for him, if you're a hating person, please try to let it go.

Margaret Verrall—blog post, 'The Impatient Gardener'

"This is giving me a powerful sense of déjà vu," I muttered, as we stood at the Vatican train station, waiting for Eduardo's men to finish checking the train so we could board. Pope Cornelius and the rest of his group stood nearby, with the all-important USSA delegation, and the accompanying cluster of bodyguards, both VSS and South American.

"Everything's going to be fine, Margo," said Bane firmly, squeezing my arm through my light cotton blouse.

No wedding outfit for this trip. I'd been meaning to put my poor skirt and blouse away until after the vote when I might have time to repair the rips, but they'd been whisked off by some kindly old ladies and returned expertly mended. All the same, I'd been to the little clothes' store and chosen a new speaking outfit, a matching light cotton skirt and jacket—blue, since people were used to seeing me in that color—with a pale yellow blouse. There was a little bit of yellow embroidery on the jacket, too. Very summery.

It was too hot for the jacket right now, though. I squeezed Bane's arm in return, trying not to frown. Should I have told him about the baby? But he was stable and happy, *finally*. The news would plunge him back into emotional turmoil. If things were still okay with Baby when we got back, that would be the time to tell him, surely?

"You've got your speeches and notes, and everything?" Jon checked.

"They're all in this bag of mine, with my laptop," I assured him. The EuroGov weren't allowing me to make any speeches in their territory, but the USSA embassy counted as South American soil, so I'd be doing a few, all the same.

Eduardo appeared and stepped off the train, trailed by Snail and Bumblebee. "All clear, on you go, everyone. Margaret, your lot in that car over there; Your Holiness, honored delegates, this car here. Jacques, Thom, you're with Margaret. Jack, everything okay here?"

Unicorn greeted this with a nod—and a look so woebegone that my heart went out to him.

"You're not cleared for physically-active duties yet," said Eduardo, in response. "You can't possibly come. Anyway, isn't a whole state's security enough for you?"

Unicorn looked slightly surprised. Not aware just how down-hearted he was looking? No doubt his head knew exactly why he couldn't come with us, but his heart felt like he was being punished for what had happened in Monaco. "More than enough," he assured Eduardo. "And yes, everything is under control here."

The railroad car interiors had been stripped out to make extra cargo space, back in the days when the EuroGov still occasionally allowed the train to go out of the Vatican onto the EuroBloc tracks and return full of provisions. But for this visit, we saw as we entered our assigned car, some actual tables and chairs had been bolted to the floor.

Bane, Jon and I settled ourselves at a table, with Sister Krayj, as Snail and Bumblebee took up positions at each end of our car, and the off-duty guards got into the other cars. Five cars was about four more than we needed, but the idea was that someone with thermal imaging goggles and a sniper rifle or rocket launcher would find it harder to figure out which car the 'important' people were in.

A heap of newspapers lay on the table, so I started

reading out the headlines, the better to ignore the fact that the train doors were slamming, the engine starting, and—*squeak-grind*—the rail portal opening.

"M.V. Back On Form!" said the first headline. With the Religious Suppression suspended, the papers could report on my blog, but I'd not seen it making many online headlines for the last couple of weeks. Eduardo had clearly put out the papers from the last couple of days, rather than take today's away with us.

The train shuddered and moved forwards. I stumbled over the next headline and Bane groped for my hand. Then we'd gone under the wall and the train was cruising serenely along, picking up speed.

Diplomatic immunity, remember?

I picked up the next paper. "Georg Friedrich pleads guilty," I read. Monaco, despite its status as a Free State, had what was essentially a justice system integrated with that of the EuroGov. They didn't have to waste any space on Detention Facilities; they just sent their criminals over the border for the EuroGov to deal with. The EuroGov no doubt were used to getting their pick of organs from those sentenced to death, so it was mutually beneficial.

No question but that Georg Friedrich was going to get the death penalty, even if they wouldn't actually be able to dismantle him. Due to the moratorium on dismantling, the EuroGov were busy disposing of their criminals by firing squad, at the moment, and complaining loudly about the waste.

"I must write something about Friedrich, once we get back from this trip," I said. I'd simply not had time since the trial began three days ago, but no doubt the trial would still be going on by then. Little chance anything I said would lead to clemency, but still...

"You're not actually going to try and get him off, are you?" demanded Bane. "After what he did to Snakey?"

"Do you think Snakey would take any pleasure in his death?" I asked quietly.

Bane was silent for a long moment. Eventually he said, "Still claims he's Resistance, does he?"

I scanned the text. I'd been too busy the past few days

to keep up to date with the trial of Snakey's killer. "Yep. Doesn't seem like he's saying much else, though."

"What's the point?" snorted Sister Krayj. "Exactly how many witnesses were there?"

"How are the EuroGov controlling the guy, though?" said Jon. "If he's one of theirs—and Eduardo's sure he is—yet they're letting him take the rap for three murders and an act of terrorism, you'd think he'd give up his cover as a Resistance fighter and plead that he was just following EuroGov orders. In which case, as the hired man rather than the instigator, it's possible he might avoid the death penalty. What's their hold on him?"

"Perhaps he's got family who're being held hostage," said Bane, frowning. "Or maybe he's being military mind-controlled. They're supposed to be getting quite good at it now, according to the rumors."

I shivered.

"More likely, he doesn't want them to delay the execution until after the Vote," said Sister Krayj dryly. "No doubt he prefers the firing squad to the possibility of the dismantler making a 'mistake' and him getting Conscious Dismantlement. All they have to do is make sure he's convinced they're going to win. Not hard, if he's already their creature."

My stomach lurched slightly as I took in what she meant. My word, she was right, wasn't she? Holding that threat over Georg Friedrich, they could make him do practically anything. Including giving up his only chance at life by playing the role of a Resistance fighter all the way to the execution yard.

He was being incredibly thoroughly stabbed in the back. Despite what he'd done, I couldn't help feeling just a tiny bit sorry for the guy.

1 month, 2 days

I'm writing to you all today from the United States of South America's embassy in Brussels. Hard to believe, isn't it? The EuroGov haven't violated diplomatic immunity and seized any of us, so I'd say it's going very well, so far!

Margaret Verrall—blog post, 'The Impatient Gardener'

"How are you, Margaret?" asked Pope Cornelius, as we met at the breakfast buffet in the USSA embassy the following morning.

"Oh, fine. The room they've put me and Bane in is incredible!" The bed was a four poster, for one thing!

Pope Cornelius smiled. "Well, it is the Brussels embassy of a major world bloc. I'm sorry you're taking the brunt of the public appearances, by the way."

I waved this aside. "That's why you brought me, isn't it? I mean, if you don't attend all those meetings, what was the point of you coming?"

He smiled again and helped himself to another cheese-stuffed *arepas.* "True. Well, good luck. More than luck, in fact. Especially tomorrow night. Just in case I don't see you again beforehand..." He raised a hand and blessed me.

I crossed myself and thanked him with very genuine sincerity. Today and tomorrow I would be busy giving talks within the embassy to various groups, and trotting around Brussels in the wake of the lesser delegates, along with Bane and Jon. I wasn't permitted to make any speeches outside, but I didn't need to. Pictures of the 'three most wanted' strolling around Brussels would speak for themselves.

But tomorrow night, *that* was the big event of our short visit, at least as far as *my* schedule was concerned. A live television debate between the head of the EGD and myself, hosted by my dear friend Reginald Hill. There was no doubt that this was when they hoped to—verbally—take me down. The Chairman himself wouldn't be present, but two members of the High Committee were two too many as far as I was concerned.

I swallowed, and decided against a second corn cake.

1 month, 1 day

"People often say to Margo, *if you'd passed your Sorting,*

you wouldn't be doing this. The hospitals need the organs—you're just being selfish. Well, I was as sure as anyone can be that I was going to pass Sorting. And being a self-absorbed teenager I assumed Margo would scrape through too. Yet I've opposed Sorting my whole life. No, it is not *selfish*. *Sorting* is *selfish*. Opposing it is *right*."

Bane Verrall— quoted on 'The Impatient Gardener'

"Ready, Margo?" asked Sister Krayj, checking the hang of her habit was concealing her nonLee.

I moistened dry lips and wished Bane was here with me, rather than already seated in the audience with Jon and Eduardo. "I don't know if I'll ever be ready for this..."

The last time I'd seen that man in person, he'd sentenced me to a hideous, agonizing death. And then he'd taken Bane's eyes; he'd tried to blackmail us both... I knew I shouldn't, but I hated him. And I must not let it show. As far as the press were concerned, I was little Miss Forgiveness, after all. They kept making my pedestal higher and higher; how long before I fell off altogether?

About another half hour, if Reginald Hill had anything to do with it...

"You'll be fine," said Sister Krayj firmly, and nodded towards the opening to the stage. "It's time to go."

Lord, please just use me as your ventriloquist's dummy tonight. Just speak through me. 'Cause I don't know what to say...

"Bee, I think you should be the one to come with me, don't you?" I said.

Bumblebee smiled, white teeth gleaming. With his dark, dark skin and blond hair, he was as far from the EuroBloc Genetics Department's stupid idea of racial perfection as it was possible to be. Being extremely tall and solid as well, he was the logical choice to have at my back, while Snail, being small and fast as a whippet, was better left to hover a few meters away backstage.

I took one last deep breath, and walked onto the stage, Sister Krayj and Bee following.

The lights were dazzling. As everyone had assured me, I

couldn't actually see the audience at all. In one way that was good, but it meant I couldn't see Bane, either.

There was Mr. EuroBloc Genetics Department, or Doctor Gunvald Anfeltsen, as I'd discovered his name was. And sitting in the chair beside him...

"Mr. Hill..." I stepped forward and held out my hand. "It's so nice to meet under pleasanter circumstances."

He took my hand, shook it, murmuring pleasantries. All soft-spoken amiability. But I'd seen his other side.

"And Doctor Anfeltsen..." I turned to Mr. EGD, who was staring at Bee with ill-concealed distaste.

With a trace of reluctance, Anfeltsen shook my hand as well, looking just as haughty as I remembered from my interrogation. His expression seemed to say, *this girl is doing all she can to destroy my entire department, and I'm supposed to sit around and make small talk with her?* I didn't miss the hard look Reginald Hill shot him, at which, Anfeltsen pasted a rather false smile on his face.

Well, you tried to destroy *me*, I told him silently. How do you think *I* feel about this?

I sat in the seat across from Reginald Hill, and Sister Krayj settled silently into the final chair, like the excellent personal assistant she was supposed to be. Bee took up position just behind me, like a comforting mountain.

"So, Margaret Verrall has graced us with her presence tonight," said Reginald Hill smoothly. "Let us get started. Obviously the main topic will be Sorting. My colleague Gunvald is the leading expert on this subject. Gunvald, to begin, do you have any questions for Mrs. Verrall?"

"Yes," said Mr. EGD. "I would like to know why she thinks it would be such a good thing to plunge the bloc back into the dark ages before Sorting. To life expectancies of around eighty years. Eighty years! Down from almost one hundred and ten! How can this be a good thing?"

"Well, Margaret?" smiled Reginald Hill.

I took a breath and began, my voice calmer than I could have imagined possible. "*Well*, I have to say that I am sur- prised a medical man of such apparently high qualifications could be so poorly informed on this subject. There is no question of life expectancies slipping back in the way he describes. These figures are taken from history, and do not reflect the advances in medicine that have been made in parts of the world that have not embraced Sorting, or at least not so single-mindedly as the EuroBloc."

I turned towards the audience as I went on, "For example, life expectancy in *comparable* African States, by which I mean, states with similar levels of development and GDP as the EuroBloc, range between ninety-five to one hundred and five years. Seeing that the 'almost' one hundred and ten years to which Mr. Anfeltsen refers only applies to the top ten percent of the population in terms of wealth, it's pretty clear that for the general population of the EuroBloc, there would be next to no reduction in life expectancy whatsoever."

Reginald Hill's smile became a little taut as the audience murmured in obvious interest and appreciation. The look he shot Mr. EGD seemed to say, *you'd better have something stronger than that.*

Anfeltsen frowned. "Mrs. Verrall, am I correct in thinking that your superstition dictates that you must be generous to other people. Generous to quite absurd degrees, in fact?"

I smiled sweetly at him. "It was made very clear to me by those nice customs agents at the station that I am not permitted to discuss my faith in any way whilst on EuroBloc soil, which this television studio, of course, is."

Anfeltsen almost glared, then managed to swap it for a would-be light-hearted smile. "Indeed, quite so." He stared at his handheld networkAccessor, clearly trying to reword his question.

Reginald Hill came to his rescue. "Margaret, would you say that extreme generosity is something that is very important to you personally?"

I could see where this was going, but still... "Yes, I would."

Back on script, Mr. EGD plunged on, "In that case, how is it that you don't support the act of incredible generosity that a reAssignee makes when they give up their organs for the good of others? A generosity you captured so well in your original short story?"

For all I'd been expecting the question, the way he put it sent a stab of rage through me. I held off answering for several heartbeats, then spoke calmly. "To start with, I defy you to find even one reAssignee in the entire bloc—in the entire world, even—who feels the way Annabel Salford supposedly felt in that story.

"No, I take that back. I've no wish to be responsible for you threatening some poor kid to make them say what you want. But suffice it to say, real people don't feel like that. Generosity is of vital importance, yes. But a reAssignee does not 'give up' their organs, in the way that an organ donor does. A reAssignee's organs are violently ripped from them and stolen, along with their very life. If a man steals your car, does generosity on your part enter into the process in any way? No. Generosity has to be voluntary. Sorting is imposed. Generosity doesn't enter into Sorting at all. Your argument is completely void."

More murmuring from the audience. A couple of brave people clapped. Mr. EGD looked sullen.

So far, so good...

After almost an hour, Mr. EGD just sat and sulked. Which counted as a point to me, undoubtedly. The only problem was, the program was scheduled to run for another hour, and Reginald Hill had now taken over. He was a lot better at it than Doctor Anfeltsen.

"Would you not agree, Margaret, that the reason the species of the natural kingdom have developed such impressive abilities—the speed of the cheetah, or the eyesight of a hawk, for example—is due to natural selection?"

"That would certainly appear to be how God did it." Oops, I shouldn't have mentioned the G word...

Overlooking what would normally have been termed proselytization, he just smiled like a cat about to pounce. "Then would you not agree that if we eliminate natural selection, the progress of the human species will stall and slide into ever increasing imperfection?"

"If we eliminated *natural* selection, there would be that danger, I agree. However, despite the best efforts of mankind throughout our entire history to do just that, we

185

have never managed to entirely eliminate natural selection. Plenty of diseases, natural disasters, and accidents still come along to thin us out.

"However, I believe what you actually mean to refer to is Sorting, which might more aptly be termed *unnatural* selection, since it is *natural* for human beings to work together and look out for one another in order to increase both their chances of survival and their quality of life. Clearly there is nothing at all natural about Sorting, so an appeal to natural selection is inappropriate."

"But surely you would at least concede that the Sorting program *is* improving the human race."

"I am not convinced of that at all, actually. Homogenizing the human race, perhaps. But one cannot measure the advancement of humanity only through the physical attributes of its members. True progress is much more far-reaching. When I look back on our history, there are many cases where people who would not have been permitted to live adult lives in our society have been the ones responsible for huge leaps forward in science, culture, or the arts. The EuroBloc curriculum edits their disabilities out of history as best it can, but if you look on an uncensored website you'll find the information.

"Just one example: several hugely important scientific theories were discovered by a scientist called Stephen Hawking—everyone's heard his name—but have they heard that he spent almost his entire life in a wheelchair, able to communicate only through a computer? Because he did. Nowadays his condition would have been picked up in the blood tests at Sorting and he would have been dismantled. Just think how much less advanced our scientific knowledge would be, without his contribution. And therefore think: far from *improving* humanity, just how much has our true progress been retarded over the last half century, thanks to Sorting?"

Reginald Hill's smile had taken on just a fractionally sour tinge, but it didn't last long. He held up a hand to quiet the murmur from the audience, his lined face kindly and cheerful once more. "Well, it's time for our break. I don't know about my companions, but I'm getting quite parched.

We'll be back in ten minutes."

Mr. EGD and I murmured our agreement, and we all got up and trooped off stage, Mr. EGD now attempting to ignore the six foot five black guy with blond hair. "There's coffee and biscuits along there," he snapped at me, pointing down the corridor. "And I hope you choke!"

"Now, now, Gunvald," purred Reginald Hill—rather dangerously, I thought. "If you'd been reading Margaret Verrall's blog like a sensible person, you'd have known she'd already demolished most of your arguments at some point over the last six months, and you might have been able to make her work a little harder."

Mr. EGD spat something very rude under his breath and stalked off.

"You know," said Reginald Hill to me, in a confidential tone, "I always said he wasn't up to it, but he *was* the logical choice. That'll teach them not to listen to me, hmm?"

With a certain amount of effort, I managed not to retort with something rather similar to Mr. EGD, simply smiling tightly and heading in the direction of the refreshments. Not that I felt like eating anything. In fact, Eduardo had advised me to eat or drink nothing outside of the USSA embassy, most especially not tonight. We didn't want them slipping something into my coffee to turn me into a giggling fool—or worse.

I waited out the break, ignoring the exaggerated relish with which Reginald Hill was drinking his coffee, slipping my own cup onto a side table untouched when it was time to go back in.

There was no sign of Mr. EGD, though his chair was still there. If he'd felt he was being publically humiliated to that degree, it was fantastic—though it did mean I had an hour of solo Reginald Hill. The man settled back in his chair, calm and confident, his eyes gleaming with something too like anticipation. Considering I'd managed to counter all their arguments pretty well so far, why was he so smug? Simply pleased to be vindicated in his opinion of Mr. EGD's debating skills? No, he knew how important this evening was, and he'd been appropriately furious about Gunvald's poor performance. He had something else up his ten

187

thousand-euron sleeve.

"So, we welcome Margaret Verrall back for the second half of tonight's special program. Doctor Gunvald Anfeltsen has unfortunately been called away on urgent business, and will not be with us again. However, another guest will be joining us for a while, although he will have to leave before the end since he has an important appointment in an hour and a half."

Huh?

Two EuroBloc security men appeared, walking a figure between them. Dressed in prison pajamas, they'd sat him in the empty chair before I recognized him.

Georg Friedrich.

Snakey's murderer.

15

A FULL ENGLISH BREAKFAST

I sensed Bee stiffen behind me, then relax as he managed to overcome the distraction. I pressed my fingertips tightly together, fighting to give no sign of the anger that surged up inside me. Was Lucas watching this on TV? How would he feel if I failed to extend forgiveness to this man? Let alone what everyone *else* would think...

Georg Friedrich shot a look of resentment at me, but when he looked at Reginald Hill his eyes were full of hate. They were blackmailing him, all right. He didn't look so tough, now, nor did he seem like some sort of mind-controlled military drone. In fact, he looked far from healthy. He still had one arm in a sling, and looked pasty and sick, not nearly so recovered as I'd assumed when I'd heard they were putting him on trial so soon.

"Hello, Herr Friedrich," I managed. "You look a lot better than the last time I saw you, but are you really well enough to be here?"

He just glared at me for a moment and looked down at the floor again.

"Well, it's not like there'll be another opportunity," said Reginald Hill lightly. "What with the sentence that was passed this afternoon."

Sentence? To my surprise, Georg Friedrich's trial had ended during the day we'd spent *en route* on the train—with him found guilty, of course—but surely they hadn't sentenced him already?

"But perhaps you've been too busy to watch the news," went on Reginald Hill. "I'm sure you'll be glad to hear that justice is to be done: this very night, no less. At nine-thirty this evening, Herr Friedrich is to be executed at Brussels Detention Facility."

The clock on the wall at the back of the stage said eight

o'clock. A chill went through me, despite the man's crimes. "But not *dismantled*, surely?" I checked. Not with the Moratorium? But in that case, what pressure were they bringing to bear...

"Why, yes, indeed," said Reginald Hill smoothly. "Brussels Detention Facility are acting in this matter as agents of the Monacan government, by whom the trial has of course been conducted. It is hardly reasonable to expect Free States to suspend their normal methods of punishment just to comply with a *EuroBloc* Moratorium on the dismantling of *EuroBloc* detainees. Naturally the Moratorium does not apply in this case."

I swallowed, and tried to keep breathing through my anger and surging emotions. Oh, I could see it now—his two-forked plan—see why he was so confident. Either, he reasoned, I would be unable to treat the conscious, much-recovered assassin with the forgiveness I'd so famously extended before, or my hatred of dismantlement would overwhelm me and I'd turn my rage on *him*. Either way, little Miss Forgiveness would be dead and buried on live TV.

Angel Margaret, help me!

"I'm very sorry to hear about your sentence," I told Georg Friedrich. Honestly.

He looked up, disbelief on his face. "The hell you are!"

I couldn't help a surprised blink. "Come on, if I wanted you dead, I wouldn't have bothered with that bandage, would I?"

He looked blank. "What bandage?"

Oh... "Uh... well, uh, you were bleeding rather badly when my bodyguard rendered you unconscious, so, uh, I put on a dressing and applied some pressure, just until the medics arrived." My cheeks were burning.

Sister Krayj leaned forward slightly. "She saved your life," she said bluntly.

Friedrich stared at me, glanced at Reginald Hill, clearly expecting to hear what had just been said roundly denied. When Reginald Hill went right on relaxing in his chair, he turned back to me. "*Why?*"

"Why? Because I didn't want you to die."

"Why not?" he demanded. "I tried to kill you!"

"I know. But if I killed you or allowed you to die unnecessarily, how does that make me better than you?"

From his expression, unraveling this was giving him a headache. "No one would have thought you were wrong," he said at last.

"I would," I said.

He frowned. "What would you do with me, then? If not the... gurney..." His voice squeaked slightly on the last word. He wasn't really so very old. Under thirty, surely? There was sweat on his brow.

"Me? Well, I'm not part of the Vatican Justice Department, but if you'd been taken into our custody, then since you committed crimes against Vatican State citizens, you'd be tried, and found guilty, but we don't use the death penalty. We'd have sent you to a secure rehabilitation farm we have in Africa. I was reading about it recently; it's much nicer than most prisons. But the only way to get out is to change. For the better. As part of your rehabilitation, you'd have had to communicate with the friends and relatives of Javier Alvarez—and the Monacan policemen, if their family were prepared to get involved—and get to know the men you killed, but you wouldn't have been killed yourself. I'm sorry you can't go there."

"*You're* sorry." He gave a bitter snort, but there was no hostility in it, now. Not towards me, anyway. "Trust me, right now even the touchy-feely stuff sounds like heaven." His voice was very strained and his eyes flicked to the clock. He'd an hour and a quarter to live. He must be able to feel every passing second, vibrating through his gut.

"Margaret," said Reginald Hill, in the delicate tone of someone pressing a detonator into a block of explosive. "Why don't you tell us all a bit about your poor bodyguard—now what was the name? Javier Alvarez?"

Friedrich looked at the floor again, clearly guessing this question boded nothing good for him.

"Well..." *Dear Lord, please help me to talk about Snakey without getting so mad I say something awful to that man...* Or to Reginald Hill, surely almost equally responsible for Snakey's death... "Snakey—that was his nickname—was a very lively guy, very full of life. He could make everyone laugh. But never at someone else's expense. He was actually really quite gentle, underneath. He ran away from his home in Spain at age fifteen to devote his life to his faith—he was never afraid of taking a risk for what he believed in. He was..." I swallowed. My throat was getting tight. "He was a great person."

"And his full nickname was Grass Snake, I believe?" said Reginald Hill. "An animal name, so... part of your Liberation team?"

"We were both part of Bane's team, yes. Snakey's partner was Gecko—my brother Kyle. It was nice to know Snakey had his back—and vice versa." Yes... and I'd been so wrapped up in how *I* felt about Snakey's death, and how *Bane* felt about it, had I ever really considered how *Kyle* must be feeling?

"And this Javier was your bodyguard on all your speaking tours, am I right? He and the British guard."

"Jack Willmott. Yes. I felt very safe with them there. Clearly I was right to feel that way. Actually..." I took out the omniPhone Eduardo had issued me as an emergency means of contact on my trips out-of-state and flicked quickly through to a photo I'd taken whilst blending in with the other queuing boats. "Here's a picture of Javier and Jack on the boat to Monaco." *Hours before Snakey was killed* hung in the air unsaid.

I got up and went to hold the phone in front of one of the video cameras, glancing at the screen that was angled towards us to check the photo was showing okay. Snakey and U, laughing. The audience murmured in sympathy, and I swallowed another lump in my throat.

I took the phone back to my seat and held it out to Friedrich. "Do you want to see?"

He looked up, but only to glare at me. "If you're trying to make me feel bad, it won't work! I was just doing my job!" He shot a nervous look at Reginald Hill. "The job my Resistance commander gave me," he added quickly.

I put the phone away, and said levelly, "Personally, I find killing for money even more distasteful than dismantling."

"Well I wasn't killing for money, was I?" snapped Friedrich. "I was fighting the EuroGov. I'm Resistance, aren't

I?"

I sat for a moment in silence. "You know," I said at last, "surely by now you've realized that even if I was dead and you'd completed your mission, the 'escape' you were no doubt promised would never have materialized, and you'd *still* be watching that clock tick your life away. After Lucas Everington, did you really think the EuroGov would allow a second high-profile prisoner to give them the slip within the space of six months? You were a dead man from the moment you accepted the job, though clearly you didn't realize in time."

Friedrich glared at me yet again. "I don't know what you're talking about, you crazy bitch!" he hissed. "You're just pissed 'cause I took out your bodyguard!"

"Much good it's done you!" I snapped before belatedly registering the fear in Friedrich's voice. Oh—afraid that if I convinced everyone he wasn't Resistance, Hill might make *him* pay for it.

I'd better leave the subject alone. It wasn't like it was within my power to save him, and I'd no wish to be responsible for anyone getting Conscious Dismantlement. Even him.

I shouldn't have snapped at him... I simply mustn't say anything else, I mustn't... *Oh Lord, help me...*

Reginald Hill still waited, smugger than ever, patient as a stalking cat. Watching, all the time, for the trigger that might set me off. Bee shifted his stance behind me, no doubt making sure his muscles weren't stiffening up. He was a good bodyguard, no question, but I still missed Snakey...

Wait a minute... bodyguard... something about that word was triggering a subliminal squeal of excitement. Not within my power to save him... or was it? The idea was falling together in my mind but—I needed information. Couldn't do anything without it... I glanced at the clock again. Barely an hour before the execution. Friedrich would be taken away within the next quarter hour, surely?

I put a hand to my stomach, trying to look un-comfortable—but not too hard—and got to my feet. "I'm so dreadfully, dreadfully sorry, but I'm going to have to excuse myself just for a minute."

Reginald Hill smiled in such a way that I almost expected to see canary feathers sticking out of his mouth. "No problem, Margaret. Herr Friedrich can stay a little longer. He'll still be here when you get back."

Trying to greet this with an expression of glumness rather than triumph, I hurried offstage. Hill thought I was getting mad—thought I was bolting in the hope Friedrich wouldn't be there when I returned. He wouldn't be letting Friedrich go *anywhere* just yet, schedule or no schedule. Good.

"Margo? Are you okay?" Sister Krayj, Bee and Snail pretty much chorused, as we got a little further from the stage.

"I'm fine," I said, very softly, "don't get in a tizz." I dived into the ladies' room, turned on all the taps to foil any bugs, and pulled out my phone again.

"Margo, everyone will think you were getting angry," said Sister Krayj, looking unusually anxious. "Who are you calling that's worth that?"

"Shss..." I said. "I've no time to explain, I need to get back out there ASAP." I pushed my handbag into her arms. "Can you find a piece of blank paper and a pen, please?" Now, the person I needed to talk to... I knew the name of their 'residence', as the large group houses in African Free Towns were termed, but I only knew the *phone number* of another residence in the same Free Town... Let's hope that was enough. I dialed quickly.

A woman answered, and spoke in an African language, as usual.

"Hi," I said in Latin. "Is there any chance you can put me through to Kangbe Residence, please? It's very important."

"Should be able to. Hold on," said the woman cheerfully, after the usual time lag. I waited... and waited... It felt like forever before...

"Kangbe Residence," said a man's voice in Latin, clearly appraised of the Underground call. "Can I help?"

"Yes, I need to speak urgently with Juwan Toure."

"He's watching the debate with the rest of us. I'll go and get him. Who shall I say is calling?"

194

"A friend."

"Oh. Okay." Footsteps echoed down the phone as the man walked away. Come on, come on...

More footsteps. "Hello?"

"Juwan? It's Margo."

"*Margo?* You're supposed to be on stage right now! Why did you rush off like that?"

"Because I needed to speak to you. No time to explain—how much do you know about EuroBloc employment law?"

"Well... I never did do that Law degree, but... *un petite.* What do you need to know?"

"What's necessary to constitute a binding contract of employment? I take it you have to sign something?"

"*Non,* you don't have to sign anything. You can have a verbal contract. All you have to do is agree that they're going to work for you. For it to stand up in a court of law, you need witnesses, though. It's pretty meaningless without any."

"That's it?" My heart leapt. Might this actually be doable? "Nothing else?"

"Well, you have to pay them the first time, before the contract is in force. That's to protect employers from discussing a job with someone and having them turn around and say they have a verbal contract."

"Pay them? How much?"

"Oh, a week, a day, an hour. Doesn't have to be much. The money changes hands, the contract's legally binding. Most bosses pay in arrears, so if they're hiring on casual workers on verbal contracts, they just pay a single hour to bring the contract into force, then pay in arrears as usual. Standard practice."

"Nothing else?"

"That's all there is to it, Margo. Written contracts, well, that's a different kettle of fish. Better protections for both parties, but things need to be signed and so on."

"Okay, thanks Juwan! I've got to go!" I ended the call and stuffed the phone and the piece of paper Sister Krayj was now holding back in my handbag. Took out my purse instead—Eduardo had given me some emergency money. I pulled out a ten euron note and tucked it into my waistband, pulling my blouse down to hide it.

"*Oh my...*"said Sister Krayj, catching up with my train of thought at last. But she checked her nonLee, helped me turn off the taps again, and followed me out without another word.

Surprise, surprise, Georg Friedrich was still sitting, sullen, trapped and miserable, in his chair. I settled myself back in my own chair and gave a deliberately slightly false smile. Keep Reginald Hill thinking his plan was working for as long as possible...

"I'm very sorry, the embassy are giving us all this wonderful South American food, but some of it isn't quite what I'm used to." Let everyone deduce what they liked from that perfectly true statement.

Reginald Hill murmured something polite and sympathetic. Friedrich went on staring at his feet. "So, Herr Friedrich," I said brightly, allowing my voice to sound slightly strained. "Did you always want to be an assassin?" Friedrich looked up, scowled, and opened his mouth, so I said, "Sorry, Resistance fighter, of course."

He looked at his feet again, like he wasn't going to reply. Come on, think... You're clearly not the brain of the German department, but you must see that talking about yourself makes you more sympathetic to the audience, and that is the only thing that could conceivably help you now. *So* little chance, of course, that he might not think it worth the effort...

No, he was looking up again. "I... wanted to join the military for quite a long time. Some type of military," he amended quickly. "But before that... well... I wanted to be a chef, actually." He made the admission as though it were something to be ashamed of.

"A chef?" I blinked in surprise. "But that's a good thing to be. Why did you decide to go in for killing people instead?" A chef... surely I could make that work...

Friedrich scowled some more. "My pa showed up out of the blue one day—not around much, my *vater*—heard my dream and went ape. Said cooking was no job for a real man and I was to forget all about it. After that I still cooked loads for fun, but I just couldn't bring myself to consider it as a serious career anymore. So I fixed on the military instead. I always liked computer games with lots of shooting." He directed another look at Reginald Hill. "Uh... I got all patriotic in my late teens, so I chose the Resistance."

"Of course," I murmured. "Can you cook any British food?"

He uncurled slightly, a hint of pride stiffening his spine. "Oh yeah, I can cook loads of British recipes. And French and Spanish. Not so much Scandinavian, but some. I'm good on Italian, too. And I make *great* German chocolates."

"Really? I wish I could hire you to cook a goodbye breakfast for the USSA ambassadors tomorrow morning. They've treated us so well, sharing their diplomatic immunity and their embassy and everything. I'd have liked to give them a gesture of our appreciation."

Friedrich congealed, sinking back into his hunched position. Thinking I was deliberately twisting that invisible knife in his back by mentioning a morning he would not be alive to see. No doubt everyone else thought the same— Reginald Hill looked ready to start purring. I simply had to bring this off, or no one would ever know any better...

"What would you prepare if I engaged you to cook a British breakfast for some high level diplomats?" I asked.

Friedrich glowered, then looked at the floor again.

"Come on," I said coaxingly, "I'd really like to know."

Perhaps remembering the audience sympathy thing again, he raised his head and spoke resentfully at first, but with gathering enthusiasm. "Well, Latin taste is heavily into hot cooked breakfasts, so I'd do a Full English, as the main dish. And I'd cook some proper porridge, made with milk, not water, and serve it with cream and brown sugar. Boiled eggs, with proper toast soldiers. And grapefruit halves. And I'd serve proper coffee, because even Brits would serve proper coffee to guests like that. But I'd have English tea as the second option, along with milk and fruit juice. Plus anything else you wanted..." Remembering this was all an empty—and cruel—fantasy, he ran down and focused on the floor again.

"That sounds perfect!" I said, ever so light-heartedly. "Will you come and cook it for me?"

"Bitch!" he muttered, without looking up.

"Oh, come on," I chirped, "won't you take the job? Say you will. I'd pay you, and everything..."

Gah, how to get one dim-witted assassin to catch on, without one razor-minded Internal Affairs minister catching on as well? If Hill figured it out, he'd have Friedrich out of here before you could say *boiled eggs*, and I'd go down in history as the mega-bitch who'd tormented a condemned man in his last hour of life. It could cost us the vote. Probably would. I tried not to swallow too noticeably. And Lucas probably *was* watching, as well. I *had* to bring this off...

"What's so interesting about your feet?" I simpered. "Surely I'm more interesting?" *Ag*, I was making *myself* sick! But I pulled the money out of my waistband and had it ready in my hand when Friedrich shot me another angry look. Hill wasn't looking at the screen and the money was hidden behind my body... I held the bank note out a little way, so Friedrich couldn't miss it, and twitched it at him. "Won't you work for me?" I cooed. "Please, *say you will*..."

His stare became blank and baffled. *Come on, think, man, think; see that I'm hiding it from Hill and remember you've just found out I tried to save your life before and don't just dismiss it as an extreme level of...*

I saw the thought enter his eyes, saw astonishment blossom, closely followed by a meteorite of insuppressible hope, the kind you try so hard to contain, because if you're wrong the agony of disappointment will be just so...

"Yeah, I'll work for you," he said quickly.

"Good, here's an hour's pay," I said, leaning forward.

Out of the corner of my eye, I saw the jerk that ran down Reginald Hill's body as he figured it out—he began to move out of his seat... too late. I shoved the money into Friedrich's hand; his fingers closed on it like it was a lifeline. Suddenly breathing as though he'd been running, he stared at Hill. So did I.

Reginald Hill made a quick gesture to the waiting EuroBloc Security men—they moved forward towards Friedrich.

I sprang to my feet, actually grabbed a handful of prison

pajama, and said all in one breath, "Herr Georg Friedrich is now in the employ of the Vatican Free State and as such comes under the diplomatic immunity of the United States of South America, so *back off!*"

The audience's bewildered silence broke into gasps, cries of shock, a roar of conversation and a few outright whoops of laughter or approval.

But I was still looking at Hill. His lined face had frozen into an unreadable mask, only the barest traces of dismay and anger leaking through. Which way would he jump?

He had only two options. Try to claim that hiring someone specifically to help them escape justice didn't make them a valid employee as far as diplomatic immunity was concerned and seize Friedrich anyway—but most other states would view that as violation of diplomatic immunity, whatever he said. Almost more importantly, for the Euro-Gov to insist on Friedrich's death when I, one of the parties most wronged by him, was fighting to save his life, would leave them looking utterly horrible. Hill would be a positive ogre to my saintly little angel.

Or he could laugh it off as the whim of a silly, sentimental girl with no appreciation for the importance of justice—and let us carry Friedrich away. Which would leave him looking a fool, but prevent the awful publicity. I'd a feeling Reginald Hill was not a man who enjoyed looking a fool. But he was also smart enough to know that just now, good publicity was worth more than anything else.

Finally, he raised a hand for silence. "Let me see," he said evenly, "You agreed basic employment terms, and you paid him. A verbal contract is therefore in force, and the USSA's diplomatic immunity does indeed extend to all Vatican employees present in Brussels. Much as it saddens me to see such a vicious terrorist go free, it seems he is all yours.

"I can only extend my apologies to the people of the EuroBloc." He spoke now to the audience and to the cameras. "I feel I have failed you. I would never have brought this Resistance terrorist together with Margaret Verrall had I know she would aid and abet his escape from justice in this underhand manner. Once again, my sincerest apologies to you all, and my assurances that if this killer ever ventures out from behind Margaret's skirts and enters EuroBloc territory again, he will be seized immediately."

Friedrich had gone so white he looked like he might pass out, and his hands were visibly shaking.

My own belly was beginning to flutter with reaction. "Thank you, Mr. Hill." I glanced at the clock. Twenty minutes, still another twenty minutes, *oh Lord, be with me...* I turned to the audience myself. "I would just like to reassure everyone that Herr Friedrich will certainly not be set loose at any time in the near future. He will go to the rehabilitation center I spoke about earlier, until such a time as he is no longer a danger to others.

"However, I will not apologize for what I have just done. I believe very strongly that rehabilitating people who have made bad moral decisions is a much preferable way of dealing with them than simply killing them. I will be happy to address any concerns you may still have about this matter. Just leave a comment on my blog."

A movement at the stage entrance... Snail had stepped into sight. When he saw me looking, he gestured beside him. There were Spitfire and Croquet, sent by Eduardo to take charge of Friedrich, no doubt. I beckoned to Snail and all three of them crossed the stage.

"I don't suppose I could trouble you for the key to the handcuffs?" I asked Reginald Hill politely.

A sour expression very nearly made it onto his face, but he directed a nod at one of the Security men, who pulled out the keys and handed them to me. I passed them to Spitfire, who pocketed them.

"Come along, then," Spitfire said to Friedrich, in a voice of professional neutrality. "Can you walk? You look a bit peaky..."

Friedrich stumbled to his feet, looking dazed. But as he got level with my chair, he stopped. "Do you really want me to cook that breakfast?" he asked, almost... hopefully?

"Uh..." *No, of course not, it was just a pretext...* I closed my mouth quickly. "Uh, naturally. That's what I hired you for, right?"

A sour smile did make it onto Reginald Hill's face, this

time, but a look of genuine pleasure covered Friedrich's as he shuffled off between Spitfire and Croquet. Good grief, he really wanted to do it, didn't he?

Reginald Hill and I made rather fierce conversation for the remaining time, he bombarding me with all the worries that would most be plaguing people, and me providing verbal ointment to soothe them—I hoped. But nothing he said could possibly top what had come before for interest and drama, and from the slight downward turn of his mouth, he was all too aware of it.

"Margo!" Bane gathered me in his arms for a tight hug. "That was amazing! We couldn't think what you were doing, Jon kept whispering, *she's being so horrible! I've never known her act like this!* I could practically feel him wringing his hands."

Jon smiled slightly apologetically. "And Bane kept saying, *she's up to something, she's up to something, can't you tell?* And then...!"

"Reginald Hill sounded like an utter fool!" crowed Bane. "You totally *owned* him, Margo!"

"I was afraid you might be cross," I admitted, into his hair, since he hadn't let me go yet, and I didn't particularly want him too. I was starting to shake all over, now. I'd run a terrible risk.

Bane snorted. "I didn't care two hoots what the EuroGov were going to do to that man. He deserved it. But you just counted coup on Hill, on the whole EuroGov! So Friedrich gets to go be all rural and productive in Africa, so what? Anyway, you were right what you said. Snakey would be pleased."

"Yes, I think he would," I said softly.

We were back in the embassy—Snail and Bee had whisked me off in a car without waiting for the others, clearly afraid of any retaliation from the EuroGov for their public humiliation. But Bane and Jon hadn't been far behind.

Eduardo appeared at last. He marched over to a mirror and peered closely at his... forehead?... then turned to leave, without saying a word.

"Uh... what are you doing?" I asked.

"Checking for gray hairs!" he snapped, and marched out of the room again.

Sister Krayj and I caught each other's eye—and dissolved into giggles. After only a moment, Eduardo stuck his head back into the room, and we tried to get hold of ourselves.

"By the way," he said. "That was brilliant."

1 month

"There can be no peace without justice, no justice without forgiveness."

Pope St John Paul II—quoted on 'The Impatient Gardener'

The impromptu breakfast was an event of some size by the time Eduardo had invited half the press in Brussels, and Pope Cornelius had rounded up various other ambassadors. I took a deep breath, tried not to clutch Bane's arm too hard, and prepared to be nice to Georg Friedrich all over again. In truth, I was very glad he was saved from execution, but it was hard to speak to him without thinking about Snakey.

Friedrich was standing behind a serving table groaning under platters of quite delicious-looking food. He was handcuffed again, in the presence of so many august guests, but looked rather pleased with himself, if even paler and more wan than before. For a sick man, he'd certainly worked hard.

Trailed by Sister Krayj, and Snail, and Bee—felt like I was leading a parade—I got a plate, and helped Bane fill his as discreetly as possible—he'd rather just pick things up and sniff them to identify them, but he couldn't really do that at an event like this. I was about to escape into the crowd with my full plate, when Friedrich appeared in front of me, Spitfire and Croquet flanking him.

He clutched a small dish, which he held out to me. "I made this specially for you. It's *bauernfrühstück* or farmer's breakfast. A traditional German breakfast recipe."

Out of the corner of my eye, I could see the last few

cameras swinging to cover us...

"Uh, thank you, that's very kind." I put my plate on the table so I could accept the dish. I thought I could see potatoes, eggs, leeks and bacon. "It looks very tasty." No need to worry whether it was safe, Eduardo had gone through the embassy kitchens and removed anything even remotely poisonous, and several people had been watching our felonious cook like a hawk the entire time.

Friedrich stepped slightly closer. "You know they're going to kill me if they can, don't you? To stop me talking," he said, rather urgently.

"We'll do our very best to prevent them," I said. No need to clarify who 'they' were. "We can't do more than that."

He seemed to find this more reassuring than I'd have done. "I could be your bodyguard, you know?" he offered abruptly, a worshipful glint in his eye that I had an uneasy suspicion wasn't a put-on. "I'd be a good bodyguard. And you don't have your usual two with you now..."

Spitfire's and Croquet's faces suddenly attained a whole new level of expressionless professionalism. I felt Bane tense beside me—I squeezed his arm slightly and somehow managed not to yell at Friedrich that the only reason I didn't have them with me was because *he* had killed one of them and collapsed a stage on top of the other.

My expression must've given my thoughts away, though, because Friedrich looked like he was reviewing what he'd just said and—belatedly—thinking better of it. His face took on something of the look of a puppy that's just made a puddle on the carpet.

I gritted my teeth together. "Once you've checked out of the rehabilitation center you'll be free to apply for such a role, if that's still what you wish." The chances of Eduardo actually accepting him... well. Stranger things had happened. Very rarely. But having a dream might make all the difference in the world to his future, so who was I to stamp on it?

"You wait!" he said. "I'll be your bodyguard one day, just wait and see!" He allowed Spitfire and Croquet to shepherd him back around to the other side of the table, thank goodness, freeing me to mingle. I made sure to add a big scoop of the German dish to my plate, first, leaving Friedrich glowing—and then looking alarmed as Pope Cornelius moved in his direction.

"I hope the adoration wears off," I muttered to Bane, as we moved away. "But I've a feeling I'm going to be getting German delicacies made with African ingredients through the post from now on."

Bane just sniggered, unmoved by my unsavory admirer. "If you don't want people to think you're the best thing since sliced bread, don't go round saving them from certain death!"

There wasn't much I could say to that.

Once it was all over, and I'd given one final talk to one final roomful of journalists, I went upstairs with Bane to pack. The train was leaving at midday. Jon, who'd packed already, went off to try and get a bit of work done: his Braille talk had been so well received he'd been busy preparing another one when this trip had come out of nowhere.

"I'd better do these 'anger exercises,' if that's okay," said Bane. "I mean, I can't do them on the train..."

"No, of course not. That's fine. I'll pack."

Bane settled himself on the luxurious carpet, slipped his earplugs in, pulled several faces to show how much he hated doing this sort of thing, and finally settled into steady deep breathing. Karen had set him a number of types of mental exercise, as well as a physical exercise program. All designed to help him stay calm or to bleed off his anger through acceptable scenarios such as slaying dragons or leaping into stormy seas to rescue children. He'd been immensely skeptical about pretty much all the mental exercises to start with, but he now conceded they weren't entirely useless—and he was working at them very conscientiously every day.

I'd just put my final things in the bag when... *Knock knock.*

Door. Who was that?

I drew my nonLee and went to answer it, looking through the peephole first, the way Eduardo had insisted, even in this highly secure embassy building. I blinked and peered again, my eyes trying to identify the person. 'Cause it couldn't be the person they were seeing. But who was it?

Cautiously, I opened the door. Stared at the man who stood there.

"Hi, Margaret. Sorry to startle you."

It *sounded* like him too. Had I lost it? I clutched the nonLee with shaking fingers and finally managed to speak. Or squeak. "You're... *dead!*"

16

BE CAREFUL

The man raised a hand and brushed a straggle of dark hair back from his forehead, baring a small white scar. "Hollywood myth that a bullet to the head is always fatal, Margaret. I may have wished I was dead over the last few months, but I'm as alive as you are, I promise—not even permanently harmed, praise the Lord."

He certainly looked alive. Thin, face lined, voice tired, eyes haunted, but... alive.

"Father Mark!" I lurched forward to hug him—he leapt back skittishly, like a deer. I stopped abruptly. Where had he been? The same place as Lucas? Horror flooded through me. "You were *alive?* I'm so sorry, I just *left* you there!"

He stepped forward again with an apologetic smile, but spoke firmly. "I'm very glad you thought I was dead or you *wouldn't* have left me, and I hear you and the rest of Animal team barely got away yourselves."

"Are you sure you're okay?"

"I really am fine. Had the best medical care Internal Affairs could provide," said Father Mark bitterly.

"Really?" I frowned. "How come they didn't execute you at once?"

"Because they identified me as that supposedly-dead Resistance jackal, and thought I might be useful to them. Took them until now to accept it wasn't going to happen. I'm fine, anyway. Well, the right-hand bit of my face doesn't work quite the way it did, but no matter. I can still smile with the left side of my mouth."

I hadn't been able to put my finger on it until he said that, but it was true. His face did seem slightly... lop-sided. "What... what are you doing here? Did they just let you go?" After what I'd done yesterday? "They should've released you months ago!"

He grimaced. "An oversight. That's the story they're sticking to. Never mind, I'm free."

I opened the door wider and shoved the nonLee back into my waistband. Carrying the gun on me whilst in my room at the embassy was the compromise I'd made with Eduardo, to give Sister Krayj some time off—and me some privacy with my husband.

Beckoning Father Mark in, I hurried over to Bane. Made sure to tread heavily on the floor and waft a hand past his cheek before touching his shoulder.

Only starting a little, he pulled out an earplug. "Margo! I'm slaying a dragon, here..."

"And doing a very good job, I'm sure. You know I've always fancied you as a dragon slayer." As the initial shock wore off my heart felt near to bursting with joy. "But there's someone here..."

Bane pulled out the other earplug and got straight to his feet, flushing slightly.

"It's all right, it's Father Mark: he's not dead!"

"*Not dead?* But... we *saw* it!"

"Didn't see what we thought we saw. Well, we did—he's got the scar to prove it, but we jumped to the wrong conclusion!"

Bane's brow wrinkled. Which was easier to believe, Father Mark alive or my having lost it?

"I'm alive, Bane," confirmed Father Mark.

"Father Mark?" whispered Bane, still stunned. He stepped forward, arms held out—and Father Mark let him hug him. Huh. Bane really seemed more harmless than me, these days?

"Sit down, Father Mark. Did you need something to eat? There's tons of leftovers downstairs. Coffee? We've got a kettle... You must've seen Eduardo, right? I'm going to ring Jon..." All the rooms in the embassy had internal phones.

Other than to give a nod to my Eduardo question, Father Mark didn't try to get an answer in. He just sat down on the sofa with Bane. Jon came tearing in not long after my phone call, with Sister Krayj in tow, wide-eyed. Father Mark let them both hug him. I tried not to feel hurt. Perhaps I'd just moved too suddenly.

I made coffee and pulled out some of the snacks provided in each room and before long the Foxes showed up, cheering and punching Father Mark in the shoulder and soon most of Animal team was in our room and there was quite a party going on, although a few members were back at the Vatican, including Mr. Liar, liar, cassock on fire.

But soon enough it was twelve, and Eduardo appeared to chivvy everyone along. People scattered in all directions to frantically finish their interrupted packing, and we made it to the station only slightly late.

By the time we got on the train Father Mark looked rather exhausted by it all. Time to change the subject and give him a breather? I dispensed more coffee for everyone, from a thermos this time, and took the seat furthest from him, 'cause he really did seem a bit edgy around me. Could it be that his subconscious wasn't quite so happy about my having left him behind?

"Did you get anything done on your talk, Jon?" I said.

"It was going okay when this wonderful distraction cropped up."

"Are people very interested in the rediscovery of Braille, or is it just that, no offence, it's Jonathan Revan telling them about it?" asked Sister Krayj.

"I think they're actually interested. People have so many questions at the moment about what will happen if they do the right thing and give up the unlimited supply of organs, and this is an answer to one of those questions. If you lose your sight, you'll still be able to read. And even write—I've got the engineering guys tinkering around with some old Braille typing devices I found in the archives, trying to get them working."

He prodded Bane in the shoulder. "Basically, I'm trying to send the message that no disability is as limiting and as hopeless as the EuroGov would like you to believe. It would be really great if Bane could show up and take his share of the credit—preferably looking happy and healthy. Though not doing himself in is a really great start—that would not be a good illustration of the point I'm trying to get across."

"Oh, nice to know you care," sneered Bane, elbowing him back.

"Apart from the more obvious objections," Jon added, elbowing back.

Father Mark was frowning in concerned enquiry.

"We've, uh, had a sticky patch," I told him, "but, um, I think we're through that now. Actually..." He was going to bump into Kyle pretty quickly. "Can we fill you in now or would you rather we kept it for another day?"

"No, go right ahead. Glad to hear it's all past tense."

I let Bane tell him most of it, which he managed to do, keeping his head down much of the time, and his voice too low for Snail and Bee, on guard at each car door, to hear him. Sister Krayj listened emotionlessly. Father Mark winced and looked sympathetic at appropriate moments, and didn't jump up and punch Bane, but I'd not expected him to.

"Oh dear," said Father Mark, when the sorry tale drew to its more cheerful conclusion. "Still, everyone in front of me looks pretty... *happy and healthy* now, so let's be thankful for that."

He ran a hand through his decidedly *un*healthy-looking hair. "Actually... now it's just you four, there is something I want to talk to you about." A difficult subject, from the slight frown lines on his brow.

"Go on," said Jon.

"Okay, well... you know I said they thought I might be useful?" He was keeping his voice low, too.

We all made 'umhmm' noises.

"Well, I think they spent most of the time, after putting my brain back together, trying to, well, I suppose the word is... program... me."

I shivered. So the rumors were true.

"Did they manage it?" Bane suddenly sat up a lot straighter.

Sister Krayj went from relaxed cat to coiled spring, staring at Father Mark.

"No. Uh, well..." His hands were actually clenching together slightly, very un-calm behavior for him. "I *really* don't think so..."

"What did Eduardo think?" Jon also had his ears turned very attentively in Father Mark's direction.

Father Mark grimaced.

"You didn't tell him, did you?" I said, dismayed. "Oh, Father Mark! That's the sort of thing he's *got* to know about!"

"What *did* you tell him?" asked Jon. "He's not stupid, y'know."

"Calm down," said Father Mark. "I *did* tell him. I said how they'd tried and failed, so decided to release me as a big propaganda exercise to get some good press. That *is* why they let me go; it'll be all over the news by now."

"So... why were you pulling that face?" I asked.

He pulled *that face* again. "I just... well, I'm sure they didn't manage it. Certain-sure. But... I remember one thing, one word, which I think they were trying to program into me as a trigger, and... I thought it might just be an idea to... test it. One of you say it and just... make *absolutely sure* nothing happens."

"And what *would* happen?" asked Sister Krayj levelly.

Father Mark swallowed. "I'd try to kill Margaret."

I swallowed too. If Father Mark, as a former trained assassin, ever came at me, there wouldn't be any 'try' about it. And it wouldn't just be me... My hand crept protectively to my stomach and I took it away quickly before anyone could notice.

"You should have told Eduardo," said Sister Krayj softly.

"You shouldn't have come anywhere near her!" snarled Bane, apparently ready to launch himself between us as a physical barrier.

"It's safe!" Father Mark almost... pleaded. "I really am sure!"

How important was it to Father Mark to believe that he wouldn't hurt me? Clearly important enough that he was prepared to hide a few tiny facets of the truth from even a trusted colleague.

"I think," said Sister Krayj, "you're right we should make certain. Let's try this trigger word out and be done with it."

Sister Krayj drew her nonLee, then stood me at one end of the car and Father Mark at the other, with herself standing near me.

"What's going on?" asked Bee.

"Nothing to worry about," she assured him—and Snail,

who was frowning from the opposite door. "Okay, what's the word?" she asked Father Mark.

Father Mark had gone a little pale. This test was clearly very important for his peace of mind. "Margaret's parish. Margaret's home town..."

Something sure to be mentioned in both our presences sooner or later.

Sister Krayj nodded, then said very clearly and deliberately, "Salperton." Nothing happened, so she said, just to be thorough, "Salperton-under-Fell."

Still nothing.

Everyone stood and waited for a bit longer. Bane's frown began to ease slightly, and a faint smile of relief spread over Father Mark's face.

"How do you feel?" asked Sister Krayj. "Any different?"

He shook his head. "No. I feel the same. Well, I just *had* to check."

Sister Krayj casually slipped the nonLee into her pocket, still watching Father Mark intently. Again nothing happened, and she relaxed. "Well, you were right. But worth checking, yes."

"Come on," I said, "Let's finish our coffee."

Father Mark gave me a side-long look as he sat down again at the table. "Sorry, Margaret."

"It's not your fault. Though you should've told Eduardo you wanted to check it out."

"That's what I was apologizing for."

"Look." Sister Krayj gave him a gentle poke in the arm. "How about we slip along to his car in a minute and bring him up to speed, hmm? Get it in before Snail and Bee, at least," she added dryly.

"You're right. I should have before, I just..." He closed his eyes for a moment. "I didn't want to be shipped off on the next boat to Africa. Really wanted to see everyone."

And you couldn't allow yourself to believe they might have turned you back into a killer?

He emptied his cup in one last big swig, put it on the table and stood up. "I'll go tell him. Coming, Pussycat?" he asked Sister Krayj. She nodded, and it felt a bit like we were on Liberations again, with the two of them second and third in command of the team.

"Ah... Eduardo expressed an intention to throw a blanket on the floor and sleep," said Snail. "He was up all night supervising Margo's new chef. Who I imagine is also asleep back there. Just tell him first thing tomorrow, *oui?* It'll be late when we get home."

"We promise we'll let you speak to him first," said Bee in his deep voice, still looking extremely suspicious about what had been going on. As well he might.

"I can hardly wait," murmured Father Mark, making Sister Krayj snort slightly.

It was indeed late when the glittering lights of Rome appeared on the horizon. We murmured sleepy goodbyes and scattered to our respective accommodation blocks. Jon walked with us to the door of our apartment, though, and stepped inside for a moment. "Thank goodness that was a false alarm, earlier," he said quietly. "D'you think Sister Krayj could've stopped him?"

"He obviously thought so," said Bane. "I wouldn't underestimate Sister Krayj."

"And she had a nonLee," I pointed out.

"Of course she did," said Jon. "Oh dear, poor Father Mark. What a horrible thing to wonder about."

"He should've told Eduardo," snapped Bane, rather less sympathetically.

"Oh, come on, Bane," I said. "He told him. Just left out that he thought it worth testing that one thing."

"Kind of important one thing! What if you'd mentioned Salperton back at the embassy, before the others arrived?"

"He didn't think anything would happen, and it didn't. You saw... witnessed... that. It's just the sort of horrendous possibility that makes one ultra-paranoid, isn't it?"

"S'pose."

"Well, good night," said Jon.

"Night, Jon."

"Night, Jon."

"Tony was a smart boy. We're not just saying that, he won every prize at school. He was funny, too. Not one of these swotty kids. Everyone loved him. Everyone said he'd be the one to find the cure for metastasized cancer—you know, the type that's spread too far to be fixed by a transplant. He'd have done it, too. But he went off to school on Sorting day, so excited that he'd soon be a New Adult—and he never came home. They said he had this tiny hole in his heart and they took him. We never saw him again.

People say to us all the time, what a waste, what a shame. And I say to them: it's nothing to do with waste. That's not why it's wrong! It's the fact that he was a good boy, an innocent boy who'd done nothing wrong, and he did not deserve to die!"

'Mrs. N.'—quoted in a blog post on 'The Impatient Gardener'

The first clock chimed two in the afternoon.

"What!" I looked up from my computer. "That can't be the time!" I'd only opened it up to post a blog entry I'd prudently pre-written before I went away, and to check what was what—but an absolute mountain of comments and flagged-up blog posts had greeted me. "I simply must go and see Lucas; he'll think you accidentally left me in Brussels!"

"Oh, let's have lunch first!" protested Bane.

Ah. Yes. Lunch had got forgotten too. "Okay, let's throw some pasta together."

Bane had been rather quiet this morning—not just, I feared, because I'd been so busy. *Lord, please don't let him get depressed again, now all the excitement of the trip is over...* I suppose we'd all been on a bit of a high in Brussels, and this was the come down.

The baby would cheer him up. But I didn't really want to give him such news over a hasty bowl of pasta. It ought to be special. I'd cook a really nice dinner, for just the two of us, and then I'd tell him. But... I eyed my laptop glumly... it would have to wait another day or two.

Jon arrived when we'd almost finished eating, and I couldn't help feeling relieved that I didn't have to leave Bane alone. The way he'd been in Brussels, I wouldn't even have thought about it, but... there was that quietness about him, this morning. And although so much had happened since, it was only just a week since he'd snapped out of that awful depression.

Jon was bursting to share something, I could tell.

"Fancy going along to the nonLee range, Bane?" he said, would-be casually.

Bane frowned, snorting in disbelief. "Uh, *no*. I can waste my time just as well right here."

"Eduardo's put in some new targets," said Jon, rather smugly. "He figured out how to shield speakers from nonLee blast. So now the targets breathe... and chat... and shuffle their feet. You can even set how noisy you want them to be. Want to go and try them?"

My heart lifted as Jon spoke—what a fantastic idea of Eduardo's!—then fell as Bane's face went hard and closed.

"Not really," said Bane shortly. "I'd have thought Eduardo would have had better things to do right now than pretending I'll ever be anything other than a danger to others with a gun in my hand."

Jon looked taken aback. "Well, right *now*, maybe. That's the whole point of *practicing!*"

"*You* don't need to practice," said Bane. "We all know *you* could hit those targets. So why didn't you come on the Liberations? Because you'd *still* have been a liability. And it doesn't matter how much *I* practice, I'll still be a liability too! So no thanks. I don't want Eduardo's pity!"

From the look on Jon's face, he wanted to punch Bane. I kind of knew how he felt. But he just said, "Clearly you don't need it. You seem to have plenty of self-pity of your own."

Bane scowled but didn't reply. Jon being Jon, he didn't take himself off in a huff, thank goodness, and the subject was dropped, but it was almost three o'clock before I was heading for Lucas's room.

I was still pleased when I ran into Father Mark and Sister Krayj. Together, so... just back from seeing Eduardo? Father Mark had looked so tired, he'd probably slept very late.

"Everything okay? Had your knuckles wrapped?"

"There was a certain amount of sarcasm," said Father Mark, "but I'm forgiven."

"Eduardo thought the test was both satisfactory and appropriate; he'd just have liked to know beforehand," expanded Sister Krayj.

"No surprises there, then."

"I have to see the shrinks, though," said Father Mark rather glumly. "Get myself generally checked out."

"Sounded like he'd told you that already," said Sister Krayj.

"He had, but I thought it might not happen. No chance of that now."

"Well, it'll do you good," I said. "Weren't you the one always trying to get Bane to see them?"

"Hoisted by my own petard," he muttered dryly. "Ah well, where are you off to?"

"I'm overdue to visit Lucas. Actually, you two would probably sympathize with each other a lot."

"Uh, with whom?"

"Oh, they were pretty selective about what news they gave you, I take it? Lucas Everington. He turned up here alive a bit over a month and a half ago. You're in a heck of a lot better shape than he is, thank goodness, but he is recovering slowly."

Father Mark looked understandably surprised by this information. "That man survived? Well, well."

"If we let Margo get to him before he goes on hunger strike again, I'll bring you up to date," said Sister Krayj.

Lucas opened the door almost the moment I knocked, and looked decidedly relieved to see me.

"Hi, Lucas, I'm sorry I didn't get here earlier. My blog has gone insane after what happened the evening before last. Did you see it?" Unicorn had said he'd make sure Lucas had a TV for the debate.

Lucas nodded, eyeing me rather intently. "You...

forgave... assassin?"

"Well, I'm certainly doing my best." Georg Friedrich had been smuggled out of the Vatican before I was even out of bed this morning. He'd be on route to Africa by now, and his new life as, no doubt, prison cook.

"Look... happy."

Huh? "Well, I am really glad the Lord showed me how to save him. But something else happened as well, something wonderful but totally unexpected. We've got a dear friend back from the dead."

He turned his head slightly to one side—oh, trying to figure out if I meant...

"Not *literally*, it's not the Last Day. It just feels like he's back from the dead, 'cause we *thought* he was dead and it turns out he *isn't*."

Lucas thought about that. "Very happy?"

"Yes."

"Good. Never mind late." He offered me the Office book. Office first, chat later. Probably stressed after the last three days.

By the time I'd finished reading, he seemed much more relaxed. We talked about one of his plants for a bit; he'd been worried about it before we left, then he asked about my back-from-the-dead friend, so I told him all about it. "...And there isn't anything wrong, and we've got Father Mark back, so it's wonderful!"

Lucas didn't look as though he thought it was wonderful. He caught my wrist and spoke intently. "*Be careful.*"

"Be careful? Of what, of Father Mark? He's not going to hurt me, Lucas. We tested it."

Lucas shook his head; he looked very unhappy indeed. "No one knew he was alive?"

"No. Well, only the EuroGov."

"And they *let him go?* Not kill him?"

"For *good press*, Lucas."

Lucas bit at his lip, frowning in the way that said he was trying to remember something. "Mark. Priest. Mark... I know this name. Former dismantler trainee, then Resistance assassin, now priest? Mark Tarrow?"

I blinked. "Yes, that's his full name. That's him."

"They ask me much about him. Want me to say I arrange with him... the escape. They *hate* this... Mark Tarrow."

I frowned. I suppose they would, if they'd identified him—clearly they had. "Makes sense. He was the one who came with Bane to rescue me from... the Lab." I said the words cautiously, but while Lucas screwed up his face for a moment, he didn't flip out. "*He* did certainly help arrange the escape."

"Yes, *hate* him," he said emphatically. "They don't let this man go. Unless for some *great* advantage."

"Yeah, like a *ton* of good press! Good press is worth votes, and votes are worth more than *anything* just now! Lucas, trust me, it totally makes sense!"

Lucas shook his head stubbornly. "No. Greater advantage. And greater revenge on him. Something more. Worse. Trust *me.*"

"I trust you, Lucas; I just think you're reading too much into this. We checked he wasn't going to hurt me, remember?"

He pointed to me and drew a finger across his throat, falling back into his sign language in his frustration. But he didn't have enough signs and went back to words, his mix of English and Latin—increasingly Latin, with the odd similar Italian word slipping in.

"Obvious. Killing you is obvious thing they want! Know you'll think of that. Know..." he waved at the CCTV camera, "know camera fellow think of that. So maybe subtler. But *something.*"

"Look, perhaps they thought they *had* programmed Father Mark. But it didn't work. We've proved that." I glanced at my watch. "I'll have to be off, anyway. I'm on the kitchen prep rotation today."

I got up to go but he grabbed my wrist again, his hand like a bony vice. "Be *careful!*"

I looked into his fearful eyes. He was still very unwell, and here I was arguing with him like he was just another person. I put a hand gently over his. "I'll be careful, Lucas. I promise, okay?"

He allowed me to draw my arm from his grasp, but I

could feel his anxious gaze on me until I closed the door.

Soon I was hanging my wedding ring on the ring tree in the kitchen and struggling into a pair of rubber gloves. Lots of potatoes awaited me in the sink. To work, then. The British cooks were on duty. Shepherd's pie. Perhaps Bane and Jon would come to the cafeteria for supper.

Would Bane and I bring our little one down for meals sometimes in the future? Of course we would... I pictured us leading a... little boy? little girl? between us to the hatch— could almost hear the little voice pleading, "I can hold my own tray, Daddy, I can..." and Bane saying, "Well, you've got to hold it steady. Careful... Got it?" and hovering defensively as our proud little one walked to...

"Margo? Earth to Margo? We've finished." The cheery voice of one of my fellow cooks dragged me from my daydreaming.

"Oh... right."

When everything was washed up and wiped down, I replaced my ring and headed off up the stone staircase to (hopefully) fetch the other two. Met Father Mark coming along the corridor at the top.

"Early bird," I remarked. "Did you not have lunch?"

He glanced over my head at the empty corridor, then he looked at me—instinct screamed: *DANGER*...

I spun around and I ran for the stairs. My mind, wailing protests, waited for the hurt cry of "Margaret!"

No cry. Just running footsteps.

Catching up fast.

17

STANDING ORDERS

I drove my feet into the tiles with every scrap of effort I could muster, running as I'd once run before—towards a small, open wall gate.

Almost at the stairs...

Footsteps so close...

I swung round the corner, leaping for the third step... Father Mark's hand clamped around my arm, pulling me up short, swinging me into the wall with a painful thud... I twisted frantically, yanking with all my strength... off balance, his hand opened, releasing me—I grabbed for the rail... missed...

Tumbling... ceiling, floor, rails spinning in front of me... pain stabbing me with each impact... turn of the stairs coming up... a glimpse of Father Mark racing after me, empty-eyed... I stumbled half to my feet, pushed off the wall and tried to reach the next flight only to stagger and crash into a small table—too dizzy, I've got to *move*... Father Mark was almost on me, reaching... I dived for the banister, threw myself over... dropped... *O-Lord-further-than-I-remembered...*

Smack...

Pain shot through my feet and hands... *a rush of displaced air above me...* I pushed off with my mercifully unbroken ankles as Father Mark landed behind and somehow I ran... sort of... winded, sense of balance betraying me...

Gasping for air...

Footsteps closer.

Cafeteria door coming up.

Breathing behind me, any moment he'd have me...

I slammed through the doors at full tilt, not slowing 'til I stood in the middle of a group of early birds and kitchen prep people. Spun around, my heart thundering in my chest.

Father Mark hurtled through the doors, saw all the people and pulled up with a jerk. Shook his head as though to clear it, blinked, rubbed his temples. Looked up and saw me, staring at him, my eyes wide with terror and exertion. The color drained from his face, leaving it sickly white. Turning abruptly, he strode through the doors and away.

"Are you okay, Margaret?" someone asked.

"Oh, fine, fine. Just... just racing Father Mark to supper."

I stayed, alternately poking some shepherd's pie around on a plate and rubbing my belly protectively, until I could leave with a group headed back to my block and my floor. God help me, Lucas's paranoia had probably just saved my life! Both our lives. But if I simply called out the guard on Father Mark, he might get hurt—or *they* might. I'd get Eduardo to come around, and I'd tell him face to face—he might not overreact if I was sat right there in front of him, safe and sound.

My hands were beginning to shake as I let myself into the apartment. Bane raised his head, relief mingling with hurt on his face.

"The vegetables put up a fight?" he asked, would-be casually.

Jon was making his deeply-indented notes on a notepad, no doubt working on his speech again.

"I'm sorry I'm a little late." My voice didn't really shake, but they both turned towards me at once.

"What happened?"

"I think..." I glanced at the now carefully locked door. "I think we may..." I opened the drawer and transferred the nonLee to my pocket, checking the charge. "...have a problem after all."

"What sort of problem?" asked Bane.

Jon, clearly determining what I was doing, made the connection. "Father Mark?"

The doorbell rang. I tiptoed up to look through the peephole. Father Mark. Well, at least he hadn't gone and jumped off the roof.

"Is that him?" asked Bane.

I took another look. Still white-faced, but it looked like

him in his head. I took out the nonLee and snapped off the safety catch, then held it behind my back. Operated the latch as silently as I could, said, "Come in, Father Mark," then skipped back to put most of the furniture between myself and the door.

Father Mark came in very slowly and closed the door behind him, as though deliberately avoiding sudden movements. Went and sat on the sofa.

"Are you okay, Margaret?" he whispered, his eyes running over me fearfully.

"I'm fine," I said. Bruised, but I hardly needed to say that. He put his head in his hands.

"Problem?" demanded Bane. "What problem?"

"Well, I can't be certain what his intentions were, but just now he met me in a deserted corridor and I was so frightened I ran away. Ran like hell, in fact."

"Thank God," whispered Father Mark. "Thank God you ran! Why *did* you run?"

"Lucas had got me primed to listen to my instincts, thanks be to God. I expect normally my brain would've interfered until it was too late."

Father Mark looked sick and dropped his face to his hands again.

"Did he hurt you?" demanded Bane.

"I'm okay," I said quickly.

"So... why did he go for you then and not yesterday?" asked Jon.

I'd been thinking about that. "Sister Krayj was there on the train. But the corridor was empty just now."

"I think they've made it so the programming doesn't kick in unless I've a very strong chance of success, clever bastards," whispered Father Mark. He'd also been thinking about it. "I could feel myself... not myself exactly... something... analyzing the situation."

"It wasn't you," I said firmly. "It was like a stranger was looking out of your eyes. That's what tipped off my brighter, more primitive self."

"But..." Bane's hand twitched towards the place where he'd carried his nonLee on the Liberations, and his head turned unconsciously towards the phone and the panic button. "How could you come here now! Sister Krayj's not h..." he broke off, looking petrified. He'd never thought he could beat Father Mark, even before.

"No," said Father Mark, in a horribly calm voice. "But Margaret's got a nonLee behind her back, and if she's the smart girl I've always known, the safety catch isn't on."

Was that, *Margaret, if it's on, take it off?*

"She has? Oh..." Bane let out a long, relieved breath.

"So... why *are* you here, Father Mark?" I asked warily. "I mean, I'm sorry, but there's no question now, you're going to have to see a doctor... *Father Mark!*"

At the word 'doctor' his head jerked back and his entire face screwed up in pain—after a moment the spasm seemed to pass and he held his head in his hands again. When he finally looked up at me, all color had gone from his cheeks. "That give you some idea?"

"They've..." aghast, I groped for vocabulary from Hollywood thrillers, "uh... implanted that response in you. To d..." I broke off as he winced in anticipation.

He held up his hands, palm up, looking bewildered. His brow was damp with sweat. "I... don't remember it! But they must've done. It's not *natural.* I tried, Margo, that's the first place I tried to..." He broke off, breathing hard. "I can't even talk about go... Lord help me!" He clutched his head some more and finally managed to go on. "Then I tried to go to Eduardo so he could take me to... but I couldn't even do that. So... so eventually I decided I would just... just come and have a chat with you..."

"Come and have a chat?" exploded Bane, still looking ready to throw himself between us, much good it would do. "Are you out of your mind?"

"Apparently, *yes,* intermittently!" Father Mark's eyes were wild, all his calm shredding away. "Margaret, I was able to come and *chat* to you," he was staring at me, hard, "do you understand me?"

My mind still reeled in horror at the situation, and what had been done to him. But he had a plan and I was supposed to be catching on... Oh. Yes. He'd told *himself* he was coming to chat with me... knowing what I'd be holding if I let him in.

I steeled myself, not sure how much control he still had. "I understand you."

So did that other thing inside him. It slid into his eyes and he was off the sofa and coming—I swung the nonLee forward and fired and immediately fired again... When he dropped to the ground, he was halfway to me.

"Margo!" cried Bane.

"I'm fine," I gasped. "Lord have mercy, he's quick!"

I half-stumbled, half-ran to the phone, because I didn't know if I'd hit that fast-moving target both times, hesitated momentarily between Eduardo and the hospital, then phoned Eduardo. "Eduardo! They did program Father Mark, only they were too clever for us! He's unconscious on the floor and he needs securing before he comes around..."

Eduardo said a word he'd never used in my hearing before, and turned from the phone to bark several orders sending guards and Doctor Frederick to my room instantly. Then demanded, "Are you safe?"

"I've a nonLee in my hand."

"Get out of there, for pity's sake!"

"No. He might come round, and I'd rather know where he is if he does!"

Eduardo snarled and hung up, then burst in an improbably short time later, hard on Bumblebee's heels. Bee was already covering Father Mark's unconscious body with his nonLee as though it were a conscious—and rabid—tiger.

Eduardo grabbed my shoulders and walked me out the door; pushed me into Unicorn's grasp when he came rushing up. "Take her to... to your apartment. Don't answer the door to anyone until I've phoned to say we've got Father Mark safely locked down in the hospital, okay?"

"Yes, sir."

"Hey, wait up!" Bane hurried after me. "I'm coming!"

"And me." Jon actually ventured to catch Bane's hand and tow him along.

Unicorn hurried me off, but deigned to wait a few moments for them before shutting the apartment door. His exertions didn't seem to be causing him pain, so he really was almost entirely better, a small plus point in what was otherwise shaping up as a really bad day.

Bane gathered me into his arms as soon as we were sitting on the sofa. "Oh, what a nightmare!" he muttered. "I was so glad he was okay. I mean... I still am, but..."

It was awkward. Was it just.

Unicorn was standing with his nonLee in his hand, attention divided between the door and the window.

"I was afraid Eduardo would overreact," I said. "Clearly I was right."

Unicorn shot me a look. "An assassin of Mark Tarrow's caliber is after you, and you think Eduardo's overreacting? Think again, Margo."

I shifted uncomfortably in Bane's arms. Even after what'd happened on the stairs, and just now, it was still hard to believe that Father Mark, the priest I'd known and loved since I was fourteen, could really hurt me.

We waited. We discussed the awful situation a few times, and then we waited some more. When Bane and Jon started to work on the next Braille talk, I took my knotted cord rosary from my pocket and said one for Father Mark, my hand straying to my belly whenever Unicorn's blue eyes weren't turned in my direction. Father Mark and the baby. I hadn't hit my stomach *very* hard... *had I?* I just wasn't sure: the tumble down the stairs was a painful blur. But the baby had been okay after... after what happened with Bane. It would be okay now. *Please Lord? Please, please, please, please, please...*

Finally the phone rang. Unicorn picked it up.

"That's Eduardo," he told us, after hanging up. "He's coming now."

"Thank goodness," I muttered. "I haven't even posted my blog yet, and I'm exhausted!"

Eduardo arrived pretty quickly, and Unicorn let him in.

"Well, Father Mark is in Mr. Everington's old room and very well secured," Eduardo said.

"How is he?"

"He came round as we were moving him. Got one look at Doctor Frederick and went..." Eduardo grimaced. "I was afraid he was having a stroke or something. Doctor Frederick had to put him under."

"He was fine when he talked about having to see a

shrink earlier," I said.

"But he wasn't talking about seeing a shrink about the programming, was he? They've done some sort of job on him, all right."

I was alarmed by his expression. "But... the psychiatrists will be able to cure him, won't they?"

"If you know of anyone here with expertise in military mind-programming, please let me know. The doctors we've got will do what they can. We'll just have to hope it's enough."

My heart sank. I didn't like the sound of that. The Underground got every kind of defector: surely there was *someone* we could get in from Africa?

"Oh, you're free to move around normally," Eduardo told me. "Don't go trying to visit Father Mark yet, though. Not until Doctor Frederick's got him stabilized." He turned to Unicorn.

"Jack, enter it into the standing orders of all guard units. Anyone sees Father Mark Tarrow near Margaret's apartment or near any place Margaret is known to be or out of the hospital, period, they shoot on sight and they keep shooting until they see him go down. No counting shots, no challenge, no hesitation, understood?"

Unicorn nodded and turned to leave—I caught his arm. "You can't do that! They could kill him!"

Eduardo eyed me stonily. "Margaret, how many young guards who just happened to be standing between you and Father Mark do you want to die, just because they hesitated? I will inform Father Mark of these orders as soon as he is well enough, and I'm sure they will be a great comfort to him."

"Well, they're not to *me!*" I snapped, but I let Unicorn go.

"I have to think about the guards too, Margo," said Eduardo, with a shrug, and followed Unicorn out.

True, but... "Stony-hearted bastard!" I couldn't help muttering, once he was out of earshot.

"He is right, Margo," said Jon. "Father Mark would rather die than hurt you, or anyone else."

"And the guards wouldn't stand a chance against him,"

said Bane. "I mean, don't get me wrong, they've got the guts, but they haven't got the experience, have they?"

"But it's not Father Mark's *fault*," I protested. "It would be wrong to kill him."

"He'd thank us."

"*I don't care!*"

"Come on, Margo," said Bane glumly. "Let's go home. Don't get all upset."

I swallowed. I *was* beginning to feel quite upset. Blast. Suppose I was just going to be emotional for the next nine months. Oh well. It was more than worth it.

What had woken me? I lay still for a moment. Bane's breathing was deep and even beside me—all the excitement and stress of the day had tired him too.

I began to roll over to cuddle up to him and go to sleep again—stopped, wincing. I hurt. In a lot of places. But it wasn't Father Mark's fault. He was in a much worse state than I was. I directed my annoyance where it belonged—at the EuroGov. When I ran my hand over my stomach, it only felt a little sore in a couple of places... better than the rest of me.

I was about to finish rolling over—more gently—when I felt a trickle of wetness between my legs. My breath caught—it felt like my heart did too. I wanted to lie down and pull the covers over me and hope when I woke up again it was just a dream. But I felt all too awake.

Hands beginning to shake, I pushed back the sheets and slid from the bed. Bane didn't stir as I tiptoed to the bathroom. Once inside I flicked the light on and locked the door.

"*Please, Lord, please, please, please...*" I whispered desperately, pretty much diving onto the toilet and dragging my pants down.

Scarlet with blood.

"*No...!*" My voice climbed before I remembered Bane and clamped a hand over my mouth to quell the sound. He mustn't know! Not... not now...

My throat was closing up and tears were squeezing from my eyes... I made a last-ditch effort to stay calm. How much blood was there? Perhaps... perhaps it wasn't...

I looked again. It would've been quite light if it was my monthly, but seeing that there wasn't meant to be *any* blood for another eight months or so...

Plop.

Oh God, was that my baby? I leapt up and peered into the toilet. A blood droplet was diffusing through the water. Not the baby, but... what was I supposed to *do?* My baby was going to... was going to come *out,* and...

I lost it then, I just lost it. I dragged the towel from the towel rail and shoved it under me and then I lay there and cried, one corner of the towel balled up in my mouth to muffle the sound. I'd never felt so helpless, even when strapped to that gurney waiting to be dismantled—there was nothing I could do, nothing anyone could do, *nothing...*

Time passed, dimly I heard clocks strike a few times and I attempted, sporadically, to get myself together. But my aching heart was still lodged firmly in my chest and my body seemed determined to cry it right out.

The chiming of another clock... Four o'clock. How long had I been in here? Surely Bane would miss me soon and wake up... He didn't sleep on such a hair trigger now as he had during our flight across Europe, but I must've been in here for *hours...*

The baby is gone, Margo. Bane isn't. All I could do now was to protect Bane, and right now that meant not letting him find out about this. Not allowing anything to tip him back into that black depression...

I managed to pry my aching body from the floor at last. There was a little more blood on the towel, and... a small bloody clot. My heart caught in my throat. That must be it. It was so tiny... I crouched down as close as I could and tried to see, but I could make out nothing. Far too early.

It was still my baby. Our baby. I couldn't just... what? Flush it down the toilet? Throw it in the bin? Even the thought made my chest clench up.

Right. Okay. What was I going to do?

Ten minutes later, cleaned up and clutching our largest serving spoon and a wooden knick-knack box, I was tiptoeing out into the corridor.

Turning from closing the door, I started. Unicorn stood

there watching me curiously, his vivid eyes shadowed in the dim night-time illumination.

"What are you doing here?" I demanded.

"I'm on guard tonight—and I might ask you the same thing."

"I live here!"

"I meant *in the corridor*. What's that?" He pointed to the box.

The word 'nothing' tried to strangle me. I didn't reply.

After looking at me rather closely for a moment he just said, "I'll have to accompany you wherever you're going, you understand."

"But Father Mark is secured..."

"Eduardo's orders, Margo. He's probably just going to put a Swiss Guard by your door from now on, but for tonight, you've got me."

Did Eduardo really think Father Mark could get loose? Or was putting U on guard tonight, although he hadn't actually been cleared of 'physically active duties' yet, just Eduardo's way of expressing confidence in him, after he'd had to stay behind instead of going to Brussels...

"Fine," I muttered, heading off along the corridor.

"Uh, Margo? Where are you going?"

"To the gardens. I've got something to do."

Unicorn raised an eyebrow a fraction and directed a meaningful look at my feet. I looked as well. *Bare. Oh, Margo, you idiot...* For a moment I stood, my mind at a standstill... if I went back in, I'd surely wake Bane...

"Well, it's not cold, is it?" I managed at last, and hurried off before Unicorn could reply. He followed, of course.

Darkness closed in all around as I left the buildings, though in the distance the Vatican wall was well illuminated, the lights of Rome twinkling behind it. I should've brought a flashlight... too late. I plowed on anyway, the dew-damp grass chilling my feet, despite it being almost June. Before I could fall over a gravestone, light stabbed the darkness. I glanced back: Unicorn had produced a flashlight from somewhere. I carried on, too drained to muster thanks, or any comment at all. I knew where I was going. There was a little secluded grassy spot surrounded by a semi-circle of bushes... yes, here.

Unicorn shone his flashlight in helpful silence as I knelt by the flower bed, laying the box beside me, and began to dig in the loose earth with the spoon, clawing the soil to one side with my hands.

A movement beside me... Unicorn had opened the box and was unfolding the hankies. "Don't touch that!" I said, so intensely that he took his hand away.

"Margo, that looks like blood. What on earth...?" He broke off as I carefully, so carefully, refolded the cloth around its insubstantial contents and closed the box. "Oh Margo... *you weren't*... were you?"

"I was," I choked. "I *was*." I turned and attacked the hole again.

"Margo, I'm so sorry. *So, so sorry...* "

I looked at Unicorn again, startled by the depth of contrition in his voice. Oh... of course... he would feel this triply, not only as our friend, but as part of our security, and even more so as Eduardo's likely successor...

"It wasn't your fault, U," I said thickly. "It was... it was the EuroGov."

It was Father Mark, said a little voice of unreason. *He knocked you down the stairs...*

Only because the EuroGov made him, I told that little voice, as firmly as I could. *He's just as much a victim as... as my...*

I went back to spooning soil. The hole was nearly ready. No one would be digging all that deep, not so close to the foot of this bush. I squared off the bottom as well as I could with my awkward implement, and gently lowered the box into place.

"Do you... want to have a priest?" Unicorn's voice betrayed something of the helplessness I'd been feeling.

"Yes," I said softly. "I do. But... after I tell Bane. But I can't tell him quite yet. And Father Mark definitely cannot know. I've got to keep this quiet. For now. Promise you won't tell anyone?"

He looked upset. "If no one knows, Margo, that will be very hard on you..."

"*You* know. You can pray for me, right? Anyway, with

everything that's going on at the moment, this is the least of our worries, isn't it?" Hard to even say that, but I had to be strong, for Bane, for the vote...

"Well, *yes*, but... promise that if you need to talk about this, you will come to me, or you will... talk to Jon, perhaps?"

"I am not telling Jon about this before Bane!"

Unicorn pulled a face. "I suppose not. But..."

"Okay, I promise."

"Then so do I. And I will. Pray."

I turned my attention back to the little box in the hole. Kissed my muddy fingers and transferred the kiss to the box.

"I love you, little baby," I whispered. "And so does your daddy, even if he doesn't know it yet..." My voice broke on the last word and I had to squeeze my eyes closed.

When I opened them again and reached for the heap of soil, Unicorn offered me something. A blue and white flower from a nearby bush. I managed a nod of thanks as I accepted it, then reached in and laid it on the little box. It was only the work of a couple of moments to push the soil back into place and make the area look undisturbed. I sat for a moment, then, feeling horribly empty.

But the semi-ceremony of the burial had steadied me a little. *Lord, please look after our baby. I suppose that's a silly thing to say, of course you will, but I have to say it anyway...*

Time to go. I was desperate to get back to Bane. But as we passed the door to Kyle's room, I couldn't help stopping. I wanted a hug from my mum so badly that just the thought brought tears to my eyes. Mum wasn't here. Kyle was...

I found myself stepping up to the door and tapping softly. And rather nervously. He'd been so angry after that terrible row... But what had Pope Cornelius said, *if we both wanted to make up...* I certainly did.

There was no reply, though. I tapped again, then yet again, a bit louder.

"Do you know where he is?" I asked Unicorn, my heart sinking.

"I'm not certain, Margo," he said gently. "Adoration, maybe? I think he might be on the rota tonight."

Oh... What was I thinking, anyway? Bane really *should*

be the first person to know about this... *Bane*... I had to get home.

I'd no sooner closed the door behind me when I heard Bane calling, "*Margo?*" He sounded scared. I rushed across the living room and opened the bedroom door.

"I'm here, Bane... I'm sorry, I went for a walk. Couldn't sleep. Unicorn insisted on trailing along behind, Eduardo's orders."

"Oh." Bane sounded reassured. And it certainly wouldn't occur to him to be jealous of U. "But... *why*, Margo? You've never gone for a walk at this time before!"

"I'm sorry, I was lying awake for hours. I just really needed to go for a walk. I thought I'd get back before you woke up."

"Well, I only woke up just now. Another few moments and I'd have called the guards."

"I'm so sorry, Bane. I didn't think."

"Well, did it work? Are you coming back to bed?" He still sounded rather disgruntled.

I wanted to go straight to him, but I was so wet and muddy. "I hope so. I'm just going to run to the toilet."

Bane sighed and flopped back into bed. "Okay..."

"Your feet are freezing!" he grumbled, when I slipped into the bed at last, trying not to grab hold of him like a depressive limpet. "You know," he added, with a suggestive nuzzle, "you really *should* have woken me. I can think of a much better way to loosen you up..."

My mood lightened, just a fraction, at the thought of trying again. Then fell. It wouldn't be the *same* baby... It would *never* be the same baby.

No point even thinking about it until I'd stopped bleeding, anyway.

"If you don't mind, Bane," I said softly, "I'd rather just have a cuddle."

Bane stopped nuzzling and gathered me close. "Come here, then, cold feet and all." I nestled my head under his chin and he rested his cheek on my hair. "This Father Mark business is so awful, isn't it? I was so glad he was alive. I mean, I still am... it's just..." He trailed off miserably.

He sounded so down it made my heart thud slightly in

fear. He'd remained comparatively up-beat since our return—but only comparatively. The confidence and excitement of Brussels was only a memory. Even with Karen's help, I kept worrying that his mood was slipping again. He must not find out. Not yet.

If only Father Mark had stayed dead, that irrational voice whispered. *Then our baby would still be alive.*

Shut up, I replied. *I'm glad Father Mark's alive.*

I am.

Am, am, am.

29 days

Did none of you read Mrs. N's conclusion? All these comments, oh, what a shame, now there's no cure for M-type cancer, perhaps IQ screening should count for more during the Sorting tests... Shame on you! Every child deserves to live! Whether they're the brainiest child in school, or the least intelligent, or the tiniest clump of cells in a mother's womb. They deserve life! Why can't you get that into your thick heads?

Margaret Verrall—blog post, 'The Impatient Gardener'

"Jon?" said Bane in a rather small voice, when Jon came round the next day.

"Um-hm?"

"Do you... want to go down to the nonLee range and practice?"

After a beat, Jon just said, "Yeah, of course."

Once they decamped—Bane muttering, "And yes, I'm an idiot, and I apologize," as they trooped out, I headed off to Lucas's room.

"Here..." When Lucas opened the door, I held out a flowery white fuchsia. Lucas suddenly looked like my favorite person in the world, compared to how my subconscious felt about Father Mark. His face brightened and he accepted it at once. "I owe you an apology. Father Mark's programmed to the eyes, poor thing. I think the fact you wouldn't let it go probably saved my life."

His eyes went wide, straying back from the plant to me. He caught my hand with his free one. "Safe?"

"I'm fine." *I* was... *Physically*... Somehow I kept my voice steady. "I listened to my instincts and I ran away, and I'm fine. Father Mark's fine too... sort of." *Not that I care, right now...* "He's in the hospital, anyway. Very secure."

Lucas frowned. Hesitated. Looked down at the new plant for a moment, as though he'd like to bury himself in its care. But finally placed it on the table. I'd never seen him part with a new one so quickly. And this was a fuchsia!

"I... look. Father Mark?" He made the gesture for look and pointed around the room. I frowned—he was nervous and it was making him inarticulate.

"You want to see Father Mark?"

He gestured again. "Secure? I look?"

I got it. "Oh, his room. You want to check if it's secure. I'm sure it is; I wouldn't worry..." I broke off and bit my lip, remembering those orders Eduardo had given. *I do care...*

I phoned Eduardo to clear it, but soon we were heading up to the hospital. Lucas walked very fast, head down, and if anyone greeted us he ran away as though expecting an attack, and waited for me around the next corner.

"They're not going to hurt you, Lucas."

He shook his head and huddled close to the wall until the next group of people had passed. "Look like... people like you. All people."

"*People like me*? What do you mean?"

"Would have been these people." He flapped a hand up the corridor. "Look like *them. All* them."

Suddenly I got it. "They look like reAssignees," I said tonelessly. "Or remind you of who they might've been in the future..."

He closed his eyes and went off at a run again, opened them in time to avoid a wall, but only slowed down when we passed a window with a plant in it.

Ah well, good thing the word 'reAssignees' hadn't put him in a worse state. Actually... this was the first unambiguous sign of remorse I'd seen. Well, actually, our "Vote No" campaign was very happily quoting the "anti-Sorting" speech he'd made at his trial, and somehow I'd understood he was sorry, but still....

Snail was on guard outside that room again, when we arrived, only this time he stood looking straight through the window, and the curtains were gone.

Reluctantly, I looked through as well. Lord! *Secure?* Father Mark was chained to the bloody bed! Thick padded cuffs circled his wrists and from the attachments on the footboard, there were more on his ankles.

"Isn't that a bit extreme?" I choked.

Snail didn't answer. Really was in guard mode. Father Mark's eyes were closed, his dark brown hair damp and sweat-tousled, hard to tell if he was awake. My nastier side was glad he was looking such a mess. Seeing him all healthy and well-kempt would be a kick in the teeth when my baby... *No, Margo, you cannot think about this. Lock it away!*

"*Fine*," I told Snail. "Lucas has permission to go in there and have a look, but I expect you know that?" Snail was wearing a wristCell, of course.

Snail nodded, murmured, "*Bien sûr*, of course, Margo," then stepped to the door, turned the key in the big new lock that'd been fitted, and opened it.

Lucas looked pretty stressed by now—maybe considering curling up against the nearest wall and pretending he was somewhere else?

"If you were him, Lucas..." I pointed through the window at Father Mark, "how would you escape, hmm?"

His gaze sharpened—reminded why he'd made this foray into the frightening world, he stepped through the door.

He was quite a while. Circling the room, he looked at pretty much everything, checked the windows, even lay on the floor on each side of the bed and gazed around—seeing what Father Mark could see? He examined the cuffs and the chains and the attachments and Father Mark and... well, everything. Father Mark opened his eyes after a while and watched him, but his eyes were so glazed it was clear he wasn't entirely with it.

Finally Lucas came out again. "With cuffs, good. No cuffs, no good."

Blast! Now Father Mark really would be stuck with the

things. Still... better cuffed to a bed than pumped full of not-so-nonLethal-in-quantity charges.

Why do you even care? whispered that little voice.

Because it wasn't *his fault,* I answered firmly, and said out loud, "Thank you." Lucas's conclusion might be unwelcome, but he'd made such an effort. From the look in his eyes, the best thanks I could give him would be to get him back to his new plant ASAP. "Shall we go?"

We got into the corridor outside the hospital and—oh no!—there was Kyle, on his way to see how Father Mark was, no doubt. I grabbed Lucas's arm to stop him bolting—really didn't want to face Kyle on my own. This morning, I was finding it hard to believe that I'd really knocked on his door like that, last night. Had I forgotten how he'd behaved? Not that I didn't *want* to make up...

"How's Father Mark?" asked Kyle tensely.

"He could be worse, I s'pose." There *was* something I really wanted to say to him, in case Father Mark did get loose and polish me off. "I, uh, didn't actually mean what I said about never wanting to see you ever again, you know."

"Really," said Kyle stiffly. He was looking at Lucas with recognition—and dislike. It made me mad again.

"I don't think you've met Lucas properly," I said coolly. "Lucas, this is my brother..." *Oh*... with a look of pure anguish, Lucas slipped my grasp and fled. I sighed. "He's a tad shy."

"Oh?" said Kyle coldly. "Looked more like a guilty conscience."

"How very perceptive of you. And why blame him for that? A good thing in the circumstances, isn't it?"

"I know what that man did to you, and you expect to just introduce him to me and have me what, *shake hands?* Then again, after *what you did the other day*, why am I surprised?"

"What I did?" I said blankly. He seemed so *angry*.

"Georg Friedrich! You put the entire vote—all our lives!—on the line for *him*. For Snakey's *murderer*. How could you?"

For a moment I wasn't sure what to say. "I'm sorry," I said at last, "when I was growing up, I was taught to forgive people, but I must've misunderstood. Clearly I was only

235

supposed to forgive the boy in the playground who stole my lollypop, not the man who cut up my face or the man who killed my friend. Must've got it all wrong."

"Oh, don't give me that!" snapped Kyle. "There's forgiveness, yeah, and then there's going right out on a limb unnecessarily because you've just got to play the hero and feed your swollen ego! To hell with the rest of us, if it had gone wrong! And now Snakey's killer has as good as gone free! How must his parents feel? Did you think about that?"

I stared at him, speechless. I felt like he'd just cut me open with a scalpel.

Snail appeared beside me, his face hard. "Kyle, turn around and clear off. You're completely out of order!"

"What, you think she did a good thing?" Kyle practically yelled. "Don't you care about Snakey?"

"I think what Margo did is a far better memorial to Snakey than what you're saying you'd have preferred." His face softened slightly. "Kyle, seriously, what's up with you?"

"What's up with *me?* What's up with my *sister*, more like!" Kyle swung around and stormed off.

I stared after him, my insides beginning to shake, my throat to close... No, I mustn't cry. If I cried it would really upset Lucas. *I am actually worried about him. Perhaps I really do forgive him now.*

The thought cheered me a little. But another thought came: *And the man who killed your baby? Can* you *forgive* him?

"Are you okay, Margo?" asked Snail, worriedly. "He was talking nonsense. *Totalement!* You know that, right?"

Did I? I hadn't even questioned my impulse to save Friedrich: it had felt so right. Could my motives have been so horribly selfish as Kyle claimed? But I hadn't *wanted* to risk everyone. *To risk Bane, my baby...* I swallowed hard. It would have been so much easier to just let the man go to his fate...

Kyle *was* talking nonsense... But he'd planted a little seed of doubt in my mind, all the same, like a burr for the devil to torment me with...

I apologize for my somewhat heated post yesterday. I was having a very bad day and I really did feel many people had totally missed Mrs. N's point.

Margaret Verrall—blog post, 'The Impatient Gardener'

"Father Mark?" They'd let me come in to see him today, though I had to stay out of grabbing distance. "Are you awake?" *Hopefully not...* I'd only come because it would look odd if I didn't.

His eyes opened slowly, as though it were a great effort to get the lids up. *Bother. Act natural, Margo...*

"Margaret?" His speech was slightly slurred from the heavy combination of sedative and tranquilizer. The psych-people hadn't been able to do anything with him yet. The doctors were still trying to adjust the drugs to enable him to communicate with them without his brain trying to cook itself.

"It's me. How are you?" *Why didn't you try harder to resist the programming?* That's what I wanted to ask. To scream in his face...

He rattled a wrist chain and tried to smile. He looked so groggy and strained... "A little tied up. And very happy to stay that way."

"They're going to sort you out, y'know." I tried to sound confident. I really did hope it was true.

He gave another crooked smile and I suddenly had the feeling he was trying to make *me* feel better. "Let's hope so." He stared drowsily at the ceiling for a while and I tried to think of something to say. Something not to do with my baby...

"See you've found yourself a protector," he said at last.
"Huh?"

"That gangly fellow prowling around in here yesterday. That's Everington, isn't it?"

"Oh. Yes, that's Lucas. I think he does worry about me a lot. He got very anxious about this whole thing."

"I noticed. Had the impression that if he wasn't satisfied

the place could be made secure enough, he'd have just pulled out that knife and dispatched me."

I gaped at him. "No way! So he's got a knife again? Doesn't surprise me; we gave him a kitchenette. But I'm sure he wouldn't have killed you!" *I almost feel like I could, when I think about...*

Stop thinking about it! Do you even remember what the word 'unfair' means?

"He's killed before," murmured Father Mark sleepily. "S'pose you can't see it 'cause you never have. Never had to, thank God." He blinked and shook his head slightly, clearly trying to wake up a bit. "I'm just saying... what am I saying?"

"I thought letting him look around would *help* you!"

"Well, I found it very reassuring." He meant it, too. "Look, that guy's not all together at the moment, Margaret. Plain enough to see. Means his inhibitions aren't as strong, his reasoning may be off. So if someone threatens you when he's there, just... don't expect his response to be restrained—or even anywhere within the bounds of *appropriate.*"

I frowned. "He's so quiet. Never threatened anyone." Wasn't sure Father Mark was *wrong*, though. Thank goodness Lucas had run off before Kyle really got started, yesterday... "To be honest, he's improving so fast. Every day he seems better, now. So... I don't think it's likely to be a long-term problem."

"Or he won't have that insanity defense for much longer! You might want to mention that to him."

18

PLAN B

Father Mark casually calling the only alternative to being chained to a bed, "Mr. Everington's plan B," had me on my way to Lucas's room straight away.

"It's *not* an option! And I'll make sure he knows it!" My subconscious could whisper as much as it liked, I *didn't* want Father Mark dead! I'd popped in to see Lucas on the way to the hospital, but this warranted another visit.

He did look surprised to see me. Pleased, though. If slightly anxious. "All right, Margaret?"

"I'm fine, Lucas." How many times had I told that lie, already? And how on earth was I going to put this? "I've just been to see Father Mark."

Lucas nodded gravely. "Brave man."

I blinked. "Yes... *Look...*" Nothing for it, blunt it was. "You're not thinking of killing him, are you?"

His eyes widened slightly and he was silent for a moment longer than usual before replying. "Room secure. All okay."

Evasive, much! "*Lucas,*" I said sternly.

He shrugged and spread his hands. "Margaret, everyone's thought about it at least once by now. The guards. The camera fellow. Bane. Definitely thought it!"

"Father Mark's one of Bane's best friends!"

"Yes." Lucas fixed me with a particularly sane look. "But you're the other half of him."

I swallowed. Stupid to think it hadn't crossed Bane's mind. No sin in a passing thought, though, only if you let it settle. *You might want to bear that in mind yourself, hmm, Margo?* "You *can't* kill Father Mark, Lucas."

"Could. Easy. He wouldn't fight."

"I meant you *mustn't!*"

"Oh." He combed his fingers through his neat blond

239

hair, staring at me gravely. "Wasn't going to, Margaret. Last resort idea. Saw it in my eyes, did he?"

"Yes, he did."

"Shouldn't have told you."

"He was afraid you could get into trouble. And he's right. Don't kill anyone, Lucas, okay?"

He stared at me and didn't answer.

"Unless they're literally about to kill me or someone else and there's no... less permanent... solution, okay?"

He smiled and nodded. "Unless," he agreed cheerfully. *Men!*

27 days

I've been thinking about Snakey's parents, recently. We've been trying to make contact with them, since what happened. I do hope that they don't feel in any way betrayed by what happened in Brussels. But I'm also convinced that however they feel about it now, Georg Friedrich's survival is ultimately in their best interests. Because only reconciliation can ever truly bring them peace, not revenge.

Margaret Verrall—blog post, 'The Impatient Gardener'

Taking my fertility chart from the drawer, I put it in my lap and opened it, thermometer in my mouth. I'd not done my checks since... My finger went to the graph, tracing the shape gently... there, that was where my temperature had leapt up on the day I'd found out... and all along here, oh, the relief of marking that higher level, day after day...

But today... today it would drop...

Fumbling the pen into my hand, I took the thermometer from my mouth, but it was no use... I had to slam the book closed. If I looked at that chart for one more second I was going to lose it.

"Okay, Margo?" asked Bane.

"Fine. And you?"

"Oh, I'm okay. I might actually be able to do something for the vote today, you know? Jon's talking about getting

240

someone to film us practicing with the nonLees, so he can use it for his 'Disabilities are only as limiting as you allow them to be' campaign. Clearly I must be improving."

"According to Jon, you're doing really well. Other than..." I hid a smile.

Bane winced. "Has everyone heard about that?"

"It was totally Trainee Wayland's fault. Even if it is a nonLee range, you don't just stroll along to adjust your target whenever you feel like it."

Bane grinned. "Yeah. The headache was the least of his problems. By the time Eduardo finished with him I think he was wishing I'd been using a Lethal!"

Lucas's faint memories of the awesomeness of St Peter's had won out against the threat of people—who looked like *them*. Point to St Peter's. Lucas was still doing his hiding and scuttling in the corridors, and he wouldn't enter the lift—too like a cell?—but we reached the mighty basilica without incident. Fortunately it was pretty close.

We walked in and he went 'wow', his eyes widening. I genuflected to the tabernacle, then stood for a moment. *Lord, Lucas is so hungry. Feed him, please?*

My hungry companion was staring at me. "Why do you go down on your knee like that?"

"Because Our Lord is here in this place. Physically present. You see that gold dove hanging under that huge bronze awning? He's in there."

Lucas thought about that, eyes intent on the 'dove' now, despite the awesome building. "Can I see?"

"Uh..." Okay, should've seen that one coming! "Well, the Host is often displayed for Adoration, but I can't just get Him out for you; a priest would have to. There's not much to see with the eyes, though. It looks like a small, round piece of crisp bread."

More thought. "So how do you know it's really God?"

"Because a long time ago, when God was among us as a human being, He told us it was."

Lucas clearly knew enough about our stream of the Underground that the whole God-coming-as-man didn't leave him bewildered, and he nodded acceptance of this answer. "God should know."

"Well, yes. Have you... read up on the different streams before, Lucas?"

He nodded. Who'd have thought? An EGD Security Major well-versed in forbidden knowledge.

"Actually," I told him, "did you know there are some people from other streams here at the moment for a big meeting with Pope Cornelius?"

He just shook his head. "Not interested. *This* is the only one that really made sense. *If* God cares. Seen a lot of..." His eyes went haunted and conscious-stricken. "Seen a lot of... of Underground executions. *Well*... seen them brought in. All very brave, whatever stream. All very certain. But this stream... something. Joy? Something... unexplainable. Always drew me. Just didn't *know*..." He shot a sidelong look at me—still didn't know. Not yet.

Did *I?*

25 days

I did three years in the EuroArmy before being recruited for SpecialOps. After another year with them, they said they wanted me to infiltrate a Resistance cell. I'd had three friends killed by the Resi-rats by then, so I was all for it.

It was hard at first, being Resistance. SpecialOps had taught me to kill ruthlessly, but the Resistance wanted me to kill the people I was really protecting. But I had my orders from HQ. *Kill anyone they want you to kill. Your job is to protect the majority. Never focus on the individual.* So I followed my orders. Hesitation would've cost me my life.

Georg Friedrich—interview for the 'Maltese Herald'

"You know, St Peter's is a bit of a breakthrough for Lucas," I told Father Mark, a few days later. "He likes it so much he sneaks along there on his own. Tucks himself away in a crevice of some ancient tomb or side altar, which does no harm to anyone, except making the guards jump occasionally."

Usually to be found in the vicinity of the 'dove', which fascinated him, though he was more normally staring at the flowers at the foot of the altar below. The Head Gardener liked flowers alive and growing, just like Lucas—he lined the old vases with plastic and transplanted plants into them for a week at a time.

Father Mark smiled sleepily. Not feeling like talking but happy to have me babble at him. Lucas was a nice safe topic.

"I had to persuade him not to remove the flowers from the altars—he kept wanting to look at them," I went on. "And the other day Father Simeon—the Sacristan, you know, he didn't mean any harm, bless him—but he was a little too persistent trying to get Lucas to put them back. Lucas went into total panic mode and ended up at the top of the tallest tomb in St Peter's."

I sighed, still half-dismayed, half-amused by the incident. "The Sacristan had to send for me and a ladder— the ladder for me, I don't know how Lucas got up there; he certainly can climb."

Father Mark smiled again in acknowledgement of this tale as I leaned to examine the plant on the bedside table. Something about it had been bugging me for several days.

"This isn't even the same one!" My plant recognition skills had improved markedly of late. In fact... "This is one of Lucas's, isn't it?"

Father Mark blinked and cranked his mind into conversational mode. "Man's been bringing me a different one every day. Don't think he trusts anyone here enough to leave one long-term."

"Lucas has been here?"

"Every day, Margaret, and my throat remains intact, so relax."

Father Mark could now just about think and talk around the nasty headache he got when doctors were present. But apart from the psychologists' necessarily brief sessions, he hadn't much to occupy him. Hmm...

Lucas watched lots of Masses from his hidey-holes, and

he was asking a lot of questions. Really good ones, too. I was occasionally having to look up the answers. Perhaps Father Mark could get him talking and handle those...

24 days

The orders came down from Reginald Hill himself. I was to travel to Monaco, still as the Resistance fighter whose cover I'd spent the last five years perfecting, and take out Margaret Verrall. If captured, an 'escape' would be arranged. I'd have to lie low out-of-bloc until the furor died down, then I'd get a new identity and return to work with SpecialOps. Out of consideration for the disruption to my life during that period, I would get a special bounty of 100,000 eurons. Of course, I knew it wasn't *really* for the 'disruption,' it was because of the nature of the job, but all the same. Who wouldn't leap at an offer like that? 100,000 eurons just for doing my duty, and I'd get out of the Resistance alive, too!

The thing they forgot to tell me was that Reginald Hill is a conniving, back-stabbing, treacherous, murderous bastard and Margaret Verrall is the complete opposite. So despite the fact I'm now stuck at this touchy-feely farm, I'm actually genuinely glad that for the first time in my life I failed to complete my mission. It saved my life.

And by the way, if I could vote, I'd vote no!

Georg Friedrich—interview for the 'Monte Carlo Gazette'

Kyle's accusations were still niggling me, however hard I tried to put them from my mind. And the opinion poll I'd just seen wasn't good news. Three points lead to the EuroGov...

Was it possible I'd actually get five minutes prayer time? I hurried towards a favorite curtained-off side chapel in St Peter's, hardly daring to think the thought too hard. Raised a hand to move aside the curtain and paused—a voice was speaking inside.

"Obviously it's wonderful when someone asks for baptism, but you must understand that I am obliged to ascertain the *motivation* behind the request."

Bother, Pope Cornelius was in the chapel with someone, and it sounded like a private conversation. I'd go to the main altar...

I turned that way, but... Wait a minute, Jon was over there. He'd not left Bane on his own, had he?

"Motivation?"

Hang on, that *was* Bane!

"Yes. Why are you suddenly asking for baptism? The truth, please."

I heard Bane's resigned sigh. I should leave... but my ears were trying to strain right through the curtain. Not all that hopefully, 'cause this was the first I'd heard of any spiritual awakening...

"Well, I'm sure Margo told you what happened, before we went to Brussels. Thing is, she's still really worried, doesn't want to leave me on my own—comes up with all these excuses, but it's obvious enough. I can't stand it that I've done this to her, made her so scared. And I know what a downer you people have on... doing that to yourself... so I thought if I got baptized, it would, y'know, maybe convince her I really *wasn't going to.*"

Pope Cornelius's turn to sigh. "Bane, wanting to reassure your wife is a commendable thing, but it is not an appropriate reason to take upon yourself something so serious and life-changing as baptism. You must know I have to say no."

Bane sighed again. "Yeah, I was honest. Look what it got me?"

Pope Cornelius's voice went a little sterner. "Do you really not realize, Bane Verrall, what it would mean to your wife, if you were to seek baptism for the *right* reasons? Unless you have another reason you are reluctant to share, no is the answer and you should thank me for it."

A long, long silence from Bane. "*No other reason,*" he muttered at last, rather fiercely. And after another moment of silence, "*Thank you,* I s'pose."

Imagine being able to actually think about spiritual matters—just think about them—without that gnawing terror that *someone might find out*. That, specifically, the Department for the Eradication of Superstition might find out. If that sounds attractive, well, don't forget that in 22 days, you can make it happen.

Margaret Verrall—blog post, 'The Impatient Gardener'

Even now, walking over the grass with the flowerbeds around me, my heart thumped too hard as I found myself thinking, as ever, about the Vote which now seemed to be hurtling towards us like an out-of-control freight train. No more restfully, my mind insisted on listing the things I had to do in the rest of the day.

Visit Father Mark—no improvement there, alas.

Check and post the blog I'd written yesterday.

Answer as many comments and comment on as many other blogs as I could.

Write that article requested by an actual EuroBloc newspaper. Absolutely must do that.

Spend some time with Bane before he forgot what his wife... sounded like.

Prayer lists, how many days had it been since I'd even managed to pick one up?

Even the crush of things to do faded from my mind as we drew close to a certain unmarked grave. *Don't think about it, Margo. Not until you tell Bane...*

But my treacherous mind was already picturing a little child, hair dark as Bane's, running across the grass, laughing...

Never. It would never be.

Maybe one day. *A* child. So long as nothing was actually... damaged—*oh Lord, let that not be so*. But never the one I'd loved so hard those few short weeks. The one Father Mark had...

"Margaret?"

A question? I shoved the thoughts into my mental 'baby

box' and slammed the lid. Until three days ago, only St Peter's, with its awesomeness and the call of the 'dove', and the hospital, with its familiarity, had seemed sufficiently non-threatening destinations for Lucas to creep from his room. But he'd finally let me tempt him out into the Vatican gardens to see where all his plants came from, and it was already clear this was going to be a permanent alteration to our routine. Because Lucas did love the gardens, but for some reason he'd only venture out there if I went with him. So we'd started going for a walk after reading the Office and doing all the questions and answers out there.

I absolutely did not mind. Nice to get outside.

What had Lucas found...? Oh, a particularly lovely specimen of... something yellow and petally... growing in a rockery. I went to look. "Is it a good one?"

His finger traced the rim of a petal. "Fine shape."

"It is very even."

That familiar flash of amused condescension flitted through his eyes. "No... *right* shape, see...." He traced the petal again, then located an inferior specimen and turned back to me. "This not..."

His eyes narrowed into instant, intense focus on something over my shoulder—he dived into me—a sinister hiss—only as I was falling in a strange slow motion did my mind catch up.

Danger...

19

JUSTIFIABLY OVER-PROTECTIVE

What Hollywood don't mention about being knocked into a rockery and then landed on by a fully-grown man, even one as skinny as Lucas, is that it's enough to drive every single scrap of air from every last corner of your lungs, and that *hurts!*

For several moments I could only gasp, mind blank in the shock of the landing... then... *hiss...* silencer? *...Lethal!* Guards... need guards here *now...*

I fought to scream, but my body thrust each lungful of air straight back out in order to heave in another. Was the assassin walking towards us right now? Lucas was pinning me down, wriggling to place the thickest part of his body— such as it was—over my head and chest. Didn't make a sound, though, damnit! Winded too?

I've got to scream, I've got to, got to... The assassin would just shoot Lucas, roll him off, then shoot me, I had to make a *noise...*

Finally! I managed to hold a breath long enough to let it out past my vocal chords. More like the wheeze of a dying cat than the scream of someone in mortal peril, but surely those guards who ever since Brussels had lurked near me oh-so-casually would hear it? *Please, Lord?*

I struggled to hold another breath, to try again... *There...* a VSS guy tore around the side of the rockery with a handful of plain-clothes Swiss Guards behind him.

"Hey! *Get off her!*" He rushed towards us, nonLee in hand. Red with fury.

Oh, Lord help us! I managed to extricate an arm, point in the direction Lucas had been looking and wheeze, "Gun!"

He jerked to a halt, face frozen as his entire understanding of what was going on was rearranged in a moment of intense thought. Then he spun around and dropped on one knee, jabbing at the others with his free hand. "You, you, you, stay here, the rest of you, follow me!" Up and off, running towards the gunman, no, no, no! *Don't get killed, please?* I could see Snakey in my mind, Georg Friedrich raising his pistol... I waited for the evil hiss, the screaming...

Three of the guards knelt in a triangle around us, nonLees out and ready, clearly positioning themselves as human shields. When I tried to wriggle out from underneath my original human shield, he resisted.

"No, stay there, Mrs. Verrall!" ordered one of the guards. "Er... if he doesn't mind."

Lucas clearly didn't mind; like trying to detach a limpet. But... something warm and wet... I held my hand where I could see it. Blood, *oh no*... "Lucas, how badly are you hurt?"

No reply. He just hunched over me more protectively than ever. Not winded, no, just flipping out. I patted his back over as best I could, but it was mostly his arm that was wet.

"Lucas is hurt," I told the presumably senior man who'd spoken before.

"How badly?"

"I can't tell!"

The guard jerked his head to the guy on the rockery side of the triangle, furthest from where I'd indicated the danger lay. "Take a look?"

I waited... Still no shots or screaming...

"It's his arm and it's not serious," said the delegated guard after what felt like an age. "It'll keep for a few minutes until the area is secure."

I breathed a little easier. Literally as well as metaphorically. I was getting my breath back. An age of waiting, then suddenly guards were everywhere, lots of VSS and a load more Swiss Guards, these ones in uniform. From the babble of noise, they'd caught the would-be assassin. Eduardo appeared, looking deeply pissed off, and started questioning everyone in sight.

Time for another attempt to extricate myself.

"Could we get a doctor over here?" I tried to ease out of Lucas's grasp—he renewed his clutching. "It's okay, it's okay now. All safe, the man's caught, come on, you can let me out now..." After quite a lot of soothing, and easing, and gentle prying of his fingers apart, I managed to slide right out.

He sat up at once, watching me intently—immense strain on his face. I slipped a reassuring arm around his shoulders, eyeing his arm. There was a bloody tear in his sleeve, and clearly another in his flesh below. But it probably really wasn't too bad. *Thank you, Lord!* But... comparing his height to mine... that bullet had been meant for my head.

"Lucas, thank you so much," I said softly. "You saved my life. Again." My stomach was turning over and my hands beginning to shake. I drew a couple of deep breaths, fighting the shock. Lucas was freaking out enough for the pair of us.

Lucas eyed Eduardo warily as Eduardo approached slowly and crouched beside us, empty hands held out in plain sight. So Father Mark wasn't the only one who thought Lucas might be unpredictable at a time like this.

"Margaret, are you all right? What happened?"

I swallowed and tried to speak calmly. "I'm fine. Lucas was just showing me a flower when he saw something— man with a gun, I assume—he flattened me in the rockery, I heard a hiss—which I'm guessing must've been a silencer, since Lucas is shot. I was terribly winded but eventually— felt like eventually, anyway—I managed to scream, and the guards came."

"Anything to add to that, Mr. Everington?"

Lucas breathed in shallow pants, a deep, deep furrow in his brow as he fought to remain alert and engaged with the world.

"He's really not going to be able to answer your questions just now," I said. "Way too many strangers around here and most of them are holding weapons."

Eduardo grimaced slightly. "Nothing we can do about that quite yet. I'm afraid you'll have to be closely guarded until we've ascertained there was only the one."

Lucas twitched slightly. I touched his hand gently and... thank goodness, there was Doctor Frederick. Quickly pointed in our direction, he deposited his big first aid satchel on the grass beside us. "Are you okay, Margaret?"

"I'm *fine*, it's *Lucas*..." I gestured to the bloody arm like a

TV-presenter.

"So it is." Doctor Frederick peered at Lucas's arm for a moment then unzipped his bag. "Right, looks like a flesh wound to me, but let's get that sleeve off..." He produced a pair of scissors with a flourish and leaned towards us...

Lucas sprang—one hand slammed into Doctor Frederick's arm, sending the scissors flying, the other reached for his throat as Doctor Frederick went over backwards on the grass.

I lunged, wrapping a restraining arm around Lucas's chest and grabbing the wrist of the hand groping for the scissors. "Lucas, stop it! It's Doctor Frederick, for pity's sake, you *know* him! He wasn't going to hurt you! He wasn't going to hurt *me!*"

A long moment... then Lucas allowed me to draw his hand away from Doctor Frederick's throat, scrambling back a few paces, where he crouched, rocking slightly, hands buried in his hair. Looked like he wanted to just run away... but couldn't because he still wasn't sure if I was safe.

Doctor Frederick sat up shakily, rubbed his neck and his arm once or twice and retrieved his scissors, a deep flush covering his face. "That... may not have been the smartest thing I ever did."

Glad he wasn't harmed—also relieved that he blamed himself.

"Waving a sharp object at an overwrought and at this moment justifiably over-protective madman?" Eduardo hadn't tried to wade into the mess. "Really wasn't, no. I think Margo had better deal with that arm for now."

Doctor Frederick handed me a small first aid kit willingly enough, promising to come and take a proper look at Lucas in the morning, and Lucas followed me uncomplainingly as I led him away, his hand shaking in mine. He needed some fuchsia therapy. He looked over his shoulder at Snail and Unicorn only a couple of times— Eduardo had deliberately chosen faces familiar to him to bodyguard me, thank goodness.

"Margo? *Margo?*"

Bane? "Bane? I'm here..."

"Margo!" It *was* Bane, on his *own*, hurrying along,

shouting my name, his stick swiping from side to side... heading straight for a gravestone...

"Bane, there's a headstone, go right..."

He went right a bit, then pretty much broke into a run. I gently detached Lucas from my hand and hurried to meet him. Didn't want any more overreactions.

"Margo?" Bane gasped, as I caught his hands.

"It's me..."

He flung his arms around me and held me as though I was the last solid thing in the world. "Margo, are you *all right?* Are you *okay?*"

"I'm fine, Bane. Calm down, everything's all right."

"I heard... there'd been an attack. You involved! And someone hurt...!"

"Lucas is a little bit shot, but thankfully it's nothing serious."

"Shot?"

"A man with a gun." I tried to keep my voice steady. "Generally known as an assassin. Only a would-be one, in this case, thank God. I suppose we shouldn't be too surprised, after what happened in Brussels."

Bane clutched me tighter. "You're all right?"

"I really am fine. Very happy to have a hug, though."

Bane managed to ease up enough to stroke my hair. "God help me, I was so frightened!"

"And you came by yourself," I said proudly.

"Uh... yeah. I just dashed straight out, y'know? Kept asking people the way. But it really wasn't that bad."

Probably didn't seem bad at all, with an enormous distraction like that! A silver lining to this horrible event?

"I... er... kind of need to get back to Lucas, Bane. He's really stressing out. I was just taking him home to bandage him up." Before Bane could get hurt by this, I added, "He knocked me out the way. Got shot instead of me."

Bane blinked and allowed me to disentangle myself from him. "You'd better take care of him. Though..." He followed me as I went back to where the others were waiting. "Why isn't Doctor Frederick doing it?"

"Because he almost got his own scissors in the throat when he tried," said Unicorn.

"Oh, hi U. Wait, he what?"

"He made for your beloved with a pair of scissors in his hand, so Mr. Everington put him flat on his back, at which point Margo intervened and was deputized."

"You're a doctor now as well as a counselor, hmm?" teased Bane, clearly light-hearted with relief. "You're racking up those qualifications, aren't you?"

"Very funny," I said—but not too grumpily—taking Lucas in tow again.

21 days

Proving whose orders this man was acting on may be difficult, but he himself will spend the foreseeable future occupied with far more peaceful and productive work, at a certain secure rehabilitation farm in Africa. Probably eating very good food, so we needn't feel too sorry for him.

Margaret Verrall—blog post, 'The Impatient Gardener'

...I started awake; drew in a convulsive breath. Sat up and wrapped my arms around my knees. My heart thudded painfully, fooled by the dream. Shivering, I switched on the light. Directed a hopeful look at Bane. Nope, still sound asleep. Exhausted by the stress of the day. As *I was*, I just couldn't *stay* asleep with these nightmares!

What is wrong with you, brain? Lucas is fine! Stop killing him! Let me sleep.

When we'd reached Lucas's room, he'd immediately sat down cross-legged on his bed, with his original beloved fuchsia in his lap and his Office book clutched to his chest, gone very, very deep inside. I'd dressed the wound, put a blanket around him, fussed with it a bit and then left him to recover—nothing else to be done, and Bane had gone on ahead to put the kettle on.

"Expect you could do with a cup of something," he'd said, with that familiar bitter note in his voice—making hot drinks wasn't something he could do yet.

But by now Lucas would have tidied himself up and

gone to bed—hours ago, most likely. He was *fine*. But my hands were shaking from the dream. All of me was shaking. I clenched my fingers together irritably.

Hang on... Something missing. My wedding ring... oh no, it was still in Lucas's room! I'd taken it off when bandaging the wound, because the cold brush of the metal was making him twitch and it was going to get bloodied. Blast. I'd just have to get it in the morning. I glanced at the clock. Two o'clock. I could hardly get it now.

But... shivering, I rubbed the back of my neck. Stupid, Margo. Lucas is fine. Safer than you, there's a camera in his room.

It's dark, though.

What on earth would be wrong? Not hard to see where the nightmares came from, tonight!

But... I'd really hate it if Bane noticed my ring was missing when he touched my hand. I could slip in and get it, and see with my own eyes that Lucas was fine...

No, what if I woke Lucas? I lay down again and pulled the sheets up to my chin. But now I'd thought of it...

Argh! Couldn't even get back to sleep now!

I struggled not to toss and turn. No need to share my sleepless misery with Bane. Oh, this was stupid! In less than five minutes my wedding ring could be back on my finger and my paranoid subconscious reassured...

Slipping from the bed, I put on my dressing gown and slippers, took the nonLee from the bedside table and stuffed it through the dressing gown belt, then crept out of the bedroom. Bane still slept soundly. He wouldn't miss me.

The Swiss Guard outside the apartment door started as I emerged. I closed the door before speaking. "Sorry. Didn't mean to make you jump."

"S'okay. Er... I'd better call someone if you're going somewhere."

"I've just got to get something from Saint Ignatius's." That was the name of Lucas's room. "There's a camera in there."

"Oh, right." The guard relaxed. "Well, I'd still better accompany you to the door."

He followed me dutifully down the flight of stairs and

in a matter of seconds, I was outside Lucas's room. Even a gentle tap would be cruel at this hour, so I just opened it and slipped inside. Moonlight illuminated the room dimly; the curtains were wide open. Never seen any sign he closed them. Good thing, because I'd not thought to bring a flashlight!

I could make out Lucas's shape on the bed, anyway, lying on his back, probably because the side he normally lay on had a hole in it, and hear his soft breathing in the silence. He'd put his pajamas on, so he must be feeling better. *See, subconscious, all fine.*

I'd get my ring and be off home. I tiptoed around to the far side of the bed and slid my hand carefully across the top of the bedside table. What? I felt around more carefully. No ring. Must've got knocked onto the floor. Crouching down, I ran my hands over the surrounding carpet. Nothing.

How long should I keep looking? Frustrating to leave without it, but moon or not, it was jolly dark in here...

I made one more pass over the carpet. Nothing. I was leaving, then. Didn't want to wake Lucas, I'd scare the life out of him. I tensed my muscles to stand, but...

A faint noise from the balcony? The wind?

No. *That* was a noise on the balcony. *And again...* a tiny scuff, thud... like... like something landing? I looked quickly over the bed and Lucas's sleeping form. My heart stopped.

Two shadowy figures were silhouetted behind the glass. One reaching for the handle of the balcony door...

My heart took off again, pounding away. Lord help us, they were after *Lucas?* He'd pissed them off, but... *what do I do, what do I do?*

If I shouted, the assassins were closer than the guard. Mouth dry, I wriggled the nonLee free of my belt and slipped off the safety catch. Cover? *Footboard...* I crawled quickly along... thank God the old bed was solid all the way to the ground...

Putting only one eye out from behind the footboard, I poked the nonLee out as well and waited. The door was open, the first man stepping through. *Wait, Margo, wait... if you don't get them both at once, you'll be for it!*

He moved into the room... *don't shoot Lucas, please*

don't shoot him yet, wait for your friend... I tried to breathe silently and not pant in terror. If he raised his pistol I'd have to risk it...

But the other man was stepping inside. Did they... yes, they had their backs to the bed... weird, but thank God! They were staring at the other end of the room...

Lord, give me strength...

I rose slightly on my knees, aimed-and-fired, aimed-and-fired...

Both men crumpled silently to the ground. *Thank you, Lord; thank you, Angel Margaret.* Now I could raise the alarm, if the camera guys hadn't noticed yet...

Wait... a thought stopped me before I could stand. *Three noises.*

I hunched down again. Change position... isn't that what they do in films? Crawling cautiously along the foot of the bed, I peeped around, towards the balcony. Was there another person? The balcony door stood open, everything was silent. Two separate feet touching down, perhaps, but one guy?

Something small and round flew through the glass door. Knobbly and one hundred percent lethal.

It rolled gently to rest against one of the fallen men...

20

DEAD AS NITS

My body lost the ability to think, it just acted. I dived into the open, grabbed that knobbly thing and hurled it through the door, into the courtyard... *No!* It struck the top of the balcony rail and fell back...

I launched myself at the bed, my fingers grabbing arms, pajamas and sheets together, using my momentum to carry us both over and off... we were falling as there was an ear-shattering crack and a load of stuff thwacked into the wall above us.

Then for the second time that day, I landed on a hard surface and a guy landed on top of me... I lay whooping and gasping—Lucas started to fight free of the bedding, gasping more in shock, eyes wild in the moonlight. I lunged weakly and caught his pajamas, stopping him sitting up enough to be visible over the bed. He looked around, peeped over the bed, ducked down again—catching on fast?

My breath was coming back, it hadn't been so bad a fall. I struggled into a half-sitting position. "Keep down! There's someone on the balcony..." But an image played in my mind, of a small knobbly object, rolling to rest against the outside rim of the door. "*Oh my God, I threw...*"

Lucas's face hovered before my eyes—saying my name, over and over...

The door flew open... Light flooded the room... Lucas was crouched in front of me, one arm shielding me... But it was the guard who was rushing towards me, eyes wide and panic-stricken. Lucas switched a very sharp kitchen knife to a throwing position, hissing wordless warning...

The guard stopped... dithered, looking anguished... Then Eduardo and a sea of vaguely familiar faces were spilling through the door...

* * *

Someone was holding a hot drink to my lips and Doctor Frederick was examining me, prodding me strategically and asking me if it hurt... I kept saying no, and sipping the drink—I could feel wonderful tendrils of warmth spreading out inside me, steadying the freezing, jelly-like maelstrom that was my insides. Bane kept his arms around me, kept kissing my hair and my face and murmuring comforting things. I pressed against him and sipped my way gradually into quietness.

Eduardo had brought me and Lucas to Jon's apartment, as a comfortable safe location. Lucas was sitting in a nearby armchair, the dishpan in which he'd laid out his poor explosion-torn plants cradled to his chest. His eyes were alert, but he didn't seem out-of-his-mind stressed. Eduardo had left most people outside and everyone in here had stood guard at the hospital and counted as a familiar face. Except Jon. Lucas had looked at Jon once, gone a sickly gray color, and was now clearly pretending he wasn't there. Because Jon was kind of a familiar face as well...

"Margaret?" said Eduardo. He'd an unusually compassionate look on his face. "I've played back the footage. I take it you were trying to throw the grenade into the courtyard?"

Lucas was giving me a rather similar look.

"Yes," I sniffed, as a few straggling sobs escaped.

"I thought so. But what on earth were you doing there at this time of night?"

"Oh..." I wrestled my thoughts into order. "Well, I couldn't sleep. Kept having nightmares in which Lucas got killed. Thought I was being paranoid after what happened earlier and tried to ignore it—now I'm thinking it was my guardian angel kicking me in the head like mad. Then I realized I'd left my wedding ring in Lucas's room. I took it off earlier when I was bandaging his arm. Oh no!" I began to panic. "It's still there!"

Lucas held up one finger in a 'hang on a minute' gesture and felt gently in his dishpan. Produced a small circle of gold with a triumphant smile. "Found it on table," he said in a low voice, clearly trying to pretend I was the only one there, full stop, though he was using Latin. "Hung it on the fuchsia so not lost."

Everyone else blinked at this choice of safe place, but I accepted the ring without surprise. "Thank you!" I slipped it back on with relief. "Are they going to be okay?" I nodded to the bowl he was nursing. "Is the fuchsia okay?"

He shrugged unhappily in response to the first question, but added, "Fuchsia not too bad. Took away from window for night."

I tried to gather my thoughts again. "Anyway, eventually I decided to just go and get my ring—check on Lucas at the same time—sounds a bit silly, I suppose, but you know what it's like when you get fretting in the middle of the night— well, *you* probably don't..." I looked at Eduardo, but the others were nodding their understanding.

"Anyway, I slipped along to Lucas's room, but my ring wasn't where I left it. I was just about to give up and go home when I heard something on the balcony, and... well, you saw the rest. But you do realize they must be after *Lucas*, right?"

Lucas was frowning in concentration as he listened, and not just because it was in Latin.

"I don't think so," said Eduardo. "No offence, Mr. Everington, but however much you ticked them off, it doesn't warrant this. They were after Margaret. She's the reason Georg Friedrich is safe in Africa giving interviews about how Reginald Hill sent him to Monaco to kill her."

"Which Hill is denying, saying Friedrich's making it up because he's so grateful to Margo for his life," remarked Snail.

"True, but not everyone believes him, by a long shot. It's done them a lot of damage. Without even taking into account the hammering Reginald Hill's ego took."

I must've still looked doubtful, because Unicorn nodded and said grimly, "The guy *threw a Lethal grenade* into a room with two of his comrades in, Margo. He was clearly under orders to kill you at *all* and *any* cost And, if at all possible, to avoid either himself or any of the others being captured—alive, anyway." For someone so thoroughly nice and honorable, it often surprised me how good U was at thinking like a bad guy. He'd have been in the wrong job otherwise, I suppose.

"They're after Margaret, no doubt," concluded Eduardo. "The question is, how on earth did they know she was in there?"

Unicorn, Snail and Bee looked me up and down analytically. I was still biting my lip at the mention of egos. Kyle had actually turned around in the corridor yesterday and gone back the other way when he saw me coming...

"Tracker?" said Unicorn.

"I would've thought so, except they stood with their backs to her—clearly they didn't know exactly where she was."

Lucas frowned. "Looking at... tea table, Margaret?"

He meant the little table by his two little soft chairs, where he sat with visitors, i.e. me, and Bane once. "Yes, I'd say that's about where they were looking."

"Fuchsia there."

"They weren't tracking the plant," snorted Bumblebee, throwing up one dark-skinned hand in a 'for goodness' sake' gesture.

"Not the plant, *imbécile*," said Snail amiably, "he just told us he'd hung Margo's ring on that particular plant, didn't he?"

"So it's the ring," said Unicorn.

"Not again!" said Bane. That was exactly how the EuroGov had tracked him back to our secret hideout on Gozo in January.

I looked at my hand in horror.

"Sorry, Margaret, I'm going to need that." Eduardo held out his hand.

Reluctantly I drew the ring off again.

"So," summed up Unicorn, "They thought she was there in that room the whole time, but they waited until the dead of night to make their move."

"Lucas, I'm so sorry!" I exclaimed.

"Not your fault," he said calmly.

"Good job you went to check on him, though." Eduardo looked like he'd be having nightmares of his own. "No guarantee they'd have left *him* alive even if they *had* realized it wasn't Margaret in the bed."

In the dark, with the ring in the room, they might easily have put a few shots into the person in the bed, and left, none the wiser. I breathed slowly and carefully for a few moments.

"Are... are all three of them... definitely...?" I trailed off, the state of the room forcing itself into my mind.

"I'm sorry, Margaret, they are dead as nits," said Eduardo. "If it makes you feel better, even the guy on the balcony who threw the thing won't have known what hit him."

"I wish they'd had nonLethal grenades," I couldn't help muttering.

"They wouldn't have used one even if they did," said Unicorn patiently. "Because people *wake up* after a nonLethal grenade, don't you know?"

Eduardo opened his mouth and the other VSS agents chorused, "*Fifty-percent-lethal grenades, U!*"

"The latest ones are up to seventy-five percent nonLethal, actually," said Unicorn. "But Margo knows what I mean."

"Seventy-seven point three percent nonLethal," said Eduardo precisely, unable to bear inaccuracy when it came to statistics.

"So who were they?" someone asked quickly, before Eduardo could give us another incomprehensible lesson about how nonLethal weapons worked. Incomprehensible to me, anyway. It was all to do with electricity and magnetism—or perhaps electro-magnetism—and I still couldn't get my head around it.

"According to their Vatican passes they were all EuroBloc nationals who'd sought sanctuary here within the last four months. We've been putting all such new arrivals in accommodation well away from the secure areas, just in case any of them were in fact EuroGov agents—so I'm not exactly surprised. Let's just hope there aren't any more of them."

Spies or not, they were people. Probably people I'd seen and had breakfast with that morning. I swallowed hard, feeling that cold, knobbly thing in my hand again.

"I'm guessing they let that assassin in, somehow,"

continued Eduardo, "then when he failed so completely, they tried to finish the job themselves with equipment he'd brought for them. I wonder who they were meant to be going after with that kit? Or whether it was just for backup purposes..." From the look in Eduardo's eyes, he'd be following up on these questions immediately.

"Well, anyway, that's enough to be going on with," he added. "You get to bed, Margaret, try and sleep. And I'd like Mr. Everington to remain here as well, just to be on the safe side."

"Take my bed, you two," said Jon. "And I suppose Mr. Everington had better have the sofa. I can sleep on the floor."

"Have my bed, Jon," said Unicorn, eyeing his boss. "I don't think I'll be getting to it now."

Eduardo smiled grim confirmation.

Lucas stared at me in desperate appeal, clutching his dishpan tighter than ever.

"Oh... Lucas needs new pots and everything. I don't think it can wait until morning."

Eduardo sighed slightly. "I'll make sure everything he needs is brought here. Just get some sleep, Margaret, you'll feel better."

"Oh, of course I will, I'll wake up, and they'll not be dead!"

Eduardo just greeted this sarcasm with a shrug.

20 days

There's not the slightest doubt these men got what they deserved. But I still can't help thinking. If they weren't fathers, they were probably registered partners. If not that, then they were surely someone's sons. But do you think the EuroGov cares about that? To them, they were nothing but tools, just like Georg Friedrich. To them, that is all any of us are.

Margaret Verrall—blog post, 'The Impatient Gardener'

"Y'know, I don't think Doctor Frederick thinks Lucas is a

chimpanzee anymore," I told Father Mark that evening, laughing as I remembered Doctor Frederick's expression when Lucas actually spoke to him—to apologize.

"I don't think anyone thinks he's a chimpanzee," said Father Mark blurrily. "People probably like him a lot better all of a sudden, though."

Bane certainly did! And we'd gained a lot in the opinion polls as news of the assassination attempts spread—at least in the early part of the day. At noon the EuroGov had launched a 'Save Sylvia' campaign, parading some cute little girl with cancer in front of the cameras. They must've had her up their sleeve, ready to distract everyone.

Bane had been pretty miserable, though, regardless of our temporary lead in the polls. "How d'you think I feel, knowing you're safer with a madman than with me?" he'd said. "Knowing if you *had* been with *me* yesterday, you'd be..." He hadn't even been able to finish, and he'd spent most of the day at the range, either in genuine hopes of improving his skills, or just because he needed to shoot something.

I couldn't help glancing at Father Mark. *I wish I liked you the way I used to. I mean, I sort of still do, but I just can't seem to look at you without thinking about...* Oops, Father Mark was giving me the searching look he'd been turning on me more and more often since...

"I dare say," I replied quickly. "I'm not actually sure the whole thing hasn't done Lucas good. He seems more confident today."

"I know what you mean. Goodness knows he was in a murderous rage earlier, though."

I blinked. "He was?"

"Wanted to kill those guys again, himself, just for putting you in that position."

"Oh." There had been a bit of glint in his eye last night that I couldn't figure out. "Did you point out that's a bit... um... violent?"

Father Mark smiled. "I did point out that if *you* could forgive *him*, he could surely forgive three guys who couldn't pay any more in this life and who were probably paying in the next as we spoke. He went away pretty quiet—even for him."

"Well, probably for the best. I've got the impression he doesn't get angry very easily—but he's got a really nasty temper when he does."

"Says the young woman who held her brother up at gunpoint."

I stared at him, startled. Not 'cause it wasn't true—no denying my temper had been a match for Lucas's on that occasion—but it seemed rather a harsh thing to say. "I am really sorry about that, y'know."

"Not sorry enough to proffer an olive branch, from what I hear."

"*What?*" I choked. "I *went* to Kyle's room just this morning, Father Mark! After what happened yesterday... well, if there was an olive branch, I wanted to take it. But I didn't see any sign of one! He just talked to me in this aggrieved, self-righteous way, like I'm a silly little girl who's obviously wrong and he can't understand why I'm taking so long to come around to his point of view! And he's so *angry...*"

Father Mark sighed. "Perhaps Kyle needs a bit more time to calm down and come to terms with Snakey's death. I don't think he's dealt with that very well."

I couldn't help a rather bitter snort at that. "You don't say." I really, really wished I'd paid more attention to Kyle, after it had happened, but it was hopeless now—he didn't even want to speak to me.

Another sigh from Father Mark. "And this thing about him lying to Jon by omission...."

"What about it?"

"Well, you obviously think that *Antonio* saw enough to figure out what happened, but all he told Kyle was that Bane had hit you."

My heart sank. I'd jumped to a wrong conclusion. Kyle hadn't done what I'd thought he'd done... But that didn't change all the horrible things he'd done *since*.

"Kyle doesn't give a damn about Bane," the words broke out: of everything, that was what hurt the most. "Bane could've died because of how Kyle acted! I tell you, it would be a heck of a lot easier if he'd just... *pinned me to a gurney, carved up my face and left me to die in agony!"*

Father Mark winced. No doubt he'd a pretty clear memory of finding me after Major Everington... after *Lucas*... had done just that. Strange feeling of disconnection... in that memory he was still *The Major*...

"And the way he was about Georg Freidrich!" My tongue rushed on. "He all but said he wanted to see the man dead! And he was *so* cruel to me! What sort of priest is he going to be?"

"He won't be one at all if he can't sort out this crisis he's having," said Father Mark quietly.

Oh. When we were little, Kyle always wanted to be a priest like Uncle Peter. Once old enough to understand what that really meant, in the world we lived in, he'd tried to forget all about the idea—but the Lord had other plans. Or so we'd all thought...

My stomach was churning. This was too much to take in. Time to change the subject, surely? I tried to think of something to say. It was so *hard*, smiling and chatting to Father Mark like nothing was wrong. Almost like nothing was wrong...

He was giving me that look again. "Margaret... I am really, really sorry I hurt you, you know. And... I know it must be hard for you to forget what I did, but... is there something you're not telling me?"

The word 'nothing' still stuck in my throat. "Don't be paranoid, Father Mark. I'm sorry if I'm a little distant. So much is happening at the moment; it's hard to take it all in." My words came out far more brusquely than I intended. Blast. I might as well have just said, "Yes, there is."

Father Mark frowned, but the little machine Doctor Frederick had set up by the bed to monitor his blood pressure and heart rate gave a little beep. Slipping the next lot of drugs into his veins. Sleep soon claimed him.

Feeling guilty, and depressed, and slightly shaken by that conversation, I set off from the hospital and found my feet taking me to Lucas's room. With a bit of a mental shrug, I knocked. He let me in without comment on my late reappearance and made a pot of tea.

I sipped gratefully, feeling the hot brew settling my

churning emotions. Lucas stared at his cooling cup in silence. The glint was gone from his eye. Father Mark really had knocked the anger out of him. Every so often, though, he glanced at a large bunch of cut flowers in a vase with a mournful look appropriate for a dear friend who's just been told their illness is terminal.

"Who sent you those?" I asked after a few minutes of this, trying not to smile. He did like his flowers alive and growing.

He got up and fetched a little homemade cardlet—the store couldn't stock luxuries like that.

"Kyle?" I exclaimed, as soon as I saw the writing. He *did* still care about me, clearly. How could I make it up with him? *Angel Margaret, please soften his heart, make him ready to listen...*

Lucas looked at the flowers again and sighed.

"Um, d'you want to keep them, or would you rather I took them away?"

"Meant well. I keep." He threw them a look which added, "Poor things," clearer than words.

Putting the card on the table, I went back to my tea. Why had I come here? It was late, I should go home, Bane would be waiting. To say nothing of the Vote-stuff needing doing.

The EuroGov had been playing a heart-rending video all day: little Sylvia talking about how she'd arrived at the hospital to have the transplant that would cure her—showing off the teddy bear she'd had packed in her bag—and how the doctors had told her she'd have to go home, they weren't allowed to do it anymore. Followed by clips of Sylvia's tearful parents confirming that yes, a transplant was their daughter's only hope. Yes, Sylvia had only weeks to live. Yes, they were just hoping against hope that their daughter could hold on until the vote... and that everyone would vote to save her. Sob, sob. No interviews with the parents whose daughter had died to supply the intended transplant...

Yes, I really should've gone straight home to carry on with countering that vile video. S'pose I just wanted a cup of tea and a moment's peace and quiet to absorb what Father

Mark had said.

No danger of not getting that with Lucas, especially tonight. Pensive. Definitely the word. He stared into space, lost in his own thoughts.

A knock on the door. Lucas went to answer it, clearly startled. Looked at the person there for a moment, then said, very deliberately, "Hello."

"Thought that silence must be you. Hello." Bane's voice. "I brought this for you."

Lucas stepped back from the doorway, a cardboard box in his hands. "Margaret here. Come in."

"Hi, Bane," I said, as he followed Lucas into sight. "I'm sorry, I was about to get back."

"S'okay," was the surprising reply. "I wasn't actually there." He jerked his head towards the sounds of Lucas opening the box and grinned rather smugly. Hang on... out and about on his own? A grin spread over my own face for what felt like the first time in hours, if not days. Lucas's face brightened—so that's what was in the box.

I went over to admire the three healthy, flowery, un-damaged plants that he lifted out, since Bane seemed so pleased with himself. Each a very different type and color but... a whiff of strong distinct fragrances... that would be how Bane had picked them.

Lucas stroked the petals and leaves and checked the soil and soon bore them to the window. Stood back and surveyed the more cheerful scene and nodded to himself. Glanced at Bane and said politely, "Thank you."

"Thank *you* for saving Margo."

Lucas considered this. Thinking the plants were un-necessary? Or the thanks were? Eventually he just said, "You're welcome." And after another moment, "Tea?"

Bane got that look people get when they're trying to figure out if the offer is sincere. "Why not?"

When we finally got home and were getting ready for bed, Bane's self-conscious air as he slipped off his light jacket caught my attention. And his cheeks were going rather pink... ah... that was why. He'd just shrugged off a shoulder holster complete with nonLee, and was placing it carefully on the bedside table. Embarrassed, but very pleased with himself.

I came up and slipped my arms around him. "Danger to everyone near you with a gun in his hand, I think you said?" I murmured in his ear. "Eduardo clearly doesn't agree."

Bane flushed more than ever. "He said I'm not to take it out except as a last resort," he said quickly. "I'm not like Jon; I can't tell who it is near me the way he can. But with the vote so close, and the EuroGov after you the way they are... he said he wanted me to be armed."

"Quite right," I told him. "I feel safer already."

"Really?" Skeptical, but not angry.

"Really," I said firmly. "Cross my heart and..."

"Don't say it!" He turned around, traced his way to my lips with gentle fingers, and stopped my words with a kiss.

For once, I forgot the tiredness that nowadays always seemed to claim me by this time of day, and kissed him back...

21

THE MAJOR'S STORY

19 days

"Our daughter Miriam couldn't walk or speak. In fact, she could understand very little at all. People often said she would be better off dead—until they met her. Once they had experienced her silent language of love and joy, they'd leave smiling and filled with a new love for life. And from then on, their faces would fall when they spoke about her coming fate."

'Monsieur P.', parent of a preKnown—quoted on 'The Impatient Gardener'

Despite lingering shock from the assassins, and the anguish about my baby that felt like it would never fade—*and* my ongoing estrangement with Kyle—I actually knocked on Lucas's door fairly cheerfully the next day, showing him the shiny new Office book as soon as I was inside. "Look what my lovely husband and friends put together all their Office tokens and got for me!"

Lucas eyed the book—then my shining eyes... oops, realizing for the first time he'd deprived me of something I really valued?

"Sorry," he said unhappily.

"It's all right, I *really* didn't mind you having that one." Glad to find I meant it, too.

Lucas frowned at the book again. "I have no gift for you. What occasion?"

"Oh..." My face fell. "No, no occasion. They just wanted to cheer me up. And my birthday—all my saint's days for that matter; y'know, St Margaret, St Elizabeth, St Anysia—are all in November, December, so they weren't going to get an

269

excuse any time soon."

Lucas had a very intent look on his face. "I know what gift I would like to give you. Wanted for long time—but simply *cannot* afford... worth so much just now..."

I was touched by the longing in his eyes. "It's okay, Lucas, there really is no occasion. And when my birthday *does* come around," *if we're still alive—shut up little voice,* "you'll have the perfect present—because your baby fuchsias will be ready by then, won't they?" He'd taken cuttings the moment he got his own room and some of them were still alive. Unlike *my* baby... *Stop it, Margo!*

He shrugged slightly, thoughts still on whatever luxury item he thought I'd like. But after a while, he focused on me again. "Feeling better, then?"

"Yes." I eyed him—still a little pensive, no glint... "What about you?"

He gave me a sharp look. "Father Mark talking to you again?"

"He mentioned you were very angry with those men."

"Yes. Aren't *you?*"

I pulled a face. "Yes. But I've been praying for them this morning."

The pensive look gained ascendance. "That's what Father Mark suggested."

"Have you been doing it?"

"No. Don't *know.* "

Oh no, the forgiveness thing again. I took his thin hand and pressed it. "I really think I *do* forgive you, Lucas. Please believe it."

He shook his head—went abruptly to sit on the bed, back to the headboard, long legs stretched out. Frowning at his shiny shoes. "I believe you think you do—but I don't know if you *can do.* You don't really know me, do you?"

I dragged one of the soft chairs over and sat. Frowned at him. "Don't I?"

"Do you look at me and see an evil coward?"

I blinked. "No."

"Then you don't know me." He spoke with such certainty.

"What you did yesterday, that was brave. You could've

been killed."

A dismissive shake of his head. "A man who is already dead cannot be killed."

"You're not *dead.*"

He just shrugged and stared at his shoes some more, so I asked, "Is this, here, now, not you?"

"Now, *maybe*... Can one really change?"

"We believe so."

He stared at his shoes some more. "I am not a very nice man. I don't know why you are sitting here with me."

"Because I forgive you."

He shook his head. "All that I've been... you don't even know."

"Then tell me."

Those memories lurked in his haunted eyes, those memories he'd struggled to hold back, to keep forgotten... should I have just said that? But he mostly looked sad...

"Should I?" He seemed to speak more to himself, and I'd a feeling I knew what he was worried about. Same reason he'd spilled his murderous anger to Father Mark and not to me.

"Yes. I can take it, Lucas. Grown up, remember?"

"All right..." he said uncertainly. "Everything?"

"If that's how much you think I need to know to forgive you."

His mouth twisted—he really did believe once I heard his story I'd be unable to forgive him anymore. Then a weary look, close to despair, crossed his face—too tired to prolong the *not-knowing* any longer, whatever the result?

"All right." He switched to English. "Well, *I was born.*" His lip quirked in a timid flash of humor, as he borrowed the first sentence of my book. "That was..." He got that look adults always get when they talk about their age. "Was it really thirty-nine years ago? Anyway, on my father's side, my family was old, gentry, you'd call it. My great-grandfather had lost all the family's money and the little manor house, and my grandfather had opened a super-market and done well and bought the manor back. My father inherited it after his parents died in a car accident, but the supermarket wasn't doing so well any more, with the latest dip—what was the latest dip back then.

"My father was very concerned with *our family name.*" More than a hint of bitterness in the way he said that. "The shop brought in enough money to keep us, but not in the style he felt necessary for *the Salperton Everingtons.* I remember them arguing all the time, my mum and my father. My mum wanted us to give up the manor, or at least let it out, and live somewhere more affordable. My father wouldn't hear of it. So things just went on as they were, and more and more envelopes came through the door marked in red.

"We were just children, my sister one year younger than me—she worried whether she'd be able to take her big doll's house if we moved, while my only real concern, other than hating the arguing, was whether we'd still have a garden. My father intended me to take over the supermarket one day, but by the time I was eleven I knew I wanted to be a professional gardener. My mum encouraged me not to abandon my dream—she could probably see that the way things were going, there might not be a shop for me to run.

"I wanted to please my father, though, like most little boys, so I started going around to the supermarket after school to try and help out, though I found it very dull. I knew we weren't making enough money—a man with a truck had actually come to the manor the day before and taken my father's car away—so when I thought up a few ways to improve things I thought my father would be delighted. But when I started to tell him my ideas, he flew into the most terrible rage. Shouting that he didn't need a child telling him how to run his business. And he hit me right across the face."

His nostrils pinched as though he could still feel the pain of the blow. "I ran out of the store and all the way home. And that night I had a horrible thought. Did he hit my mum? What if he hit my sister? It was unbearable. The next day I got all my savings together and I went to the outdoor shop and I bought a pocket knife. I wanted to be able to protect them if he tried to hurt them. An eleven-year-old with a pocket knife thinking he could take on a big man like my father." He shook his head self-deprecatingly. "But I listened outside doors after that, every evening, just in case. Started falling asleep in school—then, of course, I got a bad half-term report, and my father was angry and disappointed.

"I felt awful, because, you know, I still wanted to please him. So one day when I got a merit point I raced all the way home, hoping he'd be there, hoping it would make it up to him. Because, on some level, I felt it must have been my fault he'd hit me, even though I didn't understand what I'd done wrong."

Something bad was about to happen, I could see it in the deep line of pain down the middle of his forehead...

"I opened the door and rushed into the hall, calling to see if he was there... and he was. Hanging from the upstairs banister. Even at that age I could tell he was dead."

I sucked in my breath, shocked. Expecting some horror, but... not that.

"I don't actually remember what happened for the next hour or two. Apparently good little Lucas made an exemplary emergency call, and let the ambulance crew in and did everything just right, but I don't remember any of it. Never did.

"Well, to cut a long story short, the debtors seized the manor and the store—even Clara's doll's house—and we moved to a very small flat with a tiny balcony. My mum got a factory job—it seemed like she worked every hour of the day and night to keep us fed. I filled the balcony with plants, but Clara and I had to hang washing over them—we'd started doing most of the housework.

"I tried to garden in the undergrowth around the block of flats, but local gangs trashed my attempts regularly. I was very unhappy, but since I'd given up the idea of being a gardener, I told myself it didn't matter. The gangs tried to trash me too, of course, when they could catch me, which wasn't often. In the summer I'd used to climb down from my room to the manor garden to carry on gardening after bedtime, and climbing the side of a high-rise was no different—so long as you didn't look down. For some reason no one ever followed me, though I sometimes needed my knife to reach that safety."

I couldn't help a shudder at the thought of a childhood so bleak that clinging to the side of a high-rise could count as 'safety.'

"My burning ambition by then was to get a job that would allow me to look after my mum and Clara. I got work in a shop after school and on weekends—even before school, washing the floors. I brought back every cent I could.

"And I studied jobs. I knew starting salaries, pensions, hours, employment terms—because I was impatient, I wanted to earn as soon as I left school, and what's more, earn *enough* to look after them both."

He saw my incredulous look. "No, not many jobs like that around. There was just one—when I first saw the figures for it, I raised my eyebrows but automatically discounted it. But by the time I was sixteen, my mum was drinking too much and not eating enough. Everything was wearing her down. I was frantic for her to be able to stop slaving at the factory. So I took early Sorting and went full-time at the shop I'd been working for."

I gasped. "You took *early Sorting?* Then went to work at a *shop?*"

"The confidence of youth—or desperation. But I passed with flying colors. As for the shop, I'd been working there for so long, I was sure within a year or so I could be manager—and I was right. I did another year and a half there *as* manager, then, with the all-important *management experience* acquired, I applied for a commission in EGD Security. I knew they were always desperate for recruits."

Yes, that was the job. Very lucrative, if you could stomach it.

"I'd convinced myself by this time that there was nothing wrong with it. Desperation is a terrible tempter—or greed, call it what you will. I told myself all the usual lies people in EGD Security tell themselves. It's rational, it's for the greater good, someone else will just do it anyway... all that *rubbish*." His tone was savage.

"I didn't say anything to mum or Clara, I planned to tell them only if I was accepted for training. Clara had passed her Sorting and was just starting work, but she'd had a steady boyfriend for over a year, and I knew they were only waiting to register until they'd saved up enough money to set up home together. I wanted to be able to help with that, as well. I wanted to be able to provide for *everyone*, and the commission was the way."

"Anyway, I got a call, come in for interview, so I went. Afterwards they said I was accepted and should proceed straight to training. I could have one phone call before the transport left. So I called my mum and told her only that I'd been offered a commission and I'd tell her all about it ASAP. Deep down—well-buried by then—was the knowledge that I was selling my soul to the devil, and she wouldn't like it. I knew I needed to break it carefully—and as persuasively as possible.

"When I got there, I found the abrupt departure was only part of the test—for the three months of training, we were allowed no contact with family or friends, beyond sending a simple message to inform them of this. It was a blow, but it was the rules—they had to be able to see if we could cope with the isolation of being an officer at a Facility. I was only nineteen, and I'd never been away from Mum and Clara for even a week before, but I was determined nothing was going to stop me, so I stuck it out. I passed final testing with high marks and was officially an EGD lieutenant."

My age. They made him an EGD Lieutenant at the age I am now.

"We were allowed a couple of weeks leave then, before our first posting, so home I went—not in uniform, of course. I was glad I'd finally be able to bring Mum and Clara up to date—and desperate to see them. I'd sent a note with the day I was coming, and when I got there I had the most terrible shock. They'd arranged a party, all the neighbors were there, many of our old friends, even—all there to celebrate me getting my lieutenancy—in the EuroArmy. That's what my mum had told them. That's what she thought."

"*Oh no,*" I murmured.

"Exactly. Even in my determined state of self-deception,

I couldn't fail to be aware of the difference between EuroArmy and EGD Security. The revelation would be devastating—utterly humiliating—for my mum. I just couldn't say anything in front of them all. I was going to take mum to one side afterwards and give her the spiel. But when they'd all gone, she and Clara were hugging me and looking at me with such... such *pride*. And I couldn't do it. I said nothing."

"Oh... dear."

"Quite. I didn't do it then, so of course I never did. Over and over, I resolved to tell them the truth, but the more time passed, the harder it was. I told them we weren't supposed to wear our uniforms on leave, because of the Resistance, but my mum was always asking for a picture of me in it. I made excuse after excuse, and she believed them all."

His face twisted for a moment in shame. "Anyway, I went off to my first post, in a big city Facility, where all lieutenants go. I worked hard and diligently, and was quickly rewarded with a promotion to Captain and a posting back to Salperton. I pretty much split my pay between my mum and Clara—wasn't worrying about my own old age, not with that big pension coming to me. My mum gave up working at the factory, and went on a course for self-rehab and stopped drinking quite so much. I called them both every week and Clara was so pleased about the change in Mum—and so was I.

"Clara had got registered almost as soon as I got my commission, and she and Bill were buying a house with my help—we were calling it a loan, because Bill had his pride. But very soon she and Bill had their first child, a little boy, and they called him Lucas."

"That's nice," I said uncertainly—there was such a look of pain on his face...

"Wasn't it? I've never been happier in my whole life than when I first held that little boy. I took every scrap of leave I was entitled to, spacing it out through the year, two days at a time, so I could see him grow up. Lots of phone calls—and when he started to talk! Uncle Lucas, he called me! Wonderful, wonderful child... I think I knew I wouldn't have children of my own. I was too obsessed with providing for the family I already had to start a new one. And I'd chosen the most un-conducive career—EGD Security officers being one of the few roles actually exempt from the Stable Population Act.

"Anyway, after only a couple of years the Major at Salperton retired, and I was promoted Major and made Commandant. I got the garden for my exclusive use, which was like a dream come true, and my sister had her second child, Jill. The only thing marring my happiness at all was *dear Gladys*, the new Captain, who wasn't quite what I'd hoped for and followed me around like a..." He broke off abruptly.

"Horny puppy?"

"How do you know...? *Watkins!* He told you about that?"

"He told Jon, actually. Not us girls."

"Oh. Never mind. Watkins was a good fellow. He did something for me..." A thoughtful look settled on his face. "Something to do with a parcel. Just before they took me... Posting something...?"

"The Security Manual! You got Watkins to post it?"

His face cleared. "Yes, that was it. He didn't know what was inside. But I knew they'd seize all my post—probably recall anything still in the postal system, as well, looking for so-called evidence. So I asked him to post it from his account. Didn't hesitate. Good man."

"I think he liked you. At least as a boss."

"Liked my firm hand. He'd seen things, under more relaxed Commandants. About as sincerely well-meaning as anyone in EGD Security gets, Watkins."

"Why *did* you send that manual?"

"Two reasons. One was to get back at them for what they were going to do to me."

"How could you be so sure they'd come for *you?* It was *dear Gladys's* fault we were able to escape."

"A younger *woman* with a cheerfully plump face or a slightly older *man* who looks like a Nazi? They were always going to pick me."

I eyed his fair hair. Hollywood probably had done him a disservice there. "And the other reason?"

"Trying to make it up to you for what I'd done—and *hadn't done*. Wasn't sure if you'd actually do anything *with* it. I did wonder... Whether you'd stop. If one Facility would be enough... But it was mostly a case of *it's the thought that counts*, you know? The thing they'd most hate you to have..."

He shook his head, and from the intent look in his unfocussed eyes, he was thinking about something he remembered all too clearly. "I don't know why I didn't do it," he whispered. "When Doctor Richard took that syringe from me—you know what I wanted to do? I wanted to just take you and shove you out the wall gate myself. You'd earned it. And what did I care? I died that day, almost a decade earlier. My body's been walking around ever since, but I'm not *alive*. And I was already *for it* for losing all but one of my charges! Should have just let the last one go as well... Don't know why I didn't...

"I suppose I do, I'm a coward. I'd learned how to survive in my filthy little rut, and I was too scared to try and climb out of it. Even to save you. So I walked out like a good little automaton and left you. Knew I'd made the wrong decision as soon as I got outside. I stopped right there in the passage, and I thought about going back in and getting you out and saying to hell with them all. Maybe I'd have done it. But a guard came rushing up, telling me the Resistance were making a move, and off I ran to see about preserving the lives of the other fifty people I was responsible for. So I'll never know..."

He was silent for a long time. "Perhaps I just like to *think* I'd have done it," he said bitterly at last. "But that's why I sent the manual. It was an apology. The act of defiance I'd failed to make. Revenge. A chance. Must be the only good thing I've done in my entire life!"

He was quiet for a while longer, then, terrible, terrible pain in his eyes, he looked at me again. "So... back then everything was almost perfect. Or so I thought. Sun shining on oil produces a beautiful rainbow, but it's still oil underneath—dirty and poisonous. That's what my life was. Shining oil. One day I was looking down the Dismantling list for the day—the Dismantlers keep the detailed records, but it's the Commandant's job to keep track of who remains—intact—in his or her charge. And I came to an entry—Lucas Wherrick—my nephew's name. A coincidence, clearly—Luc was only nine and no reAssignee or murderer..."

My stomach clenched, a metal band pressed around my forehead, and my head spun, 'cause in a moment of chilling certainty I saw what was coming... My hand flew to my mouth, but he didn't seem to notice.

"Then I read the code ED-U, which means 'Early Dismantling—UnRegistered' and my eyes went on, along the line, and I couldn't stop them, though suddenly I wanted to, and the date of birth was Luc's. For a few moments I managed to cling to that safe disbelief—how *could* it be him—but it was all falling together too clearly, too easily—such short notice for their registration ceremony, so short I only just managed to be there, and that premature birth I was so worried about, until I saw the big, healthy baby boy—and I knew, I knew it was true.

"Luc was unRegistered, and they hid it, as people do if they can, to spare him from spending his short life with that hanging over him—driving everyone away from him—and it was *him*, it *was* him who'd been butchered that very day, in *my* Facility.

"And I'd not known; they'd not told me, because I was a Major in the EuroArmy, so what could I do? So I phoned her—Clara—I was half out of my mind with grief and guilt—I demanded why she hadn't told me about Luc being un-Registered—she'd clearly been crying—she couldn't understand how I knew, and I told her, *because I'm sitting here looking at his name on this list*, and she didn't understand, she said *what list, how can you know?* and I said, *because I'm a Major in EGD Security, you idiot, why didn't you* tell *me?*"

Already wincing at his naked anguish, I cringed at what was clearly a verbatim quote.

He stopped, breathing hard, his eyes dazed with memory and grief. "Well, that was that," he said at last, in a horribly collected voice. "That was the end of my relationship with Clara. And Mum. They couldn't forgive me. How could they? Clara and Bill moved away with little Jilly. Mum moved out of the house I bought her, and drank herself to the edge of the grave. Alcoholics aren't supposed to have transplants, but I pulled strings for her to have a new liver—but she wouldn't take it. Turned Conchie and died. Hating me. As I deserved."

"Why did you stay?" I whispered. "Why did you stay at the Facility? Surely you knew, then...?"

"Oh, I *knew*. I knew with one hundred percent clarity, what I'd always refused to admit. That it was evil, and it was wrong, and there was no justification for being there. I didn't even believe the 'someone else will do it if you don't' excuse any more. Because I knew, if no one else did it—*they couldn't do it.*

"But still I stayed. I couldn't face going out into the world—facing the world's disgust—trying to get a job—not that I'd have been able to. EGD Security have got you for life, no one else will have you. But since I didn't care about starving in a gutter, being a walking corpse anyway, I should have gone. But I didn't because I couldn't face leaving my garden. Does that give you some idea what I am? The most evil, cowardly wretch who ever breathed. To know as I did that it was wrong, to have lost everything to it, and to serve it still for the sake of a *garden.* "

His self-disgust was sharp enough to flay skin, and despite his words, despite what he was telling me, it was horrible to hear anyone speak of themself like that. I fumbled for words, confused and hurting for him, for his sister, for everyone he spoke of.

"How did you keep from... from harming yourself?" After hearing him talk like that...

"I'm never taking that way out! The easy way—I may be a coward, but I'll not stoop to that. Not like..." He broke off, biting his lip hard enough to draw blood.

Not like his father.

"Making my body go on living was pure torture... well, that's what I thought *then*... so I knew I had to do it. Live. Because I *deserved* it. Every moment of pain. I wouldn't run away. But the only way I could cope was if I spent most of the day buried in my garden. It was the only place I could find even a hint of peace. And I didn't deserve peace, but it was all that could keep me sane, keep me from that worst cowardice of all.

"So I stayed. And I stayed. And I stayed. I did my best for the reAssignees, but I could hardly bear to go near the boys. Every one of them reminded me of Luc. But the odd use of my old pocket knife on the guards kept serious offences very rare. I didn't care about hurting them," he was speaking almost to himself now, "they all looked like me, and I deserved to be punished, deserved it so much... it was almost a relief when Internal Affairs took me, felt like justice finally being served... except that it wasn't..." he shook his head confusedly, "I hadn't done what they said. I wished I had but *hadn't*, and I refused to lie... but what they *did* to me, I deserved..."

"Lord have mercy, Lucas, no one deserves what they did to you!"

"Is that what you'd say, if Luc had been your child? Luc or any of the thousand others?"

"Everyone is responsible for the Facilities, Lucas." Though he'd shaken my faith in this statement a little when he pointed out that if no one would do the job, the job couldn't be done...

"But EGD Security most of all," he said dully. "We are the ones who allow it to happen."

I wasn't sure what to say to that, but it didn't matter, because his control was going, tears running down his cheeks, and he wouldn't have heard me.

"Luc," he whispered. "Precious, precious boy, I loved you so much... I'd have saved you, if only I'd known! Saved you, or died trying... but they didn't tell me because I didn't tell them. My lie killed you. My job killed you. All of you... Why did I come here? All the way here? I must've been mad, to think there was any forgiveness for me... Luc, poor child, how frightened you must have been... All of you... fear and misery... And still I *stayed*..."

He brought his knees up to his chin, sobs choking off further words. Remorse. Pure remorse. I'd seen it once on Bane's face, and I was seeing it again now. And I understood, now, why he was so convinced he couldn't be forgiven. It wasn't just because his mother had failed to forgive him. It was because he couldn't even think of forgiving himself. I'd needed God's help to forgive *him* and he needed God's help with *that*, big time.

Just as I had a month earlier, I reached out and tried to put my arms around him.

He flinched away. "How can you even touch me?"

But when I made another attempt to gather him to me, he let me. "Because I forgive you," I whispered, rubbing his bony back and hugging him tightly. "And God forgives you. Please believe me."

"How could I possibly deserve it?" he whispered back.

"Lucas, none of us *deserves* it. But God forgives us anyway."

"I don't understand." His voice was thin and choked, his face buried in my hair. "Yet... I believe you *do* forgive me... but... I don't understand how it can be... I don't..."

His voice trailed off weakly and his sobs carried on for some time, before exhaustion finally silenced them. I settled him on the bed and laid a blanket over him. Smoothed his fair hair gently until sleep mercifully claimed him.

I sat and watched him sleeping for a while, his terrible story swirling in my mind. His own nephew... wasn't sure who I felt most sorry for. I'd known what he was, what he'd spent his adult life doing. The fact his own nephew was one of the victims didn't actually make any difference to *that*—it just made his own predicament more pitiable.

Thinking through the jumble of reasons he'd given for staying, my bewilderment evaporated. Paralyzed by grief, despair, anger at himself and the EGD, even at his family who'd rejected him after all he'd sacrificed for them, however misguidedly, and faced with scarcely even the prospect of survival in the world outside... *of course* he'd stayed. Or rather, *of course* he hadn't been able to galvanize himself *to leave*. He'd probably been barely able to do anything more than get through the next day. And the next. And the next...

Poor, poor man.

Poor, poor boy.

Poor, broken family.

Oh Lord, I hate Sorting. Please let us win. Please, please, please?

Opening his Office book to the page that said, "*Though*

your sins be like scarlet, yet they shall be whiter than wool,"
I left the Scriptures open on the bedside table as well, at the
place where Our Lord bids us to forgive, *"not seven times,
nay, but seventy times seven times."*

"When the Liberation team broke into our dorm we were
really scared. We'd never heard of anyone rescuing
reAssignees—no one had ever done it—so we weren't
sure what was going on. When we realized they were
taking us away—that we wouldn't have to be
dismantled—we hardly dared to believe it until we were
actually on the ship. Then we all went a bit mad. Mad with
joy!"

*Jules L., former reAssignee—quoted on 'The Impatient
Gardener'*

"You want to do *what?*" Bane pretty much yelled at
Eduardo. "You want to stick Margo up on a podium in St.
Peter's Square *right beside* the white line? What sort of
stupid idea is *that?*"

"It's not stupid," said Eduardo, un-phased. "People will
be able to gather right there on EuroBloc soil to hear her."

"Excuse me!" Bane was not mollified. "*Why* are we in
this apartment that *doesn't* overlook the walls! One sniper,
that's all the EuroGov needs. *One!*"

"I'm not saying we do it today. But in another week,
well, the EuroGov would be very foolish indeed to do
something like that then, so close to D-day. If they did, the
sympathy vote would pretty much guarantee our victory, so
this is a win-win situation."

"*Win-win?*" bellowed Bane, jumping to his feet. I
jumped up as well, thinking he was going to launch himself
at Eduardo... but instead he took a deep breath and stood
very still, fists clenching.

Eventually he snapped, "Has anyone ever punched you
in the face for what you consider to be no apparent
reason?"

"Every now and then someone tries," admitted Eduardo.

"I'm not surprised," snarled Bane. "Don't you even realize you're calling *Margo getting killed* a *win?*"

"And obviously I don't want that. But a week before the vote, I judge the chances of another assassination attempt to be extremely low. I was just pointing out that if the worst did happen, it wouldn't be a complete dead loss, if you'll pardon the pun."

Bane took several more deep breaths...

"So, are you up for it, Margo?" asked Eduardo.

"No!" said Bane.

"*Margo?*" repeated Eduardo, pointedly.

I swallowed. The thought of standing there with absolutely nothing between me and a sniper's bullet... All the same, Eduardo was right. The only thing killing me so close to the vote would achieve was a huge swell of support for our cause. The chances of Reginald Hill putting personal satisfaction over victory seemed pretty low. After all, if they won, he could kill me then...

"Bane, I know it's risky, but I think I should do this speech," I said. "We've *got to win*, don't you understand? If we don't, we're all dead anyway."

Bane... growled.

"Bane, love," I slipped my arms around him. "Bane, I really think I should do this, but I want to do it with you behind me. Please?"

He let out a long sigh and slipped his arms around me in return, holding me close. "I'd rather you did it with me *standing in front* of you," he said, resting his forehead against mine. "It would be better than nothing."

I had to smile. "I appreciate the thought, love, but I think it would spoil the impression rather, don't you?"

Lucas seemed fine when he let me in. A bit subdued, his eyes following me in... wonder? ...bewilderment? I was very careful to avoid doing or saying anything that might be interpreted as a drawing away from him as a result of his story, and gradually he became a bit more his usual self.

Sort of. He sat, his head resting against the chair back, looking as though the memories dragged up by his narration were still swirling blackly around him. Internal Affairs might actually have done him a favor, by putting it from his mind.

"What a mess I've made of my life...." he murmured after a while.

"Well, you're here now. And it's not too late to start over."

He gave me a curious look. "When would it be too late?"

I blinked. Said bluntly, "When you're dead." Saw him open his mouth again and added quickly, "*Actually* dead, Lucas. *Dead* may be the only metaphor you feel properly describes the state of your spirit, but you are *not* a dead man."

"We are spirit and body both, so how do you start again if your spirit is no more?"

He knew his Theology, all right. "I think you know the answer to that," I replied.

He sank back into silence again, a more intent, thoughtful silence. But he still glanced at me now and then, with that wonder in his eyes.

13 days

"Even when we arrived in Africa it was a while before I dared to let anyone know that I believed in God. But it wasn't a big deal at all. Everyone here believes in God. People laugh and sing while they work, and I think it's because they have God."

Martina E., former reAssignee—quoted on 'The Impatient Gardener'

I hurried along the corridor, trying to go over the talk I'd be giving in St Peter's square in—gulp!—less than a week, now, in my head. I really wanted it to be good. More than with any previous talk I'd given, I'd be putting my life on the line to give it, after all. But my mind kept bouncing back to the conversation I'd just had with Pope Cornelius. There was a bounce in my steps as well. I felt like a joyful bouncy ball. Lucas had been in such a preoccupied mood for the last few days, and now...

The bounce went out of my step as I saw a familiar cassocked figure turn into the corridor. Kyle. I drew a deep breath, gathering myself. After he'd given Lucas those flowers and I realized how much he must still care, I'd knocked on his door a few more times—but if he'd been in, he hadn't let on. I wasn't seeing him at morning Mass, so he must be going in the evening. Simply to avoid me?

I stepped forward determinedly, trying to smile—I wasn't going to waste this opportunity... but Kyle turned abruptly on his heel and walked away. No, not again!

"Kyle!" I raced after him. "Kyle, please, stop!"

"What is it?" he said ungraciously, coming to a halt.

"I just want to talk to you. You're my brother, I'm allowed to want to talk to you, aren't I?" I teased.

No answering smile. "I'm really not in the mood, Margo." He turned to go.

No... *Kyle*... "Lucas is getting baptized!" I blurted. "Isn't that great news?"

Kyle gave me a downright disapproving look. "You can't baptize an adult who isn't mentally competent to make the decision."

"Well, that's what His Holiness just wanted to talk to me about, actually. Apparently, as soon as Lucas asked him for baptism, Pope Cornelius spoke immediately to Doctor Frederick and the medical staff, but they with one accord shrugged and directed him to me."

Kyle looked incredulous. "And you told him it was *okay?*"

My turn to stare at him. "Of course. I mean, I imagine Lucas will always count as eccentric, but most of the time now, I think he's as mentally competent as you or I."

"I know he's better than he was, but it's barely a week since the man tried to kill Doctor Frederick!"

Unfortunately that had got around.

"He freaked out and overreacted, yeah, but no one is at their sanest after being shot in the arm, Kyle."

Kyle shook his head to himself, wearing that 'silly little sister' expression that had been driving me so crazy.

I took a deep breath and refused to get mad. "Kyle,

Lucas walked across Europe, for four months, starving, for *this*. To find out whether God is willing to forgive him. *He* thinks the answer is no, and I've spent the last couple of months convincing him it might be *yes* after all. If Pope Cornelius refused him, it wouldn't matter what reason he gave; all Lucas would hear is *no*. Trust me, Lucas knows exactly what he's doing. Ask Father Mark if you don't believe me; he sent Lucas to Pope Cornelius."

"Huh." Kyle made as though to walk on again.

My heart and my voice both cracked slightly. "Kyle... I'm sorry I shouted at you and... and pointed the gun at you, okay? Please, what else can I say?"

"I don't want to talk about this! I don't want to talk about anything! Just leave me alone!" This time he did stride on.

I ran after him. "Kyle! *Please!* It's less than two weeks until the vote and we've no idea if we'll win! Do you really want things to be like this between us?"

Without answering, Kyle just ducked his head and barged through the door into the non-secure area. I was about to follow him, make him talk to me if I had to hang onto his arm and physically hold him still, when I re-membered Eduardo's warning... Photos of me and Kyle arguing wouldn't look quite so bad on the front page as photos of me and Bane, but it wouldn't look *good*.

Fighting back tears, I headed for the Sistine Chapel instead and dropped onto a bench—glad there was no one else there, because, unstoppably, I began to cry. Fortunately by the time three off-duty Swiss Guards came in and knelt on the other side of the aisle, I'd just about got myself under control again.

Lord, what can I do about Kyle? He obviously still cares... The way he'd run off was almost as though the conversation was upsetting him, yet... he was so hostile...

Sitting quietly, I waited a while for my face to resume its normal color and for my mind to quiet... well, the former, anyway. But I needed to go and see Father Mark, then get back to my blog. I rose, genuflected, and headed reluctantly up to the hospital, trailed by my anxious-looking body-guard. I didn't really know the one assigned to me today, so I was glad he'd remained discreetly in the background.

I took a deep breath before opening Father Mark's door. I was even less in the mood for this emotional torment than usual...

Father Mark's smile of welcome made me feel bad about my lack of enthusiasm for his company. I tried to muster a return smile, but my emotions just felt flayed.

"Are you all right?"

"I'm okay."

"Is it Bane?"

"No. Bane's fine. And Lucas is getting baptized! But I think you know that." I tried to recapture the happiness I'd been feeling about that earlier, but it wasn't quite happening. Then the vote suddenly crashed back into my mind, as it seemed to do with ever-increasing frequency. "I hope it can be done soon."

Father Mark must've seen the fear in my eyes clearly enough. "Put your faith in the Lord's will, Margaret," he said softly.

"The Lord's will is that several million *voters* should have free will. We know the Lord will be with us, whatever, but we really don't know what's going to happen at the end of next week, do we?" The end of next week. The words stuck in my throat.

Father Mark sighed. "*True.* Don't worry about Lucas, though. If he dropped dead this very instant, it would be an open and shut case of baptism by desire. But I'm sure it can be done in the next day or two."

"Oh good." Not entirely rationally, I added, "Because if we do lose, of all the people here, Lucas is going to be one of the deadest."

Him and Pope Cornelius and Bane and Jon and... *me.* And Father Mark too...

"Hmm," agreed Father Mark wryly. "Speaking of which... Have you made up with Kyle, yet?"

"I tried again just now! He won't even speak to me!" Though *right now*, I was almost relieved, if I was honest about it. Focusing on my anger towards Kyle helped me to suppress my anger towards Father Mark. Horrible but true.

"A loving big brother *is* entitled to be angry about what happened with Bane, you know. There must be something else you can do."

Why was Father Mark going on at *me* about this? It took two to make up! So far all Kyle had done was give me more reasons to be furious with him.

"Well, I'd love to know what it is!" I snapped. Lord help me, I was not in a fit state to discuss this right now... "I've *run after him*, I've *begged* him. He *won't listen!*"

Father Mark frowned. "Margaret, I know Kyle isn't making this easy. But you've *got to* fix things..."

"I've *tried! Aren't you listening to me either?*" I was getting so angry, but I couldn't help it. The rift with Kyle was painful enough without him going on and on about it...

"I know, but you haven't succeeded. You have to do better. Things can *always* be fixed, you just have to try hard enough..."

"Always be FIXED?" I yelled, my heartbeat surging, drumming in my head, and a red haze consuming everything. *"What? If I TRY HARD ENOUGH, my BABY will be FI...?"*

I clamped both hands over my mouth and tried to physically swallow the words, eyes scrunching closed.

But it was too late.

22

OVERRATED

Oh God help me, too late! My mind spun helplessly as I sought some way to cover up what I'd just said, pass it off as meaning something other than what it really meant, but it was no use...

When I opened my eyes, Father Mark was dead white and his eyes were fixed on my face. Nothing I could possibly say would fool him.

"Baby..." he whispered, eyes moving to my empty belly. "*God forgive me*, that's it, *there was a baby...*"

The machine by the bed gave its little beep. Father Mark didn't seem to notice. "I killed your baby..." he whispered. "Oh, how you must hate me..." His eyes were losing their focus and he was fighting to keep his eyes open.

In a sudden panic I sprang to the bed and put my mouth near his ear. "You mustn't tell anyone! Bane doesn't know!"

"Sorry..." he murmured, "*so sorry...*"

Sleep claimed him. Had he heard me?

But... *O Lord, I told him*. How could I have done it? The look on his face... What sort of twisted, hateful bitch was I?

With a strangled sob, I turned and yanked the door open, racing past my startled bodyguard. Didn't stop until I panted up the last few steps of a long staircase and stumbled to Pope Cornelius's door. Hammered on it with no restraint whatsoever.

The Swiss Guard standing ramrod-straight to one side of the door gave a slight cough. When I looked at him, he shook his head, just a fraction one way, a fraction the other. Telling me to cut it out? Oh... telling me Pope Cornelius wasn't in.

I crumpled down at the base of the door, wrapped my arms around my knees and just cried softly until finally a hand touched my shoulder and a very British voice said, "Margo?" Clearly my bodyguard had called for backup.

"Where's His Holiness?" I sniffed. I needed to go to confession. I'd have liked to go before, after throwing that grenade. Now I needed it desperately.

Unicorn pulled a networkAccessor from his jacket and consulted it. "I can drop you into his schedule in fifteen minute's time, if you really need me to."

My heart sank at the thought of waiting that long with all this guilt and anguish ripping me apart, but tried to lift as well. Pope Cornelius might easily have been busy all day... "Yes," I muttered. "Please do..."

Unicorn tapped away for a moment, hopefully not disarranging all Sister Immanuella's carefully organized appointments and meetings too dreadfully, then put the Accessor away. Waved my hapless bodyguard to the end of the corridor, pried me off the floor and moved me to some chairs opposite the door.

"Margo, is it something to do with..." He spoke very softly, in English. "Did you want to talk to me while you're waiting?"

How could I tell Unicorn about this? I couldn't imagine him ever doing something so vile.

I shook my head mutely.

With a slight sigh, he put a comforting hand on my back, rubbing gently. "We'll just wait, then." Fishing in his pocket with his free hand, he came out with a rosary. I concentrated very, very hard on his quiet voice, trying to stop other thoughts breaking in, and by the time footsteps trod up the stairs I was actually mumbling along, just about.

As Pope Cornelius approached, looking us over with some concern, I lurched to my feet. Oh no, Unicorn had probably just overridden the poor man's morning coffee break, or something... Why didn't I think of that?

"Margaret, come in," he said, waving me towards the door, which the Swiss Guard had just unlocked.

I headed that way, but Unicorn paused Pope Cornelius with a quick, "One moment, Your Holiness..." He murmured something else, and I caught enough words to realize that he was giving permission for Pope Cornelius to act on one particular piece of information Unicorn had previously passed on under the Seal of Confession—but only with me.

Of course... VSS all had to confess to priests with top security clearance. And Unicorn had felt so guilty about my loss...

"...because I think she won't want to actually tell you," Unicorn concluded.

He was right. Until I could tell Bane, to tell even my confessor felt like a betrayal.

Frowning slightly, Pope Cornelius followed me, no doubt working out whether the Seal of Confession actually *allowed* him to act on Unicorn's permission. He sat me straight on the sofa and went to put the kettle on. He returned quickly with two mugs of coffee, but my unoccupied mind was already turning back into a maelstrom of guilt and self-recrimination.

"I need to confess..." I blurted, as soon as he sat down.

"All right, but I give you permission to drink that coffee while you do it. Come on, start sipping."

He'd added plenty of milk. And sugar, I found, when I obediently took a big sip. It wasn't how I liked my coffee, but a papal order was a papal order, and shock was shock, and apparently shocked was what I looked. It was how I felt. So shocked with myself I hardly knew myself.

The hot coffee was good, though. I took another gulp, then the words began to tumble out. "Bless me, Father, for I have sinned, I... I told someone something. Something I'd sworn to myself I would never tell them because it would be kinder to just... stab them to death with a table knife! But I told him! I told him... *viciously*... with the deliberate intention of hurting him... punishing him... being... being avenged on him... And I can never take it back..."

"Did you tell him calmly, in a premeditated way, after making a decision to do so?"

"No... No, it was in the heat. I got so angry. I just blurted it out..."

"This thing you told him, was it true?"

"Yes... *Sort of.* Well, no, only *physically*. He *wasn't* responsible. And I know that. Most of me knows that... That's why I was so determined he shouldn't know. I wasn't going to let him know, I wasn't, I thought I'd die before I let him find out! And *I* told him!" My voice trailed off into a near sob.

Pope Cornelius sighed and directed a stern look at my mug. I swigged more coffee, trying to keep myself under control.

"Some people would say that it is usually better to know the truth, however painful," he said, after supervising a few more mouthfuls.

"Not this! No one needs to know this! Not when it wasn't his fault. I just can't get rid of this anger! Sometimes I feel like I *hate* him... *It's so unfair of me...*"

"And you think you could feel like this and him not sense it? Isn't it better that he knows *why?*"

"No." I shook my head. "Thinking I'm a little uncomfortable with him because of something that he did, and knowing *this* are *totally different.* They don't even fit on the same pain scale. They just don't!"

Pope Cornelius sighed again. "Well, you may be right, but what's done is done. And your motives for telling him may not have been good, but it sounds as though you didn't really mean to do it."

"The moment I actually did it, I did! Just not the second before or after." It was so clear to me, now, how Bane had come to hit me. Just that *split second's* loss of control... of reason... of love, even... All one's anger and grief and loss and frustration escaping in one poisonous surge...

"It was ill meant, alas, and I will surely set you a penance for it. But it's a rare person who never says a hot word in anger. The driving force behind it was... I suspect... unusually powerful. And however badly the truth hurts, I imagine the person in question will prefer to know it. So you will say your penance, and then you will forgive yourself, do you understand?"

I blinked. Nodded slowly. Despite rushing here for confession, the idea of being forgiven for *this* seemed extraordinary. Oh dear, was this how *Lucas* felt? But what had I tried so unsuccessfully to tell Bane? *There are no unforgiveable sins...*

So, perhaps...

"Do you have any other sins to confess?" asked Pope Cornelius gently, when I focused on him again.

"Um... yes. Three dead guys."

"I am not setting you a penance for *them,*" said Pope Cornelius, very firmly. "Anything else?"

"Kyle..." I said uncertainly. "I mean, I forgive him, I *do...* but we haven't *reconciled.* He won't *talk* to me..."

"Then so long as you are truly endeavoring to love and forgive him wholeheartedly, the failure to reconcile is not your fault. Though you should keep trying, of course. Anything else?"

"I expect so, but my head's mush..."

"That will do, then. For your penance, you will visit Father Mark every day, since he is someone who is in special need of love and care right now. You will also forgive yourself. And you will say a rosary specifically about this anger that you feel for someone. Okay?"

I nodded. Pope Cornelius was acting on Unicorn's permission in that he wasn't asking me a load of questions, but he clearly wasn't prepared to make his knowledge explicit.

So I said my Act of Contrition, then he gave Absolution, and incredibly, I was forgiven for what was quite possibly the most horrible thing I'd ever done.

Forgiven, yes... but I would surely regret it forever.

12 days

"We'd been hearing so much about the Liberations, the warden took all our radios away. We used to fantasize about it; we even held 'Liberation drills' where we'd practice getting everyone in line. But those of us who understood the odds—how low they were—knew it wouldn't really happen.

"Then one night this little canister smashed through the window, with folded up instructions inside—and it was really happening, to us! We were being Liberated!"

Francine le G., former reAssignee—quoted on 'The Impatient Gardener'

I wanted to visit Father Mark on my own the following morning, but Bane and Jon nixed that by suggesting we all go along together. In a way, I was relieved not to have to face him on my own. But...

Please God, don't let Father Mark blurt out something in front of Bane...

When we arrived, though, we found doctors and nurses clustered around Father Mark's room. A seriousness in the way they were talking and moving...

"What's happening?" I caught Nurse Poppy's sleeve.

She gave me her professional face, but her eyes were unhappy. "We think he had a small heart attack earlier this morning."

"Heart attack! He's far too young!" *Oh Lord, is this my fault?* "Did he... do you think he... got a nasty shock, or something?"

Doctor Frederick noticed my raised voice and came over. "You perhaps don't fully understand the condition he's in," he said, addressing all three of us. "Nasty shocks never exactly help, but they're pretty much redundant in this case. His body is under truly extreme stress, thanks to the conditioning, *twenty-four hours a day.* The drugs we're giving him—hardly harmless in themselves—can only *reduce* the symptoms of the panic. What's happened is pretty much inevitable."

"Is he going to be all right?" asked Bane urgently.

"Well, it doesn't look like there's any *very* serious harm done, so in the short term he should be fine. But if we can't undo the conditioning, then there *is* no realistic possibility of any *in the longer term.* He'll have another heart attack, a stroke, something. No one's body can cope with this sort of strain indefinitely."

"But... can't you do *anything*?" asked Jon.

"It's a tight place. If we take him away from the hospital, and the doctors, there's no hope of a cure, but the conditioning won't kill him. If we keep him here, there's a chance of a cure, but he may well die before we can manage it. The truth is, we need a military mind-programmer or Father Mark has only a matter of weeks. And that's if we're lucky."

Good, whispered that little, still-not-wholly-exorcised voice.

"Eduardo is searching for one in the safe towns of Africa," Doctor Frederick added, "but he doesn't think we should get our hopes up. It's an incredibly rare and specialized profession and we probably simply don't have one."

We met Eduardo as we headed away from the hospital.

"Ah, Margo," he greeted me. "Am I right in thinking that you've already prepared your talk?"

"What, the one for St Peter's Square next week?"

"Yes, that one."

"Uh... yes, why?" I said uncertainly.

"You haven't seen the news yet today, I take it?"

"No..."

"You know Sylvia Elendale?"

"That little girl with cancer they've been parading over the news? 'Vote 'Yes' to save Sylvia,' and all that twisted line of argument?"

"Yes, her. She died suddenly last night. The EuroGov are milking the situation for all it's worth. I think you should take a few minutes to work Sylvia's tragic death into your speech and then get out there and do it, this morning."

"This morning?" The fear in Bane's voice was impossible to miss. "It's still twelve days until the vote! Is it safe?"

"Not entirely," said Eduardo, honestly. "If we'd given the EuroGov forewarning we were doing it, I'd say it was a total no-go. But they're not expecting it, so hopefully by the time they can deploy a sniper, it'll be over. Plus there's a big difference between trying to assassinate Margaret in public, as opposed to in private. Think of the videos, the pictures... The bad press would outweigh what they've just gained from that little girl's demise, despite the fact that twelve days is enough time for public sympathy to wane."

I swallowed. "Exactly how bad is it?"

Eduardo grimaced "You can sit and watch the counter on the online poll ticking up in their favour. It's bad. She was a sweet little girl, and the EuroGov are making jolly sure not to draw attention to the fact that another sweet little girl would've had to die to save her."

I took a deep breath and managed to keep my voice steady. "I suppose I'd better get out there and remind everyone, then."

"Please Bane," I said. He'd insisted on coming to St Peter's Square with me, but... "Stay here, behind the wall. I don't want to be worrying about you, too."

Bane scowled, but after we'd exchanged a long kiss and a tight hug, he remained where he was as I followed Unicorn to the gate. It was kind of nice that U was back on physically active duty—except that I didn't want him to get hurt. Again. I could feel Snakey's absence so keenly. And... right now it just kept replaying in my head: how Friedrich had shot him—and he'd been dead. Just like that...

"We'll wait here for a moment," said U. "Cardinal Akachi is just warming the crowd up for you."

"I hope he doesn't take too long," I couldn't help saying. Eduardo had sent a notification of the imminent speech to the main newspapers fifteen minutes ago, enough time for most of them to make it here. But someone would have tattled to the EuroGov. Where was the closest army base where a suitable rifle might be obtained? How long to get a trained sniper to there, and then to here?

Stop it, Margo, I told myself. *To pull off this type of assassination you need time to plan. If they just turn up, our guys will take them out.* I glanced at the wall and the rooftops of the Vatican, where a considerable number of VSS agents and Swiss Guards lay, scanning the crowd, the road, and the overlooking buildings through the sights of their nonLee sniper rifles. One of them was probably holding the very weapon I'd used during the Liberations...

Actually... "U?"

"Umhmm..." Most of U's attention was already on his surroundings, although we hadn't left the safe interior of the square yet.

"What if..." my voice was rather small, "what if an assassin just decides to stand behind a nice, nonLee-proof window and shoot through it?"

"A couple of our guys have Lethals, Margo," said U gently. "Just in case."

Oh. Of course Eduardo thought of that, Margo. Just go over your speech and stop stressing. Make sure you've got it right...

But I hadn't fixed things with Kyle... Or Father Mark...

"Okay, Margo? You're up..." U's voice.

My hands were damp with sweat. So was my brow. My head felt funny. *Oh, please Lord, don't let me pass out...* I just had to walk out there and do my speech. Easy-peasy. I'd done it plenty of times before. But I couldn't seem to move. Having failed in a private assassination, who was to say the EuroGov *wouldn't* take this rare opportunity for a public one?

"Margo?"

The crowd was waiting. *Come on, Margo. Either you go up there and say your thing and, please Lord, swing things back our way, or you go out there and someone shoots you dead and we win the vote and everyone you love will be safe... Win-win, right?*

I let out a long, steadying breath, and walked forward.

Angel Margaret, please watch over me.

Lord, be with me...

"If Eduardo comes up with any more of these bright ideas, I swear, I am going to punch him," said Bane, his arm still around me. He'd hardly let me go since I returned from that podium, alive and well, even whilst I tried to cook lunch.

I slipped my arm back around him. "No you won't. You'll just take a deep breath and speak reasonably to him, like you did last time."

"It was a close thing," muttered Bane.

"This really *was* necessary, Bane," said Jon. We were on our way back to the hospital—*and I still hadn't managed to give the pair of them the slip, blast it!* "The opinion polls were doing a nose dive. Anyway, either the EuroGov were caught off guard, or they thought better of it. No harm done."

"No harm done!" snorted Bane. "Margo, has my hair turned gray?"

"Completely gray," I said solemnly.

"And mine's gone a bit white around the temples, has it?" joked Jon.

"That's right," I said, still mock-serious. "You both look very distinguished."

"I wonder what Lucas's hair looks like?" said Bane dryly.

I winced. "I'm kind of hoping he might not hear about this."

But when we went into Father Mark's room, Lucas was already there—and from the look he gave me, he had heard all about the speech. Thankfully, seeing Jon, he gave him a wide berth, and slipped away without saying anything. One of his new undamaged plants stood on the bedside table, replacing the poor grenade-swept one he'd had to bring the day before.

"Father Mark, how are you?" we all tried to ask at once, but I tilted my head at Bane and put my finger to my lips, in case Father Mark hadn't heard the last thing I'd said the day before.

Father Mark inclined his head to me in acknowledgement of this silent communication, sober-faced. And very pale. They hadn't taken the tubes away. "Oh, I'm all right. No serious harm done, didn't they tell you?" His eyes didn't move from my face. I sat beside the bed and took his hand, held it tight, trying to tell him how sorry I was for what I'd said, with just my eyes. From the way he stared back, he was trying to tell me something similar.

His tone hadn't convinced Bane. "Don't give us that hogwash. Even not-serious harm is bad news when it's your heart; you think we don't all know that?"

"Fine, so I've received notice that my earthly tenure is coming to an end. Happy?" It was the usual bold sort of thing he'd say, but he didn't sound bold. He sounded... totally resigned. As though he'd been stepped on by a giant. And I was quite, quite sure that the giant was not the heart attack. The giant was *me*.

8 days

"My daughter has a chronic but treatable condition, but is able to lead a normal life. If Sorting is abolished in a week's time, she will be able to go on leading it. If Sorting is retained, she will be sent away to die. So please, please do not tick that 'yes' box unless you could happily look me in the eye while you do it!"

Senora Y., mother of a preKnown—quoted on 'The Impatient Gardener'

"Margaret, you try and reason with Father Mark," Doctor Frederick greeted me, as I arrived at the hospital a couple of days later.

"Uh... about what?"

"The plan we've come up with, for saving his life."

"Sounds good, but what is it?"

"He goes off to the secure farm in Africa, safely away from you, where he can live a reasonably normal life under much-reduced guard, until such a time as we find someone who can help him."

I blinked. Why hadn't we thought of that sooner? "Why isn't he going for it?"

"He's afraid it won't be safe. He's being very stubborn, too."

"Oh. Well, I'll certainly *try* and persuade him." I wouldn't have to keep visiting him then, would I? I truly did not want him to die, but I still couldn't look at him without thinking about my baby. And I don't think he could see *me* without thinking about the same.

Father Mark had the bed only halfway up, today, and his face was pale and sweat-dampened. Had the psychologists been in here recently? His eyes moved tiredly to me as I sat beside the bed—a slight pinch of pain tightened his face. As usual.

"Oh, hello, Margaret." He sounded tired too.

"Hi. How are you?"

"Fine," he said, as though it was a matter of no concern whatsoever. "When's the baptism?"

"This afternoon. Lucas seems in a bit of a daze. After everything, I think he was still sure Pope Cornelius would laugh in his face."

"Well, in a few hours, his soul will be cleaner than the

day he was conceived." Father Mark smiled in memory. Ah yes, another thing he could sympathize wholeheartedly with Lucas about. "I'm sorry I can't be there. Tell him I'm praying for him."

"I will." Quite a few people were happy about this. Of course, it made a very pleasant interlude in the horribly tense run-up to the vote... That would be another good thing about the Africa plan, get Father Mark out of here before D-Day, as it'd become known. "Father Mark..."

"Here we go."

"This Africa plan sounds just the thing to me. Why don't you want to go?"

"Why?" He shook a wrist and spoke with more feeling than he had for days. "Because it involves taking these cuffs off, that's why."

"But you won't need them over the sea in Africa!"

"Won't I? And first you've got to get me to a ship." He cut off my objection. "No, Margaret, it's not safe. I was *very* good at my job, trust me."

"But if they put you under? So you don't even wake up until you reach Africa?"

"And what's to stop me coming straight back?"

"It's a secure center! You'll still be *guarded*..."

"What did our quiet friend say about my security?"

"Only any good with the cuffs," I admitted reluctantly.

"Exactly."

"But you only go for me if you *see* me—*and* when you have a chance of success. If you're over *there*..."

Father Mark shook his head. "No. Perhaps when you're around, it's happy to lie in wait. But if I'm suddenly on another *continent?* Who's to say it won't kick in and bring me straight back here?"

"If you immediately went AWOL, the guards here would be waiting for you. I'm prepared to take the risk!"

"Well, *I'm not.*" His tone was absolute but his eyes were haunted. "I don't want any more blood on my hands, Margaret."

"But if you stay here, you'll die..."

"So be it." I caught my breath in pain and his voice softened. "I can't live like this, Margaret, with my will not my own. Never knowing when or whom I might kill."

"It's not *you*... If I can see that, why can't you?"

"Because if I agree to be set loose, knowing my condition, then I *am* responsible. Perhaps I wasn't... *that time*. But I would be now. It's not like I can break free by myself, Margo. The doctors say my body is actually programmed to destroy *itself* if I try to go against the conditioning—blood pressure, heart rate, everything would rocket through the roof. I thought I was well up on military matters, but I wouldn't even have thought it possible." He shook his head ruefully. "So you see, there's only one option. The doctors have to keep trying. And if they can't cure me, then they can't, that's that."

"This is your life we're talking about..."

"No, we're talking about my soul, which is much more precious. I won't change my mind on this, Margaret. Now, please don't be upset. Go and enjoy the baptism."

"But..." The machine beeped and I leaned over him in desperate appeal. "Please consider..."

Something in his eyes...

I jerked back.

Not quite quickly enough.

23

ST PAUL

A blinding pain as Father Mark's head cracked into my face—I reeled away, clutching my nose. Hot wetness spilled over my fingers. Staggering back against the wall, I watched him, as the door flew open and Bee and Snail rushed in.

I held out a hand quickly, my other hand groping in my pocket, "It's okay, only a nosebleed. Just need a tissue..."

Bee was not reassured, emotion darkening his deep brown skin even further. "For Pete's sake, Margo, you must be more careful! Or you won't be allowed in at all!"

"It's all right, Bee. Please, you two, go..." I'd been watching Father Mark's head thrash from side to side, now it lay still on the pillows, turned away from us. Snail and Bee went back outside, with obvious reluctance. I approached the side of the bed, tissue clamped to my nose—keeping my distance.

Father Mark's cheeks were wet. "I'm sorry," he whispered. "I'm so sorry... For... for *everything*..."

Father Mark, crying? It was horrible.

Why shouldn't he cry? whispered the voice. *You still can't even open your chart book without breaking down...*

I mentally shoved the voice aside and said gently, "It's only a nosebleed..."

"*Only a nosebleed?*" He looked at me, his eyes tortured. "If you hadn't moved, your nasal bone would be in your brain right now!"

And I'd be dead. He didn't need to add that, I could see it in his eyes. I swallowed. "*I'm* the one who should be sorry, Father Mark. That was terribly careless of me."

He shook his head once more, eyes groggy as the drugs sucked at him. "*Africa?* I should just tell our quiet friend about your poor baby and bare my throat..."

I frowned. How *would* Lucas react to the news that

Father Mark had inadvertently caused the death of a friend's child? Anger... or considerable sympathy?

"You might just get a hug instead," I told Father Mark.

Sleep took him.

Still frowning, I touched my nose gingerly and swallowed again. How safe *would* I feel with Father Mark loose, even a continent away?

Lucas's baptism was to be included in the evening Mass. Nice and quiet. Nose tended with an icepack and face washed, wearing the best of my tiny selection of skirts and tops, I knocked on Lucas's door at quarter to six. He opened the door after only a moment, looking very neat, even for him. But still looking at me as though he was just waiting for what'd been promised to be snatched away.

Until his eyes narrowed. "What happened to your nose?"

"It got a bit of a knock," I said dismissively. "But it's fine. And *no*, it wasn't Bane. You look smart, anyway. Where's your bit of white, though?" His crisp shirt was blue.

"For *innocence?*" He raised an eyebrow, pain in his eyes.

"It's traditional for baptisms." I went over to the white fuchsia and gave him a questioning look. He sighed and nodded, so I pinched off a single white flower, and tucked it into the buttonhole of his pocket. "There. Something white, and your plants get to send a representative. Are you ready to go, then?"

He stared at me, almost warily.

Lord help us, he really, really didn't think it was going to happen, did he? I took his hand. "Do you trust me, Lucas?"

He nodded, but... I put my arms around him and gave him a big hug, 'cause I'd noticed he was more easily convinced by physical contact—harder to lie with your body, I s'pose. He was tall enough his flower survived unscathed.

"Come on." I drew him gently after me.

"Mr. Everington has a friend who is unfortunately unable to be here tonight, and so has asked if he might be present through the homily." That's what Pope Cornelius had said when he went up to the lectern, displaying a piece of paper. "So I must admit to a slight feeling of déjà vu, but these are Father Mark Tarrow's words, not my own."

Lucas still looked as though he'd been hit between the eyes with a cricket bat. With his conviction of his own worthlessness, clearly it hadn't occurred to him that the compassion he'd shown towards Father Mark might've earned him one more friend than just me.

It was even distracting him from all the potted fuchsias at the foot of the altar. Ranulph, the kindly head gardener, had outdone himself.

Most people would take it only as a nice touch, but Lucas had asked me once what God looked like, and I'd explained that we couldn't possibly comprehend it, but while *understanding* that, everyone had some image which represented God, an old man with a beard, a pure light, or something they considered as close to perfection as was possible in this world. And Lucas had promptly looked at his purple fuchsia. I'd been amused at first, but really... if fuchsias were his idea of perfection...

Pope Cornelius had now come down from the lectern to stand beside the portable font. "Could the candidate and his chosen godparent, please approach?"

Lucas sat frozen, so I took his hand and tugged; he lurched to his feet and followed me. Amusingly, I was to be the 'godparent.'

Once I'd got my timid soon-to-be godson to the font, we joined in the Litany of the Saints—or I did—then Pope Cornelius stepped right up to the font and beckoned us closer. I squeezed Lucas's hand reassuringly, then let go and stepped back, just a little.

"Lucas Everington," said Pope Cornelius, with a gently encouraging smile that would've reassured the most nervous of catechumens. "Do you reject Satan?"

A long moment of silence. *Come on, Lucas, I know there's rather a lot of people here, but you can do it. For this, you can...*

"I do." Just audible.

"Do you reject all his works?"

"I do." A little louder.

"And all his empty promises?"

"I do." That was actually quite firm. Lucas knew all about his empty promises.

Pope Cornelius was continuing, "Do you believe in God, the Father almighty, creator of heaven and earth?"

For a moment I could see Uncle Peter on that gurney, speaking those words, moments before the commencement of his execution ...

Lucas glanced at me, saw my reassuring smile. "I do," he said. Quite clearly.

I beamed. He went on with the last two responses, equally firmly, then Pope Cornelius beckoned him to bend over the font, and pouring the water on his head, once, twice, thrice, made the sign of the cross there.

"Lucas Everington, I baptize you in the name of the Father, and of the Son, and of the Holy Spirit."

"I'll, uh, just go back to the apartment with Jon, shall I?" Bane directed a rather unsubtle wink in my direction once Mass had finished, but fortunately Lucas showed no signs of moving from the kneeler, let alone looking up.

"See you there."

"Jon?" Bane got up from the pew. "Are you there?"

"I'm here..." Jon took Bane in tow—Bane still hated to be adrift in St Peter's, though with his newfound confidence elsewhere, he seemed less embarrassed about admitting it."

I knelt for my post-communion prayers and some serious thanks and praise for Lucas's acceptance of new life, until finally Lucas stirred and looked up. He'd stopped crying, but still looked dazed. A stunned, happy dazed.

"See," I said gently.

He blinked. Smiled hesitantly, as though he could hardly remember how. "So you were right. Sorry I didn't believe you. Are you waiting for me?"

"Take as long as you like, I'm happy."

"It's okay. We can go now."

We headed up the stairs of our block, but when we reached his floor I took his hand and drew him upwards towards my apartment. "Uh-uh, you're coming up to my place for your party."

"*Party?*"He looked horrified.

"A very little one," I said quickly. "Very, very little. Only people you know. But you've got to mark an occasion like this with *something*. Come on..."

I towed him determinedly upwards, smiling at his resigned mutter of, "*Yes, Godmother.*"

Since Jon was attending the party primarily as our friend, to help with things, I was a little surprised to find him waiting outside the door of the apartment. A murmur of conversation was coming from inside, and Jon's head turned as he strained to identify us. "Mr. Everington?" he said.

Lucas seemed to have forgotten to breathe—no, deliberately hiding from Jon.

"Straight in front of you," I said helpfully.

"Right. Well, I just wanted to say... congratulations. And..." He bit his lips for a moment. "And... peace be with you."

He held out his hand.

7 days

"The world thinks some things are unforgiveable. When we remind them that they're not, they don't know what to think."

Fr. Mark Tarrow—quoted on 'The Impatient Gardener'

"Are you sure about this, Lucas?" I said, as Snail clipped a little microphone to Lucas's collar. I couldn't help shooting Eduardo a slightly appealing look.

"You are aware, I trust, Mr. Everington," obliged Eduardo, "that this is not as safe for you as it was for Margaret? You do not have the same level of public sympathy to protect you."

Lucas simply shrugged. Then murmured, "Understatement." But he was determined to go up onto that podium and speak. And this very morning, before he, "lost his nerve," as he put it. Not that it was assassins he was bothered about—just all the people. He looked pale and strained, and he was breathing too fast.

"You don't have to do this," I told him.

"If God can forgive *me*, I can do *this*," he replied.

"I could publish your statement on my blog..."

"People will think you wrote it."

"Well... are you *sure* you don't want to at least take some notes up there with you?"

He shook his head again. "No. They'll think you wrote them."

I sighed. He had a point. Supporters of Sorting would be quite happy to believe that the madman was simply reading lines he'd been fed by Margaret Verrall.

"All right, well, I'm going to go up and give you a little intro, then you can make your speech."

He went even whiter. "Not *speech*. Can't. Too many words. Just... a few sentences."

"Of course. Well... good luck. May the Holy Spirit be on your tongue."

I went through the gate and mounted the podium with a bit more confidence than last time. With a bare week to go, it would be an extremely foolish EuroOfficial who couldn't see that assassinating me right now would hand us the vote. Lucas, on the other hand... well, it still wouldn't look *good*, would it?

"Thank you for coming along," I said. A big crowd had gathered, despite, once again, the rather short notice. A mob of press were at the front, jostling for position. But over to one side... A small knot of people were shouting anti-EGD slogans and holding up photos... Oh no, they were pictures of their children, of dead reAssignees... Could Lucas cope with that?

I struggled not to scowl at them. Lucas was speaking *against* Sorting and they were still picketing him? Unbelievable!

I'd just have to ignore them, and hope Lucas could do the same. "Lucas," I continued, "Lucas Everington, that is—was, as you probably know, baptized yesterday. And the Holy Spirit is prompting him to say a few words to you all this morning. Just a very few—his torture at the hands of the

EuroGov's Internal Affairs department has left him very nervous of strangers and of crowds, so I leave it to you to imagine how much effort it is taking him to come up here today. Since his words will be so brief, I think it's also safe to say that he will have chosen them with great care.

"I'll hand over to him now. Please make him feel welcome." I managed not to glare at the protesters as I left the platform and looked around. Lucas was peering around the gateway, face more gray than white, by this time. Should I take his hand and lead him to the podium? No, it would look totally like I was putting him up to it. If he couldn't do it, better I just blame the EuroGov, and post what he wanted to say on my blog...

But no... Lucas was stepping into view, jaw and shoulders rigid, and walking forward. I gave him an encouraging smile as he passed me, and continued on my way back to the gate, the better to emphasize that he was acting of his own free will.

Unicorn hustled me right behind the wall, out of sight, ignoring my protests... but Eduardo promptly handed me a networkAccessor showing live feed from a camera.

Lucas had got up onto the podium, and stood, entwined fingers white with the pressure he was putting on them. His head turned slightly from side to side as he eyed the crowd, panic in his eyes. His head jerked as he registered the protesters and he began to shake slightly. I could tell he was fighting the urge to flee into himself and hide. For a moment, watching him... writhe... I thought he would simply physically flee instead...

Then he closed his eyes tight, and grew a little stiller. Praying? With obvious effort, and without opening his eyes, he began to speak.

"My name is... Lucas Everington. I was Commandant of Salperton Facility for... more than ten years. In EGD Security for... fifteen years... I am very, very... So sorry... to the parents..." He broke off, chest heaving, a couple of tears running down from his tight-closed eyes. Was he going to break his fingers? Or break down entirely...

Just when I was sure he couldn't go on, he finally did. "I... I cannot express that... I'm sorry. I just want to say...

something about... greed. What you are all fighting, right now, as you... try to decide. Is greed..."

He took another deep breath, "Greed tells us... that once we have what we *want*... what we've convinced ourselves we *need*... it will be worth... whatever price... we paid to acquire it. But greed is a *terrible liar!* Some prices are... are always *too high*. No matter what benefit... need... we pay it for. Greed lies! Don't choose lies. Or you will be... dead things walking around... like I was... until yesterday. Thank you..."

Eyes opening at last, he pretty much bolted from the podium and was almost through the gate before the crowd could even start clapping.

I stretched out on the grass, basking in the sun like a lizard. Lovely. After that stressful start to the morning, we'd brought all the leftover party snacks out into the garden for a picnic brunch, and I'd managed to coax Lucas into joining us—it was the remains of his party, after all, and he looked thoroughly wrung out by the morning's exertions. He'd settled himself near some flowery shrubs as far away from Jon as possible, but he clearly remembered he was forgiven.

The baptism and the party had given us such a nice— albeit brief—break from the looming vote... *no, not thinking about that right now.* And we weren't sitting too close to... *no, not thinking about that either.* I really should be doing my blog, though... Soon. The time it took to eat up the party food wouldn't make any difference.

Pushing a bowl of chips over to Lucas, I started feeding some others to Bane, who seemed to find it necessary to suck my fingers regularly, and said nothing about coddling. But when the snacks were all gone, he frowned in Lucas's direction. "Y'know, there's something I've been wanting to ask you—how *did* you escape from that Detention Facility after your trial?"

"Septic tank," I said, grinning.

"Not really!" said Bane.

"Yep."

"But how did you get out of the *cell?*" Bane persisted.

Lucas sighed—still not keen on long speeches, let alone

after this morning!—but he continued, "Well, everything from that time is hazy. I only remember snatches. But I recall enough about the cell to reconstruct how I must have done it.

"I could have simply hot-wired the card scanners," he went on, "but even if I sauntered along casually would have had to be lucky not to be noticed on the monitors. I suspect not that way. Not when there was a hatch into the sewage downpipe in the wall of my cell."

"That wouldn't have been big enough for you, surely?" said Bane.

"Very skinny, even then. And the EGD fit stupidly large pipes. Saves them a lot of time unblocking them, but if they starve a prisoner long enough... I think I had to dislocate my shoulder before getting in. Hurt on and off half-way across Europe." He flexed it thoughtfully. "Must have reset it afterwards, not very well."

"So you wriggled down the pipe?"

"Yes. More dangerous than the other way. Not with regards to getting caught, but could easily have got stuck, suffocated, or drowned. Not that it mattered."

"You got the hatch back in place," I remarked. "There wasn't a trace of where you'd gone."

"Or they didn't want to admit to it," he said dryly. "They probably figured it out in the end, when they checked the camera footage and found nothing. Anyway, have a dim memory of the septic tank, of trying to climb out with my shoulder hurting, so quite sure that's how I got outside the compound itself. Then just ran... shambled... Found rock and stuck on that until I found a stream, then stuck in that as long as I could, and times that by a couple of thousand kilometers..."

"Remind me never to try and keep you somewhere you don't want to be," murmured Bane.

The snacks were all gone.

Just a few more minutes...

24

AN IMPOSSIBLE PENANCE

Shutting the apartment door behind me, leaving my bodyguard—Unicorn today—to take up position outside, opposite the Swiss Guard, I sniffed appreciatively. Lunch was ready. Jon must be here. They were both in the kitchen, arguing amiably enough about the best way to carry a tray level.

"Hi, smells nice," I told them.

"Oh good," said Bane, "we can eat."

"You're quiet, Margo," he said before long. "What's wrong?"

"Pope Cornelius was at the hospital to anoint Father Mark."

"Damn."

"Yeah," I said sadly. He could die at any time, now... "And how does that make me different from anyone else?" he'd say, if I bewailed that fact to him.

We were all quiet for some time. Bane looked particularly miserable. Would some guilty part of him greet Father Mark's death with relief?

"I just don't understand why that heart attack affected him the way it did," said Jon after a while. "It's like he's totally given up."

"I never thought anything would faze Father Mark," said Bane, frowning in agreement. "But you're right. He puts a brave face on, but underneath... you can tell he just doesn't care. I don't understand it either."

"Has he said anything to you, Margo?" asked Jon, when I didn't speak.

"What? Oh. No. Perhaps... perhaps he's just tired. He obviously went through hell with Internal Affairs, though he doesn't talk about it."

"True," sighed Bane. "But it still doesn't seem like him."

Another glum silence fell.

"D'you remember that super-fast anointing he gave Margo in the Fellest?" said Jon at last, with just a slight smile.

"It was pretty fast," agreed Bane.

I'd been thinking about that as well. Perhaps it would make the subject for my next blog post. Out of consideration for Father Mark's feelings, we'd not told the world exactly what was wrong with him, only that he was seriously ill in the hospital as a result of his time in the EuroGov's tender care. But I could write about anointing.

Although the internet papers and TV channels were already reporting on his mini-speech, it was Lucas's baptism that was all over the papers today. The worst EuroPocket papers, as we called them, were stridently declaring it to be a publicity stunt and a sham, and predicting dire consequences for Lucas if we won the vote; other papers were more positive. But whatever their stance, they were pretty enthralled. We'd see what they had to say about his speech in the morning.

I got my blog written just in time to race to one of the grand old reception rooms for a video interview alongside Pope Cornelius and Cardinal Akachi—with a major EuroBloc network, no less—then I snuck back to the hospital. Vote or not, who knew how long we had left with Father Mark? It hurt to be around him, yes, but that was partly why I went. I couldn't bear for him to die while I felt this way about him. It wasn't his fault, so why couldn't I forgive him properly?

Of course, if I really believed it wasn't his fault, why did I feel I *needed* to forgive him...?

"*Margaret,*" he sighed, when he saw me (after the usual look of pain flashed across his face—a mutual feeling, alas). "You've got better things to be doing."

"I wanted to come and see you."

"I'm fine, really."

"I *saw* Pope Cornelius arrive earlier."

He sighed again. "I see. Well, then, you'll know I really am fine."

"And you'll know why I'm here again."

He sighed once more. He still looked sweat-streaked

313

and weary, but he seemed more peaceful than he had earlier. Had he confessed about killing my baby, or had he done that already? Had Pope Cornelius given him a penance? Or had he said ever so firmly, "I am not setting you a penance for *that*"?

"It's not that I'm not glad to see you," he said more softly, and probably no more truthfully than I could have done. "It's just the vote. I've been hoping I might still be here to know the result, but if you keep this up, I'll start wishing to depart immediately and spare you the distraction."

I snorted. "You really think that wouldn't be a bigger distraction?"

He just shrugged. He had a point. Was his emotionally agonizing presence more distracting than the agonizing emotional blow that his death would be? Or *should be?*

From the way he was looking at me, he was working up to yet another, "There's nothing I can say that will make it any better, but I'm so, so sorry," speech. "If you really want to make amends in the slightest," I snapped, "then could you try *not dying?*"

He looked startled, then smiled slightly. A genuine smile. "A priest is not allowed to set an impossible penance, so nor are you," he said lightly.

"Well... at least... at least *care*, would you?"

He smiled again, very gently, and suddenly I felt more like a little girl than a grown-up married woman. "Margaret, this is not so bad, you know. A downright wonderful way to go compared to what I've expected for so long. As I would think you'd particularly appreciate."

Even a thought of that gurney, and I shuddered. What could I say? He was right. "I'd rather you didn't go either way," I muttered. "Not just yet."

"I will go when I am called and not begrudge it," he said softly. "But in truth, I would rather stay. Does that make you feel better?"

It should—to know that I hadn't completely stamped out his will to live—but it didn't. In a way it just made it worse.

Click.

I sat there for a little while once he was asleep, a deep-rooted panic in my gut. I had to go now, I really did, back to my computer, but... would this be the last time I saw him alive?

That was the question I found myself asking at the end of every visit for the next two days, but still he hung in there. Pale and strained and... I was no longer in any doubt that he was in much more pain than he let on. I prayed fiercely for him, for a mind programmer, with much less of the 'Your will, Lord' than I should've done. And for the strength—the *reasonableness*—to forgive him.

Kyle had been getting such a... hunted... look whenever I managed to catch sight of him that I'd taken the decision to back off and give him some space. He didn't want to talk to me, but he was talking to Father Mark. Hopefully he'd work through the anger and relent. *Soon, Lord? Any chance he could do it really soon? Like, in the next week?*

I was working almost nonstop at my laptop, anyway. But Lucas had noticed everyone else worked, and he just "sat in his room eating," as he put it. Not that he ate a lot. Ranulph, the head gardener, was happy to allocate him an old disused greenhouse in which to raise plants for us to sell. So I stole an hour with Bane to help Lucas finish setting it up. Bane helped with the heavy lifting, and I chased spiders. Lucas was taking more cuttings from his precious purple fuchsia and beginning crosses of the most promising Vatican varieties while we were still finishing off.

When Ranulph dropped round and got Lucas talking plants, Bane and I bade our goodbyes and left them to it.

5 days

"The EGD would have it that anyone with fewer than five perfectly functioning senses is somehow less than human. Exactly what, then, is someone like me? With only four (slightly more than!) 'perfectly functioning' senses. Am I a gorilla? A dolphin? EGD logic fail."

Jonathan Revan—quoted in an article by Margaret Verrall for the 'The Parisian Voice', reprinted in 'The Madrid Tribune'

Ring-ring.

Bane went to get it. Good. I was busy at my computer, as ever—but the familiar fear coiled in my belly... Not Father Mark... Not Father Mark...

"Hello? What? *Really?* That's brilliant! *Isn't it?* Why not? Oh... I s'pose... can we come over? Okay." Bane hung up, and turned to me, excitement and caution warring on his face. "Some defector just walked into St Peter's."

"So?"

"Says he's a mind-programmer."

"What?" I hurtled out of my seat. "That's *wonderful!*"

"Ye-es," said Bane warily. "Bit convenient, isn't it? We haven't had a mind-programmer join us for... the whole history of anyone in Africa, as far as Eduardo's been able to discover, yet right *now...*"

...when we needed one so badly... "Eduardo's suspicious?"

"He's not too happy. I'm with Eduardo on this one, it stinks to high heaven. Anyway, he said we can go over if we like, see what we think of the fellow."

The defector was sitting behind a table in the interview room dressed in an expensive and totally un-rumpled suit, looking... un-rumpled. An average-sized man, in fact, pretty average in every way.

"So how do we even know he *is* a mind-programmer?" demanded Bane, after I gave him a description. We were invisible in the observation room.

"His ID checks out," said Eduardo. "Though naturally I've no intention of letting him know I know that."

"Easiest test is to put him in with Father Mark and see if he does any better than the psychiatrists," I said.

"Easiest, maybe—also riskiest."

"Riskiest? What risk? If he strangled Father Mark with his shoelaces, it wouldn't make a whole lot of difference, at this point."

"He's one of the ones who programmed Father Mark in the first place. I ran his name and photo past Father Mark already."

That shut me up for a moment. Hadn't expected that.

"So what reason does he give for defecting?" asked Bane.

"Says he feels bad about what he did to Father Mark and other people. But he also gives the impression that he doesn't think the EuroGov are going to win, so it may be self-serving, when you get to the bottom of it. He may feel if we knock off Sorting and Religious Suppression it won't be long before we get to Torture—and that's how I'd class his previous work."

"Has he asked for money?"

"He wants a comfortable house in Africa, and to be left off the chore rotation of whatever free town it's in. And a written assurance that he won't be sent to 'Friedrich's touchy-feely farm' as he puts it. An astute enough request, since he participated in the torture of at least one Vatican State citizen, not that we try defectors for past crimes, as a general rule."

"Well, that all shows good character," I couldn't help saying.

"Quite. He does not come across as a savory customer."

"But he's the only mind-programmer we've got. It's try him, or let Father Mark die."

"Well, no need to ask what you think we should do. Any opinion, Bane?"

Bane chewed his lip for a moment. "If we let this guy at Father Mark, and he says he's cured him, we'll have to do some seriously careful tests before letting Father Mark loose. Might still need to relocate him far from Margo. But we have to try."

Eduardo frowned, as though secretly hoping someone would come up with a reason good enough to justify keeping the guy away from Father Mark. "Jack?"

Unicorn shrugged, blue eyes troubled. "We've got to try it, sir. Margo's right; he can't make Father Mark *worse*."

Eduardo sighed. "All right, it's undeniable. I don't think any of us could stomach not making use of him, in the circumstances. Let's get him up there, then."

He went out of the room and almost immediately reappeared in the interview room. "Hello again, Doctor Reynar. Sorry to keep you waiting. It's been decided to grant you a

317

temporary visa to remain. However, as you probably know, Father Mark Tarrow is here in the hospital, and it will be a condition of your visa that you cure him."

"Of course," said Doctor Reynar. "But you understand, there will be certain things which I require."

"I don't think you're in a position to dictate terms, Doctor Reynar," said Eduardo coolly.

"No? I don't think *you* quite understand the scarcity value of my particular set of skills. If I choose to walk back across that white line, the EuroGov will welcome me with open arms. My art is a delicate one. I have my conditions, or I will not work."

"Oh, he's charming, isn't he?" muttered Bane.

I grunted agreement, equally revolted by the oily tone and pompous words.

"Still, Father Mark's life," I reminded him—and myself— after a moment.

"Yeah," said Bane, wholeheartedly. No, he really didn't want Father Mark to die. Not *really*. Nor did I.

"Reasonable terms regarding your medical work will of course be met," said Eduardo. "Now, can you start at once? The situation is urgent."

Doctor Reynar heaved a big sigh. "Am I not to have a cup of tea and bite to eat?"

"I'll have it sent up to the hospital. In the meantime, you can begin assessing your patient."

"Very well," said Doctor Reynar irritably.

"Caring fellow," I muttered.

"We didn't need to meet him to know that," said Unicorn dryly.

True. I offered thanks to God guiltily tinged with wariness. Had the Lord really sent this man to us, or was the cause something less benevolent—or at least more human?

Eduardo called round later in the day and from his expression and irritable manner, he shared my lack of certainty. "Well, it's good news," he said without preamble. "He's got the panic response stabilized."

"Already?" Too good to be true, surely?

"It would appear these characters leave themselves

metaphorical back doors and shortcuts," said Eduardo. "We haven't just taken his word for it—he got pretty sniffy about it, but we tested it out. Father Mark can be around a doctor now without the drugs in him."

"My goodness," murmured Bane, "then his life is saved?"

"So long as we don't offend dear Doctor Reynar," said Eduardo bitterly.

"Then... he probably really can undo the programming that makes Father Mark try to kill me?" I asked.

"He says it's more complicated; reckons we're looking at several weeks. But he seems totally confident about the eventual outcome."

"So, as long as we win..." Bane broke off. Swallowed.

Five days. Opinion polls now varied widely. In some, we were clear winners. In others... I swallowed too, feeling nauseous. *Again.* Of course, I'd probably have my head in a toilet for half the day by now, if it wasn't for Fa... for the EuroGov. Now I was just stuck with stress giving me some of the downsides without any of the upsides...

Lord, stay with us...

2 days

As a former reAssignee I want to add my voice to all those you have heard over the last six months and beg you—do not dismiss us as imperfect, for every human being is imperfect. Do not dismiss us as unimportant, for no human being is unimportant. And do not, *do not* imagine that you can raise your children in a society that treats children as we and countless others were treated, and that they will be *safe.*

No child is safe while Sorting continues.

No adult is safe while there is no Religious Freedom.

Margaret Verrall—blog post, 'The Impatient Gardener'

I had written far into the night, pouring myself into a set of posts for the next two days. What might be my final posts. I'd now done everything that I could do through my writing to help make the case for an end to Sorting and Religious Suppression. The day of the vote itself would be split between live interviews and Eucharistic Adoration, for which I kind of hoped Bane would join me, otherwise we were hardly going to see each... be with each other.

But right now, I was admiring rows of neatly potted plants and trying to understand an explanation about how Lucas had taken the pollen of one variety and used it to pollinate another variety, and how this would result in new hybrids.

"So when will they be ready?"

He looked amused. "Not yet, Margaret. The plants have to make the seeds first, then I plant the seeds, then the new plants grow. Then none of them may be very good, so you try a whole load of new combinations, and each time keep the best ones. You have to be patient to get something really good." He shot the purple fuchsia cuttings a look of rather parental pride.

I smiled. "Well, my blog title says it. I'm a very impatient gardener. If you could call me a gardener with my success rate."

Success rate... Doctor Reynar was reporting good success with Father Mark. Unfortunately, his claims were no longer such as could be tested. Doctor Reynar hadn't let me see Father Mark for three days, now, but I suppose the whole forgiveness thing was no longer quite so urgent. Unless we lost the vote... Still...

Doctor Reynar couldn't do anything worse to Father Mark; his motives, unsavory as they might be, checked out; everything we'd been able to check checked out and still... the whole thing left me so uneasy.

"Margaret?"

"Sorry. Just thinking about Father Mark."

"I wouldn't let Doctor Reynar near... near a *seedling.*"

I stared unhappily up at him. "I *know,* but what choice do we have? Father Mark could easily have been dead by now, without that man."

"I don't trust him as far as I can pick him up and throw him."

And considerably physically recovered though Lucas might be, he certainly couldn't do that.

"I *know*. But what do you suggest? Let Father Mark die?" Lucas frowned. "I don't want Father Mark to die."

"Well, then!" I stroked a fuchsia's deep-veined leaves absently for a moment. "Y'know, I don't think it would be half so bad if I could *see* him. At least then I'd be able to tell if he really seemed to be improving..." I trailed off. "Well, I couldn't tell he was programmed until he made a move, so maybe not. I'd just feel better."

"That man won't let me in. Won't let anyone in."

"What about Eduardo?"

"No."

My turn to frown. Unicorn was keeping us up to date, but he'd not mentioned that absolutely *no one* was allowed in. "That doesn't seem... *necessary*. I mean, Doctor Reynar had assistants when he did what he did to Father Mark the first time. Not that I know anything about mind-programming..."

"Eduardo should insist."

"He can't, can he? Doctor Reynar has us over a barrel. I just wish *someone* could speak to Father Mark. Check *he's* happy with what the guy is up to..."

Lucas turned his head slightly to one side and eyed me rather intently. My heart lurched in mingled hope—and fear that our need for reassurance could actually do harm. But... I didn't trust Doctor Reynar as far as I could throw him, either. Bane, Jon and I had sat with him in the cafeteria several times to try and find out about Father Mark's progress, and he didn't improve on closer acquaintance. So... "D'you think you could... get in there?"

Lucas smiled faintly.

"Okay, ask a stupid question. But without anyone knowing you'd been there? We mustn't lose Doctor Reynar!"

Lucas pulled a face, as though he'd love to lose Doctor Reynar but his reason disagreed. "Don't worry," he said simply, then added, "Tonight."

I bit my lip, but didn't take back my request. The programming didn't relate to Lucas in any way; how could it possibly do any harm?

Lucas adjusted a couple of pots for a few moments, back and forth. Something on his mind?

"Margaret... something's been bothering me."

"What?"

"Well, when you do wrong, you do penance, yes? After you're forgiven, as... as an apology, to show how sorry you are."

"And it has a purifying effect on oneself, yes."

"Well, what do you do when... all your wrongs are far too many to ever be put right?"

I took his hand and gave it a squeeze. "You've just been baptized, Lucas; all your sins are gone. You don't *need* to do anything."

"But if it's partly an apology... what if you *want* to do something?"

"Um... well, I don't suppose there's any reason you can't. So long as you do understand it's not *necessary*. Anyway, genuine sorrow is the most important thing: over and above that, we just do what we *can*, and leave the rest in God's hands."

"Do what we can?"

"That's right. However little or however much. And even the little is totally voluntary for you right now."

He nodded thoughtfully, then snagged a spider that was trying to move back in and carried it outside.

1 day

I'd like you all to take a moment to imagine something. Try to imagine the hope that's burning right now in the hearts of thousands of parents across the EuroBloc. The hope that their child might live. Imagine it, and remember that feeling, and don't forget it when you vote tomorrow.

Margaret Verrall—blog post, 'The Impatient Gardener'

A hand was shaking my shoulder... my eyes flew open in the darkness, my heart thudding. A voice calling urgently... "Margaret! Margaret?"

"*Lucas?*" I pushed myself into a sitting position and fumbled for my bedside light. "*What are you doing here?*"

"What on earth?" said Bane. "How'd he get in?"

"He's *gone*," Lucas said straight over us. "*Listen*, he's *gone!*"

My mind was still attempting to lurch into action. "Who's *gone?*"

"Father Mark!"

25

GONE

"*Gone*," repeated Lucas insistently, "Guard in a heap on the floor and he's *gone*."

Felt like a bucket of ice-cold water had just been chucked over me. I shoved back the sheets, grabbed the nonLee and swung my legs out of the bed. Bane snatched his holstered nonLee, then dived for my bedside table, where Eduardo had installed an extra phone after the assassination attempts, swiping the handset out of the cradle, tracing his way to the red hash button and pressing it.

Then he scrambled off the bed after me and began to hustle me across the room. "Into the bathroom, until the guards arrive, quickly..."

Lucas clearly approved of this plan, since he held the bathroom door open, followed us in and bolted it behind him. Only then that I noticed the knife in his hand. Two nonLees and one knife. Theoretically ought to be enough, but let's hope the guards got here quickly. Having a key in the possession of our door guard was deemed a greater security risk than not having one, so they'd have to wait for the Officer of the Watch or kick the door down.

"Is the guard okay?" I asked.

"Unconscious." Lucas's eyes stayed on the bathroom door. No windows, hence Bane's choice. "Not bad, I think."

"How the hell did he get loose?" hissed Bane. I took his free hand and pressed it tightly, seeing his terror. I—*and* Father Mark—were in terrible danger.

"Smarmy bugger helped him," said Lucas. "Simple, with help; without, *no*."

Better if Lucas had raised the alarm at once, instead of rushing straight to me... well, maybe. If Father Mark had turned up here while we were asleep...

The sound of a key in the front door, the soft padding of quite a few feet. A very anxious voice calling, "Mrs. Verrall? Mr. Verrall!"

Not Father Mark's voice. Or the smarmy bugger's.

"We're in the bathroom," I called, drawing back the bolt.

The door opened a moment later and a Swiss Guard officer stared down the barrels of two nonLees, and very happy he looked about it. "Mrs. Verrall! You're all right!"

The guard who'd been outside when we went to bed peered anxiously past his superior. Saw Lucas and demanded, "How the hell did *he* get in here?"

"How *did* you?" I asked Lucas.

"Window."

"Oh."

The officer looked horrified. "Is the apartment insecure?"

"Not especially," said Lucas.

"His other name's Houdini, remember?" said Bane, very fast, "But Father Mark's loose; worry about *that!*"

The guards went white. The officer began to give orders, and soon I was literally completely surrounded. A few more moments and a dressing-gown-clad Eduardo was shoving his way into the tiny room. So he *did* sleep!

"What's going on?" He raised his wristCell to his ear, listened for a few moments... "Damn! He's gone, it's confirmed."

"Is the guard all right?" I asked urgently.

"Choked senseless, but he's come around, seems to be no permanent damage." Almost unconsciously he turned to Lucas and demanded, "*How?*"

Most people would've recoiled and said, "How should I know?" but Lucas just looked thoughtful. "Simple. Doctor Reynar did some new programming. Then loosened one of the wrist straps—couldn't *undo*, no keys for the cuff, but could loosen straps, like when they turn him. Made it long enough to get around guard's neck. Middle of night, programming kicks in, Father Mark pretends some distress, guard rushes in..." He shrugged eloquently. Father Mark's guards had carried the cuff keys in case of emergency. Hadn't occurred to anyone that someone might *help* him...

325

"Damn!" muttered Eduardo. "Simple." Then he frowned at Lucas. "You went up there?"

Oops, we were caught. "I'm sorry, I put him up to it," I said quickly. "I *just* wanted to know if Father Mark was all right."

"How did you plan to get past the guard?"

"Didn't," said Lucas. "Climbed up to window."

"Ah."

My stomach turned over. What a climb! Lucas clearly didn't think anything of it, but I must be more careful. The things that man would do to please me...

"If he's loose," said Bane tensely, "and not in control of himself, then where the hell is he?"

Why isn't Father Mark here yet, in other words.

"We're checking all the cameras," said Eduardo. "If he's on the move, we'll find him. That guard wasn't unconscious for long."

Another cold shudder ran down my spine. If Lucas had been a moment sooner...

"Sir..." Unicorn pushed his way into the room and handed Eduardo a networkAccessor. "Here, tunnel four. Camera feed from the last few minutes... *look...*"

Lucas and I craned over Eduardo's shoulder as he ran the video. A dark figure slipped along a passage, found a spot on a large portrait, swung the portrait out, revealing a doorway in the wall. Scrambled up and through. The portrait swung back into place.

"He's leaving the state?"

My astonishment was echoed on Eduardo's face. "Jack, send a team down to tunnel four. To advance with extreme caution: check he's really gone. Someone go over the footage between that moment and now and someone else keep their eyes glued on that portrait, in case he comes back. Off the top of my head, that was the only tunnel I'd given Father Mark the location of, so he can't just slip back in along another one..."

"But he's left?" I said again. "Are we sure he's really programmed? Could he just be... trying to get away from me?"

"He had help to escape," said Bane.

"*Smarmy bastard,*" said Lucas emphatically. No, I didn't trust the smarmy bastard either. He'd done *something.*

"I think it's time we had a little chat with Doctor Smarmy. I'm off to his room." Eduardo stopped, and shot me a conflicted look.

"We're coming!" I said fiercely. "I want to know what he's done to Father Mark!"

Eduardo pursed his lips for a moment, clearly concluded that at least it would keep me under his eye, nodded and led on.

By the time we reached Doctor Reynar's room, Snail and Bee—no doubt called suddenly back onto duty—had appeared, with Jon following behind, all looking as though they'd pulled their clothes on in about thirty seconds flat.

Doctor Smarmy answered his door in his pajamas, though, putting on a good show of innocent bafflement. I'd half expected him to be gone too.

"Oh, be quiet," Eduardo cut him off. "We know perfectly well that you loosened at least one of Father Mark's restraining straps before you left the hospital last night."

"What if I did?" said Doctor Reynar unexpectedly, with an unconcerned shrug.

"That piece of paper we gave you only covered *past* crimes," said Eduardo grimly. "So if you did, you are looking at a lengthy prison sentence."

Doctor Reynar laughed. "What, all two days of it?"

Yet another chill ran down my spine. He was so confident we were going to lose...

"A lot longer if we win," said Eduardo calmly. "And a lot of polls seem to be in our favor, so I think your confidence is misplaced."

Lucas was staring hard at the pompous doctor. He hadn't liked the 'two days' crack either. Bane clasped my hand tighter, his nonLee safely holstered again.

"That's true, I suppose." Doctor Reynar didn't *sound* as though he thought it was true. Didn't sound worried at all.

Lucas began to hustle me towards the room's balcony doors.

"*Lucas...*"

Hey!" protested Bane.

"You look pale, Margaret, you need some air..."

"I'm *fine*..."

"Better out here."

I almost protested again, but bit my tongue suddenly. I wasn't *pale*, I didn't need *air*... and Lucas knew that.

Eduardo, with a glance to check that Unicorn was following me, continued his interrogation of the smug prisoner, as Lucas opened the doors and walked me out; stood me in a corner of the dark balcony. "Take a few deep breaths and you'll feel better," he said almost absent-mindedly, and hurried back into the room, where Bane's efforts to follow me had shifted the group most of the way to the doors. Unicorn shook his head to himself, clearly chalking this strange behavior up to over-protectiveness.

"Why don't you tell Eduardo what he wants to know?" Lucas cut in harshly. My eyes flew to his hands—empty, thank God; the knife was in his pocket.

Doctor Reynar laughed in his face. "You lot are pathetic. You can't make me tell you anything. Two days, and you're all dead, and I'm a rich man."

Lucas sprang, bearing the man straight through the doors and clean over the balcony rail. I leapt forward and grabbed Lucas's belt to add my weight to his, because although he had a good two-handed grip on Doctor Reynar's collar, Doctor Reynar clearly weighed quite a bit more than him, and Lucas's knees braced under the stone balustrade were the only thing stopping him going over as well.

An eruption of oaths from the room behind us, barely audible over the doctor's screaming: "You can't do this! You can't do this! You people don't do this sort of thing!"

"*Madman*, remember?" panted Lucas.

"Help me!" shrieked the doctor, presumably to Eduardo and the others.

"What can they do? If they come near me, I'll just let you go. So start talking. Something seems to have happened to my muscles in your masters' tender care and I can't hold you for long," Lucas said.

"You're bluffing."

"How many stories up are we, Margaret?"

"Uh... six."

"My grip is going, Doctor. You have about thirty seconds..."

Long moments of terrified gasping. Lucas *wasn't* bluffing about not being able to hold on much longer. His face was tight with strain. Craning around him, I saw Doctor Reynar's collar slip a little in his grip...

"The Chairman! He tries to assassinate the chairman, we win the vote..."

The blood drained from my face and I clung tighter to Lucas's belt.

"Keep talking," snapped Lucas.

"The pre-vote speech tomorrow evening in Brussels. Chairman walks past, Mark Tarrow drops from a first floor window and tries to kill him. *Father* Mark Tarrow. Live on TV. Bodyguards know which window, so he won't succeed."

Lucas's fingers were white, every tendon standing out. The collar was slipping again... "Which window?"

"Hotel Champagne, room one-oh-eight, I swear, I swear, please, please don't drop me, I was just following orders. *You* must understand that: *following orders?*"

"Wrong answer," snarled Lucas, and let go.

The guards lurched forwards in dismay, but Unicorn and Eduardo didn't move—they'd figured it out. The wail was almost instantly cut off by a thud, followed by a rising torrent of relieved sobbing, increasingly—and reassuringly—interspersed with a lot of swear words. He'd figured out he'd been had, and he wouldn't be swearing if he'd not told the truth.

Eduardo and Unicorn joined us and we all peered over the balustrade, but it was too dark to see the next balcony down, the ornate curved front of which protruded further than the one on which we stood.

"You didn't have to drop him, Lucas," I said, being a dutiful Godmother.

"Did. Couldn't pull him up again. Couldn't hold on. Do him good."

I hid a smile.

"Some of you get down there and secure the pompous git," said Eduardo, rather unprofessionally.

Several guards bounded off, and Eduardo shepherded me back inside, seeming distracted. I was rather distracted myself. Assassinate the chairman! Heaven help us, the git was right, even an *attempt* by one of *our* people would lose us the vote. The vote was the day after tomorrow—no, *tomorrow*, now. No time to try and explain anything. As for that... we'd not told anyone about Father Mark's programming. To try to explain now... even the only mildly suspicious would be skeptical.

"Mr. Everington," Eduardo was saying sternly, "that is *not* how we get information from people in this State."

"Do you *get* much information?"

Eduardo's lip twisted rather cynically. I'd a feeling Eduardo actually got a lot of information from people, simply by listening to what they thought they *weren't* telling him, but it wasn't very quick. "I mean it, Mr. Everington. If you ever do anything like this again, I shall have to do more than smack your wrist."

Lucas listened solemnly—held out his arm. Literal. Bane was right.

Eduardo looked startled, but obliged with a not-entirely-nominal smack. Miffed he'd had to stand by and let that happen, even if his more pragmatic side had stopped him intervening once the guy was hanging there. "*Don't* do it again."

"If you don't stop him, there won't be any *again.* "

Eduardo pulled a full grimace this time, then looked around as the guards frog-marched Doctor Reynar back into the room. "Ah, Doctor," he said icily. "Feel like expanding on what you told us a moment ago?"

Doctor Reynar clamped his lips together and glowered. We weren't getting any more out of him. We didn't really need to. He'd spilled the beans and he knew it.

"All right, take him to the cells. He's unhurt, is he?"

"I imagine he has a few bruises; he seems to be walking okay."

"Take him away, then. Make sure a doctor sees him—but in the cell."

"Sir."

Doctor Reynar was hustled out as Eduardo turned to

Unicorn. "Keep the security high on the Verralls' apartment, not that I think Father Mark's coming back, and get a team ready to go after Father Mark. Briefing in fifteen minutes, followed by immediate departure."

He strode out of the room and Bane drew me after him. "Come on... We have to leave this to the experts. Where's the door? You need some more sleep—lots of blogging tomorrow..."

"I've written everything already..." But I steered him towards the doorway, Lucas trailing behind like a grim-faced ghost and Unicorn going ahead like a suspicious guard dog, Snail and Bee and several other guards tagging along as well.

"Whoa," said Unicorn suddenly, holding up a hand to halt us. "*Sir?* What is it?"

Eduardo was standing in the passage, speaking urgently into his wristCell: "Main gate, please *respond...*" He waited only a moment before snapping, "All wall posts, call in *now...*"

More silence.

The guards suddenly closed in around me, drawing their nonLees. Bane put an uncertain hand on his...

"All guard posts," said Eduardo into the wristCell, "repeat, *all* guard posts, we have a situ..."

Something small and circular bounced around the corner and rolled to rest just in front of us—I caught only a glimpse before Bee had flung himself on top of it, curling into a ball. Unicorn changed an abortive move in that direction to a lunge at me, and carried me to the ground, Eduardo and Snail landing on top of him split seconds later, followed by two more guards. *Ouch...*

Lucas was hurtling towards me too... but at the last moment he swerved into Bane, carrying Jon to the ground as well in a jumble of sticks and long limbs. I wanted to scream their names but had no breath... then several well-muscled torsos were rammed completely over my head and I could see nothing... I could only wait for the bang...

The heap of protecting bodies twitched oddly; a strange sensation tickled my feet, swept up to my head, my ears rang and darkness closed in around me... Then...

331

I lay, panting, head aching... I'd heard no explosion. Had I actually passed out? No... But my human shields had become dead weights, limp and unresponsive. *Oh Lord, please don't let them be...*

Wait a minute... No explosion... Round and... smooth... With some effort, I dragged myself far enough out to see. No blood. Not even on Bee, and I could see his chest moving up and down. NonLethal grenade? Why was I still conscious? I heaved myself free and sat up. Promptly regretted it as a sledgehammer attacked my brain and my insides tried to revolt.

"Margo?" came a weak voice from nearby, promptly followed by another familiar voice, also rather thin.

"Bane? Are you okay? Where's Margo?"

"Sitting up, I think. I hope. *Margo?*"

"It's me, Bane," I gasped, as the nausea eased. I was about to crawl over to them when a foot scuffed just around the corner. I had time to hiss, "Play dead!" then draw my nonLee, and throw myself flat just before two SpecialCorps soldiers appeared, nonLee rifles cautiously raised.

"Looks like we got them all," said one, in Esperanto.

"I thought I heard something," said the other, not lowering his rifle. "They look like security guys; let's put a shot in them all, just to be sure."

"Right..." The first one raised his rifle as well—the other guy was taking aim at Bee... I pushed myself up just enough to aim, and fired twice.

Thud. Thud. Two heavy bodies hit the carpeted floor.

"Thank you, Lord," I whispered, beginning to shake, though adrenalin was now pushing away the sickness and headache. I fired into them both again to keep them down for several hours, then scrambled over to Bane, Jon and Lucas. The three of them had fallen behind the rest of us and must have been largely shielded, but not quite enough to save Lucas, who was unconscious as well.

"Were those assassins, Margo?" asked Bane, sitting up with a barely-smothered groan.

I stared at all the soldierly kit hanging from the very soldierly figures and remembered what Eduardo had been saying. There seemed to be a strange echoing in my head. "I think it's worse than that. They're soldiers. I think the EuroGov are annexing us."

"What?" said Jon. "Not right now; not *before* the vote!"

"Yes," said Bane, frowning. "It makes sense. If they take us over *now*, there's no way we can stop Father Mark, so we'll definitely lose the vote. *And* they can be sure none of us will escape afterwards. They can claim it's to ensure neutrality, of course, and promise to withdraw if we win. But we won't win. Not if..."

Not if Father Mark made it to Brussels. And... I glanced at Unicorn's unconscious form.

"Oh no! U never had time to pass those orders on. No one is going after Father Mark!" Something rather like despair washed over me. The State was under attack, had perhaps fallen already, and the people who most needed to be awake were lying senseless on the floor. Fifty-percent lethal grenades, Eduardo had once dubbed them. Would he and the others even wake up?

I glanced at Bane and Jon. They were both now sitting up, looking as dizzy and sick as I felt. The State needed the head of security and his best men—instead... it had us three.

I was struggling to force my aching brain into gear when Jon's head came up. "Quick!" he breathed. We staggered to our feet and slipped into a nearby room, leaving the door ajar. More footsteps were approaching along the passage.

The feet paused outside.

"Good grief," said a scornful voice. "These idiots put themselves out with their own grenade."

"Perhaps they had no choice. Lot of nonLees lying around here," said another voice, more mildly. "We'd better collect them up. And keep your voice down, we're not supposed to wake anyone."

Clinking and rustling sounds as the two soldiers searched Eduardo and the others and gathered the fallen nonLees.

"We'll have to take these idiots' toy guns too," said the first voice, more quietly this time. "Can't leave them lying here."

"Yep. Okay, let's get on."

The footsteps retreated.

"Blast it!" snarled Bane. "Why didn't we pick the other guns up?"

"I don't think any of us are at our best after that grenade," I said. "At least we've still got ours." I tried to bully my brain into action again, but the conclusion it kept reaching really did make me want to throw up. I thought it through twice more, with no change to the solution.

"We may be the only people still free and conscious who know about Father Mark," I said at last. "What's happening here is totally irrelevant in the long term, if he isn't stopped. So one of us has to go after him. Obviously it will have to be me."

Bane drew a deep, deep breath, then stopped. He bit his lip almost to the point of drawing blood. Jon just looked extremely grim. After some more deep breaths, Bane finally said, "You can get out of the State easily enough; we know the location of several passages. But how will you get to Brussels?"

"Train. I need the escape rucksack from the cupboard at home. Everything I need is in there. I could chance it without the wig, but I've got to have that money."

"Let's go, then."

It was horrible leaving the others there like that, collapsed on the floor, but what choice had we? Speed was everything, now. *Lord,* I thought, fighting the despair, *please be with us... We can't do this by ourselves...*

We made it down the stairwell without meeting any more soldiers, but a quick peep into our corridor showed no fewer than four members of SpecialCorps, standing around our door. The crumpled body of the Swiss Guard who'd been left on duty had been shoved to one side of the passage, but from the fact that they'd taken the time to bind and gag him, he was probably just unconscious.

I pressed Bane and Jon back. "Shss," I breathed. "Go upstairs again..."

Safely up on the landing, I murmured the bad news to them. "...and they're armed with nonLees as well; the EuroGov are clearly trying to make this bloodless—for now—but I don't understand why they're just standing there," I concluded.

"Because they think we're in there, of course," Bane murmured back, not looking puzzled at all. "You heard those others: they mean to completely take control while everyone's asleep. Who knows, in the morning they may even plan to trot you and Pope Cornelius out to do your speeches just as planned, and pretend they aren't really occupying us. All those soldiers have to do is put on some Swiss Guard uniforms and hold a gun to my head off camera and I should think you'll cooperate, seeing that you were planning on making the speech anyway."

I shrank from that vision, then dragged my mind back to the more immediate problem. "I don't think I can get all four of them before they get me."

"Then I'll take the nonLee," said Jon. "When I give you the signal, switch off all the lights. You can do that without being seen, right?"

I glanced down the stairs to the bank of light switches on the landing below. "Yes. Could be a little illumination from the other landing, but you'll be at the dark end so I doubt they'll be able to see you. Not in the first few moments."

"Good. Let's have it, then." Jon held out his hand for my gun, but Bane gave him his. "If they do see me, they're only holding nonLees, right?" *Four* nonLees, though. Panicked soldiers, firing blindly... From Bane's expression, he was making the same calculation. So was Jon, because he added briskly, "I'm expendable, anyway. Let's move."

No time to argue: right now, we were *all* expendable. "One moment. Have you got a hanky?" I was still in my dressing gown. Jon produced one from his trouser pocket and I bound it quickly around the nonLee. "Okay, here it is. Don't let the hanky slip off; it's covering the power gauge. The glow might give you away."

"Right," said Jon. "Once we get down there, kill the lights when I tap my finger on the barrel like this... Then pray."

"Don't forget to take the safety off," said Bane. At Jon's frosty silence, he added, "Seriously, mate, it's easily done!"

"Come on!" I urged. "Every moment Father Mark is

getting further away!"

We crept back down the stairs, trying not to let our feet scuff on the carpet. Positioning Jon just out of sight around the corner, I moved to the switches, took a deep breath—*Lord, watch over Jon!*—and clicked a nail against the wall to let him know I was ready.

I saw him take a deep breath too—just one—then his finger tapped the nonLee. Using both hands, I swiped all the switches off together, plunging us into darkness.

Startled oaths from around the corner...

No sound of Jon moving, but then...

Thud. Thud.

Thud.

Another oath, cut off... *thud.*

A moment's utter silence... I waited. Jon was probably listening, checking they were really unconscious.

"Okay." Jon's voice, coming softly from inside the corridor.

Relief rushing through me, I flicked the lights back on and hurried after Bane, who'd already joined Jon. There were the soldiers, crumpled in heaps just like the unfortunate Swiss Guard. I picked up the nearest nonLee and used it to put another shot into them. No point emptying the powerMag of the weapon I was used to.

"They all out?" asked Bane.

"Like the lights were," I said. "Good job, Jon."

Jon just shrugged. "All that swearing, how could I miss?" he said modestly. "Like shooting ducks in a barrel."

"Come on," said Bane. "Let's get them inside before someone comes. Then they'll assume this lot have just wandered off."

"I only need to grab my bag..."

"It's better if they don't know we're loose. At the moment they're going for stealth. If they think you're about to slip through their fingers, they'll lock the whole place down."

"Okay, you're right. I'll get the door."

Door open, I made to help them, but Bane just said, "Get your bag, quickly; we can manage."

It was the work of a moment to take the small bag of

escape stuff from the little cupboard by the door. Actually...

"I'd better get dressed while you finish with them," I said in a low voice. "I can't go to the train station like this!" I slipped into the bedroom, dragging my dressing gown and nightie off with frantic fingers. Had the EuroArmy seized VSS HQ yet? Did they have access to all the cameras? We needed to be so, so quick...

I reached for my skirt, then grabbed my jeans from the drawer instead. I needed to blend in out there. I slipped into a clean top, yanked on my shoes and grabbed a jacket, only to drop it back on the bed and pull out my nonLee as the window swung silently open. I raised the gun, heart pounding, finger tightening on the trigger...

A glint of metal... a knife raised to throw... and a thin, familiar face... "Lucas!"

The knife was being lowered, he'd recognized me in the same moment. He eased through and dropped lightly to the ground, though his movements seemed rather stiffer than usual. "Margaret, are you all right?" He broke off, said, "Excuse me," stuck his head back out the window, and was violently sick.

Oh yes, post-nonLee symptoms. I could sympathize. I slipped my jacket on as I waited for him to recover himself.

"Are you all right?" he demanded again, as soon as he had.

"Fine, Lucas. I was so well shielded I didn't get knocked out, same with Bane and Jon, thanks to you. Are the others awake?" I asked urgently. Please say they were—and not in EuroGov hands. Would the EuroGov try to wring security secrets from Eduardo?

Still, perhaps they wouldn't realize immediately who they'd caught... because Lucas was shaking his head. "Unconscious. Sorry. Just me."

Bane appeared at the door. "You woke up, huh? Good. Thanks for knocking me over, by the way.""

"Are you all right?" asked Lucas.

"Me?" said Bane, gripping his nonLee rather fiercely, "Oh, I'm fine. Young dogs pick up new tricks, y'know."

"Old dogs too, sometimes."

Bane looked startled for a moment, as he realized Lucas

had made a joke. "So they do. Here..." He pulled a com-mandeered nonLee from his pocket and held it out. "You'd better have this. Let's move..."

I grabbed the rucksack and we all headed for the door.

"How did you take out all these fellows?" Lucas looked from the unconscious soldiers to me.

"I didn't. Jon did. I switched off the lights suddenly and he got them all before they knew what'd hit them."

Lucas greeted this with a rather predatory smile of approval.

Fortunately the nearest secret passage wasn't far away. We raced down the final flight of stairs, peeped around the corner, and hurried into the lower corridor. There was the cupboard. I found the first bit of woodwork to press—to engage the cupboard with the door behind, without which the cupboard would just move like any other cupboard, revealing an apparently innocent stretch of wall—then pressed the second and heaved... it swung away, leaving a rectangle of darkness.

We piled through the opening as fast as we could, pulling it closed behind us before anyone could come along.

It was one of the older, lesser-used passages, with no lighting. I reached into the bag, then stopped, my heart sinking. "Oh no, I put the torch out on the window ledge to charge—and I hadn't brought it back in yet!" I said. "I take it no one else has one?"

Lucas muttered a no, since it was too dark to see a head shake.

"We don't need one," said Bane dismissively, taking hold of my arm. "Come on..." Stick presumably bumping against the wall, he strode off down the passage at his normal speed.

"Ur... this way," said Jon awkwardly, clearly taking Lucas in tow.

For a while there was just the quick brush of our feet on the flagstones, and the sound of our breathing, then after perhaps a kilometer, Bane jerked to a halt. "Whoa! It's a corner or..." I could hear him feeling around. "No, it's the door. Finally."

He hauled the door open—still no light beyond, but when I stepped through and felt the walls, I found a light switch and flicked it. Light! We were in a cellar.

Lucas stepped through behind, squinting in the brightness. A slight pinch at his brows suggested his headache was ten times worse than mine, but he was soon looking around alertly. "How long have we got to get to the station?"

I paused in the middle of fishing hair clips from my bag, and looked at him. "*We?* You can't come with me, Lucas. You're far too recognizable."

From the mulish look on his face, he wasn't impressed by this argument. "Lucas, you don't have an ID card; you might as well just slit your wrists. And you will get *me* caught, do you understand?"

The stubborn look slipped into one of pure misery.

"I'm sorry," I said softly. "It's just the truth."

Fumbling in frantic haste, I began to fasten my hair up as carefully as I could.

"Cheer up, Lucas," said Bane. "You could look as inconspicuous as anything—which you so don't—and have a perfect ID, and you'd still have to stay here with us."

Jon turned his head towards Bane, frowning slightly. "Why?"

"Because we three have a job to do."

"We do?"

"Yes. We have to retake the Vatican."

26

THE PANTHER IN THE WINDOW

Only a slight widening of Lucas's eyes betrayed how he felt about Bane's statement, but Jon's jaw frankly dropped. "I... usually hate to use the word, but, surely it's *impossible*. *Us* three? The place must be crawling with EuroArmy."

I was thinking the very same thing, but then I saw Lucas's eyes narrow, a look of intentness covering his face.

"No, it's not," I said. "Lucas has a plan."

He gave a slightly wry smile. "Well, I have an *idea.* "

"Good," said Bane briskly, as I yanked a blonde wig from the bag and started pinning it into place. "First things first, have you both got a nonLee? And you keep that knife of yours in your pocket, Lucas, okay? Obviously the situation is totally different to how it was at the end back in Gozo—there was absolutely no hope of success then even if we did fight, so we'd have been killing people for nothing—but right now, even leaving aside all the normal moral considerations, the EuroGov are using nonLethals. For political reasons, yes, but it will still look really bad if *we* kill anyone. So lethal violence can only be our last resort, understood?" He tilted his head particularly at Lucas, looking endearingly stern.

"Understood," said Lucas gravely. "I have a nonLee, anyway."

I wanted to stay and listen, but... No time. I clapped a football cap over my wig, pulled low over my forehead, and put a pair of sunglasses on my head, ready to use as soon as I got somewhere light enough.

"I have a nonLee too," Jon was confirming.

"Good," said Bane again. "So, Lucas, enlighten us?"

"Well, we play to our strengths," Lucas said.

Right... I turned towards the stairs. Yikes, no! I took the nonLee from my waistband and tucked it into the bag.

Made myself take stock from head to feet. Nothing else incriminating. Oh yes, just one more thing...

I hugged each of the others, quick and hard, and kissed Bane. "Don't you dare get killed," I said. "Any of you!"

Bane held me so tight I thought he wasn't going to be able to let me go after all. But finally he whispered, "If we lose, don't you dare come back!" and released me.

I hurried away up the stairs before I could lose my nerve or give in to curiosity and stay to hear more about their plan. If I didn't stop Father Mark, it wouldn't matter if they succeeded or failed.

The stairs led up to a hallway with a front door. Opening it, I stepped out into the street as boldly as I could. Now, which way? Bother, should've checked the map before coming out...

I walked briskly a few streets, then stopped to consult the map of Rome in the bag. I was several hundred meters from the Vatican—the station was quite a walk. Didn't know when the first train was, so I'd better step on it.

Rome still slept, the streets were deserted. As I neared my destination, I began to see the odd person, mostly trundling suitcases in the same direction, so at least I knew I wasn't lost.

Roma Termini—I saw the sign over the door at last and hurried inside, slipping the sunglasses on as I entered the lit area. Screens... there. Brussels, Brussels... there... 04:52... Platform 5. It was a twelve hour journey, right? Next train not until... 06:02... my eyes flew to the clock... 04:48... *Lord!*

I ran for the ticket office. "Brussels, please," I gasped in Esperanto, swiping my fake ID card without a second thought. *Quick... quick...*

The reader beeped happily and the sleepy-eyed ticket clerk glanced dispassionately at her screen and deigned to move her fingers over the keyboard slightly faster. "Return?"

"Uh... yes." Though with an unconscious Father Mark to lug along, I'd probably have to 'borrow' a car... Still, just in case I had to get out of Brussels in a serious hurry...

I handed over rather a lot of the emergency Eurons Eduardo had given me, accepted the ticket and legged it for platform five. Dived on board and hadn't even taken a seat when the doors hissed closed. Too close! But I'd made it.

It was only when I'd settled into a seat in the mostly-empty carriage and my heart rate had gone back down and I'd started to relax that it hit me what I'd done.

I'd left the Vatican.

I was on EuroGov territory.

And this time, I had no diplomatic immunity. If they caught me...

I forced the wave of fear back down. Father Mark had risked the same for me when he helped Bane rescue me from inside the Lab itself, back at Salperton Facility. Risked much more for me, what with the current moratorium. And it wasn't just Father Mark's life at stake, was it? But my body insisted on flooding me with panic and adrenalin. I scowled, tried not to fidget, refused to burst into tears, and kept my face determinedly turned to the window.

The train raced on. The carriage filled up a bit. The ticket collector came by, and checked my ticket without even looking at me.

Seven o'clock. What was happening back home? Were Bane and Jon and Lucas okay? Captured? Hurt? Was it even possible that they could actually be... winning? From the determined set of Bane's spine as he marshaled his unlikely troops, they were going to go down trying. *O Lord, keep them safe...*

Eight o'clock. I checked my ticket. Arrival time... 16:34. I might even be able to be waiting for Father Mark at the hotel. How was *he* going to get there? Oh Lord save me, could he be on this very train? When would he have got to the train station?

As long as Father Mark didn't see me, it would be fine. But if he did... I couldn't pull out the nonLee on the train, it would spell disaster for both of us... but it would be equally disastrous if he went for me... especially for *me*... Why hadn't I thought this through?

Wait... over there, a leaflet of train times. I got up casually and went to pick one up. Carried it back to my seat and had a look. 01:52... no, 03:52... Could he have made it for that train? What time had Lucas woken us? About three o'clock, surely? There was a pretty good chance, then.

There wasn't really anything I could do about it, anyway. Not like he'd have any reason to walk up and down the train.

Nine o'clock. Oh dear. Almost a twelve-hour journey and I didn't have a book.

Well, I'd better pray. Pray for Bane and Jon and Lucas, for Unicorn and Eduardo and the others—what would a fifty-percent-lethal grenade have done to Bee? Pray for everyone at the Vatican. And for the vote tomorrow, and for me and Father Mark. For the Chairman, even... Was Father Mark's attempt really meant to fail? If Reginald bloody Hill had come up with this, perhaps he meant to step into the Chairman's vacated shoes...

Not my problem; nothing I could do about it, anyway. Father Mark was my problem right now.

The day crept past. I prayed and prayed some more. I pounced on abandoned newspapers and magazines. Quite a lot about the vote: evenly balanced in opinion. Prayed again.

I was so tired... but I fought against sleep. All it would take would be for me to start sleep-talking. Even if I didn't speak some dangerous name, I might use Latin...

All the same, I was dozing when the train stopped with a jerk. My eyes fixed on a station sign and I sat up straight, sleep forgotten.

Brussels.

I took a surreptitious look at my reflection in the window. Wig straight. Hat pulled forward over my scar. How would Lucas feel if I got caught, after refusing his help?

Stop it, Margo. Stop thinking like that. It won't help. Get off, find Hotel Champagne, save Father Mark.

I consulted a tourist map on a display board on the platform—I'd been to EuroSquare when I was here before, the obvious location for the speech, but not Euro Boulevard, where the speech was actually going to take place—no doubt to avoid memories of the January protests that had led to the vote. So... Euro Boulevard... there... I was here. Not far. Good. Already quarter to five.

Off I hurried, trying to move with the confident step of one who knows exactly where they're going. Fortunately the directions were simple, and I didn't have to crane around too much for street names.

Here it was. Euro Boulevard. There was the podium for the speech. The Chairman's car would drive in along that bit of road, stopping *there*... he'd walk along the side of that building... yes, Hotel Champagne, said the sign.

I worked my way through the crowd already gathering, slipped across the road through the gaps where the crowd control barriers hadn't been put into their final position yet, and strolled casually into the hotel.

Expensive place. I probably didn't fit in very well. Confidence was the key. There were the lifts... I'd head that way with my breeziest air... *uh oh!* Barriers ran across the lobby, funneling everyone between two rectangular arches. WeaponScanner arches. Oh... *damn.*

Some other department of the EuroGov had noticed this building was the perfect place for an assassin, too. Father Mark didn't *need* a weapon. I did. But no amount of confidence would get me through with a nonLee in my bag.

I stopped and glanced around the foyer for a moment... *What, what could I be looking for?...* ah-hah! I moved determinedly to a stand of business cards, selected one for a taxi company, and strolled out of the hotel again.

Now what?

Slipping down a back street let me reconnoiter the Hotel's second accessible side. There was a service door, but it was locked. No weaponScanners beyond that, no doubt, but I had neither lock picks nor crowbar.

What to do?

I could... go back to the lobby, put my bag on the floor to get something from it, and casually slide it under one of the sofas while no one was looking. Then go up and... what? Get Father Mark's attention and run like billy-ho, beat him to the lobby and get my bag, run outside, lure him down the back street and shoot him?

I'd need a lot of paper to write down all that could and probably would go wrong with that. Starting with the whole *outrunning* bit. I'd barely beaten him along half a corridor, when he... I swallowed a sick lump of rage-pain, and tried to think.

What other option was there?

I'd have to wait here—surely someone would come out, and I could slip in, even if I had to shoot them with my nonLee. I hunkered down behind a refuse bin, and waited.

No one came out. I could hear the crowds growing and glanced at my watch. Quarter to six! *Please Lord! Let someone come out?*

Minutes crept by. Ten to six. Lord, it's the *speech* that starts at six; when will the Chairman *arrive?*

My blood froze in my veins. He could arrive at any moment. And once I saw that car pulling up, it would be too late. There was no more time. I had to get up to room one-oh-eight, even without the nonLee. So long as Doctor Reynar hadn't undone the original programming—unlikely— I'd hopefully be sufficient distraction to allow the Chairman to pass under the window un-attacked.

I licked dry lips. Father Mark was fast, fast like Lucas. Could I really outrun him, even with a head start? In the distance, the crowd began to cheer.

Bane, forgive me. My heart accelerated in my chest, but I was already running down the back street. I yanked the bag off over my head and chucked it at the base of the wall, then pushed my way with a total lack of charity through the crowd to the hotel entrance.

Cool as a cucumber... I walked in, straight across the lobby, through the right hand weaponScanner arch and up the stairs. As soon as I was around the turn, I ran again. Skidded to a halt on the first landing, my eyes desperately searching the signs. Rooms... 51-100, 101-150... *there*. I sprinted through the corridors, my eyes skidding over door numbers, *come on, come on, drive slowly, car, drive slowly, let the Chairman wave, take your time...*

There...

I hadn't got a door card! *Oh no...* I reached out and turned the handle. It opened. Ah, not locked. One less com- plication when programming Father Mark...

Pulling off my sunglasses to show my face, I stepped inside, making sure the door wouldn't swing closed, and looked around.

Father Mark crouched in the open window, behind the curtain, like a panther about to spring, his gaze intent on something below. He'd not heard me over the sound of the crowd...

"Father Mark," I said clearly.

His head jerked around, his eyes widened—for a split second, I saw terror in them, then that other thing slid back in and he sprang...

I was already moving, but as he leapt, his hand reached out, grabbing a cushion from the window seat and throwing it with tremendous force... it struck the door squarely, knocking it closed. I lunged for the handle—felt him hurtling up behind me—had to get out of the room or I was dead but... had to *move* or I'd be dead *sooner*—I leapt away—too slow, he carried me to the ground, knocking the air out of me, not like screaming was an option anyway...

I twisted, trying to get to my feet but he was on me, his hands closing around my neck. I tried to kick him, thrust him off with my feet, but his weight held my legs immobile. I couldn't breathe, pain around my neck, I struggled frantically grabbing his hands, trying to drag them off but it was hopeless, too strong... of their own volition, my fingers began to claw at the backs of his hands, but his knee caught me in the stomach and the last of my air was forced out of my closed throat and with nothing to replace it, my vision began to gray out, can't breathe, can't breathe, can't breathe, can't breathe, air, air...

I writhed with increasing feebleness in an agony of panic and pain, one thought whispering in my head... *Bane, I'm so, so, sorry... so, so, sorry...*

Something else, as well, something important, air, please, air, air... important... to do with that blurred shape above me, something I hadn't said, needed to say, wanted to say... No breath for speech, blackness creeping up to swallow me, but I managed to mouth, "*I forgive you...*"...'
Hope he saw, hope he remembered...

Blackness won.

27

FROZEN VEGETABLES

My neck hurt. A lot. My chest too. I was gasping like a fish. Even my back ached, nothing compared to the rest. I dragged my eyes open... an unfamiliar ceiling. Fancy cornice... expensive wallpaper... *where on earth?*

I rolled over, wheezing. Why was I this out of breath?

Oh... I froze, then turned my head, quickly scanning the room. That was why...

Father Mark lay half-propped against the nearest wall, his chest heaving. His face was a horrible gray color and his lips were almost blue. Eyes half-closed.

I scrambled up onto my knees. Was I up to running away? No strength in my body at all... He looked so ill... "Father Mark?"

Father Mark's eyes opened all the way—filled with intense relief. "Margaret, are you all right?" he whispered. One hand was clutching his chest...

"Fine..."

The look of pain in his eyes deepened, they closed for a moment and he slid a little further down the wall.

I started to scramble towards him without thinking... Stopped. "Is it... safe?"

He opened his eyes again, his hand slipping from his chest as though it was too much effort to hold it there. "I think so. Be careful..."

I was already beside him. I waited for him to take this in, watching his eyes warily—nothing happened so I got an arm around him and maneuvered him onto my lap before he could slide all the way to the floor. His skin felt cold and clammy.

"Father Mark, tell me how to help you?" I pressed his hand urgently. "What do I do?"

"Did you mean it? Did you...?"

347

"Yes. Yes, I meant it," I whispered—and it was true. "I forgive you. Please... tell me what to do?"

A joyful smile settled on his lips, though the pain still lurked in his eyes. "I'm free, Margo," he murmured. "Do you realize? I'm free of it. My own again... Thank you... *so much*..."

"*Me?* It wasn't me, if you've broken free of it, it was *you*... Now what do I *do?*"

"Pray with me..." Had to strain to hear him. "You know the one..."

"No! No, tell me how to *help* you? *Please?*"

His eyes lost their focus—his hand tightened around mine, just a little, as though checking I was still there. Another spasm of pain crossed his peaceful face and his hand loosened again... Was he even still conscious?

Heart aching, I bowed close to his ear and began to pray. "At last, all powerful Master, You give leave to Your servant to go in peace, according to Your promise. For my eyes have seen Your salvation, which You have prepared for all nations, the light to enlighten..." His body changed from weakly alive to deadweight in my arms, his last breath fluttering my fake locks, then no more...

I clawed short, dark hair back from his damp forehead, touched his slack face in desperate appeal, whispering useless, useless words... "Please, please don't be dead, please don't be dead, *please*..."

But his gray eyes stared up through me, through the ceiling, through all earthly things and there was nothing for me to do but hold him and rock in silent misery.

Not *again*.

A sudden silence from the open window and the sound of a clock striking drew me back to thought. I had to get out of here...

I went on kneeling, paralyzed by indecision. I couldn't carry Father Mark's body—couldn't just leave him... Apart from my natural reluctance, it would be a gift to the Euro-Gov. They'd claim their own security forces had killed him as he came to attack the Chairman, and if the vote was as finely balanced as I feared, it could be enough. Getting his body out of here was almost as important as stopping him jumping out that window had been. So *think*, Margo!

My mind was slow with grief. Wheels... wheels would be a start. This was a hotel, so... laundry trolley? Everyone would be at a window here or there, listening to the speech—I could look out for an apron or something, but above all, I must just be quick.

Hurry, Margo! Perhaps they'll assume Father Mark didn't get here in time, but they'll come to check sooner or later...

The door opened—my heart catapulted up to my throat... *what the?* A team of paramedics rushed—quietly—into the room. They stopped dead when they saw me, gaping, then, recovering, the first one crouched beside me and placed two fingers on Father Mark's neck... I did a double take. *Spitfire?*

"Too bloody late," I whispered. But thank God they were here. Did this mean Bane and the others had *succeeded?*

A pair of them placed a stretcher-gurney thing on the floor, Spitfire swiftly but gently closed Father Mark's eyes and they heaved him across. At which my mind concluded I didn't need to worry about anything further, and I could go back to Feeling Awful.

Quickly fastening straps to hold him onto the stretcher, they arranged a medBlanket over him, strategically pulled half across his dead face, deployed the stretcher's wheels... then Spitfire was shaking me gently. "Margaret? You need to play the concerned relative, you understand?"

I nodded dully. That wouldn't be hard.

Spitfire plonked my cap back on my head and pulled me to my feet, moving me into position beside the stretcher, and we were off. I jog-wobbled alongside, occasionally remembering to peer anxiously at the supposed patient—*oh, Father Mark!*—but the corridors were deserted. We went down in a service lift and came out of a door into that back street. An ambulance was parked there, into which the stretcher was loaded.

"Wait..." I croaked, as Spitfire urged me in. I pointed. "My bag... down there. NonLee. Fingerprints..."

He understood. Better not to leave stolen weapons in the vicinity of the Chairman with my fingerprints all over. He murmured an order and Orange ran for the bag. As soon as he'd piled in, we were off. I caught a glimpse of what looked like EuroGov security hurtling out of the service door, just as we pulled away. Too late.

Well... we still had to get out of Brussels.

"*Bane?*" My voice was hardly audible, but they understood what I was asking.

"I don't know," said Spitfire apologetically. "The state was still in EuroBloc hands when we left. We snuck out."

"How..." I broke off, wincing, but again he guessed what I wanted to know.

"Eduardo crept into our apartments and woke us. We had no time to talk about anything other than the mission. But if Bane was okay when you left, I don't see why he wouldn't still be okay."

Clearly they thought I'd left Bane sleeping peacefully in our bed, or something... My heart sank. They knew nothing. Well, not *nothing*... Eduardo was alive, and well, and somehow free, or had been when they left. That wasn't nothing. But whether Bane and the others had freed him or whether he'd just woken up in time to avoid capture, like Lucas... No way to know if any of them were alive or dead.

Bane...

Jon. Lucas. *Kyle.* Oh, Kyle. Kyle who was still avoiding me...

I stared at Father Mark's body and went back to feeling numb. *Lord, watch over them. Please watch over them...*

We stopped quite soon and a couple of the guys jumped out, and wiped a quick mix of street dust and oil over the number plates. Good point...

Lord, watch over them.

Long minutes of forcing our way through traffic with the siren on, and doubling along back streets with it off, and finally we were out in the open countryside.

"Where's the bloody forest?" snarled Spitfire after a while.

"They don't have so much around Brussels, lucky blighters," said Trombone.

But finally, suddenly, sheltering trees loomed around us.

Lord, watch over them.

Spitfire was on his phone. "Our location's coming up on your screen? Good. How far away are you?" There must be another guy... "Okay, we'll be ready. Oh, wait, stop at a supermarket and buy a whole load of frozen veggies, would you? Yes, frozen vegetables. Any kind. Oh, about..." He shot an awkward look at the blanket-shrouded shape. "About enough to pack around a dead body, okay? Yes. Yes, it is. I know, me too."

We pulled off down a dirt track and soon came to a halt. Spitfire urged me out and sat me on a log, posted a guy on either side of me, and went back to the others. "Clean it all out, that's right... leave it tidy. Take some photos, so we can prove we left it undamaged. Start getting some of the kit off, give it a shake, fold it..."

The ambulance cleaning went on in front of me for some time, barely registered. Eventually Spitfire's voice came again, more loudly, "Oh good, here's Discus..."

An innocuous white van was pulling up. Discus jumped out, opened the back and started to hand out the guys' own clothes. When it slowly sank in that some of the guys were blushing and seeking the inadequate shelter of the ambulance, I turned around on my log, and stared unseeingly into the forest instead.

Lord, watch over them.

Soon I was being loaded into the white van.

Hang on... where was Father Mark...?...

Spitfire saw me looking around anxiously and stamped gently on the floor. It *sounded* solid, but I knew what he was about to say before he said it. "Secret compartment, Margo; don't worry."

That was all right, then.

Lord, watch over them.

There wasn't a lot of space in the back, with five of the guys and me, so I stretched out on the floor and alternated between dozing fitfully and staring miserably into space. Spitfire tried to get me to talk, but soon gave up. I just felt so numb.

The first couple of times I actually managed to nod off, we came to a road block, and they woke me and stuffed me into the secret compartment with Father Mark, who'd been

351

packed around with frozen peas and wrapped in a foil blanket.

"Too many roadblocks," muttered Spitfire. "It's insane; they *must* know she's out here somewhere."

"They've had a very close look at the CCTV footage from the hotel lobby, I s'pose..." said Trombone.

"Here's another one," called Discus from the front.

In practiced fashion, the guys took up the floor panel.

"I'm so sorry, Margo." Spitfire looked horribly guilty as he pressed me once again into the cramped space with only a corpse for company. "But we just can't risk it."

I did agree, though I didn't feel like talking about it. I lay there in the darkness, shivering inside a foil blanket of my own, holding Father Mark's cold, stiffening hand through the joins in the blankets in an attempt to ward off the terror, and wishing, wishing, wishing it was still warm and alive. *Lord, watch over them.*

"This is mad," Spitfire was saying, as they hauled me out again. "Our IDs may be perfect, but they probably got a rough idea of how many of us were in the ambulance. Pretending to be a hard-up band on our way back from a gig may have worked so far, but if they even ask to see our instruments? I think we should pull off somewhere nice and quiet in the forest, and give things time to calm down."

"Well, you're in charge," said Trombone.

"I was hoping for slightly more feedback than *that.*"

"Well, obviously we're keen to get home and help," said Geranium. "But this is really, really tempting fate. I think we should stop."

"We'll be no use to anyone if we get caught," agreed Boeing. "And we've got Margaret's safety to think about."

"Okay, Discus, find us a quiet spot, preferably under the shelter of the trees in case the Eye of Sauron passes over."

Things got extremely bumpy for a time, then we were stationary. The guys started to pass around field rations, but I wasn't hungry. *Lord, watch over them.* I lay down again, and after a while I slept.

...Daylight filtering into the van... I stretched, aching all over, touched my neck tenderly—regretted it—and finally glanced at my watch. One o'clock. I'd been asleep for almost *ten hours!* If the team had slept they were awake again now, playing card games and munching more rations.

Spitfire sat me on one of the bench seats and insisted on smearing some salve from the first aid kit on my neck, much good it was going to do. I endured. The numbness still hovered around me, and anyway, talking hurt rather a lot.

"Radio?" I rasped, but Spitfire shook his head.

"We have to assume all methods of communication are compromised," he said. "I'm sorry, Margo."

I nibbled at a ration bar for a bit, but swallowing hurt a lot too. After a while, I had to make a run for the doors— there was very little to come up; I'd barely eaten the day before. I gave up on the ration bar after that, because throwing up made talking seem painless, and I still felt a little queasy.

I joined the guys in a rosary for Father Mark, only mouthing it myself, and by early evening, Spitfire decided we'd carry on and see if the roadblocks were gone. Relief surged through me as we moved again.

Bane... Are you okay? It was an ache in my gut, I needed to know so badly.

Jon? Lucas? Kyle? Everyone?

Lord? Watch over them. Get us safely home?

The roadblocks were gone. We drove sedately, at the speed limit. A police car would get more than it bargained for if it pulled this van over, but still, unconscious coppers would provide a trail for the EuroGov.

It was a very long night. I dozed fitfully and, embarrassingly, had to get them to pull over twice for me to be sick, though my stomach was empty. I reassured them in a croak that I didn't get motion sickness, it was just stress. *Or grief.* First Snakey, then my baby, now Father Mark... And no way of knowing if Bane and the others were dead or alive... It was all simply too much. We stopped once to buy a new load of frozen veggies, and every moment of that long journey, I was keenly aware of what lay under the floor. I'd failed. Father Mark was still dead...

When at eight in the morning, the twinkling roofs of

Rome appeared through the windscreen I'd scarcely ever been so happy to see a place, despite not knowing what awaited us. Of course, unlike most cities, Rome had checkpoints to get in. Something about the Underground's headquarters nestling in the center...

Back into the makeshift morgue. Father Mark's hand was limp again; rigor mortis had passed. I'd not imagined the interminable nature of the journey.

After a while Spitfire lifted the floor a crack. "The checkpoint barriers were just open, no one there. But stay down there in case of a random check, okay? Not far now."

I muttered an affirmative. My throat was beginning to improve a little.

Finally, finally, we pulled to a halt in a garage and they hauled me out one last time. Carefully, they lifted out Father Mark's body as well, laying it down in the corner before drawing their nonLees and opening a concealed door.

I wanted to sprint along the passage, I was so desperate to find out what had happened, but I allowed them to go ahead, advancing with extreme caution.

Lord, watch over them. Lord, let them be all right...

The passage seemed to go on forever. Nothing but the dim illumination from the flashlights and the sound of our breathing...

"Halt, who goes there?" The sharp challenge came from ahead. Everyone froze and dropped to one knee, nonLees held ready. Several guys pressed me to the wall, shielding me with their bodies.

"Identify *yourself,*" demanded Spitfire.

"You're supposed to go first," said the voice.

"Uh..." Sounded like Spitfire was frowning. But the challenger was right. "Agent Gedro, VSS number five, six, eight, three, two." Spitfire sounded nervous. If it was a SpecialCorps soldier, a grenade would probably come rolling round that corner... "Identify yourself, please?"

"Agent Fallon, VSS number four, seven, seven, six, three. Advance and be recognized."

Spitfire's dark silhouette rose and disappeared along the passage. We all waited for a bang, a thud...

"Ferrari!"

"Spitfire!"

That was definitely the sound of manly back-pounding, not someone collapsing on the floor. We all hurried forward.

"What's happening?" Spitfire was asking Ferrari, AKA Agent Fallon. "Is the Vatican back in our hands?"

"Yes, everything's fine," said Ferrari, waving the question away. "Go right along, everyone will be delighted to see you. Wait, where's Father Mark?"

Spitfire sighed. "He's dead," he said softly. "Trombone, Discus, nip back and get him, will you?"

I was already rushing along the passage. *Wait, I didn't actually ask if they were all okay...* But surely he'd have said... I raced on, the guys jogging alongside, the walls passing in a blur.

Finally I was scrambling up through a knee-high opening... and there was a group, heading straight for us. My eyes snapped to the solid figure in front, a thin stick waving in front of him.

"*Bane...*" I lurched to meet him, pretty much fell on him, and at long last, burst into tears. He managed to get hold of me as my legs threatened to give out entirely.

"Margo?" Checking he wasn't about to passionately embrace the wrong weeping female?

"It's me," I sobbed. "I'm a bit hoarse."

He settled his arms around me and held me close. Inhaled deeply. Stroked my hair, kissed my face, kissed my hair. Rocked me to and fro, and hugged and kissed me some more. I just clung to him and cried and cried and cried.

"Oh, Margo," he sighed at last. "You're safe..."

"That's my line," I whispered, smiling through tears of joy.

"Yeah..." he said, wiping my cheeks dry with his thumbs and kissing my forehead. "But it's okay, Margo, everything's okay."

I stared at him. I was overjoyed to see him, alive and well. But he looked so... *happy?* Ferrari had clearly reported our arrival. Didn't Bane know...?

"You know I failed, don't you? You do know Father Mark..." I broke off, swollen throat closing even more.

Bane's face fell. "Yes, I know. You tried, Margo. You'll have to... have to tell me what happened."

"Then why do you look like you want to grin from ear to ear?"

He blinked, looking astonished. "Margo, don't you understand, we *won!*"

"Won?" I said blankly.

"The *vote,* Margo! We won the *vote!*"

28

TEAM BETTER-LATE-THAN-NEVER

"They announced it on the radio just now," Bane added.

I stared at him, comprehension finally dawning. "We *won?*"

Ridiculous as it might seem, Father Mark's death and my fears for Bane and the Vatican had driven the vote from my mind entirely. But as we'd sat in the forest, kicking our heels, the EuroBloc had been voting. Each tap of each ballot terminal had flashed a vote almost instantly to the EuroBloc mainServer, where the carefully imported—and neutral—Vote Verification Technicians had been watching over the counting program. The EuroGov must've run out of things to insist they double-check—they should've been able to make the announcement at about five past midnight.

I flung my arms around Bane and hugged him yet again. "We won!"

He swung me from side to side in celebration. I buried my face against his chest, a tight bubble of joy inside me, but despite my relief, my mood only lightened slightly. Father Mark was still dead. And so was our baby. And Snakey. Eventually I detached from Bane and looked around again; registered the pair of green eyes fixed on me like those of an anxious cat. And the autumn-haired figure with an equally attentive ear cocked in my direction. "Oh, Jon, Lucas... I'm fine, really."

Lucas stepped over, hands running from my head down my arms, as though he had to have physical confirmation of my well-being.

I gave him a hug. "I really am all right. What happened here?" I hugged Jon as well. "How did you re-take the state? Is anyone hurt? Is Kyle okay?"

"Kyle's fine." Eduardo had just come up behind me, Unicorn and Snail beside him.

"U! Snail!" I hugged them too, not caring if they were on duty. "And Eduardo... you're all okay. The grenade didn't hurt you, then?"

Uh oh... The question made their happy expressions slip.

"Bee... hasn't woken up yet," said Unicorn quietly.

"Oh no. How bad is it?"

"It's too soon for Doctor Frederick to say," said Eduardo. "But some level of brain damage looks all too likely."

"Oh no," I said again, helplessly "What he did was so brave."

Unicorn nodded, his face very sober. Yes, if Bee hadn't beaten him to it, he'd have been the one curled up over that grenade...

"So... what did happen?" I asked.

"Well, we woke up—well, all of us except poor Bee, that is—piled in one of the cells," said Unicorn. "Not the one Doctor Reynar was in, the other one. Doctor Reynar was whining to be let out, but they weren't having any of it. Weren't risking anything upsetting their plan until they were sure the state was secure. We tried to escape, until they threatened to shoot us all if we didn't knock it off. Since there were as many of them out there as there were of us, and them all armed, there wasn't much we could do. Fortunately for us, Bane's little commando team were getting busy."

I turned to Bane and made an encouraging noise.

He went slightly red, but spoke with increasing enthusiasm. "Well, Lucas figured our only chance was to play to our strengths—and clearly he was right. So he took a look around double-quick, before it could get light, and found where Eduardo and the others had been taken. We couldn't get to the light switches without being seen, though, so Jon and I hid just outside the cell block, whilst Lucas slipped off to the main power transformer..."

"...a junction box..." corrected Lucas.

"Okay, box, whatever. Eduardo really needs to hire Lucas as a consultant: he already knew the weak spots.

Anyway, Lucas shinnies his way up to this item of strategic electrical importance—attached to a pole, I believe it was—and *poof,* he shuts off the power to the section where we're hiding. The guards reacted the same way they did earlier, lots of swearing, so Jon and I just strolled in and sent them all beddy-byes. Then I listened out for trouble whilst Jon found the right keys and got the cell unlocked."

"I couldn't believe it when this voice whispered, 'Don't attack me, it's Jon!' and the door opened," put in Unicorn. "Thought I was having hallucinations from the nonLee, or something. No offence, you three."

"None taken," said Jon. "It would never have crossed my mind we could do it, either. Bane just refused to believe we couldn't."

"Because we *had* to," said Bane, blushing charmingly, and hurrying on, "Anyway, once they were out, Eduardo just said, 'Jack, see about re-taking the state,' and off he ran to find some guys to send after Father Mark, then locked himself in a cupboard with a laptop to hack the ambulance system so the guys could borrow one and look official. By the time he reappeared, it was all over.

"Personally," Bane went on, "I could've understood U thinking that was rather a tall order he'd been given, but he just sent guys off to various places to scout around, shut the rest of us up in a broom cupboard with him to wait for them to come back, and forbade us to say a word."

"I needed to think," said Unicorn.

"Yeah, by the time the scouts came back, I think he'd formed a plan for each possible scenario, because the moment they'd all checked in, he was deploying his troops. The EuroGov had spread their soldiers thinly through the accommodation corridors, just patrolling to stop anyone who happened to wander out of their room from raising the alarm, but they were heavily guarding the Swiss Guard barracks, the Vatican Police barracks, and of course, the armory and VSS HQ. But they didn't have access to the camera room—I should say camera vault—because they'd have needed explosives to get in quickly, and that would wake everyone. So U deployed four guys to the barracks and four to the armory, and sent Jon with them."

"In case we could use the trick with the lights a third time," said Jon. "He took Bane with *him* for the same reason—you know that Eduardo's going to make all the guys practice blind-folded with the audible targets, from now on? He's already appointed me and Bane as instructors!"

"Anyway, U sent Lucas to protect the Holy Father," went on Bane, looking equally pleased, "Which just about killed the other guys. but the fact was that Lucas could get to him, and they couldn't, so we persuaded him to go in the end."

"Persuaded?" I queried. "Didn't you want to do it, Lucas?"

Lucas shrugged slightly and Bane went red again. "Lucas, er, had kind of appointed himself my bodyguard. But I managed to convince him that you'd rather he went to Pope Cornelius."

"Oh. Lucas, thank you so much for thinking about Bane, but... well, they were right. You had to go to His Holiness, in the circumstances."

Lucas shrugged again. "Well, I did go," he said.

"Glad to hear it. I take it Pope Cornelius is okay, then?"

"Right as rain," said Eduardo. "Some panic-stricken soldiers did burst in eventually to try and take him hostage, but Lucas just shot them."

"Right so... uh, Jon went to the barracks, Lucas to the papal apartment—by an external route, I presume—and... where did you go with U, Bane?"

"Oh, we went to the Exchange."

"The Exchange?" I echoed. "Isn't that where the telephoneServer is?"

"That's right. Only two guards there, we took them out easily. Then U gets on the telephone system and puts a call through to every occupied residential room. People answered and got a recorded message saying, 'Hold for a security announcement.' When virtually everyone had picked up, he got on the phone himself, announced that the EuroArmy were in control of the state—that they were right outside their rooms, in fact—and ordered them all to go out and take them down with whatever they had handy—as nonviolently as possible, obviously.

"So..." Bane grinned, "about thirty seconds after U hangs

up, the corridors are full of angry young nuns..."

"Waving frying pans..." put in Snail, eyes gleaming with amusement.

"Priests with, what did you say, Snail? Tennis rackets?" put in Jon. "Lay people with walking sticks..."

"One guy was throwing dinner plates," added Snail.

"Anyway," said Bane. "Total chaos ensued. Of course, most people just got shot with nonLees, but that was the whole idea, it turns out. U's really a rather ruthless fellow, you know. Because by the time U's small teams of armed, trained agents made their move, there were whole heaps of unconscious bodies everywhere, but the EuroArmy had empty powerMags."

"It was the only way," said Unicorn softly, his face grim.

"Was anyone hurt?" I asked, alarmed to see everyone else's faces sobering as well.

"Three fatalities," said U quietly. "All old folk—weak hearts, all of them. I said old folks were to stay in their rooms, but they went out anyway." He sighed. "I knew they would. Five other heart attack cases are in the hospital at the moment. Father Mario's the worst, but it looks like he'll pull through."

Three dead... and Father Mario and four others very ill. And Bee... Still, who knew what the EuroGov would've done if they'd still been in control when we won the vote...

"Anyway," concluded Bane, "Once the Swiss Guards were freed, that was it. Game over. Though from the sound of it some of the EuroSoldiers were actually quite glad to be rescued from the little old ladies with their rolling pins."

"Divine wrath of God personified," muttered Snail, and grinned.

"But what happened to *you*, Margo?" asked Bane. "What's wrong with your throat?" Bane's concerned fingers moved in that direction.

I fended him off. My speech was improving, but it was still very sore to the touch. "Father Mark tried to strangle me," I said simply.

He went white. "Weren't you going to shoot him on sight? Didn't Spitfire and the others get there in time?"

"Spitfire and the others... well, they were Team Better-

Late-Than-Never, I'm afraid, so I was on my own. And there were weaponScanners in the hotel lobby, which meant I had to ditch the nonLee. I hoped to get in the back way instead, but no one came out, and the Chairman was coming, so I had no choice."

"Oh my God! You used yourself as bait..."

He sounded so horrified I slipped an arm around him and squeezed. "*Really* didn't have any choice."

Eduardo looked ill as well. "How did you get away with it?"

"Well, obviously I *didn't*. He got me, choked me unconscious—suspect he was exerting enough influence over his actions to choose a nice slow method in the hope he'd be interrupted—but it appears he managed to interrupt *himself*. 'Cause I came round and he was collapsed and in a very bad way, but he was so *happy*, because he'd broken free, and I could go near him again, but..." my voice wobbled, "whatever was wrong... something to do with his heart, I think... it was too bad and he..." I buried my face in Bane's shoulder; I could feel it all over again, him dying in my arms...

"I see," said Eduardo softly.

I took a couple of deep breaths and managed to finish, "I was just getting in a panic, trying to figure out how to find a laundry trolley, and get him out of there when the team showed up and took care of all that."

"Right. Well, I can debrief you more thoroughly later, but that will do for now. Oh, this is all top secret," added Eduardo sternly. "Not a word. Understood? Margo? Bane? Jon?"

"What about Lucas?" said Bane.

"That goes for Mr. Loquacious as well. You lot can go. Team Better-Late-Than-Never, come along for debriefing."

The team winced in unison, and followed him.

Telling the story seemed to have given me the shakes. I let Bane lead me out, and a few short minutes later I was sitting on the sofa in our own home—happily the unconscious men had been removed while I was away—and Bane was putting a mug of tea into my hands. I sipped appreciatively for a while and Bane sat beside me looking—

it slowly sunk in—oddly pleased with himself. I glanced around... no, I'd not imagined Jon excusing himself. I'd been a little surprised he hadn't stayed...

"Did *you* make this?"

"I did," he said rather smugly, then shrugged self-deprecatingly. "Jon and I had to do something this last week whilst you've been so busy."

"Well, it's perfect. How did you do it?"

"Well, I boiled water, I put tea in the pot..." I slapped his arm lightly and he laughed. "Okay, okay, actually it's just lots and lots of practice. You pour cold water into the teapot *over and over* again until you can hear when it's full. Then you do the same with the mug until you know what *that* sounds like when full. Ten minutes later you've forgotten—start again. Really boring, basically."

But he'd stuck at it and there was pride in his face. Not being able to make hot drinks for himself or for me might not seem like a big deal, but I'd a feeling it'd been one of things that stung the most.

"It's a perfect cup of tea, Bane, thank you."

He kissed my hair and I rested my cheek on his shoulder. The tea was slowly thawing me out inside and settling my stomach. We'd *won*. How happy Father Mark would be about that. How happy that he'd not been the one to derail it all...

And I'd forgiven him. I had. I could think about my poor baby and Father Mark at the same time, without that gnaw-ing anger trying to swallow me whole. The pain... the pain was undiminished. Doubled, with Father Mark's loss. No wonder I felt so sick.

We'd won. I'd not really thought beyond the vote, not in anything but the most generalized terms. Suddenly the rest of our lives were spread out in front of us. Freedom... *We'd* not be going back into the EuroBloc, but still. Freedom for the Underground. A constant fight to keep that freedom awaited us; no doubt that would be a lifelong struggle. But. We *won*.

After lunch the next day we ventured down unfamiliar corridors to the mortuary in the basement. Father Mark's funeral was to be tonight, and Bane wanted to pay his respects. We joined a subdued line and waited—mostly members of Animal, and other first-wave Liberation teams. Eventually it was our turn.

It was a small room with clean-cut stone walls, nothing there but the coffin on its trestles and a simple crucifix on the wall. They'd dressed Father Mark in his cassock, all neat and ironed, brushed his dark hair and folded his arms across his chest, so his very body would bear the sign of the cross into eternity. His seven stealth stoles, bits of colored yarn he'd used during his years as an Underground priest in the EuroBloc, had been braided colorfully into one and put in place around his neck.

They'd not used eye cups, or make-up, or any of the things nonBelievers use to lie to themselves; he looked dead, all right, but he was a very presentable corpse, and there was a bizarre comfort in that.

I dragged my eyes away from the body of our friend and glanced at Bane as he made a frustrated noise.

"This is useless! I can't *see* him!" Familiar sentiments, but I frowned as I tried to analyze his voice. "Oh well," Bane sighed, stepping forward, his hands tentatively tracing the coffin sides and finding Father Mark's face. "I don't really know what he *felt* like. But it'll have to do."

Something was gone from his tone. Frustration, anger, irritation, they were all there. What was *gone?*

Despair.

Realization washed over me. There was no despair in his voice. Like he no longer secretly felt his blindness was the end of his world. My heart pounded with joy and relief. Karen North, Bane, I, we were winning. Everything was going to be all right.

Thank you, Lord!

"You're lurking, Lucas. You can join us, you know." I'd finally registered the furtive movements at the corner of my eye as we got settled in a pew ready for the Requiem Mass. "Unless you'd prefer the company of St Norbert..." A nook behind St Norbert's statue was one of his favorite hidey-holes.

He sidled into the pew, slid warily past Jon and Bane and sat beside me. He must've *sounded* furtive too because Bane leaned around me to say, "Y'know, Lucas, we had a big lunch earlier; I doubt Jon could fit you in, he's too full."

Lucas looked intent for a moment as he unraveled this, then he actually smiled. "Nothing on me, anyway."

"*That's* true," I said. "You've got to remember to eat more."

He shrugged. "More interesting things to do."

"Perhaps, but eating's *important.*"

"Yes, Godmother."

That got a snort from Bane, as ever. Even Jon smiled slightly. But we all fell silent, then, attention returning to the trestles standing before the tomb rail, awaiting the simple coffin. I felt so down. Why did I have to be so *moody?* Hormones again? Perhaps now all the stress of the vote was over, I'd level out.

Oh no, not again! Can't we start? But it was no good, I was going weepy...

"I wanted so much to save him," I whispered into Bane's shoulder.

"I know, I know," he soothed, rubbing my back and looking anxious. I didn't want to put that look on his face.

"I'm okay," I sniffed, unconvincingly. "I don't know why I'm being like this. I'm just so sad..."

Lucas was staring at me with his head on one side. "But... this is a very happy day for Father Mark, isn't it?"

I blinked, my tears abruptly petering out. Rubbed at my cheeks with my sleeve, my mind in turmoil as intellect fought with emotion. Finally I reached out and hugged him tightly.

"I said something right?"

"Very right. Reminded me what really matters. It's human enough to feel sorry for oneself at a time like this, but I've got to remember to be happy for Father Mark as well!"

Lucas nodded and smiled serenely. "With God."

"With God, Lucas. He is."

The Mass was simple but the choir sang beautifully.

Pope Cornelius did the homily—reminding me painfully of how he'd given the homily at the last Requiem Mass for Father Mark. My throat tightened at the memory.

Afterwards we processed out to the Vatican Gardens in the setting sun to watch the coffin lowered into a freshly-dug grave, tucked away in that pleasant bush-encircled corner that meant so much to me. They'd asked me to choose the spot, and it'd felt right. They were both victims of the EuroGov, after all. A wooden cross was set up, to mark the foot of the grave until the headstone could be planted. Once it'd rotted completely away, it would also indicate that the headstone could be moved to join the others around the walls, and the space reused.

Oh no, I was feeling sick again. Since when was I squeamish?

Kyle was there at the funeral, of course, and I tried to reach him, but he disappeared into the throng, deliberately or not, I couldn't tell. Should I go and look for him? No, not right now. I was feeling too emotional. I went back to Lucas's room instead, because I felt I could use a few minutes of his cheerfulness. Sorry as he was to lose one of his only two friends, he was possibly the only person who was actually managing not to begrudge the Lord Father Mark's company.

I drank tea, trying to settle my rebellious stomach, and admired his healing plants, listening a little absently to their progress reports.

"Margaret?"

Blast, I'd tuned out completely. "Sorry, Lucas."

"Worried?"

"Not really. Just thinking about Bane's eyes. Which is stupid. Especially since... well you know, just earlier today, I realized things really are going to be fine. For Bane. For me. For us. Without his eyes. But still, the thought of them sitting somewhere in the EuroGov's grasp keeps creeping back into my head."

"Worth a lot less now," said Lucas softly.

"Don't remind me. I think that's why I'm dwelling on them so much. Because what can they use them to gain, now?" I sighed. "Well, *we're* not getting them back. There's no point thinking about it. What were you saying?"

He blinked and sipped his tea. "I sold a plant. Yesterday."

"You did? What did you sell?"

"One of my first fuchsia cuttings. The cafe owner from outside the square came to buy a plant—just to savor the permanent lifting of the Religious Suppression, I think. And chose the little fuchsia."

"Well, congratulations. You're in business."

"Yes. I do hope he looks after it." Lucas heaved rather a sigh himself, then offered me the biscuit tin.

I waved it away hastily as a waft of sweet biscuity smell assaulted my nose. "No, thank you, I... *oh, blast...*" I ran for the toilet.

Grrr, go away stress. Father Mark's buried, the vote's won, so clear off!

My not-very-full stomach now empty, I sat back on my heels and pulled off a wad of toilet paper to wipe my mouth. Looked around to find my gangly host leaning on the doorframe, watching me with rather less panic than I might've expected.

"Are you having a baby, Margaret?"

"What?" My heart clenched so hard it took my breath away, and I fought to keep tears from my eyes. "No, of course not."

"Why of course not? That sturdy young man is your husband, isn't he?"

My cheeks caught fire, but there wasn't much I could say. "Yes, but... I'm not, anyway. It's just stress."

"Oh." Looking disappointed, he offered me a bony hand and drew me to my feet. "Okay now?"

"Yes, sorry about that."

"I think it was worse for you."

Eduardo actually looked the tiniest bit amused the following morning as he handed me a EuroPocket paper. I took a look at the photo and blinked in surprise. Someone had snapped me hugging Lucas in St Peter's yesterday. How was this *front page?* I scanned the headlines and text. Oh...

"What do you think of that?" Eduardo almost smirked.

367

"They don't know what to make of it, do they! Bane, Jon, it's a picture of me hugging Lucas yesterday. You know the EuroPockets have been swearing up and down that this forgiving Lucas and baptizing him is all a big publicity con, and as soon as we won we'd lock him up and throw away the key and I'd never go near him again? Well, now they've got this photo and they're floundering. Why did they print it, though?"

Eduardo gestured to the other papers on the table. "They've all got a shot of it, so they felt they had to try and come up with some sort of explanation. They really are struggling, though. They know we have as much reason as they do to hate him."

"And they *really* hate him, don't they," I muttered, scanning a few EuroGov quotes. They didn't come straight out and say it, but it came through somehow. Reginald Hill was quoted at poisonous length, even calling Lucas a "consummate deceiver capable of taking in even the scheming minds of the most seditious."

"They'd rather people think Lucas has taken us in than that he's genuinely repented, and we've genuinely forgiven him," I snorted. "I think it's getting a bit thin."

"Well," said Eduardo, "Most of the papers seem to have finally ruled in our favor on this one."

"Bring one over to read," suggested Jon, turning back towards the serving hatch.

Soon we were settled at a table and I was devouring cherry tomatoes, and reading the article to the others. Why didn't I used to like these things? They tasted good. I'd better eat more than just those, though. Continental breakfast today. I ate a slice of ham and started on the croissant. And then... Oh *no*, not again... "S'cuse me. Back in a tick..."

I almost flattened Kyle as I hurtled from the cafeteria and dived into the ladies.

"Margo?"

He actually spoke to me! But I couldn't stop...

"Sorry, must dash," I yelled over my shoulder, hurrying into a cubicle and promptly losing all the tomatoes and ham. This was getting ridiculous! I wasn't even feeling stressed this morning! I was still very sad about Father

Mark, and my baby and Snakey, of course, and we were all worried about Bee, but the general post-vote euphoria had been buoying my mood...

"Are you all right, Margo?" Kyle stood in the outer doorway, frowning at me.

"I'm fine, really. I'm just stressed out."

"Oh. I wondered if you were pregnant."

I flinched as my heart knotted up again. "No, I'm not! Why does everyone keep asking..." I stopped with my mouth hanging open, the answer to this question hitting me like a slap in the face.

"*Uh*... got to go..." I raced back into the cafeteria and grabbed Bane's arm. Gave a distracted nod to Sister Mari and Sister Krayj, now sitting there as well. "Come on, Bane..."

"What? I haven't finished..."

"Doesn't matter, come *on.*"

"*What*... are you okay?"

"I'm *fine*..."

Giving in to my efforts to drag him from his seat, he located his croissant, used it to wave bemused resignation to the others, and followed me.

Was it possible? Actually possible? So soon?

"What's up?" Bane asked, once we'd threaded our way through the tables and reached the corridor outside.

"Tell you in a minute." There were people everywhere, and he was bound to repeat what I said at the top of his voice. Someone even followed us into the lift, so I kept silent.

Oh... Kyle had been *speaking* to me—grudgingly—and I'd just run off... I shouldn't have done that... hadn't even thought... Too late now.

When we got out of the lift Bane sniffed, clearly catching some tang in the air. "Are we going to the hospital?"

"Yes."

"I thought you said you were okay!"

"I *am*, relax!" No possibility of taking my own advice, I felt I was about to explode with needing to know...

I towed him into the waiting area—all the staff were at breakfast, good—and took another pregnancy test from the box. Or the same one, recharged, for all I knew.

369

"Then what are we doing here?" demanded Bane.

"I want to do a pregnancy test."

"A..." He dropped the croissant. "You think you're...!"

"I think it is possible."

"But... I thought you said... And we... Your chart..."

I tried to choose my words carefully. "Well, I haven't been looking at my chart as often as I should have been." Not at all, it still made me cry... "I've been so busy and stressed. And now... well, I'm feeling sick all the time, I'm tired all the time, I'm moody and I'm suddenly rather sure that your renewed interest in certain parts of my anatomy doesn't account for how sore they are."

"Unlikely," snorted Bane. "You keep falling asleep before I can even say *goodnight, Margo.*"

"Exactly. Watch it..." He'd trodden on the croissant. I bent to pick up the pieces, but he found my hands and gave me a push.

"No, you've convinced me; do the test, I can't stand the suspense..."

"Okay." I pulled the thing out of its box and stuck my finger in it. "Done."

"Don't you need to... um... go in the bathroom, or something?"

"It's a blood test, Bane. The new type of test."

"Oh. Right."

We tidied up the croissant and sat on a seat to wait.

"Oh, Margo, Bane, did you want to see someone?"

I stuck the little device hastily behind my back as Nurse Poppy arrived, probably back from breakfast herself. "Oh, no, we're just, er, we're fine."

From the gleam in her eye and the fact that she accepted this and bustled off, she'd caught a good enough look at what I held.

Beep.

My heart was pounding so hard I could hardly breathe. "Lord help me, I'm afraid to look..."

"Well, *I* can't!"

"Yes, okay. Right..." I drew a deep breath and took the test from behind my back.

29

A DOUBLE MEASURE OF PRECIOUSNESS

My heart lurched... "Oh my!"

"Oh my *which?*"

"Bane, you're a daddy." *Again!*

"*Oh my*..." he whispered—abruptly bent forward and put his head between his knees.

"Bane? Are you okay?"

"Fine," he said faintly.

"You are... happy?"

"Of course I'm happy. It's just... wow." He sat up slowly, his hands slipping around my waist to cup my stomach.

Nurse Poppy drifted into the waiting area with a mug of water and began watering the plants. That was the job of the gardening team, so I wasn't too surprised that she was craning to try and get a look at the object in my hand.

"Poppy, it's positive, okay?" I held it out to her. "But don't pass it on; it must be less than a month. Is there a proper obstetrician here?"

Poppy looked half-pleased, half-embarrassed. "Well, Doctor Carol is a competent obstetrician. She's the only one in the state at the moment."

"Is she in today?"

Nurse Poppy glanced towards the schedule on the wall behind the nurse's station as though to jog her memory. "Yes, she'll be in soon. Ooh, Margo, I'm so happy for you!"

She hurried off and Bane paused his gentle explorations of my tummy. "What did you mean about less than a month?"

"It's not normal to tell people until you're three months along. Once you get past that, you can be... you can be much more certain everything's going to be all right." My voice

371

wobbled, despite all my efforts, but this clearly seemed perfectly understandable to Bane, who looked so horrified that I added quickly, "Most... most people get through the first three months no problem, Bane. It's just a precaution. We can tell Jon; a few people like that."

Bane relaxed a little and began running his hands over my belly again. "I can feel the bump already."

"You won't be able to feel it, yet!" I laughed.

"I can," he insisted. "There is definitely a bump here. You used to have a really flat tummy."

I peered down skeptically. Actually... my stomach did stick out a bit. "Well, I must've put some weight on, that's all. It can't be the baby, Bane. It must be less than a month."

"Don't you know exactly how old it is? From your chart?"

He was right, I ought to know. I'd only been energetic enough to engage in baby-making a couple of times since I'd lost our... but I literally hadn't looked at my chart since then. I'd been going on the theory that it was so close to the vote that it didn't really matter.

I was saved from answering by Doctor Carol's arrival. She had nothing more pressing to do, and soon had me on a bed for an ultrasound.

"There *is* a baby?" demanded Bane eagerly, almost before she could place the probe on my goo-smeared belly.

"Oh, there is definitely a baby. Right there, see, Margaret..." I peered hard at the mass of black, gray and white lines on the screen and could make out a small shape. Doctor Carol touched some controls and it grew larger.

"Is that... I think I can see the head! And an arm... Legs!" I could make it out so clearly! "Bane, I can see the baby! It's so well developed! Oh!" I gasped and clutched Bane's hand. "I can see it moving!" I could feel nothing, but there on the screen... The little shape kicked lazily... waved a tiny hand... Oh, if only Bane could see this...

Doctor Carol slid the probe back and forth for a few moments, smiling as Bane hung on my awed descriptions. "Looks like a healthy eight to nine weeks, to me," she said.

I stopped staring at the screen and stared at her instead. "Eight to nine *weeks?* That's two months... Are you *sure?*"

Doctor Carol looked bemused. "Positive, Margaret. That's an eight- to nine-week-old fetus. And look, you've got a nice little baby bump starting."

I stared at the screen again. The baby was incredibly well developed. But... eight to nine weeks ago... was when I'd *conceived* the first baby...

I felt the blood drain from my face. My hands flew up to cover my mouth. "Eight to nine weeks?" I squeaked. "Our baby's really eight to nine weeks old?"

Doctor Carol nodded patiently.

Shock and joy crashed over me, exploded me from the inside out—I clung to Bane and burst into full-out sobs.

"Margo? Margo? What's wrong?"

"I'm happy," I managed to gasp. "I'm just so happy! Our baby's eight to nine weeks old!" It was all I could do to hold in the words: "Our baby's alive! *Alive!*"

"Um... yeah, I'm happy too. It's fantastic..."

I sensed rather than saw the anxious look he turned in Doctor Carol's direction, but I simply could not get hold of myself. I cried and cried as though all the pain and anguish of the last month was being washed out by a wave of joy.

Doctor Carol smiled, though she looked a little surprised by my hysterics. "Now is probably a good time to mention, Bane, that your wife will be very emotional throughout her pregnancy. It's the hormones."

"Oh... Right." Bane sounded relieved. Of course, he'd had practice with me being hormonal. He rubbed my back and held me closer. "There, it's okay, Margo. Our baby's eight to nine weeks old and it's wonderful, isn't it?"

"Yes," I sobbed. "Yes, it is..."

Eventually Doctor Carol brought me a clean hankie and repositioned the probe on my belly.

Distracted by the baby, I managed to stop crying at last. "So, um," I gulped, "is there... is there anything I shouldn't do?" I felt as anxious as though I actually had miscarried before—and I wanted to find out what *had* happened, that terrible night. If I could do so without Bane catching on. I would tell him about what had happened—*what I thought had happened*—but when we were on our own. "I imagine I should be really careful not to fall down or anything?"

Doctor Carol smiled again. "You don't need to worry much about falling over, certainly not yet."

"But... I thought if you fell down early in pregnancy you were very likely to lose the baby?" My voice shook slightly, despite all my efforts.

Doctor Carol's gaze suddenly became intent and she opened her mouth to speak. Had she just figured out why I'd reacted so strangely to the baby's age? *She had...* I tilted my head at Bane and shook my head, giving her a meaningful look. She closed her mouth again.

After another second she said, "You've been watching too many films, Margaret. Early in pregnancy is the least likely time to miscarry due to an external impact. The tiny little baby is tucked down between your pelvis in a great big fluid-cushioned sac. You could pretty much bounce up and down on your stomach, and it wouldn't hurt it at all."

I swallowed, suddenly remembering Father Mark driving his knee into my stomach the other day. But... apparently it was unlikely to have done any harm. "I suppose... if I had any bleeding...?"

"Come to me at once, yes. But not all bleeding is a miscarriage, so don't panic beyond all reason. You're well past implantation bleeding, but there can be other types. You can even get tissue or clots, sometimes, and it's not necessarily anything to worry about. But come back another day when it's sunk in properly, and we'll have a proper talk."

I stared at her, stunned. My bleeding, my clot—not my baby, my *clot!*—must have been like that. Nothing to worry about... Unless Father Mark did shake things up a little, despite what Doctor Carol said. But... only a little.

My baby was alive!

Doctor Carol let me gaze at the baby on the monitor for a bit longer, explained that in medical terms I actually counted as eleven weeks pregnant, because of the date it was counted from, and eventually sent us away clutching a lovely monochrome image of the new life inside me.

"I owe Lucas *another* apology," I remarked to Bane.

"What for?"

"He asked if I was pregnant yesterday, and I totally

dismissed the idea."

"Well, I don't mind if you tell him."

"I think I will. He won't pass it on."

"Mr. Loquacious," grinned Bane.

I had to smile. It wasn't true that Eduardo had no sense of humor. "Well, I could pop and see him now, or we can go straight home and get Jon to come round." I wanted to bring Bane up to date, too, but I wasn't in that much of a hurry to dampen his happiness, even temporarily.

Bane looked torn. "Well... Go and see him first, if you like. We'll be ages with Jon, won't we?"

A few minutes later I was outside Lucas's room, the scan in my pocket. He let me in, eyeing me rather critically. Wondering if I would need his bathroom again?

"Lucas, you were right!" I was too euphoric to beat around the bush. I took out the scan and held it out to him. "I am having a baby!"

He took the image at once, looking so happy you'd think I'd told him he was having a baby himself! Not very surprised, though.

"There, that's the baby..." I pointed eagerly... his finger beat me to it. "Oh... it took me a moment to make it out, first time!"

Pain flashed through his eyes, momentarily eclipsing the joy. "My sister used to send these to me." He broke off, shook his head, and peered at the image again.

My fingers twitched to have it back, to look again at this hard evidence that my baby was safe inside me. Perhaps he sensed my eagerness, because eventually he returned it.

A knock at the door.

Lucas opened it and stepped back. "Hello, Bane. Congratulations."

Bane came in, looking slightly embarrassed but mostly still overjoyed. "Hello, Lucas. Have you seen our baby photo? I had to come and see it again—well, not see it, but—Margo, where are you, describe it to me again, go on..."

Trying not to smile—after all, I was no different, wanting to look at it over and over—I retrieved the scan, which Lucas had got hold of again. "I'm sorry, we do want this! I'll get one for you next time, if you like."

A big smile spread across Lucas' face, at that.

I launched into yet another description for Bane, then finished, "And, er... do you mind if I tell you whether it's a boy or a girl, because I kind of know and I'd rather not have to try and stop it slipping out..."

"I thought we weren't going to find out!"

"My fault," confessed Lucas. Bane looked bewildered.

"Yeah, um, Lucas told me. I didn't realize anyone could interpret an ultrasound, so I didn't think to brief him. I'm sorry."

"Oh. Well, you'd better tell me, then."

"It's a boy."

"Wonderful!"

"You wanted a boy?"

"Well... not specifically! It's still wonderful! But—oh no, I hadn't thought!" His face fell and he swung abruptly into panic. "What if the baby's in danger and I can't *see* that! What if..."

"Calm down!" I hugged him. "It's going to be fine. Jon will help you."

"He doesn't know anything about looking after babies!"

"Well, no, but he's very good at figuring out how to do things, isn't he?"

"Yes... but I... Oh, I'm not going to say it; it doesn't help!"

He didn't *need* to say it. From the solemn look Lucas directed at us, he heard the silent cry as clearly as I did.

I wish I could see.

I made a celebratory pot of coffee whilst Bane phoned Jon. Let's hope I could keep it down.

"Hi, Jon," Bane was saying in the other room. "Will you come round? We've got big news! Oh, but don't tell the others we've got big news, because you can't tell anyone yet, okay? What? Well, not me *personally*. Yes, Margo is. Are you going to come over? We've got a photo and everything! I know, but Margo's good at describing it!"

He came to join me in the kitchen.

"He guessed?" I asked.

"Yep."

Jon showed up quickly and managed to maintain apparently genuine interest throughout a blow-by-blow account from Bane of how we'd found I was pregnant and three descriptions of the scan from me. When Bane urged me to a fourth description, he did finally roll his eyes to heaven and mutter, "Six and a half *months* of this?" which made me giggle.

Bane simply picked up the scan again and waggled it in his hands. "It's just so amazing!"

Jon's face screwed up—definitely trying not to laugh. You could see his point—happening right now in millions of families around the world.

"It's still amazing, *Uncle* Jon," I pointed out.

His face straightened and softened, at that. "I s'pose it is, isn't it? Uncle Jon, huh? It's wonderful, wonderful news. I thought you weren't going to try and start a family until after the vote, though?"

"We're *so* not going into that." Bane went red.

"The Lord had other ideas," I said simply. By way of my un-regretted carelessness...

"Let's sit here..." I guided Bane to a bench near that grassy corner of the garden where Father Mark was buried. Where *just* Father Mark was buried. I rubbed my bump, joy choking me yet again, then glanced at Bane. How would he take this?

"Bane... I, uh, I didn't just want to come for a walk. I wanted to talk to you. I, um, need to tell you something. Please, please don't be... too hurt... or... *angry*... that I didn't tell you before, okay? I wanted to tell you so much, but I was just so scared that it might... well, depress you again. I was terrified. So please don't be too upset..."

Bane's brows had drawn together slightly. I could practically see his ears straining. "Are you about to tell me why you lost it like that in the hospital?" He'd accepted the apparent explanation at the time, but he knew me too well...

"Um... yes."

His brows drew together a little more, rather shrewdly. "And... why you went for that midnight walk?"

"Yes," I said softly. "I am."

* * *

When I'd finished Bane sat frowning, and I tried to identify the emotions flitting across his face. Hurt and anger, yes, what did I expect? But also anguish, and guilt...

"Margo..." he said after almost a whole minute's silence— thinking before speaking, that was new since we'd started seeing Karen North. "I really... I don't know what to say. I... *do* feel hurt and angry and... I wish you'd told me, obviously, but... I suppose I can see why you didn't. Mostly... I think mostly I'm just furious with myself for getting in that state and not being there for you. I should have been there to... to... *to do this*..." he gathered me into an all-enveloping bear hug and pressed his cheek to mine.

"Oh Margo," he whispered into my hair, "Didn't anyone know?"

"Well, Unicorn knew. He was bodyguarding me, remember? Try stopping a VSS agent checking inside the mysterious box you're burying at the dead of night."

"Unicorn. Well... good. I hope that made it... a little easier."

"I suppose it did. It was all pretty awful, to be honest, but it turns out I made a huge mistake and everything is fine. More than fine! So... well, I was always going to tell you as soon as possible, and now I have, so we can forget about it and concentrate on the baby."

Bane's hand found my bump. "Yes... but you can talk about it to me if it's on your mind at all, okay?"

"Now who's all for counseling!" I teased.

He just shrugged. "Margo, the worst thing for me about, well... this..." he waved a hand in the vicinity of his empty eye sockets, "is not being able to protect you any more. I feel so *useless*, it drives me crazy! And I get why you didn't tell me, but in future, you *will* tell me, won't you? Let me be a man in the only way that's left to me, and support you."

"Oh, Bane," I hugged him. "*Of course* I would normally talk to you."

"I know I haven't actually been all that approachable, these last few months. But... I've turned over a new leaf and, well, you always accuse me of being overprotective and I know I am. But please don't start doing that to me, will you?"

"I won't, Bane, I promise." We snuggled close for minute.

"Not that I'm asking you to let me walk into walls, mind you," said Bane more lightly, when we released each other again.

"Like I would."

Sister Krayj and Sister Mari came around for dinner later. Sister Krayj was still especially sober-faced in the light of Father Mark's death, and what with Bee, so I tried to tamp down the spontaneous outbreaks of beaming as I let them in. I still felt ready to burst with happiness. Bane had taken what I had to tell him better than I'd expected, and our baby was alive!

"How's Bee?" I asked Sister Krayj immediately. Bee had woken up the previous night, but his condition was sobering, even in my euphoric state.

"Same as earlier. Still not recognizing anyone. But it's not all bad, it seems. He hasn't lost language, and he remembers what things are, and most crucial things with regard to normal functioning. But at least for now, his memories are almost totally gone. Oh, there was one good thing. You know he didn't recognize Snail yesterday?"

I nodded. It'd nearly killed Snail. Heart-rending to watch.

"Well, when Snail went in again today, Bee remembered him—only from yesterday, but Doctor Frederick says that's still a very good sign, because it means his brain remains capable of making new memories. And Bee knew Snail was his friend, too. Couldn't remember anything to back up his conviction, but he knew it."

"Any long-term prognosis yet?"

"Well, Doctor Frederick is already confident he'll be able to resume a fairly normal life. Perhaps even transfer to the Vatican Police." A less demanding role than VSS... "But whether he'll ever get the memories back... it's basically a wait, pray, and see."

I shuddered. Poor Bee. What would it be like to have a past that was blank? Would you even be the same person, still?

"Well, take a seat," I said, "the food's ready..."

But Sister Krayj made a beeline for the dresser and picked something up. "Do I congratulate you both?"

"Oh no!" I sprang across, grabbed the scan, made to put it behind my back, realized the pointlessness of this and brought it out again as Sister Mari hurried across to coo over it. "Yes, you do, but please don't tell anyone; he's only eleven weeks."

How many people had I said that to, now? I'd phoned Kyle several times, to tell him the news, hoping the baby might somehow heal the breach, but he wasn't answering. He might be out, but I'd a feeling he just didn't want to speak to me after the way I'd run off earlier. I'd have to catch him in person. I'd told Eduardo, though: he *hated* not knowing stuff. I suppose I'd actually only told one extra person, then, unless one counted intent.

Bane came in from the bedroom and hastily made a beeline for where we stood by the dresser.

"Too late," I told him. "They found it."

He looked sheepish. "Sorry."

"Never mind." A knock at the door. "That'll be Jon and the food's ready."

I'd cooked a rather less than usually cheesy macaroni cheese—no one used the word bland, but it was. It stayed down. Lovely.

Underneath the table, Bane's hand was searching for my wonderfully occupied belly. I guided it there and laid mine over it, hands covering a double measure of preciousness...

"But we *won*..." Sister Mari's plaintive tone drew my attention back to the conversation.

"We may have *won*," Sister Krayj managed to be impatient and amiable at the same time, "but it's not like we've fixed everything that's wrong with the world. Religious freedom, yes—but the EuroGov haven't even returned our church buildings. And they'll take back even the territory we've gained if we give them an inch—politically and geographically."

"Offence may be the best form of defense," said Jon. "We need to keep the pressure on *them.*"

"You're not out of a job yet," said Sister Krayj, since Sister Mari still looked unconvinced. "And Margo certainly isn't."

My hand paused in rubbing my bump through my blouse. "Huh? Oh, I'll probably wind down the blog a bit, y'know. I'm going to be otherwise occupied."

"Well, don't wind it down too much." Sister Krayj sounded decidedly disapproving.

"I'll still do a bit..." I waved reassurance with my unoccupied hand. "But there are plenty of other voices out there, y'know."

"There's only one Margaret Verrall," said Jon.

"At this rate there'll be no one left to tell when it gets to three months," I said to Lucas as I arrived the following day.

He shrugged. Then his gaze gravitated to my belly and a soft smile took up residence on his face. Thinking about the baby made him almost as radiant as it made me. But there was a guarded look in his eyes which wasn't so nice to see, as though deep down he couldn't really believe I'd let him near my son.

I leaned forward until I managed to intercept his gaze. "You're going to be Uncle Lucas again, y'know."

He stared at me, eyes suddenly shining with tears. Whispered, "Second chances..." Thinking of Father Mark's homily? He stepped forward and took both my hands in his. "You are an amazing person, Margaret Verrall."

I ducked my head, embarrassed. "I think most people are amazing, if they'll just let themselves be."

"Some are more amazing than others," he murmured, slipping his arms around me and holding me tight for a moment. He pressed a gentle kiss on the top of my head before stepping back and waving me to a seat.

He set a pot of tea down a few minutes later. "I've got some advice I wanted to give your husband, actually."

"Well, why don't you tell him?"

He poured carefully. "I'd rather you just passed it on. Don't want to preach at him."

"Okay. Don't think he'd bite your head off, though."

Lucas shrugged. "Well, this is just from observation, and

from my own complete failures, but I think the most important things he must do are to look after you, look after the baby, and look after his own conscience."

"Um, okay, I'll pass it on." I sipped at my tea—so far, so good. "How's the greenhouse going?"

"Well, nothing's ready yet, of course." He sounded slightly sad—now who was being impatient! "Ranulph is very interested in the idea of selling the plants, though. Says now there's peace, he may have time to do some crosses of his own."

"I thought you two would hit it off."

"He seems very nice. So many nice people here. I met this nice but scary Sister this morning. Just came up in St Peter's and said she thought it was time she met me."

Nice but scary... "Sister Krayj?"

"Yes. Reckon she's done some damage in her time, but her heart's in the right place now."

"Remind you of anyone?"

"Father Mark," he said, a little sadly. He did miss him.

"Anyone else?"

"Me too, I suppose."

"Yes. We're big on second chances here, y'know."

Sitting down at my computer when I got home, I tried to work. I'd not blogged much since I got back, having a bit of a rest, though I'd done a few short posts in thanks and praise for people's votes. But people were still reading and it seemed rude to stop entirely—*I've got what I wanted so I'm not going to speak to you anymore?* Maybe not.

I'd got pretty well stuck in when a sudden hammering on the door made me jump almost out of my skin. I dashed to the door and checked the peep hole. Jon.

"Who?" asked Bane.

"Jon." I opened the door.

"Is the place burning down?" demanded Bane, as Jon stepped inside. He'd made Bane jump too.

"No, it's not that, something amazing has happened!"

"We already know that. We won the vote and Margo's having a baby."

"Yes, I know," Jon dismissed these momentous

happenings with a flap of his hand, "but *another* amazing thing! I've just been having tea with Pope Cornelius, and d'you know what he said?"

Bane got a very intent look, but stayed silent.

"What?" I asked, baffled.

"He said... he asked had I thought about the seminary?"

"Oh." I blinked. "Would you... like to go to the seminary?"

"Would I! Yes! I've always *wanted* to... but how could I? So I said to him, what use is a blind priest? And he said, well, everything's changing now, with priests not being hunted anymore, so there's no reason why I shouldn't be considered."

"So what did you say?" asked Bane, smiling.

"I said I'd like to be considered, of course! So it's not definite or anything. There's this whole selection procedure to discern whether you may be called; they don't take just anyone! But I can try! You've changed the world, Margo, and I can *try!*"

I shied away as he tried to throw his arms around me. Enough accolades! "For pity's sake, Jon! *I* have not changed the world! God has changed the world through a whole, whole load of people who went into ballot booths and found the courage to vote in accordance with their conscience! Not *me!* Don't you dare say that again!"

Jon blinked, brought slightly back to earth by my anger. "Sorry, Margo. I just meant... The Lord has worked through you too. Quite a lot..." He seemed to think better of this line of argument. "Sorry. The world *has been changed*. Are you happier with that?"

"Yes, that's better." But I let him hug me and my return hug was genuine. "I'm really happy for you, Jon. I'd no idea that's what you wanted." How arrogant was I, worrying he was in love with me? Sounded like I'd never been what he wanted *most!*

His face lit up again. "Well, I tried not to... to even think about it. How could I inflict myself upon the persecuted church? But now everything's different!" He hugged Bane too.

"I'm really glad," said Bane. "I did think, maybe, *now*...

I'm glad I was right." Then he nudged Jon and added, "You've just got to persuade them to *take* you, eyeless wonder."

"Thank *you!*"

Too many accolades sloshing around online, as well. Absolutely mortifying. I'd been working on a blog post before—and especially after!—Jon's visit, except one visit to the bathroom, sigh. Struggling to hit the right tone. Didn't want to come across as too stern, but really did want to nip it all in the bud. *Savior of future generations of reAssignees*, one blog was calling me. Simply ghastly.

Ring-ring. Ring-ring.

Bane had his earplugs in, saving the world again, so I dragged myself away from the computer. "Hello?"

"Margo? It's Unicorn."

"Hi, U. What's up?"

"A SpecialCorps Lieutenant and some soldiers just showed up at the gates, asking to see Mr. Everington. We duly informed Mr. Everington, and he toddled off down there."

"He *what?*"

"Exactly. He's a free man so we could hardly stop him, and Eduardo's got some guys there to make sure the Euro-Gov don't try any funny business, but I think you should get down there and make sure he doesn't wander over that white line."

"Right away!"

Pretty much dragging Bane behind me, I tumbled through the main gate a few minutes later. Skidded to a halt as a couple of VSS guys immediately barred my way. I peered between them and caught my breath.

Lucas, looking, if anything, even more than usually immaculately turned out, stood right beside the white line that marked the border between Free State and EuroBloc, speaking to a EuroLieutenant standing just the other side. He had a small box in one hand and seemed to be scrolling down the screen of some tiny gadget he held in the other.

"What's he doing?" I asked, spotting Unicorn.

Unicorn turned very baffled blue eyes to me. "Buying

something, I think. He rejected the first box—they must've been trying to fob him off. He seems happy with this one, though."

Buying something? With *what?*

Lucas closed the little box and snapped the clasps securely shut. Turned towards the gates—saw me and smiled.

"Lucas!" I called. "Come over here!" Surely the Euro-Lieutenant could just grab him and pull him over the line? It would take a full-out gun battle to get him back, and those soldiers were all carrying Lethals...

Lucas said a couple of words to the Lieutenant; the Lieutenant called over one of the soldiers, who left his rifle with his comrades. Lucas handed the soldier the box and watched closely as he crossed the line, came up to me and held it out. I took it automatically... Lucas was far, far too close!

"Lucas! Come here, *please?*"I really didn't like the way the Lieutenant was watching him...

Lucas just smiled at me again. "If there's anything you feel I should forgive you for," he looked amused at the very idea, "I do."

My stomach knotted with dread. "Lucas, what are you *doing?*"

The Lieutenant said something I couldn't catch. Lucas made a "patience" gesture and looked at me again, a long look, like he was trying to memorize me.

"What I can," he said.

And he stepped over the line.

30

A WONDERFUL FRIEND

"*No...!*" I screamed.

Too late. The soldiers grabbed Lucas, the muzzles of their rifles pressing into him on all sides. Nothing we could do—everyone nearby had seen him step over that line of his own free will...

An argument immediately broke out among the soldiers—someone had forgotten the cuffs. Lucas stood passively—but his eyes moved constantly, wandering here and there, and despite the fact he'd just handed *himself* over, surely he was analyzing his chances of escape?

Ignoring the blame-casting soldiers, the Lieutenant raised a wristCell to his ear for a moment, then turned to an expensive limo pulled up on the double red lines just the other side of the road. At his command, the soldiers marched Lucas across to it. The window slid down, revealing—shudder—Reginald Hill. Lucas's shoulders hunched; his head lowered slightly.

"Well, Mr. Everington, here we are once more." Reginald Hill's chill, smug tone carried to our ears. "Think you're going to get your way again, do you?"

Lucas's spine straightened, that instinctive fear draining away, and something rather like a smirk settled on his face. "Too late. I've got what I want."

"*Have you,*" said Reginald Hill savagely. "We'll see." He beckoned to the Lieutenant and said a few quick, quiet words. The Lieutenant started, then saluted and turned on his heel. Barked an order to the soldiers. Lucas looked faintly amused—the smug expression slipped almost entirely from Reginald Hill's face.

I was dimly aware of Unicorn filling in Bane in an undertone, but my attention was riveted to the slender figure being hustled over to the windowless wall of the building facing St Peter's Square. The soldiers stood him in the middle of it and backed up, forming a line. Lucas's head turned one way, then the other—thinking of making a break for it? But the distance was too great.

Another order from the Lieutenant and the rifles came up. I started forward—Bane's arms wrapped tightly around me, his hand pressing my belly—I lurched to a halt, held hostage by the tiny life inside me. What could I do, anyway? Pull out my nonLee and make an unprovoked attack on EuroGov troops? Throw everything away...

Lucas...

I stared as though sheer wanting could spirit him to safety. He stood quietly, the breeze ruffling his neat blond hair, looking down the muzzles of those guns, his head high and his face unafraid. Noticing my gaze he smiled at me—*everything is all right, Margaret...*

The Lieutenant's voice cracked again, and so did the rifles.

The bullets slammed Lucas back against the wall; he left a smear of scarlet on the white stone as he fell, landing face down on the pavement. His head moved, turning slightly, his arm crept out towards something... With a muttered curse, the Lieutenant strode forward, jerked his pistol from its holster and fired twice into the center of Lucas's back. The reaching hand fell to the ground and was still.

Dimly, I heard another order, saw out of the corner of my eye the soldiers march away, get into their transport up the main street, drive off... but I couldn't look away from that forlorn figure, lying on the ground. Finally my head turned, almost against my own volition, and I stared into a cruel, lined face, smiling malignant triumph as it disappeared behind a rising window. The limo followed the soldiers' truck and I slipped free of Bane and ran across the line, ran as fast as I could, though it was far too late...

A circle of guards managed to outrun me, rushing to secure the area... I dropped to my knees beside the blood-splashed wall, caught Lucas's shoulder and rolled him over. His green eyes stared blankly, his chest smashed, once crisp shirt bloody and torn... His hand trailed... I followed his last line of sight... a cafe... hanging baskets... and a little fuchsia with purple flowers...

My heart shook, my mind blank with horror and bewilderment. I was whispering "Why?" over and over...

Bane's arms wrapped around my shoulders, hand knocking the box my left hand clutched, forgotten, to my chest... He was speaking, but I couldn't make out the words.

Peeling the box from where it was practically imbedded in my flesh, I fumbled with the clasps. A solar panel nestled on the lid—it was a powered transit box of some kind. I got the lid up at last and a cloud of cold vapor escaped. A freezer box. Some sort of plastic packet lay nestled in the ice, and beside it the little gadget Lucas had been looking at—a DNA probe? The beginning of the last readout still showed on the screen:

Blake BLANK-BLANK

Then the first line of Bane's genetic code.

It felt like my heart had been hooked on a fishing line and yanked up my throat and out of my body... I slammed the box lid down, wrestled with the clasps until they closed, and shoved it into Bane's hands.

"What *is* it, Margo?" he asked again.

"*Your eyes,*" I choked, then the pain overwhelmed me and I threw myself on Lucas's body. Someone was wailing in inarticulate anguish. Me...

Eventually hands began to try and drag me away, but I clung to him, trying to gather his broken form in my arms as though I could somehow protect him. I held his head in my hands and stared into his empty eyes and said his name over and over again...

"Margo! *Please!* We have to go, it's not *safe!*"

The anguish in that beloved voice finally penetrated my grief. The hands were getting ruthless, I was about to be lifted off the ground, corpse and all. Tears blinding me, I slid the lids down over the unresponsive green eyes—let Bane drag me to my feet and away.

When we got across the white line I stopped... did I still have legs? Couldn't tell.

"Lucas, what have you done...?" I whispered.

The guards were carrying that limp form quickly across the square. I threw up on the ancient paving stones, and when I tried to straighten again, I just fell into blackness...

My head lay in Bane's lap. The coffee table was just in front of my nose—we were on the sofa. A dull fog surrounded me... what was wrong?

Then I remembered. Lucas was dead, his chest smashed by EuroArmy bullets. Dead, because he'd sold himself to the EuroGov to get Bane's eyes... for me.

I'd never felt anything like this agony. I'd heard guilt made any grief a hundred times worse, but I'd not understood. I clung to Bane, I sobbed, I cried out, couldn't stop because I couldn't get away from that crushing knowledge— *my friend is dead because of me*. I'd have given fifty years of my life to get that knowledge out of my head.

"Should I get Doctor Frederick?" Jon's voice eventually, soft and anxious.

"No, leave it a bit longer." Bane. Sounding terribly subdued, but his hands didn't stop their efforts to gentle me. "You know what he said. She's had the most terrible, terrible shock. Let her get it out."

Sheer exhaustion eventually dropped me back into his lap, not my efforts to get hold of myself or his to comfort me...

...The coffee table again. The memory was there this time and so was the exhaustion. I lay staring at the table without seeing it.

Bane fussed with the blanket he'd laid over me, cocking an ear. "Are you awake, Margo?"

"Umhmm."

"D'you want to just... lie quietly?"

"Umhmm," I managed again.

"Okay..." He began to stroke my hair.

Don't know how long I lay there, felt like hours. His hands ran over me soothingly, on and on. My mind seemed almost at a standstill, the awful truth slowly, slowly soaking in like water dripping onto dry soil.

Lucas.

Dead.
For.
Me.

At long last a few agonized words squeezed from my lips. "*Why did he do that...?*"

Bane made no reply for so long I actually looked up at him. Saw his tortured face.

"I would never have wanted that, Margo. Haven't I said all along I wouldn't risk anyone getting killed?"

Another long moment of pain, and I managed to reply. "It's not your fault, Bane. You didn't put him up to it."

I stared at the coffee table some more. Eventually Jon came back from wherever he'd been and made hot drinks. Bane sat me up a bit and began pouring weak tea down my throat. It revived me a little—not sure if that was a good thing just then. I rested my head on Bane's shoulder and tried not to think, period.

After a while Jon began to speak quietly to Bane. "Seems it's actually a simple operation. Doctor Frederick can perform it, no problem. The really important thing is the nerveFusion solution and the muscle stimConnect gel; you can't do it without them. But there's a small amount of both here and Pope Cornelius has authorized a dose—both obscenely expensive, apparently."

"So how long will it take?" asked Bane. Then pressed a kiss to my hair. "Margo, I hope you don't mind... I just thought it would be nice if I had them in for... for the funeral. If it's okay with you..."

Afraid I'd think he was being insensitive, arranging things before my tears had dried?

"It's all right, Bane," I said tiredly. "He didn't do that so you could put them in the freezer and forget about them."

He looked relieved. "So, Jon?"

"Well, you have to have a general anesthetic. That's as risky as it gets. After the operation they have to keep you deeply sedated for twenty-four hours, to prevent your brain trying to move your eyes while the solutions get your nerves and muscles together properly. Once they wake you up, your eyes will be sore for a few days, but the muscles will finish healing quickly."

"So if I had the op tomorrow morning... I'd be awake again a little later the next day?"

"Yes. I asked Pope Cornelius about the funeral and he said it can wait 'til evening the day after tomorrow, no problem. He's going to leave Margo in charge of all that, providing that's what she wants."

"Right. When would Doctor Frederick need to know? 'Cause I want to see how Margo is..."

That jerked me from my daze of misery again. "I'll be fine, Bane. Arrange the op."

"I just don't like to think of me lying there for a day and night, useless as a lump of lard, when you're feeling like this..."

"Just make the arrangements, Bane. I'll be busy organizing the funeral, anyway."

"Well... I suppose I could still put it off if I really felt I had to."

"I'll go and sort it out, shall I?" offered Jon.

"Yes..." Bane had a very intense look on his face, but spoke haltingly. "Wait... Jon, I... I've been thinking... well, after having *no* eyes, anything's better... and they're out of my head already. Would you... like one?"

Jon froze, eyes widening. A long, frozen silence. I hardly dared breathe.

"Bane," said Jon softly at last, "if I live to be a hundred and fifty, I'll never forget what you just said. But I'm content as I am. The Lord *gave* me a pair of eyes, remember. Attractive ones, so everyone tells me. Anyway," he laughed, "you're a wonderful friend, but you're rubbish at biology."

"Huh?"

"We're not the same tissue type, silly."

Bane's empty eyes widened. "Didn't even think of that. So busy wrestling with myself..."

"Thank you, Bane, anyway. And I promise never to reveal your intellectual lapse to another living soul!"

Thanks to the herbal tea Bane coaxed down me before bed, I actually slept for most of the night. Awaking at dawn, I wept into my pillow for a while, reluctant to wake Bane by crying on him. It would put him off having the operation.

And however much I might wish Lucas hadn't done it, I knew he'd like it if Bane was there at the funeral with that oh-so-expensive gift already in his head.

Taking a couple of painkillers in the vague hope it might numb my pain—my head was pounding anyway, a minor discomfort in comparison—I managed a reasonable degree of composure when Bane woke up. He'd had some of the herbal tea himself, because he might be less grief-stricken, but he felt pretty bad about this.

Bane wasn't supposed to have breakfast before the anesthetic, but I managed to make and eat some plain toast to demonstrate that I was okay to be left to my own devices for twenty-four hours, then it was time to go.

"Ah, Bane, hello," said Doctor Frederick, when we arrived at the hospital, Bane with his dressing gown on over the patient gown they'd given him. "We're all ready. If you just get yourself onto that trolley in front of you, we can get started..."

"All right, all right..." He hopped on. "Oh, I'm going to feel like a numpty lying on this thing..."

"If you'll lie down," said Doctor Frederick, "we can get you anaesthetized and you won't know any more about it."

"Yes, *all right.*"

Nervous about the op, poor love. However safe people tell you it is, not a nice thing to have to offer oneself up to in cold blood.

He found my hand, drew me in for a kiss. "See you tomorrow, Margo. *Literally, please God.*"

I kissed him again, fiercely. "See you tomorrow, Bane."

"Nighty-night, Bane, have a good sleep," said Jon.

"Ha ha," said Bane. "Look after Margo."

"She'll be fine, Bane. Lie down."

"All right, but I feel like a prat." He lay down at last, the doctors converged, and the nurses hustled me and Jon from the room. Soon they wheeled Bane out and away.

Jon slipped an arm around me and gave me a quick squeeze. "Okay, Margo?"

"Yeah. You said the op would take less than an hour?"

"That's right."

"I'll just wait here then, find out how it went."

We sat in the waiting area and I tried not to think too hard about what'd happened yesterday. Tried to pray instead, for Bane, for Lucas, for this new world we suddenly lived in... After a while I turned my thoughts to the funeral I was supposed to be arranging. What would Lucas want?

It was less than forty-five minutes before they trundled Bane back from the operating theater and we followed them to a private room. Bane was still completely out of it, of course, and something like a sleep mask had been put over his eyes.

"Everything went fine, Margaret," Doctor Frederick re-assured me. "The eyes were in perfect condition, they went back in nicely, we used plenty of gel and solution; should heal up well. Nothing for you to worry about. We'll wake him this time tomorrow and he should be able to see again."

I checked my watch. Ten o'clock. It would be a long twenty-four hours. I kissed my sleeping husband's cheek and Jon and I headed off at last.

"So, um, what do you want to do now?" asked Jon.

"I'm really not sure. I've never organized a funeral before."

"Well, there's all the stuff like hymns, readings and so on. Need to pick a spot for the grave; don't imagine he'd want to go in the catacombs. And, uh, you'll need to give them some instructions for laying out the body..."

"I'll do it," I said shortly.

"Margo... won't that be rather... upsetting?"

"*I'll* do it. Should be someone who... who gives a damn!"

"Margo, I'm sure there's hardly anyone here now who *doesn't* give a damn, y'know."

"I'll do it. And I suppose I'd better do that first. I'll need some things from his room. You really don't have to trail around after me, you know. Actually... d'you think you could find a piece of wicker trellis or something, for a bier? Reckon he'd rather go straight in the soil than be shut in a box."

Jon hesitated, clearly feeling he ought to stick to me like glue. "Okay. I'll see what the head gardener's got."

* * *

Lucas's room was eerily silent. No scuff of shoes on carpet as he hurried to fill the kettle. No rustle of plant or Office book leaves.

A fat envelope stood propped against the purple fuchsia's pot—on it, in curly handwriting familiar from long hours poring over a certain manual, was written one word.

Margaret

31

GROWN-UP-ITIS

I picked the envelope up and tore it open with shaking fingers; took out four sheets of paper.

Dear Margaret,

I hope I make it back before you ever have to read this, but I suppose I probably won't. I will be coming, if I can. If I can't, I'm sorry. I know everyone will say, poor mad man, but I know what I'm doing. I know what I want, and I can finally afford it.

I would not risk this wonderful new life for anything less precious, but for this, I am happy.

Thank you for saving me, Margaret Verrall—you will say you were just the instrument that brought me to

God's salvation: that is so, thank you just the same.

If you are reading this and you know that I am definitely not coming back, don't worry about me. Someday we will meet again in the Divine garden.

All my love,

Lucas Paul Jameson-Everington

_P.S._

Please look after my plants.

Turning over to the next pages—closely written, front and back—a huff of laughter escaped me despite the tears streaming down my cheeks. One page for me, three for the plants. Detailed care instructions for each one, by the look of it. No one could say he didn't know me now!

I gave the fair hair a last brush and frowned. It just didn't look as neat as when he did it. I tried again, but the hair began to get staticky and cling to the brush. I was making it worse. I took the brush away and smoothed the strands back into place with shaking fingers.

An unbearable pressure had been building in my chest as I worked. Jon was right. This was really, really hard.

They'd already washed the body when it arrived, and bound the shattered chest round with bandages to prevent... seepage. So I'd been spared the sight of those holes. Lucas was now dressed in his smartest shirt and trousers, in matching blue. They didn't look quite smart enough either, but it was the best I could do. I'd slipped a handful of seeds inside the shirt, just over his heart. Perhaps they wouldn't grow at that depth, but it seemed like something he'd like.

With a silent apology to the dead man, I'd also placed a single cut stem of purple fuchsia, with a few hanging blooms, under his crossed arms, but there'd be no other cut flowers around, I'd charged Jon to make sure of that. Ranulph and one of his assistants had brought along a very serviceable wickerwork bier and shifted Lucas's body onto it, so I really was done, wasn't I?

No. One more thing... I picked up Lucas's Office book, which I'd brought from his room, lifted his head and slipped it underneath for a pillow. There. Right now he looked more like a corpse than ever for some strange reason, but... all done.

I placed a kiss on his cold forehead, then, the need to keep going, *to finish,* gone, I sank right down on the chill stone floor, buried my face in my knees and began to cry. Kept whispering, "*Lucas, I'm so sorry...*"

Even though I knew he wasn't.

"Margo?" Jon's hands found my shoulders. "Margo, have you been here this whole time? Margo, you're freezing! Come on, let's get you out of here..."

He hauled me upright and aimed me pretty accurately towards the door. I rested my head on his shoulder, my legs moving unthinkingly. The world seemed to have become very blurred and hazy, a long way away from me...

...Jon holding something to my lips. Something hot. I sipped automatically—warm liquid ran down my throat—I seized the mug and drank greedily.

"Are you with us again, Margo?" Jon's hands hovered anxiously around me.

"I'm okay," I whispered, in-between sips.

"You weren't, you were seriously spaced out."

"Margaret, will you have a little lunch?" Pope Cornelius waved invitingly to a plate of sandwiches. I blinked. Didn't even remember walking up to the papal apartment. "They're nice and plain..."

Cucumber sandwiches. My face screwed up as I fought against tears—I buried my face against Jon's shoulder.

"Oh... oh dear. Margaret? What did I say?"

Jon sniffed. "Oh, are they cucumber? I think, er, *he* may have used to make those..."

"Oh, I see. I'll take them away."

"No, no..." I protested. "Don't waste them, I'm just being silly..."

"I won't *throw* them away, Margaret," he said gently, "but you're not being silly. I'll bring something else."

The Supreme Pontiff disappeared into his kitchenette, plate in hand. Returned after a while with another plate of sandwiches. Plain ham, fortunately. I didn't feel hungry, though.

"Well, baby is!" Jon shoved a sandwich into my hand.

Oh. Yeah.

I began to munch. Cautiously. But it stayed down. Was I past the worst of the morning sickness, or had the stress been making it worse, after all? Not that I wasn't stressed now...

I put the plate to one side, pain bubbling inside again. "*How*," I couldn't hold the words back any longer, "*how* did I give him the impression I'd rather have Bane's eyes than him, alive? What sort of friend am I, that he could've believed that?"

"Oh, come on, Margo," said Jon. "He did *not* believe that. He knew jolly well you'd hate the idea, that's why he didn't tell you! I'm sorry, but this is a classic case of—no offence, your holiness—*grown-up-itis*..."

"*We're* grown-ups, Jon."

He made an impatient gesture, "You know what I mean. He was doing that thing parent-types do where they know *perfectly well* what *you* want but they think *they* know better than *you do* what will be best for you. He thought having a husband who could see would be better for you than having an eccentric plant-lover underfoot, that's all."

I buried my face in my hands. "He was so pleased with himself." I could still see him, standing there, looking into the muzzles of those guns. "*So* pleased with himself..."

"Shame he couldn't get away. He was so good at that."

"That was his plan. Hand himself over and then escape. He knew it might not work, though. The EuroGov isn't completely stupid."

"Still, he wouldn't have expected..."

A brutal, on-the-spot execution.

"No." But he hadn't cared, because he'd, what'd he said? *He'd got what he wanted.*

I suddenly felt overwhelmed with exhaustion. Checked my watch. Only two o'clock. "Jon, I'd like that hymn about love springing up like wheat, or however it goes... But I'm not sure I can face choosing all the other hymns and readings right now..."

"It's fine, Margo. We can do it."

So that was that. Still twenty hours till Bane would be awake.

And Lucas would still be dead.

"You two put me to shame, y'know," I whispered to Father Mark. I'd come to the gardens to choose the grave site and just ended up sitting down beside the fresh grave. "Both facing death with a smile on your lips. Wish I had your faith. When death comes near me, I just feel scared."

The little circle of bare soil over the center of the grave had been empty last time I'd been here, waiting for its irrigation pipe. Now the pipe was in place, and a fine white fuchsia had been planted there. Looked familiar... I leaned closer... yes, the white one I'd given Lucas to thank him for saving my life from Father Mark. Very appropriate. So Lucas had finally given Father Mark one of his plants...

My eyes ran around the little secluded corner. I still thought it was the nicest place. "You know, there's plenty of space here and I know you won't mind," I told Father Mark, who could surely hear me, wherever he was precisely. "You two can keep each other company."

So that was that.

                              * * *

Only so long one could sit on a sofa and stare into
space, and only so many times Jon could say, "Are you okay,
Margo?" before one snapped.

Eduardo had dropped around to give me a couple of
framed photos of Lucas, both taken from security cameras,
but properly printed on photographic paper. His way of
commiserating. I spent a while looking at them, before
turning to the newspapers he'd brought.

Glad to see the papers thought the summary execution
shocking and awful. Plenty of press hanging around St
Peter's Square these days—they'd got the whole bloody
business on film. Most had stills of me weeping over Lucas's
body, a couple had smaller insets of the execution itself,
which made me have a brief, weary cry on Jon's shoulder.
But when I looked at the pictures again, finally, I got mad.

I opened up the laptop and placed one of the framed
photos on the desk as I waited impatiently for it to boot. So
much for winding down the blog. Reginald Bloody Hill had
just given me a new objective.

Capital Punishment in a 'Civilized' Bloc: Contradiction in Terms?

                              * * *

I woke as a hand brushed my shoulder. "What the... Oh;
Margo?"

"Good morning, Jon," I said sleepily. Shifted and almost
fell off the edge of Bane's single hospital bed. "Whoops!
What time is it?"

"It's nine o'clock."

"Bother, I missed Mass."

He shrugged. "Yes. But... well, there's... there's one tonight, isn't there?"

Lucas's Requiem Mass. Hadn't exactly *forgotten*, but
still, the reminder was like a blow to the stomach.

"D'you want to come and get a spot of breakfast? We've
another hour to wait."

"*I* don't, but I s'pose baby does. I need to get dressed,

though." Oh no, now it'd be me sneaking around the corridors in my dressing gown!

"Crept in here in the night, huh?"

"Couldn't sleep."

"Right."

By the time we came back, the medical staff were congregating. Almost time. They were doing something with the tubes. Stopping the sedation?

Soon Bane's breathing speeded up and the mutter from the doctors said he was awake, but he didn't stir or speak.

"Patience." Doctor Frederick noticed my anxious expression. "It takes time to come fully awake from a general anesthetic. You could try talking to him now, though."

"Bane?" I leaned closer. "Bane? Are you awake?"

"Hmm? Margo?" he murmured.

"Yes, it's me. How do you feel?"

"Groggy..." He lay still for a few more minutes, then suddenly, his hand was reaching towards the eye cover. "Hey, aren't I supposed to be able to see?"

Doctor Frederick caught his wrist. "All in good time. We need to ask you a few questions about how your eyes are feeling, then we can dim the lights and get them uncovered. If you're feeling sufficiently with-it, now...?"

"Yes, come on..."

Definitely waking up properly!

"Okay, well, how *do* your eyes feel?"

"Kind of ache, to be honest. Like someone scraped around the inside of my eye socket with a hand file."

"Good-good," said Doctor Frederick cheerfully, "that sounds about right. Now, I want you to move them nice and slowly, tell me how they feel."

Bane winced slightly. "Well, the ache gets a bit sharper..."

"No really intense, stabbing pains?"

"No."

"They feel like they're moving all right?"

More wincing. "Seem to be."

"Okay, well, I'll say this before we take that cover off and you get all distracted—the pain will prevent you from straining the healing muscles, so it's better if you don't take any pain relief over the next few days if you can possibly help it, all right?"

"Okay, no painkillers; can we get the thingy off?"

Doctor Frederick smiled. "Okay. Uh, Poppy, would you get the lights... Right..."

He unhooked the eye mask and Bane screwed his eyes up in the dim light. "Wow, that's bright! Oh thank God, *light!*" He winced and squinted for a little longer, and gradually began to open his eyes all the way, struggling up into a sitting position. "Margo? Margo, where are you!"

I shifted to sit on the bed and leaned right up close to him. "I'm here!"

His hands rose to cup my face. "I think... I think I can see you! Can we have more light?"

Poppy obliged.

Bane squinted impatiently, trying to peer at me before his eyes could adjust. "Margo, I can see you!" His fingers traced my face, his own a picture of wonder. "I can *see* you!"

I stared into chocolate brown eyes, stared at those familiar flecks of lighter and darker brown, radiating around the pupils, black as night; those brown eyes, slightly blood shot, but focused on my face...

Oh, Lucas, thank you so much!

We passed a leisurely morning, first waiting for Bane to undergo various checks and tests, then for him to completely shake off the anesthetic, after which he was finally discharged. He steered a slightly erratic course along the corridors to start with, as though his brain was confused by the visual information coming at it. By the time he got home and navigated his way into his clothes, he seemed steadier, though he kept giving joyous mutters of, "I can see!" at spontaneous intervals as we ate lunch with Jon.

"Margo, I can see that!" he said yet again, as we passed an ancient tapestry on our way to the basement.

"Glad to hear it!" Then my smile faded as I remembered where we were going.

Bane's face sobered as well as we reached the door to

the cold stone room. He paused for a moment, then squared his shoulders and opened the door. Went to stand by the bier lying on its trestles and look down at the dead man.

"Goodness knows he's been through it since I last set eyes on him," he muttered at last.

"Four months starving in the forest." My throat was tight again. "And he never would remember to eat much."

Bane stood there, forehead knotted in pain. "He's given me the most incredible gift," he whispered at last. "And I can *never, ever* repay him."

"He told you what he wanted of you, remember."

"Yes... Yes, I suppose he did." He glanced at me, then at my belly. Look after Margaret, look after the baby, look after your own conscience. The words I'd passed on, little dreaming... Pain crushed my chest again.

Bane touched one still hand in hesitant thanks and farewell. "I'm sorry. And... *thank you.*"

My head was swimming—was I going to faint? I dropped hastily to my knees, terrified I might fall and hurt our son, despite what Doctor Carol had said...

"Margo!" Bane swung around and crouched beside me, catching me in his arms. "*Are you all right?*"

"I'm okay..."

"You're not... not *bleeding* or anything?"

Began to shake my head—thought better of it. Still spinning. He looked so frightened. "No, no—I think I'm just tired, Bane..."

"I'm not surprised; all the things Jon says you were doing yesterday! I'll take you to Doctor Carol..."

"No, Bane, really, I think I just need to sit down for a bit."

He looked doubtful, but gathered me up in his arms and got to his feet. "Oh Margo, you've lost weight. I really have given you a hard time, haven't I?"

I rested my head on his shoulder—what a nice pillow it made. "Bane, you definitely cannot take sole credit for the hard time I've been having recently, okay? Please don't go on a guilt trip."

"Well, I'm taking you home, I'm going to make you a cup of tea, and you're going to rest until tonight, okay?"

"Fine by me..." Felt like I'd been stampeded over by a

herd of deer, driven over by a train and torn to shreds by a bear. Like the whole of the last six months had just fallen on me at once.

Bane hurried through the corridors with only the occasional weave and soon deposited me on the sofa, plying me with cups of tea and dry toast, then tucking me up with a blanket. *Yes, I might just close my eyes for a minute...*

"Margo?"

"Hmm?" I dragged my eyes open. "Is it time?"

"No, not yet. I'm just popping out, okay? You carry on resting."

"Okay..." I murmured. Sleep sucked me back down, but I thought I heard Bane give a rather fierce mutter of, "*Because I've had enough of this...*" as he stalked towards the door. Huh? I really ought to find out what he meant...

...Voices were talking, rather awkwardly. Familiar voices. Bane must be back.

I opened my eyes.

What the...?

Kyle.

Sitting there drinking tea.

32

GREATER LOVE

What was he doing here?

"Are you awake, Margo?" Bane sprang from his seat and crouched beside the sofa.

"Is this supposed to be a pleasant surprise?" I said to him, under my breath. Though, in the face of Lucas's generosity, any remaining anger seemed to have withered and died. I'd been trying to speak to Kyle, anyway...

Bane just shrugged. "I hope it might turn into one," he murmured back. He made to sit back in his chair, but I caught his hand, so he sat on the sofa instead and I used his lap for a pillow.

An awkward silence fell. I stared at Bane's knees, looking for the right words. My anger had died, but not the hurt. I'd tried so often to make up, and been rejected every time...

"Um, thank you for inviting me to tea, Margo," said Kyle eventually, in a tight voice.

"Bane invited you," I said shortly, still not looking up. "I didn't know anything about it."

Silence fell, even heavier than before, and I regretted my rebuff. I wanted Kyle to be here, talking to me, didn't I? Yet I couldn't pretend the pain wasn't there.

"Bane is neglecting his duty as host," said Bane after another long moment of silence, easing out from beneath me. "I'd better make a fresh pot of tea." He picked up the pot—still mostly full, surely—and disappeared into the kitchen, closing the door behind him.

Right, it was just Kyle and me. Now I really had to say the right thing... *Lord, help?*

A rush of dark fabric... I looked up, startled.

Kyle knelt beside the sofa, hand half-extended as though he'd been about to touch me then hesitated. Such a look of anguish on his face... "Margo, I'm sorry, okay? I'm really, really sorry. I didn't tell that lie you thought I did, but as for the rest, I was a useless, horrible brother and a dreadful Believer right when you needed both so desperately and I'm really, really sorry and... and..."

"Kyle, shut up," I said.

His face fell into something too like despair... then I managed to lurch free of the sofa and throw my arms around him.

"Stop apologizing, Kyle," I muttered into his hair, as he remained stiff with shock. "It's okay. I'm sorry too. I... I've let you down as well."

He relaxed and wrapped his arms around me, rocking me slightly. "Oh Margo! I'm sorry. I should've helped you. I should've helped you both! I'm useless!"

"You're not useless, Kyle. You just... misdirected your protective instincts."

"Well, that's a nice way to put it," he... sniffed?

I drew away slightly and looked him in the face. "Please don't cry... Big brothers aren't supposed to cry, right? Everything's okay now, isn't it?"

"Yeah." He drew in a big shaky breath. "Yeah, everything's okay... No thanks to yours truly," he added under his breath.

I collected another fraternal hug, then he saw me very conscientiously back onto the sofa, sitting beside me, since Bane was still clattering around in the kitchen.

"Kyle," I said after a moment. "*Is* everything okay now?"

Kyle sighed, his face strained. "It'll be better now, I think. I just... I got myself in such a knot. Emotionally. I'd never had a proper best mate, before Snakey. When he got killed... well, we've been taught over and over that if something big happens we should talk about it. But I didn't do it."

"I'm sorry if... you didn't feel I was there for you after Snakey died." I said, my heart aching with guilt. I hadn't really thought about Kyle, not until we went to Brussels... "I *really* let you down."

"Not like I let you down, Margo."

"It took two of us to mess things up this much, Kyle."

"Margo, it was mostly me. Stop being so nice."

"No, Kyle, a good sister would have checked her brother was okay when his friend got killed protecting her!"

"You must've been pretty upset yourself."

"Everyone was. No excuse to be self-absorbed."

"I think you were more husband-absorbed, actually. Hardly wrong, in the circumstances. I overreacted, Margo. I *did* know Bane had only hit you once and it wasn't likely to happen again, I just didn't want to admit it because it was such a relief to let the anger out. And what I said to you, Margo, it was just the most hurtful thing I could think of to punish you for saving Friedrich—and managing to do what I couldn't, but knew I should. The way I've behaved... I think I am going to withdraw from the seminary, Margo. I just can't imagine that I'm fit to be a priest."

"What?" Dismay filled me. "Don't do that! So you made a mistake with your emotional health. You won't do it again, will you? Priests are only human, you know!"

He shook his head. He looked so... subdued. Tired. Resuming his grueling training when the rest of the seminary returned to the Vatican now the vote was safely won probably looked very unattractive. But he'd surely regret the decision later.

"Kyle, if you really think it was mostly your fault, will you do something for me?" I asked.

"What?"

"Promise me that before you make any decision about your vocation, you'll talk to Pope Cornelius about this. Tell him everything you've just told me. Consider what he says. Promise?"

He eyed me with obvious reluctance. Knew as well as I did that Pope Cornelius would make him see sense—and he wouldn't end up giving up his vocation.

"Promise?" I insisted. Kyle would learn from his mistakes and go on to be a great priest, I was quite confident of that.

"Alright," he sighed. "I promise."

I slipped an arm around him and he slipped an arm around me, and we sat for a while in silence, until Bane returned from his epically slow tea-making.

"I'm glad you two managed to have a civilized conversation, actually," I couldn't help remarking.

Kyle smiled crookedly. "Well, when someone says, hi, here I am, hit me if you want to, then we can talk, it's surprisingly hard to actually do it. So we skipped straight to the talking bit. And he said if I didn't stop making you miserable, he was going to hit *me*. Then invited me to tea. I thought I'd better accept. Seeing that... well, Father Mark's not here to mediate anymore, so we've got to sort ourselves out. After how I've behaved, I... honestly didn't realize you cared that much, the way you ran off, the other day..."

Oh... Bane hadn't mentioned the baby yet, then... I'd better explain... But Bane had put the pot down and gone over to the table by the door. "Snail gave me a parcel for you," he said, coming back over and sitting in the armchair. "Here you go."

A parcel? Who would be sending me parcels? Could it be from... Mum and Dad? My heart leapt. Of course, the last parcel I'd had I'd thought that, and it had been from Lucas... But this one wouldn't be... Pain momentarily pierced my happiness.

"Oh, Snail said don't get too excited," said Bane quickly, clearly seeing the hope on my face.

"Oh." My excitement dwindled again. Though not my curiosity. I peeled up the pre-opened flap and slid out a cardboard box that had been neatly cut and glued by hand, by the look of it. I opened it... "Ah. Don't get too excited. Right."

Five rows of delicious-looking chocolates nestled mouthwateringly inside, exquisite but with that subtle air of being handmade. Something slid underneath the box and I pulled out a sheet of paper and unfolded it.

Dear Mrs. Verrall,

That sounds rather formal but the counselor said I should put it like that what with you being married. Thank

408

you for saving my life● when you didn't need to at all. I'm sending you some chocolates that I made for you. I hope you like them. They just don't seem enough. I will come and be your bodyguard as soon as they let me.

I am working in the kitchen 3 sessions a week now. When I arrived they said everyone has to do normal duties for the first 6 months. Then I cooked some Austrian buns and they said if anyone wanted to swap duties with me they could do it even before the 6 months were up! I will cook my 'famous' Full English later this week, after which I reckon I'll be in the kitchen every day!

I'm quite surprised by how it is here, actually. It's really not so bad. Some of the guys don't agree! The religion is hard to get my head around. I'm trying, though, because I reckon I'll need to be up on that to get picked as your bodyguard.

I hope the interviews I did helped you win the vote. I just stood up and told the truth, the way the Pope guy told me in Brussels. He said some stuff about everyone having choices, so I'm trying to make choices that will make me more like you and less like Reginald Hill.

I'm hoping to send you some scottish shortbread biscuits soon. It's harder than you'd think. I made you one lot of chocolates already● but the other guys ate them before I could get them posted. Clearly they weren't paying attention in the session about why we shouldn't take things that don't belong to us. That's not something I've ever done, by the way.

Auf wiedersehen,

Georg Friedrich

"It's from Georg Friedrich," I said. "Shall I read it out?" I glanced at Kyle. "Oh, I can read it to you later, Bane." I paused. "What am I saying? You can read it yourself later!"

Bane grinned.

But Kyle said, "No, it's okay. Just read it." Clearly working on forgiving Friedrich at last.

"Okay." I read the letter aloud, but when I'd finished Kyle looked more deflated than ever. "Are you okay, Kyle?" I asked.

"Yeah." He blew out a long breath. "Yeah. Listening to that letter makes me feel about this tall, is all." He held finger and thumb very close together. "I made excuses in my head, but really, I just wanted him to pay. But I hear that and... he's just a human being. It's really... sobering."

"Well," I said awkwardly, "I s'pose I'd already had some practice at seeing bad guys as people, what with Lucas. But trust me, when I put that bandage on him, I wasn't even close to forgiving him properly. Even in the TV studio, I wanted to do the right thing, yeah, but I didn't exactly have lots of warm fuzzy feelings for the guy. But I hope he can make something of his life after all."

I could smell the chocolates. And they weren't actually making me feel nauseous. "I'm going to try one of these. Who wants one?"

A single chocolate was missing from one corner. Had the VSS guys analyzed it in their little lab, or had one of them taken the much tastier, but riskier, option of simply eating it and holding on to the parcel for twenty-four hours while checking for ill effects?

Bane reached for a chocolate at once; Kyle after only a slight hesitation. For a few moments we all chewed in silence.

Finally Bane said, "Quite definitely wasted in the military." And reached for another one.

I'd have liked another, but... better not push it. The morning sickness wasn't entirely gone yet. Morning sickness...

Time to tell Kyle about the baby!

"Thank you, Bane," I murmured, when Kyle had gone. "It *was* a nice surprise after all."

He brushed this off, looking pleased with himself. And spent the rest of the afternoon vetoing any attempt of mine to get off the sofa, except once when I had to dash to the bathroom after an overly ambitious biscuit—at least the chocolate had stayed down—and another half hour when he slipped off on (another!) mysterious errand of his own.

After all the tea, dry toast, cuddles, lying down and making up I felt able to face the ordeal ahead. At least until we reached St Peter's and I began to notice all the nooks and crannies Lucas had loved; all the fuchsias Ranulph had placed around the basilica...

I was crying into Bane's shoulder before the bier was even brought in. Since when was I such a... *faucet?* I blamed the darling little boy inside me.

Kyle had joined us in our pew, and now patted my hand awkwardly. "I am, uh, really sorry about this, you know, Margo. I know he was your friend."

I gave his hand a squeeze and tried to collect myself.

It was almost time to start when I noticed a man and a woman standing behind the rope barrier that separated the

'State' part of the basilica from the 'Public' part, eyes searching the pews. "Kyle!" I gasped, pointing.

Kyle looked as well—his eyes widened and the next moment we were both on our feet. Bane jumped up as well—"*What...?*"—then he saw them too, and we were all scrambling out of the pew and racing across the marble floor.

"Mum! Dad!" I tried not to scream it at the top of my lungs. Reaching them, I flung myself into Mum's arms, just managing not to flatten her.

"Dad!" I hugged him too; hugged Mum again. I'd missed them so much.

"Bane, darling!" said Mum. "Oh," she gasped. "*Kyle!*" For a few minutes everyone was just hugging each other over and over.

"Oh my goodness!" I said at last, standing back and looking at them properly. It was so good to see them! They looked older and worn—unsurprisingly, alas. I knew how harrowing being on the run could be. Well, they were safe now. "When did you get here?" I asked.

"We literally strolled into St Peter's Square—ever so innocently—just now," said Dad.

"I feel like my head's still going around," said Mum. "The last bit was the worst—getting into Rome." She shuddered. "We handed over our last assets to a succession of taxi drivers to get ourselves put in touch with one with a nifty secret compartment in his car, who brought us in, quaking with terror the whole time."

"That's what we did! But I thought they'd got rid of the checkpoints? That didn't last long."

"Probably because of the Resistance," said Bane. "Or that'll be their excuse."

"Yeah. Oh... I think we're about to start," I said. "You need to see Eduardo and get visas and everything, but it'll keep until after the Requiem..."

"Requiem?" Dad looked startled, but Mum was looking closely at my barely dry face.

"Who is it for, Margo?" she asked gently.

"You really haven't been reading the papers, have you?" said Bane. "You didn't notice the team of military janitors attempting to clean the blood off the pavement out there? They've been at it for ages, apparently."

I swallowed. Mum was giving Bane a sideways look. Just noticed that he had his eyes?

"It's for Mr. Everington," said Kyle.

"That EGD Security major?" exclaimed Dad.

"He was a very good friend of Margo's. He sacrificed himself to get Bane's eyes back."

Dad looked at Bane and did a double-take. "You can see!"

"Thanks to Lucas," said Bane somberly.

"Well, it sounded like he'd turned over a new leaf," said Dad, after a moment of obvious struggle. "I expect you befriended him too, did you, Kyle?"

Kyle shot me a panic-stricken look. Didn't know what to say, or didn't know what I would say?

"Kyle didn't know him that well, actually," I said. "Lucas was awfully shy, and with the State running on minimum staffing levels, Kyle was ever so busy."

"Lucas grew on one," said Bane—rather glumly.

"Well, we'll be very happy to attend his Requiem," said Mum.

She looked so tired, though...

"Are you sure, Mum? You could both go straight in and get settled, put your feet up..."

"Nonsense," said Dad. "If this chap was your friend, and sacrificed himself to get Bane's eyes back, we must attend his Requiem Mass. We can keep going for another hour."

I hugged them both again, delighted that they'd accepted Lucas, even if posthumously.

The organ began to play.

"Uh oh, we're about to be run down by the bier," said Bane, shepherding us all along the aisle. We genuflected quickly and filed back into the pew. Jon got up when it was clear it was going to be a huge crush, and slipped off to find a spot further back. He'd remained in his seat for the reunion—he'd never actually met my Mum and Dad, after all.

"Thank you; sorry, Jon," I whispered, as he passed me.

The entry procession was indeed coming. Ranulph had

offered to be a pall bearer, with Unicorn, Snail and Eduardo volunteering as well. No need for more, with no coffin and an undernourished corpse.

The bier was placed on trestles in front of the balustrade of St Peter's tomb and Mass began. I tried to concentrate. Pope Cornelius had chosen the readings in the end, and they were beautiful. Psalm sixty-four, perfect. The reading from Corinthians about love. And the famous reading where Our Lord says, "No one has greater love than this, to lay down one's life for one's friends." The homily was beautiful too, though I didn't hear half of it. I caught "...act of incredible generosity..." which made me cry again, despite my joy at my parents' unexpected presence, and "...brutal and summary execution..." made me cry too, but clearly Pope Cornelius was giving the press something to chew on.

Afterwards, Pope Cornelius came round to the front of St. Peter's tomb. Huh? Only then did I notice the portable font standing there.

"It's not normal to combine a baptism with a funeral," Pope Cornelius said. "However, in this particular case, it did seem appropriate. Could the candidate and his chosen godparent, please approach the font?"

Bane gave me a look almost shy. "Um, would you be my Godmother, wife?"

Mum and Dad gasped in delight.

"Really?" I whispered.

He shrugged. "Yeah, well, I probably should've... *got done*... sooner, but... well, I was just so furious... with God, with... *everything*. Lucas has kind of... given me a kick up the backside, to be honest. So yeah, *really.* "

Embarrassingly, there was then a slight delay whilst I cried all over him.

Finally, we got to the font.

"Do you reject Satan?"

"Do you reject all his works?"

"And all his empty promises?"

Soon we were at the Confirmation. I mopped my eyes, put my hand on Bane's shoulder and muttered, "What name, Bane?"

"St. Luke," he muttered back.

By some miracle I just managed to squeak, "St. Luke," to Pope Cornelius before burying my face in my hankie again.

We went on with the Requiem Mass and most of the tears I shed were sad ones, but for a short time, as I knelt to receive communion and Bane knelt to receive beside me, they were tears of joy. By the time they'd laid a clean white sheet over the bier and the body, and we got up to process out after it, I'd almost run out of tears. I walked, my arm around Bane and Bane's around me, dry-eyed, Kyle and Mum and Dad and Jon following behind.

A familiar voice seemed to be murmuring in my head, "But... this is a very happy day for me, isn't it, Margaret? I'm with God."

Yes, you are, Lucas. Yes, it is.

The bier was lowered carefully into the fresh grave. Kyle took Mum and Dad in tow when the ceremony was complete, and everyone else drifted away, but I stood, watching as the gardeners filled in the hole. Only when they began fitting the turf back on top did I let Bane lead me off to the reception Jon had arranged.

I went back there later the next day with Bane, clutching the small purple fuchsia from the cafe. Unicorn had ventured across the white line to try to buy it back for me, but the cafe owner had immediately made a gift of it.

A little circle of soil had been left, same as on Father Mark's grave, and the irrigation pipe had already been extended from one to the other. I dug a little hole, put the fuchsia in place and watered it carefully, trying to remember everything Lucas had ever said and everything he'd written in his copious notes.

Finally I brushed off my hands and stood up. "There we go. Hope it doesn't die."

"I'm sure Ranulph will keep an eye on it as well," said Bane.

"I hope so." I stared at the mound, with the turf that didn't quite cover it. "It's stupid," I said, "considering how little time I really knew him—let alone *liked* him—but... *I miss him so much.*"

"A friend is a friend," said Bane. "Sometimes I don't

think it matters how long you know them."

"I think you're right."

He put his arms around me and hugged me tight. "Anyway, he's reached his happy ever after, isn't that what you'd say?"

"Yeah... What you'd say too, yes?" I traced the sign of the cross on his forehead with my thumb.

He blinked. Looked intent for a moment. Then his face softened. "Yeah, I s'pose I would." He leaned his forehead against my scarred one. "Hope there are plants in heaven, or he'll probably escape and come back here."

A laugh sputtered from me. "He's so not going to want to come back here, Bane!"

"That's better," he murmured, encircling me.

I turned to lean back against his loving bulk and before long his hands strayed to my belly.

"Well, at least we have a name, now," he added softly, rubbing my bump gently. "Grow strong, Lucas."

"Lucas Mark?"

"Yeah. Lucas Mark Verrall."

"We're really looking forward to seeing you."

"*Both* of us seeing you," added Bane.

"Yeah, both of us. You've got your Uncle Lucas to thank for that, little Luc."

"We'll have to tell you all about your Uncle Lucas," Bane told my bump, so seriously I had to smile a little. "And your Uncle Mark. And..."

I listened to his happy voice and watched the purple fuchsia's leaves stir in the breeze, the sun warm on my face.

Thank you, Lucas.

Thank you, Lord.

Thank you so much...

Don't miss the I AM MARGARET
companion volume

MARGO'S (ATTEMPTED) DIARY & NOTEBOOK

Includes the Novella, VISITORS.
(SNEAK PEEK below)

I was walking along the side aisle of St Peter's when I noticed the man balancing a proCamera on his twisted, claw-like left hand while he took a shot of the main basilica. I stopped dead—looked more closely... it *was*...

When I waved a hand behind my back, a guy who'd been drifting along behind, apparently admiring the paintings, and another who'd knelt to pray at a side altar as soon as I stopped both seemed to lose interest in what they were doing and headed towards me. I hastily made another gesture, the one that meant, *I think it's fine, just pay attention*, and their interest in art and prayer returned to them just as abruptly.

I went a few steps closer to the man with the camera. *"Watkins...?"*

ALSO INCLUDES:
UNDERGROUND LATIN PRIMER—MAPS—PSALMS—
'PROCAMERA' MASS KIT DIAGRAM—PRAYERS—ETC.
(Plus a lot of graffiti from Bane!)

COMING SOON!

Paperback: ISBN 978-1-910806-14-2
ePub: ISBN 978-1-910806-15-9

unSeen

Find out more at: www.IAmMargaret.co.uk

A prequel to the **YESTERDAY & TOMORROW** series

SOMEDAY

CORINNA TURNER

All proceeds go to AID TO THE CHURCH IN NEED

Ruth and Gemma have a Physics exam in the morning.
Becky and Allelluia have college entrance tests.
So it's an absolute nightmare to be woken by the fire
alarm in dead of the night.

But for them, and for 272 other girls from Chisbrook Hall
girls boarding school, the real nightmare is just
beginning.

Because 'al-Qabda' are taking them all away.
Whether they want to go or not.

OUT NOW!

READ
2 SNEAK PEEKS!
→

Paperback: ISBN 978-1-910806-16-6
ePub: ISBN 978-1-910806-17-3

unSeen

Find out more at: www.Y&T.co.uk

SOMEDAY

SNEAK PEEK 1— *GEMMA*

I open my mouth to reply to Annabel... break off, eyes widening at the sight of a uniformed—armed!—soldier rushing up the stairwell.

"Outside!" he yells, in some sort of thick, inner-city accent. "Hurry up, everyone out!"

"Is there actually a fire?" gasps Annabel, her ridiculously long hair tumbling all around her again as she almost drops her hair tie. "Not just mice chewing wires again..."

But Ruth frowns slightly as she looks at the soldier—yeah, he's not a fireman.

He sees our expressions. "There's been a bomb threat. *Out*, now! Where is everyone else?"

"There isn't anyone else," Annabel says over her shoulder, taking off down the stairs as though... she's just heard there might be a bomb in the building.

The soldier looks annoyed—yells after her, "Where are the younger ones?"

"Year seven are at an adventure training camp," I reply, but I start down the stairs as well. Bomb threats are usually hoaxes but I'm so not risking it. Not the way things are at the moment. "Year eight, IT camp; year nine, French exchange; year ten, Venice, English trip. It's just us and the sixth form."

The soldier swears loudly, and starts herding us back down the stairs, giving me a push to hurry me along.

"Hey!" I protest. "If I fall and break something and you have to carry me, it's going to take even longer, isn't it?"

Ruth shoots the man another looks and trots on down the stairs, guiding Yoko with her, like she's more scared of the soldier than of the bomb. And though I'd never admit it, I do kind of respect her opinion—at least on anything that doesn't concern the divine Sky Fairy.

The man's scruffier than any soldier I've ever seen—and since when do they dispatch armed men to evacuate civilians?

ALLELLUIA
"Quit shoving, would you?" I snap at the man who's

chivvying us towards the assembly point. "Think I wanna stay in there with a bomb, huh?"

"Hurry up," he says.

That's all he's said since he met us outside the sixth form block and I'm sick of it.

"Jesus loves you too," I tell him.

He smacks me across the head and I gasp in pain. Did this soldier seriously just hit me? Then I see the assembly point ahead and the words evaporate from my mind.

There's a row of trucks and a couple of horse vans—horseboxes, they call them over here—pulled up in the parking lot, and more soldiers are forcing girls into them at gunpoint. Everyone looks scared—a few girls are crying. *Lord, what is going on?*

"Show us some ID!" Miss Trott is yelling. She's the senior housemistress. "You are not taking these girls unless we see some ID! Where are the police? Where's bomb disposal?" She grabs a soldier's arm, "ID, *now!*"

The soldier un-shoulders his rifle and casually smashes the butt into Miss Trott's face. She crumples to the ground in a horrible, boneless way. I jerk in a shocked breath—then grab Jill and Karen. "*Run!*"

I shove them towards the wood and dive at the soldier who hit me—after a moment of confusion, I'm rewarded by the sound of Jill and Karen's running footsteps on the gravel path. The soldier shoves me away so hard I fall, tearing pajamas and knee. *Ow...* Blood oozes brightly across my black skin. But Jill and Karen have disappeared into the dark.

The soldier swings back to me—my heart freezes in my throat, everything freezes as he brings up the rifle and cocks it, hate filling his angry eyes...

SNEAK PEEK 2—*SAM*

We've spent hours trailing through any bit of woodland that can be accessed by road and we're scratched and footsore and frustrated. And hot. Of course we know ninety-nine percent of the searchers in the entire country won't find anything *and* we're being given the least likely areas, what with us being, like, the eighty-eighth line of defense or something—but I suppose we're all hoping—and dreading what we might find, at the same time.

Movement up ahead... my mind snaps back to the job at hand, heart lurching in hope-fear. It'll be nothing... it'd better be nothing, we're all unarmed... Take more than this for them to issue live ammo to university students.

The biggest excitement of the morning approaches... in the form of a teenage boy riding bareback—and bare-footed—on a black and white pony. He rides right on up to our fatigue-clad selves in a way that makes me pretty sure he's heard nothing about the terrorists.

I can't help asking, "Why aren't you in school?"

"I don't go to school. I'm home-schooled. Or..." He grins. "Caravan-schooled."

"Oh, you're a gyp... traveler, right?"

"Half. My dad's a hippie. Traveler-wannabee, as my mum would say."

"Right. Well... Have you seen any horseboxes or vans back there in the woods?"

He gives me a funny look. "You're soldiers, right? Why are you looking for vans?"

"Yes, territorial army, strictly speaking—but we're just university officer cadets. We're looking for the two hundred and seventy-six schoolgirls who were kidnapped this morning. Or rather, the vehicles they were taken in, almost certainly abandoned, by now."

The boy greets this with a nod. "So this is like a role-play, or something, right? That you're doing for training? Is it okay for me to tell you where they are, then, or are you supposed to find them yourselves?"

"No, they've really been taken. By Islamist fanatics... *Wait*, are you saying you've *seen* some vans back there?"

"Yeah," he says slowly, eyes very wide. Then he shakes his head as though to banish his shock and turns the pony, puts it to a canter, calling over his shoulder, "This way..."

"Wait!" I yell. "You need to wait for us. Those men are dangerous."

He pulls the pony to a halt and looks us up and down. "And what are you going to do, spit at them?"

I try not to grit my teeth too hard. "We can at least make a cautious approach," I tell him, then call to the others,

"Okay, stay in your line but we're following the pony. Double-time."

When the boy finally slips from the pony's back and throws his reins over a bush, we catch him up. "This way," he whispers, and glides off silently through the trees.

We follow, sounding like a herd of blundering elephants in comparison. But we soon come over a slight rise and there below us is a clearing...

My heart begins to pound. Three vehicles. Two white vans and a blue horsebox... God help us, it's an exact match! I hesitate, torn. We're under strict orders to call for armed backup if we find anything, but... I try the radio again. Nothing. No signal on my phone either. What have we got to report, anyway? There doesn't seem to be anyone here. It may be nothing to do with the kidnapping.

"Wrexham, come with me," I say softly. "We'll circle the clearing and see what we can see. Everyone else, stay here. Tanner, you're in charge. If someone shoots us, bug out and phone for help as soon as you can get a signal."

I pick up a sturdy branch and move down the slope towards the clearing. A stick's better than nothing, right? Henry Wrexham follows. The gypsy-boy has slipped all the way to the edge of the clearing and is peering from behind a bush. I'd better try and get him to stay back.

But as I move down towards him, I find that I can see the backs of the vehicles, and they're all open, the roll backs up on the vans and the ramp down on the horsebox. A prickle of unease runs up my spine. Okay, so it's really hot today, but it could just as easily be pouring rain. Why would someone leave their vehicles open like that?

The boy glances at me when I stop beside him. "Someone brought two really big vehicles up into this clearing sometime this morning," he tells me softly, pointing. "You can see the tyre marks. Looks like semi-trucks. Totally unsuitable for that track."

Another cold prickle.

"Change of plan, Henry," I say. "We'll..."

But then a thin cry comes from the horsebox: *"Help..."*

YESTERDAY,
THEY WERE SCHOOLGIRLS.

A prequel to the YESTERDAY & TOMORROW series

SOMEDAY

CORINNA TURNER

CARNEGIE MEDAL AWARD NOMINEE

INTRODUCTION BY
ANN WIDDECOMBE

FOREWORD BY
IGNATIUS KAIGAMA
ARCHBISHOP OF JOS, NIGERIA

ACKNOWLEDGMENTS

There are so many people I would like to thank for their help with this series. So here goes!

My UK proofreaders: my mother, of course, my most fearsome critic—Mrs. 'this is so boring, cut it' Turner—along with Georgina 'Miss Picky' and Lucy 'there's a day missing here somewhere (again)'.

The team at Chesterton Press in the USA: the invaluable feedback from Regina Doman and Andrew Schmiedicke, and the work of their fantastic team of proofreaders: Joyanna, Rebecca, and Rose.

Also Kim S., for identifying the 'Britishisms' in the first UK editions of THE THREE MOST WANTED and LIBERATION.

And Dr. Liz T., for her role as a medical consultant, especially with LIBERATION. However, I did not run every single medical issue past her, so all errors are one hundred percent mine.

Also Fr. Paul C., theological consultant extraordinaire!

And my brother, for the way my website keeps on mysteriously running.

My Guardian Angel, of course, the Holy Spirit, and St. Margaret Clitherow, the patron of the series.

Everyone I thanked at the end of book 1, plus Rachel and Aaron who I actually *forgot to thank* for the prototype of book 1's tagline! How could I?

And last but not least, Bernard S. and the lovely librarians of the Chartered Institute of Library and Information Professionals for the CILIP Carnegie Medal Award 2016 nomination for LIBERATION.

And to anyone (else!) I have forgotten, huge thanks and groveling apologies!

ABOUT THE AUTHOR

Corinna Turner has been writing since she was fourteen and likes strong protagonists with plenty of integrity. She has an MA in English from Oxford University, but has foolishly gone on to work with both children and animals! Juggling work with the disabled and being a midwife to sheep, she spends as much time as she can in a little hut at the bottom of the garden, writing.

She is a Catholic Christian with roots in the Methodist and Anglican churches. A keen cinema-goer, she lives in the UK with her Giant African Land Snail, Peter, who has a six and a half inch long shell and an even larger foot!

Get in touch with Corinna (and Peter!)...

Facebook/Google+: Corinna Turner

Twitter: @CorinnaTAuthor

or sign up for a news and exclusive content, including an I AM MARGARET short story (coming soon) at:
www.IAmMargaret.co.uk

DOWNLOAD YOUR EBOOK

If you own a paperback of *Bane's Eyes* you can download a free copy of the eBook.

1. Go to *www.ChestertonPress.com* or scan the QR code:

2. Enter this code on the book's page:
MXB73477G

3. Enjoy your download!

CPSIA information can be obtained
at www.ICGtesting.com
Printed in the USA
LVHW042123030419
612847LV00001BA/88/P